LOVE,
LOVE,
LOVE

LOVE, LOVE, LOVE

Language of Love
Deborah Reber

and

Cupidity
Caroline Goode

Simon Pulse
New York   London   Toronto   Sydney

SIMON PULSE

An imprint of Simon & Schuster Children's Publishing Division

1230 Avenue of the Americas, New York, NY 10020

This Simon Pulse paperback edition December 2010

Language of Love copyright © 2010 by Deborah Reber

Cupidity copyright © 2005 by John Vornholt

SIMON PULSE and colophon are registered trademarks of Simon & Schuster, Inc.

For information about special discounts for bulk purchases, please contact Simon & Schuster Special Sales at 1-866-506-1949 or business@simonandschuster.com.

The Simon & Schuster Speakers Bureau can bring authors to your live event. For more information or to book an event contact the Simon & Schuster Speakers Bureau at 1-866-248-3049 or visit our website at www.simonspeakers.com.

Designed by Mike Rosamilia

The text of this book was set in Garamond 3.

Manufactured in the United States of America

2 4 6 8 10 9 7 5 3 1

Library of Congress Control Number 2010922977

ISBN 978-1-4424-0313-0

Cupidity was previously published individually by Simon Pulse.

Language of Love

To Derin and Shelly,
who read, listened, and laughed in all the right places

Acknowledgments

Many thanks to the fabulous team at Simon Pulse, who encouraged me to walk on the wild side and give fiction writing a try, especially Anica Mrose Rissi and Michael del Rosario, who held my hand along the way; my fabu friends and family who shared in the process; and my agent, Susan Schulman, who believed in me from the start.

1

How did I get myself into this mess? I stared up at the ceiling, looking for an answer. Of course, I knew it wasn't up there. In fact, I already knew the culprit behind my predicament was none other than Molly Harris, my BIF. In Molly's case, BIF stood for "bad influence friend"—the friend who gets you to do all kinds of things you wouldn't normally do but do anyway because that friend holds some sort of voodoo power over you.

To further complicate matters, Molly was my BFF, too. We'd been friends forever, or at least as far back as second grade, when Molly moved onto my block and I had an instant ally in my very testosterone-filled neighborhood. There were boys to the left, boys to the right, and one particularly annoying little boy in the bedroom next to mine.

Molly had me at hello with her shiny blond hair, cornflower-blue mischievous eyes, a grin that made you believe anything was possible, and a confidence that said she'd be president someday if it weren't for the countless scandals she's bound to have a hand in between now and age thirty. We'd been through it all together over the years, and though she could certainly be a bit, shall we say, self-involved, at her core Molly was a good person. When it came down to it, I knew she'd always be there for me.

To be fair, Molly didn't get me into this mess alone. In fact, I actually started it. After all, I'm the one who decided impersonating a Hungarian national was a good idea. But I was just having fun. This? This situation I was in now? Not fun. *Definitely* not fun.

It all started today after school. I met up with Molly at her locker, where she was pulling on her raincoat and reapplying her lipstick, and we figured out a plan for the rest of the day. As usual, Molly's mom was on a business trip—Hong Kong or Tokyo (it's hard to keep track)—and her stepdad wouldn't be home until at least eight o'clock. The plan was to hang out at Molly's house, get some Thai takeout, and catch up on a backlog of seriously good reality TV.

We hopped on the number four bus for the first leg

of our journey to Molly's neighborhood of Wallingford, which she'd moved to right after her parents' divorce when we were in fourth grade. The bus was packed, so we squeezed into the rear, claiming a tiny piece of real estate for ourselves and our overstuffed backpacks. We added to the hot air fogging up the bus windows by trading horror stories from the school day—Molly's uncomfortable standoff with a substitute in gym (Molly refused to wear her swim cap) and my continuing inability to bring up my cultural studies' grade.

By the time we stepped off the bus at Virginia and Third, I was sure we'd been teleported to the Gulf of Mexico during hurricane season. Having lived in Seattle our whole lives, we were more than used to the rain. And like every other Seattleite, we never carried umbrellas, thinking there was no storm that couldn't be weathered with a decent raincoat and a pair of wellies. Except for, apparently, today. And since we had ten minutes until our bus connection, we decided to seek refuge in the corner Starbucks. The added bonus? *Caffeine.*

As we basked in the warmth and contemplated the assorted goodies on display while we waited to order, Molly brought up my cultural studies grade again. "What's up with that, anyway?" she probed, shifting my attention from sugar cookies back to my bleak academic reality.

"I have no idea. I just don't get how Ms. Kendall can be such a cool person in real life, yet such a tyrant of a teacher."

"She must be on some sort of power trip," Molly mused.

"Yeah, well, I wish she'd get over it already. If I don't kick butt on this last unit on Eastern European history, I'm going to get a D." My voice sank. We both knew what that meant. I had 99.9 percent convinced my parents to let me go to Europe with Molly and her mom this summer, but they told me I had to score Bs or higher in all my classes. We'd made big plans . . . Paris, London, Madrid. The fate of my unstamped passport lay in Ms. Kendall's finely manicured hands.

"I just don't know what else I can do—I turn in all my homework; I study for the tests," I rambled on. "You know, I bet someone who's actually *from* Eastern Europe couldn't even get a B in her class."

"Um . . . isn't your dad Hungarian, Janna?" Molly asked.

"Well . . . yeah."

"So doesn't that make *you* Eastern European?"

"Kind of, I guess. But I'm talking about someone who's *from* from Eastern Europe. As in, just off the boat," I explained.

I started speaking in an Eastern European accent. "I'm

sorry. Which countries are former Eastern Bloc again? France? Mexico? *Alaska?*"

Molly giggled, egging me on.

"Please tell me why zis communism so bad?" I continued, laying it on thick. "And does zis Iron Curtain I hear of come in different fabrics?"

I was on a roll by the time we reached the front of the line and ordered our lattes with fat-free soy, plus a caramel marshmallow thingy for me (I'm a slave to sugar). Molly snagged a tiny table by the window so we could watch for the bus while waiting for our drinks. We had just dumped our bags on the floor and sat down when two boys—two very *cute* boys, I might add—walked up.

Now, it's not all that unusual for random guys to hit on us, or more specifically, on Molly. It's that whole blond, blue-eyed, mischievous smile thing. Plainly put, most members of the male species are drawn to Molly like dogs to a bone. Me? I was pretty much used to my place in our friendship. I was the classic sidekick—the best friend who tried to act as if it wasn't painfully obvious to everyone that she was nothing more than an accessory to the main attraction. It wasn't that I was ugly. I had nice enough honey eyes that come close to matching my light brown wavy hair. And I'd even been told I had a warm smile. But put me next to Molly and I've got "plain Jane" (or "plain

Janna") written all over me. And that was generally okay by me.

Today, however, was different. First off, these guys didn't come across as your typical supercool guys with heaps of attitude who thought they were all that, like the ones who usually hit on us (I mean, on Molly). Cute? Yes. But more in a boy-next-door-tussled-hair way as opposed to leading-man-chiseled-cheekbones-six-pack-abs way. For whatever reason, something about them was different enough to make us take notice.

But the *real* difference? Today *I* was the one being hit on.

"Hi there," cute boy number one said.

Having just shoved my entire caramel treat into my mouth, I remained mute and wide-eyed as Molly flashed him a winning smile.

"Well, hi there," she answered flirtatiously.

But the boy, dressed in an army jacket, jeans, and black Converse, flung his hair out of his eyes Zac Efron–style and stayed focused on me. Caught off guard, I continued chewing my caramel marshmallow in slow motion, in part because it was sticking to my teeth (perhaps I should have taken a bite instead of eating it whole?) and in part because I hadn't a clue as to what to say.

"I couldn't help but notice your accent," he went on. "So, what country are you from, anyway?"

What *country* was I from? I squinted in confusion.

"Your accent?" he continued. "I overheard you talking before. Wait, let me guess. Somewhere in Eastern Europe? Russia?"

Realizing the source of the misunderstanding, I finished swallowing the caramel and was about to set the record straight when Molly blurted out, "This is Janna! She's an exchange student from Hungary!"

I faced Molly with a look of quiet panic. She returned my gaze with a ridiculously big smile and that damn twinkle in her eye that I'm powerless to resist.

"Hungary? That's so cool!" He was clearly impressed with my apparent heritage. "I'm Julian, by the way. And this is Spence." He motioned to cute boy number two behind him.

I froze. I was at a crossroads, and I had to choose a path. I could turn Molly's declaration into a joke and admit I'd never been east of the Rockies, or I could succumb to the message Molly was sending me telepathically (and with several strategically placed kicks under the table). And then, in a split second, fueled by unfamiliar-cute-boy attention, adrenaline, and little else, it was done.

"Sank you," I responded in my most authentic Hungarian accent, which, come to think of it, I'm not sure I've actually even heard before. "I like America veddy much," I added for good measure.

Julian smiled. "I dig the accent," he said. "Where do you girls go to school?"

I sank into my chair and let Molly do the talking, too shocked I was actually going along with the ruse to say a word. I felt slightly guilty about the whole thing, but there was no turning back. Molly was already in full flirtation mode with Spence, and, being completely honest, the fact that foreign intrigue had magically made me more appealing to at least one very cute member of the opposite sex prompted me to keep my mouth shut. By the time our bus pulled up five minutes later, cell-phone digits had been exchanged and we'd planned to connect at a club where Julian was deejaying Friday night.

The sound of my cell phone snapped me back to my bedroom ceiling, back to reality. When I glanced at the clock and saw it read 10:01 p.m., I knew it could only be one person . . . Emmett. If Molly is my BIF, then Emmett can only be described as my GIF—*good* influence friend. Emmett had rounded out our friendship trio ever since Molly, Emmett, and I sat together in Ms. Lacey's French class in seventh grade. We'd congregate in the back of the classroom to discuss the guests' plight on the previous day's *Oprah* and commiserate about the complications of past perfect verbs. Somewhere along the way we became a threesome.

The best thing about Emmett? He's kind of like that gay best friend every girl wants—he's your biggest fan, thinks you always look fabulous, tells it to you like it is, and is fiercely loyal. Although it should be pointed out that despite Emmett playing this role in my life, he's not actually gay. Either way, I don't know what I'd do without him. Emmett gets me in a way that nobody else does, not even Molly. And I loved the fact that I could be so close to a guy without having to worry about uncomfortable weirdness or anything. With Emmett, no topic was off limits, which is probably why we invented the Nightly Rant or NR. Every night at ten o'clock, Emmett and I engage in sixty seconds each of let-it-rip bitching, moaning, dumping, and ranting about any and all frustrations, insecurities, and annoyances. It was kind of like tele-therapy, only free.

Despite the existence of NR rule number two, which clearly stated there were to be no judgments and no advice doled out during a rant (unless said advice was requested, of course), I just wasn't in the mood to bring up my perplexing predicament. Not yet, anyway. I still didn't really even know how I felt about everything and wasn't sure how Emmett would react when he found out what I was doing all because of a guy.

"Hey, Emm," I said wearily.

"Hi, you. How's tricks?"

"Tricks are okay," I responded halfheartedly. "Ready to rant?"

"Ready to rant," Emmett replied. "Who's first?"

"Why don't you go first?"

"Okay. Here's me." He paused briefly before diving in. "First of all, I don't understand how people waiting in line to buy ice cream, *ice cream*, for God's sake, can be so uppity and impatient. Don't they realize that imbibing sugary sweets is inherently a *happy* thing to do? Don't they know that since this stuff is frozen, one can only scoop so fast before getting a hand cramp or a brain freeze? Oh, and my dad is still pressuring me to spend a few weeks with him this summer in Hotlanta. And I know he doesn't actually want to spend the time with me . . . it's all about showing my mom that he cares. Which he doesn't. Send a singing telegram . . . it's cheaper. And . . . what else . . . ? Wait. I know I have one more thing. Oh, yeah. If the sun doesn't make a brief appearance in the next day or two, I may actually *want* to move to Atlanta. All I'm asking for is a five-minute sun break. Five minutes. Is that too much to ask?"

Silence.

"Hello?" Emmett asked. "Are you still there?"

"Yeah, yeah . . . sorry. I'm just tired. Okay, here's me. Big surprise here, but I'm really annoyed with Henry. He deleted all my shows to make room for a *Powerpuff Girls* marathon on Cartoon Network. And I just got back my test in cultural studies, and I did okay on it, but not good enough to get my grade up to a B. It's just totally unfair that I might not be able to go to Europe with Molly because of the Bosnian War. Especially since it ended more than ten years ago."

I was running out of things to say. With only one big thing on my mind, I scrambled to come up with decoys.

"And . . . and I had some disgusting garlicky sausage on my pizza tonight, and I keep burping it up." Pause. "That's it."

"You sure? You still have seventeen seconds left."

"Yeah, that's it."

Emmett didn't buy it. "You sound more upset than lost TV shows, your ongoing battle with Ms. Kendall, and bad pizza."

"Sorry, I'm just kind of out of it. I didn't sleep well last night."

"Alrighty, then. Go to sleep already. I'll talk to you in the a.m."

"'Kay. Good night, Emm."

"Good night, Jan."

I hung up the phone and toppled onto my bed, the headboard banging against my already scuffed-up wall in protest. I closed my eyes and tried to quiet my mind so I could get some sleep. Not an easy task when you were as confused as me. I kept getting the overwhelming urge to chicken out and call the whole thing off before it even got started. But, even so, I had to admit there was an ever-so-small part of me that wanted to see where this unexpected development in my social life took me. And then the words Scartlett O'Hara famously spoke in my most favorite classic movie of all time, *Gone with the Wind*, popped into my head. "I'll think about that tomorrow. After all, tomorrow is another day." Sounded like a plan to me.

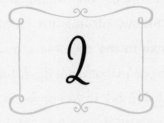

2

I awoke the next morning to the sound of a furious buzzing. And when I opened my eyes to find out what was going on, I found my brother Henry spastically scrubbing his teeth with an electric, astronaut-shaped toothbrush mere inches from my face. Even worse, I was getting sprayed with the blueberry mint foam that was spewing from his mouth.

Sadly, my unpleasant wake-up call was par for the course—I was well aware of the fact that I remained my younger brother Henry's greatest source of entertainment. (Apparently I was even funnier than cartoons). At eleven, and five years my junior, Henry was a piece of work. His precociousness, extensive vocabulary, and ridiculous knowledge of even the most inane trivia made him extremely dangerous. He knew just how to push my buttons, how to manipulate any situation for his own benefit. At the same time he was a typical boy with a love of potty humor and physical comedy. Farting on my pillow, playing his harmonica in my ear, pretending to puke in my shoes—my rude awakening this morning was just one in a series of disturbing scenes startling me from peaceful slumber in recent weeks.

"That's disgusting!" I growled. "Mom! Get him out of here!"

"Henry, please leave your sister alone," my mom said calmly, peeking into the room.

"Okay." Henry leaned in close. "Bye bye, sis." Toothpaste shot out of his mouth with each drawn-out syllable.

"Argh!" I grabbed a pillow and took a wild swing, but Henry scooted away before I could connect.

I sank back into my warm bed and asked God why he had plagued me with a brother who was such a colossal pain in the butt.

"Honey?" My mom came into my room and slowly pulled up the shades. "I know you find your brother frustrating, and it can't be easy being a big sister," she said with exaggerated empathy.

Here we go again. First she was going to validate my feelings. Next, she'd be giving me choices about how I could deal with my brother, so I'd feel "empowered and in control of my life."

"But," she continued as if on cue, "you can either accept the fact that your brother isn't as mature as you are and expect him to do annoying things sometimes, *or* you can choose to let yourself be shocked and upset every time he does something you don't like. It's up to you." She waltzed out the door. Then, as if she'd already moved on, she called back, "Dad's making pancakes for breakfast. Come down when you're ready!"

And just like that she was gone, the credits rolling on another predictable episode of *Perfect Parenting with Stella Leavenworth.* These routine interactions with my mom always left me even more annoyed. Intellectually, I knew she had the best intentions, and I also knew for a fact that she paid some parenting coach a ton of money for tips on handling sibling conflicts, but sometimes I would've appreciated some real emotion instead of her lame Mrs. Brady imitation.

With a resigned sigh, I shifted my bum over and slid my legs up along the wall next to my bed. Fixating on an old cobweb in the corner, I took five slow, deep breaths—in through the nose, out through the mouth. My yoga instructor swore doing this "legs up the wall" pose for five minutes each morning would start your day on a positive note.

Despite the fact that mine had already started out crappy and I had only one minute for the pose, I figured, what the heck? I needed all the help I could get.

I hurriedly got ready for school but unfortunately miscalculated my exit strategy. With too many minutes to spare, I was forced to suffer through "quality family time" at the breakfast nook (another brilliant idea from my parents' coach). In attendance this morning? My dad, Troy, a techie who worked at a downtown advertising firm and was frequently MIA due to his regular trips to San Francisco and Los Angeles. I was usually happy to see him at breakfast since it was such a rarity, but I was still feeling prickly from the toothpaste incident. Then there was my mom, Stella, who made an effort to sit with Henry and me every morning, no matter what crisis might be happening at her design studio. And, of course, there was Henry. You've already had the pleasure of meeting him.

But I knew neither QFT nor my brother was solely responsible for my mood today. The real source was the uncomfortable pit in my stomach that had been lingering ever since what I'd already dubbed "the Starbucks incident." I had hoped a solid night's sleep would have resulted in an improved outlook on the whole mess, but no such luck. I was still panicked at the jam I'd gotten myself into.

"Whatcha got going on today, Jan?" my dad asked,

flipping a buttermilk pancake off the griddle and onto my plate.

"Not much. Just suffering through another day of higher education at its finest."

"So tell me. What's happening with that cultural studies grade? Will we be bidding you bon voyage two months from now or not?"

"I'm working on it, Dad." I had to figure out some way to get my grade up, although I was still annoyed about my parents' inflexibility on the matter. I mean, surely traveling to Europe in and of itself was way more educational than anything I could ever learn in a book. But I knew trying to get them to reconsider their terms was a waste of time. Thanks again to their pricey parenting coach, they practiced what's called "consistent parenting," which basically meant there was no such thing as wiggle room when it came to my parents' decrees.

"All right, well, let me know if I can help with anything," he said.

Yeah, maybe you *could take my final essay exam in cultural studies.*

"Thanks, Dad." I silently forced down three bites of pancake before pushing my chair back and grabbing my backpack off the floor. "I've gotta go," I said, taking a big swig of my smoothie. "Thanks for the pancake."

"You're welcome. Bye, pumpkin!"

"Have a good day, sweetheart!" my mom called.

"Yeah, have a good day, eat fart!" Henry called.

Sigh. I could still hear Henry laughing at his stupid rhyme as I bounded down the steps of my front porch. I powered up my iPod and zoned out to vintage Cure for the short walk to Delmar High, looking forward, for once, to the distraction of school.

My plan of immersing myself in schoolwork as a way to stop fixating on the Starbucks incident actually worked. After a morning of thoughtful note taking and overeager participation, I felt almost back to normal by the time I dropped my books off at my locker and headed to lunch. *Maybe Molly forgot about yesterday. I'm probably doing my usual thing of making a big deal out of nothing.*

Feeling lighter than I had all morning, I turned into the caf and immediately spotted Molly just sitting down with Emmett at our usual table against the back wall. I could see Emmett had already scored us my favorite sandwich—a chicken, cheddar, and avocado panini—and neatly split it in half for the two of us to share. He'd even grabbed me an ice cold Diet Coke. That boy knew me all too well.

To those on the outside, Emmett and Molly probably

seemed like unlikely friends. Molly was super-outgoing, flirty, and had a, shall we say, "big" personality, while Emmett's approach to life would probably fall into the "less is more" category. Too tall for his own good and blessed with thick locks of dark, chocolate hair he was constantly brushing out of his eyes, Emmett was introspective, thoughtful, and a bit reserved. But since Molly and Emmett practically grew up as siblings (their parents were in the same birth class), they had found a way to make it work.

"Yo, what's happenin', hot stuff?" I sat down next to Emmett and reached for my lunch.

"Not much. What's new with you, sexy mama?" Emmett replied.

"*I'll* tell you what's new," Molly interjected. "Janna's got herself a new boyfriend. *That's* what's new."

I caught Molly smirking at me as she tossed a stack of paper across the table, just missing my lunch.

"Whoa, what's this?" I shoved my panini out of the line of fire.

"What are you talking about?" Emmett asked simultaneously.

I turned to Emmett. "Nothing," I said decisively while trying to ignore the monstrous pile before me.

"There's a lot more where that came from," Molly said.

"But I thought this would be enough research to get you started."

"Get started with *what?*" Emmett probed, leaning over my shoulder for a closer look. "*The CIA World Factbook?* Hungary Tourism dot-com?" He looked at me with a blank stare. "What am I missing here?"

I ignored him and turned to Molly. "Seriously? With all the extra work I've got to do to get through the rest of the semester, you actually think I'm going to read all of this?" Clearly my hope that Molly had forgotten about yesterday's events was misplaced optimism. But I certainly wasn't prepared for the dissertation on Hungarian norms and cultures she had apparently been up all night pulling together.

"You have to! Otherwise Julian will know you're not from Hungary!"

Emmett jumped in. "But Janna's *not* from Hungary." Then, as if questioning his assumption, "*Are* you?" Pause. "And who's Julian?"

"Well, technically speaking, I *am* of Hungarian descent. My dad's mom spent her childhood there before coming to the U.S.," I said defensively, trying to ignore Emmett's penetrating stare. I sighed and put my head down onto the table in defeat.

"I honestly don't get why this is such a big deal, Janna,"

Molly continued. "Haven't you always said you wanted to live in a foreign country? Well, this will be kind of like that, only reversed." I looked up and gave her my best glare before hiding my head again. "And anyway, we just have to go out with them one time. Twice, tops. By then Julian will already like-like you, Spence will be head over heels in love with me, and you can tell Julian the truth. But you can't do that just yet. You've gotta reel him in first."

Side note: Whenever Molly started comparing scoping guys to hunting or fishing, I knew I was in big trouble.

"Excuse me for interrupting, but what the hell is going on?" Emmett asked, sounding more than a little annoyed.

I didn't dare look up, choosing instead to peek through the table cracks and count crumbs on the dingy floor. Anything to avoid the look of disappointment I knew was spreading across Emmett's face as Molly explained the situation. Emmett might expect this kind of thing from Molly, but I knew he held me to a higher standard.

"Nice," Emmett said coldly, his voice dripping with sarcasm. "Or should I say"—he paused, looking over my head to the top of the research pile featuring English to Hungarian translated phrases—"*Jó.* And for the record, I can't believe you didn't say anything about this last night, Janna. You totally broke the 'no keeping secrets' rant rule. But maybe deception is your new MO and it's no biggie—"

I sat up to defend myself. Emmett may have been right, but I could only take one person beating me up at a time. And today that person was me.

"Whatever . . . it's not *that* bad. Anyway, it doesn't matter. Picking up girls at Starbucks? They probably don't even remember our names." I turned to Molly, my voice picking up steam. "So, we just won't meet them on Friday night, and—"

I was cut off midsentence by the vibration of my cell phone. We all whipped our heads around in unison, homing in on the shaking electronic device. Synchronicity happened in my life all the time—I already knew who was texting me before I picked up the phone.

Hey Janna, it's Julian. Remember me? C U Friday at Rental in Capitol Hill @ 8.

I shut off my cell and reached for the pile of research in front of me. It was going to be a long week.

3

I successfully avoided Emmett for the rest of the afternoon—I didn't have the energy to deal with his looks of disapproval. Having your conscience walk around in another person's body? It's a tricky thing. I'd never really minded before, since I trusted Emmett and his sense of right and wrong so implicitly. But now I was in uncharted territory. I knew I should feel terrible for what I was doing, and believe me, I did. But I had to admit, I also got a little thrill every time I reread the text message from Julian. Hence, utter and complete avoidance of the person whose very presence reminded me of the unsavory path I was going down.

Emmett was so annoyed, I wasn't even sure he'd call for our NR that night, but rant guidelines clearly stated only certain events could preclude our two-minute nightly check-in. Among them: a preapproved excuse for special occasions (sleepovers, late concerts, and vacations), being on one's deathbed or otherwise unconscious, or the occurrence of a catastrophic natural phenomenon such as a meteor crashing into the earth temporarily shutting down all forms of cellular communication. Most nights, the rant was on.

But Emmett did call, and so I plowed through my grievances first, mostly avoiding the elephant in the room other than to say I felt I was being judged too harshly by one of my best friends (without naming names, of course). Emmett also stuck to topics outside the realm of duplicitous, Hungarian facades, at least until he got to the last item on his rant list.

"And lastly, I'm annoyed that one of my best friends is refriending me on Facebook, and as a Hungarian impostor, no less," he said. "Why didn't you tell me your middle name was Ika Ilka? And here all this time I thought it was Grace."

"What are you talking about?"

"You tell me. I just got a friend request from Janna Ika Ilka Papp, who's hometown is Budapest, Hungary, and pathetically only has one Facebook friend named—"

"Molly Harris," I answered for him. "I've gotta go."

"I thought you might. Talk to you later," Emmett said smugly.

I'm not what you would call a frequent Facebooker. In

fact, it was Molly who had set up my account and gotten me started, which was why she had my password in the first place. It's not that I was anti-FB or anything—I just didn't feel like putting my life out there for the rest of the world to see and judge. I'd leave that to people like Molly and my ex-pageant-queen mom, who seemed to thrive on attention and assumed that most people found their everyday lives terribly interesting.

I flipped on my monitor and tried logging on to my Facebook account. Nothing. I tried again. Still nothing. I went to Google and searched under the name Janna Papp and found what I was looking for. A link to my new profile.

Molly, what have you done? I hesitantly clicked on the link, almost afraid of what I'd find when I got there. A second later I was staring at the page of someone who looked like me but I didn't actually know. Despite my ambivalence toward social networking, this little Facebook development made me none too happy. I clicked through the tabs at the top of my profile and started reading about myself:

Religious Views: Roman Catholic
Activities: Equestrianism, frequenting bathhouses, bird watching, traveling, hanging out with friends
Interests: Traveling to the United States, learning about other cultures, foreign languages

Favorite Music: Béla Bartók, Franz Liszt, Hungarian folk music

Favorite TV Shows: *Barátok közt, Celeb vagyok, ments ki innen!*

Favorite Movies: *Van Helsing, Casablanca, Dirty Dancing, Juno, Final Destination*

Favorite Books: *The Metamorphosis,* anything by Gyula Illyés, *Are You There, God? It's Me, Margaret.*

About Me: I come from Budapest, Hungary, and am now living in Seattle, Washington, in the United States. I am an exchange student living with a very nice family. I am in eleventh grade.

Face flushed, I speed-dialed Molly, my heart rate pounding louder with the passing of each unanswered ring. Finally, she picked up.

"Hey, I was just going to call you!"

"What did you do to my Facebook account?" I demanded.

"*That's* what I was going to call you about. I had to make a few adjustments to your profile." Pause. "Well, actually, I had to go ahead and create a new profile for you. We didn't have a choice."

"What do you mean 'we didn't have a choice'? And what happened to my old profile?" I asked.

"I had to delete it," Molly answered somewhat sheepishly.

"You *deleted* my Facebook account!?"

"I had to! It was only a matter of time until Julian started poking around trying to find you, and if he saw your old profile it would have blown everything! Anyway, it's not like you're ever on it. I mean, you only had twenty-seven friends. We can easily re-create your old profile when this is all over."

"And so now I have *one* friend," I said. "Like *that* doesn't make me look like a serious loser."

"If he asks, you can tell Julian this is your American account and you just opened it. Besides, I sent out a select few friend requests for you, so you should have a couple more soon."

I stewed in silence. This wasn't the first time Molly had taken my personal life into her own hands, but this particular invasion of privacy felt especially brazen. Yet, as was also often the case, I found myself being swayed by Molly's logic. Of *course* Julian would look me up on Facebook—I had been planning to do the same thing myself and check out his profile before Friday night. But, logical or not, I wasn't about to drop it that easily. I scanned through my fake profile in search of ammunition.

"And why exactly do I frequent bathhouses?"

"Bathhouses are extremely popular in Hungary. If you'd read the research I gave you, you would know that already," Molly said. "Besides, I had to make the profile look real."

"And what's up with these movies? He's going to think I have multiple personality disorder or something."

Molly laughed it off. "It shows you have a broad range of interests, that's all. Guys like that."

"And I supposed the TV show *Celeb vagyok, ments ki innen!* is something everyone in Hungary watches?"

"But of course . . . it's the Hungarian version of *I'm a Celebrity, Get Me Out of Here!*" Molly replied matter-of-factly.

Defeated, I hung up the phone and stared numbly at the screen. This was already getting way more complicated than I'd ever imagined, and our actual date was still three days away. The Starbucks incident was one thing. But seeing my big lie glare back at me from the computer screen was a whole other cup of latte.

I was just about to shut down my computer when I got an e-mail from Facebook—a friend request notification from none other than Julian Barnes. I clicked on the link and accepted, immediately going to Julian's page to start reading about him. I double clicked on his profile picture to get a closer look. It was a blurry, artistic shot of Julian behind a deejay booth. He looked cool. And cute. Definitely too cool and cute for me. I went back to his main page and saw he had two hundred forty-seven friends. Popular, too. *What am I getting myself into?* For the next half hour I poked around his profile, reading up on his favorites and flipping through his photos. I knew he was probably doing the same thing with me, although he clearly wouldn't gain much insight into who I was. Suddenly I was grateful for Molly's quick thinking, not to mention nervously excited about the presence of this new guy in my life. And as I got to know Julian better on paper (or on computer, as the case may be), my little complicated situation started to feel like it might be worth it after all.

4

By Thursday I was starting to feel slightly more comfortable in my newly cast role of intriguing foreign exchange student. Molly and I had spent Wednesday afternoon prepping, dreaming up a few fake Hungarian childhood memories involving holidays spent visiting castles in the countryside and my mom's infamous Hungarian goulash, just in case Julian asked me about my life "back home." To make sure my accent was on spot, we watched clip after clip of actress Zsa Zsa Gabor on YouTube, although I used it only as inspiration, since Zsa Zsa was a little more la-di-da than I was going for.

Though all this preparation for the role of a lifetime was clearly pushing me way beyond my comfort zone, not all of the Hungarian homework had been a bad thing. For starters, it occurred to me that I might be able to parlay my newfound in-depth knowledge about Hungary into an extra-credit project for cultural studies and therefore attain the B that I so desperately needed. And then there were the necessary wardrobe updates.

Since Hungary has a large gypsy population, Molly insisted I needed to have a personal style that was part Euro chic, part hippie chick. We spent hours picking through the racks at consignment shops in the U District, eventually piecing together the perfect Bohemian outfit for Friday night: an embroidered, empire-waist tank top with tiered cotton skirt, accessorized with a patchwork hobo bag and funky necklace.

Of course, I knew my new look was sure to raise some eyebrows, as Henry confirmed later that night when he barged into my room as I was trying on the ensemble.

"What is *that*?" he said.

"What is what?"

"That." He was pointing to my necklace.

"What do you mean? It's a necklace with the om symbol on it," I said, defensively. "It's Hindu."

"Hind *who*?"

"Hin-du!" I scowled. "What are you doing in my room, anyway?"

"Easy, sis." He slowly backed toward the door like he'd just been cornered by a wild animal. "I just wanted to tell you to say hi to Jimi Hendrix for me when you get to Woodstock. Peace out!" He flashed me the peace symbol before I slammed the door in his face.

I turned back and looked in the mirror, unclenching my fists and trying to shake off the residual Henry annoyance energy (no small feat). As I took in my reflection, I realized I actually felt great in the outfit. Exotic. Foreign, even. It was almost like slipping in to the clothes completed my transformation. The idea of being an intriguing citizen of the world was starting to grow on me.

Molly's dedication to helping me prep for Friday night was typically obsessive, but I knew her primary motivation wasn't my love life at all. Rather, it was Spence, with whom she'd been flirting via text message since we'd met. Molly's love life being dependent on me must have been an unusual predicament for her, but more than anyone I knew, Molly had a relentless can-do attitude. She intended to get her man, no matter what. Which is why, I suppose, she gave me a final homework assignment to ensure I was one hundred percent ready for the big night.

"*Method acting?* What's that?" Molly had called me late Wednesday night, excited to share her grand scheme, which had apparently hit her like a load of bricks halfway through

Heroes. Her high level of enthusiasm naturally made me wary.

"I learned all about it in drama camp last summer," she explained. "It's where you totally immerse yourself in your role. Like, you live, sleep, and breathe the character you're playing. Serious actors do it all the time. Even when the cameras aren't rolling."

I knew why she wanted me to do it—Molly wasn't going for a passable performance. She had her sights set on an Oscar.

"What exactly are you suggesting I do?" I asked.

"I think you should spend all day tomorrow in character as Janna Ika Ilka."

"All day?"

"Yes, all day. Well, of course, unless you get called on in class or you have to do something with your family. But other than that, yeah. I think it'll be great practice."

An Oscar didn't interest me, but surviving Friday night's date without humiliating myself did, so I agreed to go along with it. The afternoon was going to be tricky, though, since Emmett and I usually went to see old movies at the revival theater on Thursdays after school. Today the 1953 classic *The War of the Worlds* was showing. I could only hope that the real war wouldn't be between the two of us.

Ever since Tuesday at lunch, Emmett had been acting

fairly weird toward me, and I didn't like it one bit. Of course, we'd had disagreements before, but this one felt different. To be fair, I'd barely even seen him, since he'd spent every spare moment including lunchtime working on the yearbook, which he was art directing. I figured we just needed to spend some quality time hanging out in order for things to go back to normal. I was kind of hoping he'd actually see the funny side of my predicament today. Heck, maybe he'd even like the new Janna. But as soon as our outing began, I knew I was out of luck.

We had just caught up with each other as the bus pulled up, so the first words out of my mouth were spoken to the driver. After climbing aboard and flashing my bus pass, I quietly thanked the driver in my best Hungarian accent. My response didn't go unnoticed by Emmett, who slowly turned around, squinting his eyes.

"I'm sorry . . . did you just say *'sank you'*?"

I lowered my voice and leaned in. "Not so loud, Emm," I whispered in my regular voice. "I'm practicing my Hungarian accent today. Molly thinks it's a good idea for me to spend the whole day in character."

Emmett rolled his eyes. "Of course she does. Because to Molly, there's absolutely nothing wrong with what you're doing. I just can't believe how easily she's manipulated you into thinking this is okay."

"Can't you just go along with it for today? *Please?* The only thing that will be different about me is my accent. I promise." I paused. "Hey, I have an idea . . . why don't you pretend to be an exchange student, too? Seriously, it's kind of fun."

Emmett's dagger eyes told me that wasn't going to happen.

"I've got to be honest, Janna. I don't understand why you're doing this. Yes, I know you have a hard time standing up to Molly when she gets one of her big ideas, but it seems to me like you're actually okay with all this, which I totally don't get," Emmett said. "I mean, why would you pretend to be someone else to get a guy? It just doesn't make sense."

I turned to look out the window, not sure of how to respond. The truth? It didn't make complete sense to me, either. What I did know was that I liked the fact that there was a cute guy out there who was interested in me. I mean, who wouldn't like that? But there was more to it than that.

"I don't know how to explain it. It's like, have you ever wished you could have a fresh start and just be someone else for once?"

"I guess so."

"This is kind of like that. Do you realize that this is the first time a really cute guy has ever actually been interested

in me? I don't know. I guess something about it feels exciting. Like I have a chance to be seen as really intriguing and,
you know, a catch."

Emmett looked at me, his brown eyes boring right
through me. "What makes you think a cute guy wouldn't
see all those things in you without you having to actually
pretend to be someone else?" Emmett sighed in resigna-
tion. "Whatever . . . it's your life. Don't worry . . . I won't
blow your cover."

I looped my arm through Emmett's and leaned in for a
squeeze, glancing up at him with a devilish grin. "You are
best friend a girl could vont," I said, laying the accent on
thick.

I swear I heard a chuckle slip out.

I decided not to press my luck with Emmett, though,
and kept my alter ego in check until we got to the theater.
For his part, Emmett patiently stood by while I bought a
ticket and some Junior Mints, although the temptation to
screw with me was clearly too hard to resist, because while
paying for my snack, he loudly blurted out, "Gee, Janna,
I hope you can understand what's happening in the movie.
After all . . . there are no Hungarian subtitles!"

I ignored the confused looks from the other movie-
goers, grabbed Emmett's arm, and dragged him into the
theater. Frankly, I was looking forward to two hours of

focusing on the drama on-screen instead of the drama in my own life.

By the time the credits rolled and we headed over to Café Allegro for a cinematic debrief, things between Emmett and I seemed almost normal, which was a relief. In fact, he even seemed to be okay with my speaking with an accent. It was only when my cell phone pinged to indicate I had a text that things started going downhill.

We were in the middle of discussing whether or not a hoax regarding an alien invasion on Earth could be pulled off today when the message came in. Instinctively, I grabbed my phone and stared at the message. It was from him. From Julian. I hadn't heard from him since the text he sent me at lunch on Tuesday.

Hi Janna. Julian here. Reading Kafka in English class. Thought of u. C u tomorrow?

A cute boy was thinking of me. I thumbed out a quick reply—☺ **Yes, c u tomorrow!**—only noticing Emmett's grim expression once I was finished and tried picking up our conversation where we'd left off.

"Who was that?" Emmett probed.

"What. Oh . . . nobody. I mean, it was a text from that guy."

"You mean the guy you're going out with tomorrow night who thinks you're from Hungary?"

"Yeah, him."

"I'm sorry, is it just me or did you get all giddy and girly when he texted you? What's his name again?"

"Julian," I said, unable to suppress a grin.

"There it is again . . . that embarrassed-excited-flushed-face thing."

"I'm just nervous, that's all."

Emmett's tone seemed to change. "So, do you really like this guy? Or is it just the fact that he's paying attention to you?"

I thought about his question. "I don't know, Emmett. I don't know if I like him yet or not. And who knows if he would actually like me if he knew the truth? I guess you could say I'm interested in knowing more."

"More about what? Why he feels the need to stalk foreign girls?"

I rolled my eyes and shook my head at him. Emmett was clearly upset, and I wasn't sure why. One thing was for sure—I didn't like the turn this conversation was taking.

"Look. All I know is, he seems like a nice guy. Yes, I think he's cute. Yes, I like that he's interested in me. And yes, you're right. There's a good chance he only likes me because he thinks I'm from another country. He might be

some total exchange-student-loving loser for all I know."
Why did Emmett always make me feel like I had to
explain myself? "I just don't understand why you're acting
so uppity. Is it really so terrible that I'm doing something
spontaneous and out of character? Seriously. Maybe you
should try it sometime."

I got off my soapbox, and an uncomfortable silence
ensued. Emmett suddenly became intensely interested in
measuring the depth of his latte foam with his wooden stir-
ring stick, while I looked over his shoulder and studied the
abstract collage art on the wall.

"Look, can we *please* just let it go and move on?" I asked
after a minute.

Emmett looked up, a forced grin plastered across his
face. "Sure, consider it forgotten."

We hung out at Allegra for another fifteen minutes
more before heading out, Emmett explaining that the yearbook had put him behind schedule on preparation for finals
and he had to get back to work. I knew the truth, though.
Emmett and I were in murky waters. Even though I knew
I hadn't changed, it was clear that Emmett wasn't so sure.
And as we said good-bye on the street corner, I had to
wonder if the Starbucks incident was going to have bigger
repercussions than I ever could have imagined.

5

There are many things I enjoy doing on a Friday night. Circling around Capitol Hill in Molly's VW Beetle fruitlessly searching for a parking spot was not one of them. On top of that, we were late, and I was a nervous wreck.

While getting ready back at Molly's house, I had come up with a half-dozen excuses for calling off the date, from being infected with the swine flu to the death of my pet goldfish, but Molly was having none of it.

"You see, the thing is, I don't actually think I can do this." I was sitting on Molly's bed watching her carefully apply fake eyelashes. They looked great. "I'm being serious here. I feel like I'm going to throw up."

"You're not going to throw up," Molly said. "You're just anxious. You'd feel this way even without the Hungarian thing. I mean, it *has* been a while since you've gone out with a guy who's actually interested in you, right? Anyway, I've got a barf bag in my purse, just in case."

I gave Molly my signature blank stare, perfected after years of living with Henry.

"But what do we really know about these guys, anyway? What if Julian is some lech who just wants to go out with me because he thinks Hungarian girls are easy?"

"Well, I'm actually hoping Spence *is* a lech who thinks Seattle girls are easy." Molly laughed flirtatiously.

"That reminds me, don't you *dare* leave me tonight!" I said. The last time we'd gone out on a double date, Molly had ditched me early on, leaving me to fend for myself with unquestionably the most self-absorbed drone on the planet.

"I give you my word," Molly replied. "Look, don't worry . . . I've got your back! And don't forget—you're from another country, so, really, you can just relax and let the Americans do the talking. Just smile a lot, laugh at Julian's jokes, look intriguing, and you'll be *fine*. I promise."

But now that Molly was squeezing into a tight parking spot and the point of no return was upon us, I wasn't so sure. Molly shut off the car and adjusted the daisies peeking out of her dashboard vase before turning to me excitedly.

"It's showtime!" she sang.

We walked the two blocks to the club and heard the drumming pulse of the music before we hit the front door. I closed my eyes and stopped for one last second, trying to banish my nerves.

The dark club was teeming with people, and the multicolored strobe lights made it hard to see two feet in front you. Molly and I found the bar and snagged a stool to lean on, a buoy in a stormy sea. We hadn't been at the club for more than two minutes when Spence materialized.

"Hey," he said with a smirk he obviously thought was sexy. "You guys made it. Come on over—we have a table." Molly gave Spence a flirty smile and reached for his hand as he led us through the hordes of people to a little round table off to the side.

"Where's Julian?" Molly asked as we sat down, straining to have her voice heard above the music.

Spence pointed toward the deejay booth at the front of the club. There was Julian, standing behind a table strewn with electronic equipment. Clad in jeans, a T-shirt, and headphones, he looked just like he did on his Facebook profile picture. It was obvious by the look of focus on his face and the way his body moved with the rhythm that he was completely engrossed in what he was doing. We listened

as he seamlessly cross-faded one track to another, inject-
ing a new energy into the place. The music was fantastic
and unusual, alive with beats and rhythms I'd never heard
before. By the energy of the people on the dance floor, I
could already tell Julian was great at what he did.

I stole another glance at him and felt my stomach flip
when he looked up, smiled, and signaled he'd be done in
five minutes. I smiled back shyly and whipped around, my
knee beginning to unconsciously bounce like a Mexican
jumping bean, the only thought in my head the repeating
theme of *Oh my God, why am I doing this, oh my God, why am
I doing this . . .*

Molly must have sensed my mood shift, because she
calmly rested her hand on my knee. I looked into her eyes
and she steadily returned my gaze, willing me to relax. I
took another deep breath and turned my attention to the
dance floor, giving Molly a chance to talk to Spence and
allowing me to think about something other than what I
would do when Julian sat down.

A few minutes later Julian's voice came on over the
sound system. He thanked everyone for coming out and
pitched an upcoming gig before turning over the booth to
another deejay. And then, there he was. Sitting down. At
our table. Next to me.

"Hi there!" said Julian.

"Hallo," I said softly.

"You made it. I was starting to think you weren't coming," he said.

I laughed nervously, shrugging my shoulders. I was hoping to keep the talking to a minimum, praying Julian would assume my English comprehension wasn't great and not engage with me too much.

"I'm all done with my set," Julian said slowly, enunciating every syllable. "Do you guys want to stick around here or go somewhere we can actually hear ourselves think?" He turned to check in with Molly and Spence, but they had just gotten up and headed to the dance floor.

Julian turned back to me and shrugged. "I guess we're staying here."

I smiled, studying his face. I had seen him so briefly during the Starbucks incident, plus I was so focused on internally freaking out at the time, I really didn't remember much about his appearance, other than thinking he was extraordinarily cute. Clearly, I had a good memory.

Tonight Julian looked even better than I remembered. He was a typical Seattle boy in some ways—tall and lanky, with longish brown hair—although his fashion sense was slightly more urban and edgy than the standard Northwest fare. He wasn't quite punk or Goth (no guyliner or anything), but he definitely had his own unique fashion aesthetic. His eyes were a light, grayish-green, and I found it hard to turn away from them once they were focused on mine. He had beautiful skin, a slightly crooked smile, and red, full lips. As I looked at him more closely, I realized this guy was more than good-looking. He was drop dead gorgeous. Which made me all the more skeptical. *What was he doing with me?*

"So, how long have you been living in Seattle?" Julian asked.

"Since September," I answered in my practiced accent. "And you?"

"I've lived here for about ten years. I moved to Seattle from Chicago when I was six years old," he answered. "Well, now that you've been here for almost a year, what do you think of the Emerald City?"

"It is veddy nice," I replied. "I like to be near so much vater."

"Where in Hungary are you from?"

I had been expecting this question. "Budapest." I pronounced the capital city in the proper way: *Budapescht.*

"Well, you have water there, too, right? Isn't Budapest divided in half by the Danube River?"

My heart stopped. *Yes,* I wanted to say. *Yes, it is.* But how did he know so much about Budapest?

As if reading my mind, Julian continued, "I've actually been to Budapest before. My family travels a lot, and we did a whole Eastern Europe trip a couple of summers ago. We only spent a few days there, but I remember thinking it was a very cool city."

Great. An expert on my adopted homeland. "Yes, it is great city." Suddenly, I was feeling even more nervous than before. What were the chances that Julian had visited Hungary before? What if he brought up something I wasn't prepared for? Luckily, our conversation was interrupted by Molly and Spence, who had just come off the dance floor. Molly was already aglow, face plastered with her trademark cute-boy-induced grin.

"Yo, Julian, let's get outta here," Spence said, grabbing his coat.

"Cool. We're ready." He turned to me. "Right?"

"Right." *As ready as I'll ever be.*

We headed out and meandered around the bustling neighborhood of Capitol Hill, trying to come up with a plan for where to go next. Seattle isn't exactly known for its nightlife, but this part of the city had no shortage of cafés and restaurants and people milling about. The light rain that picked up helped us make a decision, and we ducked into a diner on Broadway near the community college, waiting a few minutes before being led to the only open booth in the place. We didn't realize until we scooted in—Julian and I on one side, Molly and Spence on the other—that the table was most likely vacant because of its proximity to the portable karaoke setup in the corner, not to mention the nearby drunken college student belting out Nirvana's "Come as You Are."

Julian and I looked at each other and burst out laughing. "Well, at least we'll be able to talk more easily now," Julian shouted.

I chuckled and opened the menu, pretending to read the listed food items but not actually doing it on account of being completely distracted by Julian. I didn't know if it was his presence, energy, sex appeal, or just really good cologne, but any time he leaned in close to ask me a question or look over my shoulder at the menu, the hair on my arms stood on end in his honor. I couldn't be positive he was feeling it, too, but I think I finally discovered the true meaning of chemistry.

Despite this nearly paralyzing physical response I had to Julian, I was actually starting to loosen up. Between the ridiculousness of the karaoke singers (and I use the word "singers" loosely), Molly and Spence's over-the-top PDA, and the fact that I'd had four Diet Coke refills in the span of two hours, I was feeling chattier than I would have expected. In the lull between over-the-top performances, Julian and I talked about the best and worst parts of Seattle, school, and Budapest. Hoping he would view me as a mysterious European, I steered the conversation back to him at every opportunity. Plus, Molly has always said there's nothing guys love to do more than talk about themselves (well, *almost* nothing), and Julian seemed happy enough to oblige me.

I found out that Julian went to the Collins School, a private academy known for its rugby team, serious endowment, and class after class of graduates going on to Ivy League schools. Admittedly, I had a slight chip on my shoulder against private school kids, if for no other reason than their schools seemed to be a lot nicer than public ones and I assumed all the kids who went to them were privileged richies. But Janna Ika Ilka didn't have those prejudices against private school kids. Heck, for all I knew, she might even be one. Therefore, I decided to lose the chip and let it go.

As Julian continued talking, I became increasingly comfortable with my role of Janna Ika Ilka. I can only assume this shift occurred because my alter ego was inherently more interesting than I was. With every look and smile from Julian, the message that someone found her attractive came through loud and clear. Embracing the freeness of being someone else, I stopped worrying so much and did my best to savor the attention and circumstances. I almost felt a little like Cinderella, that is, if Cinderella had been a lying poseur. But there'd be plenty of time to deal with that reality. For tonight I was going to stay in the moment as much as possible.

The four of us had just finished picking through a ginormous basket of cheese fries when the karaoke guy made an unexpected announcement. "Next up, it's Julian and Janna, singing 'I've Had the Time of My Life,' the theme song from *Dirty Dancing*!"

Julian stopped talking midsentence to look at Spence, who was laughing his ass off.

"Dude, that is so lame!" Julian laughed, reaching across the table and throwing a mock punch.

"You know you love this song, J. Oh wait a sec, it's your *mom* who loves it. Oops." Spence laughed.

"Julian and Janna! Calling Julian and Janna! Come on up! Let's give them a big hand, folks!"

Julian looked at me with a resigned but entertained look on his face. "I'll do it if you'll do it."

I looked at Molly, who apparently had gotten swept up in Spence's deviousness. "Hey, Janna, isn't *Dirty Dancing* one of your favorite movies?"

Julian slid out of the booth and held out his hand for me. I was at yet another crossroads. Before tonight, if you were to ask me what type of situation would strike terror and fear in my heart, singing karaoke would have been near the top of the list. All those people? Staring at me? Listening to me? Most likely *laughing* at me? The threat of public humiliation jogged painful memories of the one and only time my mom had forced me into a pageant and I was struck with a paralyzing case of stage fright. So, karaoke? There was no way. But when I saw Julian looking at me with those gorgeous eyes and holding out his hand, I knew I couldn't say no. Or at least Janna Ika Ilka couldn't.

A second later the music was playing and Julian was crooning out the first line of the song. I knew the second line was mine. So I did what any shameless karaoke singer in a room full of strangers at a random diner on a Friday night would do. I sang. Loudly. Ridiculously. And with an accent, of course.

An hour later the four of us were standing next to Molly's car facing what I always felt was the awkward time of any first date—the good-bye. I hated the uncertainty of such moments, unsure about how the actual parting of ways would transpire. Would there be a handshake? A hug? A nonchalant nod of the head paired with a "See you around?" Perhaps in avoidance of the inevitable, Julian and I focused on laughing about our pitiful karaoke performance. Or maybe we were just trying (unsuccessfully) to ignore Molly and Spence, who apparently weren't suffering from awkward-first-date-good-bye syndrome at all. No—they were leaned against the hood of the car making out like Spence was going off to war.

I turned to check on whether or not Spence and Molly had broken free of their lip-lock long enough to come up for air, when suddenly Julian leaned toward me. I froze. Was he coming in for a kiss? Maybe he did think that Hungarian girls were fast. Did he not know I hadn't actually ever had a real kiss before and that the very idea of it scared the crap out of me? Thank God I didn't have to find out. In a move I found both classy and unexpected, Julian lightly kissed me on both cheeks, Euro style. I loved the way his soft lips felt against my cheeks, his warm breath so close to my neck. My body responded with an involuntary off-balance sway paired with the tingles. Julian pulled back and steadied me when he grabbed my hands with his.

"I can't believe I just met you right before you're about to leave Seattle . . . that really sucks." Despite the darkness and fog that had settled in, Julian's light eyes shined brightly toward me. "So, when do you actually go back to Hungary?"

I felt a stab of guilt as my mind raced for a date. Into it popped the day Molly and I were slated to leave for our trip to Europe, assuming I got my grade up.

"June twenty-seventh. More zan vun month," I replied

hopefully. I may not have known where this was going, but part of me definitely wanted to find out.

I heard Molly unlock the car and pop open her door.

"Ready, Janna?" she called.

"Yes." I turned back to Julian. "Sank you for tonight."

Julian raised my hand to his lips, giving it a gentle peck. He put his other hand behind his back and bowed down in mock chivalry, before helping me into the car and gently closing the door.

"I'll call you," Julian said through the door.

Molly started up the car and we waved good-bye before pulling away. I waited until we were a solid two blocks from the guys before letting out a bloodcurdling scream.

"I know, right?" Molly laughed. "See, I told you you could pull it off!"

I was laughing now, too, in disbelief, in giddy excitement, in shock. "I can't believe I just did that. Can *you* believe I just did that? I can't believe I did that!" I tended to repeat myself when I had full-on spaz attacks. "I mean, did you see me? I sang karaoke!"

"I know. I was there, remember?" Molly rolled her eyes as she laughed. "Pretty impressive, really, considering your history with performing. Maybe you won't even have to worry about stage fright anymore!"

"Um, yeah, let's not go there, okay?" I leaned back in

the seat and closed my eyes, letting out a long sigh. "Oh . . .
my . . . God. I'm *so* relieved that's over. I still can't believe I
actually did it. Do you think he really believes that I'm from
Hungary?"

"Of course he does. You were great tonight. I actually
think he likes you." Molly sounded almost surprised but
pleased at the possibility. "And what about Spence? Did
you see how into me he was? God, he is so gorgeous! And
damn, can that boy kiss!"

Now it was Molly's turn to let out a giddy scream. I
laughed with her and then turned to gaze out the window
as we drove back to Molly's house. I was happy one of our
favorite songs started playing on the radio, because Molly
cranked up the volume and focused on singing along rather
than continuing our conversation. My head was swimming
with a combination of guilt, excitement, confidence, and
anxiety. I needed a few minutes to decompress.

By the time we pulled into Molly's driveway I was in
a silent daze, and I half walked/half floated into the house.

"Hey, girls! How was your night?" Molly's mom called
from the den room as we passed by the doorway.

"Great," Molly replied.

"That's good. By the way, there's some leftover Judy's
in the freezer if you need a little snack," she said. Molly's
mom may not have been home much, but when she was,

she was the coolest mom around. No curfews, no prying, no coaches. Plus, she had an addiction to the best homemade ice cream in Seattle, which definitely worked in our favor.

"Thanks, Mom," Molly said. "Good night!"

"G'night!"

An hour later Molly and I were sprawled out on her futon listening to tunes and finishing off what had been a pint of mint ice cream with chunks of Thin Mint Girl Scout Cookies (a true match made in heaven). We were engaged in an in-depth date recap. Usually these discussions consisted of me validating Molly's feelings and agreeing with her about whatever impressions she had regarding her crush du jour. But tonight I really needed to talk about me. And Julian. And me and Julian. And what it all meant. At first Molly was relatively patient and engaging in said conversation, but after a while I could tell she was ready to get back to talking about more interesting things. Like herself.

"I just wasn't expecting any of this to happen," I said.

"Any of *what*?"

"*This*. Like, I think I *like* him. And he's so much more incredible and cute than anybody who's ever shown interest in me before," I said. My forehead crinkled with worry. "To be honest, I don't get why exactly he likes me. That is, if he even *does* like me."

"He does . . . trust me. I saw the way he looks at you," Molly said.

"But do you think that's just because he thinks I'm someone else?" I wasn't sure I wanted to hear her reply.

"Well . . . probably . . ."

That was definitely not the right answer. Molly must have realized this because she quickly back-pedaled.

". . . or maybe not. It's too soon to tell."

"But come on, how much longer can I really keep this up? I mean, I did kind of like being Janna Ika Ilka tonight." I rolled my eyes at the sound of my new middle name. "But I also feel terrible about lying. What's Julian going to do when he finds out the truth?"

"Look, we're just having fun, right? *I'm* having fun. Are *you* having fun?"

"Yes." I had to admit, I was.

"Well, then, let's worry about that when we *have* to worry about that. Anyway . . . Julian might end up being a loser and be out of the picture before you even have to tell him the truth, right? So, just keep it up for one more week and then we'll re-evaluate," she said. "I promise, it's all going to work out."

"How can you be so sure?" I answered skeptically.

"I just am. Now can we talk about Spence?" she asked. It was clear that Molly was done placating me.

"Sure."

"Thank you!" Molly said, exasperated. And with that, she launched into a forty-five-minute highlights reel of her date with Spence, from their first kiss to the fact that he'd already dropped several hints that he was thinking of bringing her to his junior prom. I lay down and closed my eyes, inserting the occasional "Oh, really?" and "That's cool" at appropriate times, while my mind went through a highlights reel of its own.

A slow smile spread across my face as I thought back to the diner and our song, the way Julian had kissed me so delicately on each cheek. Just thinking about it gave me the same tingly feeling I'd had earlier. Who knew a kiss on the cheek could be so sensual?

Tonight had been perhaps one of the most unusual nights of my life. And while the fake accent and boho clothes probably had something to do with it, I had felt more confident, outgoing, and pretty tonight than I had in a long time, especially when hanging out with a guy. And that was something I could definitely get used to.

6

The rest of the weekend dragged by, in part because I was starting it out with a serious sleep deficit thanks to the sleepover that didn't actually involve sleep, and in part because I was wondering when and if I was going to hear from Julian again. I knew better than to expect a phone call the next day (Molly had educated me in the dos and don'ts when it comes to going out and frequency of communication), but a quick text would have been nice. You know, a "Hey, thanks for last night," or "Just thinking about you and wanted to say hi," or maybe even a little "How is my Hungarian gypsy love goddess today?"

But instead of texting with Julian, I spent most of Saturday holed up in my room working on my extra-credit project for history class. Ms. Kendall had agreed to let me write a paper on Hungary's move from communism to capitalism to boost my cultural studies grade, but I only had a week to get it done. Thankfully, my paper gave me the perfect excuse to duck out of my family's regular volunteer obligation of cleaning up one of the beaches along Puget Sound, which, frankly, I just wasn't up for. Small talk with Mom and Dad and other perfectly nice strangers for an entire afternoon? No thanks.

On Sunday the sun made a rare May appearance, and in honor of the glowing orb in the sky and because I was ready for a break from any and all things having to do with Hungary, I didn't protest too loudly when my mom and dad recruited me to help prep the garden bed for the vegetables we'd be buying at the edible plant sale later that day. They didn't have to twist my arm too hard—I actually liked gardening.

I had been working outside for a few hours and had nearly finished weeding and mixing the fresh compost into the garden when Henry shouted from inside the kitchen.

"Hey, Jan, who's Julian?"

Adrenaline raced through my body. "Huh?"

"Somebody named Julian is calling your cell!"

I dropped the mini spade and sprinted for the house, leaving a trail of dirt in my wake. I ripped the phone out of his hands and ran for the bathroom, slamming the door behind me.

"Hallo?" I answered, doing my best to sound as if I hadn't just competed in the two-hundred-meter dash.

"Janna? Hey, it's Julian."

"Hallo, Julian." I willed my heartbeat to steady.

"Hey, listen, are you home?"

"Yes. I am at zee house of my host family." I was surprised at how seamlessly I slipped into Hungarian mode.

"Well, I hope you don't mind a visitor. I'm actually on your front porch. I went for a bike ride and was passing right by your neighborhood, so I thought I'd swing by and say hi. Is that okay?"

Shoot. Why had I given him my address when he'd asked where in Queen Anne I lived? I looked into the mirror. My hair was piled on top of my head in a too-high ponytail and I had dirt smeared all over my hands, arms, and face. To top it off, I was wearing a ratty U.S. Olympic Team T-shirt circa 2004. Could I possibly look more American?

"Hello? Are you still there?" Julian asked.

"Yes! I am here. Sorry. I be out in one minute, okay?"

"Cool!" Julian hung up.

I frantically flipped on the faucet, violently scrubbing the dirt from my skin as best I could. Unfortunately, simple soap and water was no match for the dark layer of mud beneath my fingernails. Oh, well. It was the best I could do. I quickly dried off my hands and face and yanked out the ponytail holder, leaning over to shake my hair with my fingertips before standing up and flipping it over. I turned back to the mirror for another look. Frizz city. But barring the unlikely appearance of a magical fairy godmother with a transformational wand, there was only so much that could be done. I tried to flatten out the crooked wisps shooting in every direction and with shaky hands pulled my hair back into a low, more sophisticated ponytail.

I grabbed my phone and instinctively dialed Molly's number. She would tell me exactly how to get through this. *Ring.* She'd tell me to just be myself, only with a Hungarian accent and much cooler. *Ring.* Then she'd remind me that most guys aren't very bright, so I should let Julian run the conversation and things would be fine. *Ring.*

"Hi, this is Molly! Leave a—" I hung up at the sound of her overly cheerful outgoing message. I was on my own.

I slowly opened up the bathroom door and peeked into the kitchen. While I knew my current physical state was disastrous, my biggest concern at the moment was actually the location of Henry. Like a shark smelling blood, Henry surely knew something was up. If I was going to pull this off, I had to keep the little brother at bay by throwing some chum into the water.

"Hey, Henry," I said sweetly. "You should check out the new game I just downloaded on my iPod Touch. It's on top of my desk in my room."

Henry emerged from behind a potted ficus tree in the kitchen, eyeing me suspiciously.

"You want me to play with your iPod Touch?" He was clearly in a state of disbelief.

"Yeah, why not? I downloaded a game called Invader Raiders I think you'd love."

"And *why* exactly are you letting me do this?"

"Why wouldn't I? I know how much you like my iPod Touch, and I just figured that you'd wanna try this game. But it's okay if you don't want to . . ."

"No, no . . . I do! Excellent!" Henry bounded up the stairs.

Hook, line, and sinker. And now on to more pressing matters.

I slowly walked to the front of the house and looked back at the stairs one last time to make sure Henry was safely out of view before opening the front door. Julian was perched on the bottom step of my porch, and he turned around the minute I opened the door. His light eyes sparkled with genuine happiness when he saw me. That, coupled with the fact that he looked as gorgeous as ever, made my heart flutter.

"Hey," he said, smiling.

I smiled back. "Hey." I sat down beside him on the steps, keeping my arms loosely crossed in a lame attempt to cover up my ridiculously patriotic T-shirt. I couldn't believe he was actually here. At my house. To see me. He looked like he just walked out of a J. Crew catalog, with his short-sleeve shirt and loose cargo shorts. I especially appreciated the opportunity to check out his arms and legs, which, for a slender guy, were toned and muscular. It was all I could do not to gape at his awesome physique.

"I am mess," I said, waving a hand in front of my hair. "I work in za garden today."

"That's cool. What are you growing?"

"Lettuce, tomatoes, and peas, I sink," I answered quietly. It felt odd to be speaking in my Hungarian accent at home. Neighbors who'd known me since I was in diapers could walk by at any moment. Plus, there was my nosy brother to worry about. He would only be distracted with shiny electronic devices for so long.

"Nice. My mom's a total urban farmer. She's actually a locavore," he said.

"Locavore?" I repeated. "What is zis?"

"It's like someone who will only eat food that's grown locally. I guess you could say she's a little extreme." He turned to me and smiled shyly. "So, did you have fun Friday night?"

"Veddy much fun." I blushed, looking down at my lap. "And for you?"

"Yeah, definitely. In fact, I think that was the most fun I've had going out in a long time," Julian said.

I was just about to respond when the sound of a long, low belch reverberated from the side of the house.

Julian laughed. "What was that?"

I pretended I hadn't heard anything as my face turned red. I was running out of time. "Vat vas vat?"

Then we heard it again. This time it was louder. And closer.

"That." Julian turned around just in time to see Henry fall out from behind a rhododendron.

"Well, hello there. You must be Julian!" Henry walked over with a mischievous smile and stretched out his hand for a firm handshake.

"That's right. And you are—"

"Oh, me? I'm Henry, Janna's—"

"Host brudder!" I blurted out in an anxious accent.

Henry looked at me in confusion. "Your *what*?"

I laughed nervously. "Well, you like brudder to me." I turned to Julian. "Henry is son of my host family."

I watched as Henry put two and two together. In a split second, his confusion shifted into unabashed delight, for he knew he had me. The windows of opportunity had just been flung wide open, and I could be certain Henry would take full advantage.

"Henry, come please." I stood up and beckoned him into the foyer. "Please excuse, Julian. I be right back."

With exaggerated grandiosity, Henry slowly shook Julian's hand again, no doubt just to prolong my torture. "*So* nice to meet you, Julian. Come again anytime!"

"Uh . . . thanks."

As Henry walked into the house, I smiled quickly back at Julian before closing the door and grabbing Henry by the shoulders, trying to assert control over a situation I knew could go south, and fast.

"What's with the accent, sis?"

"Look. Just stay out of my business for once. I *mean* it. Can you please just do that?" If I sounded desperate, it was because I was. And Henry knew it.

"Of course I can. What are *brudders* for?" He paused. "But it's gonna cost you."

"Cost me what? What exactly is it that you want?"

"Hmmm. Let's see here. It's a big, big world, you know." Henry pursed his lips and looked up at the ceiling as if it were the location of a giant toy store.

"Don't push it, Henry. Just tell me what you want and then get out of here," I said furiously.

"Well, let's see . . . I have been wanting the Lego Star

Wars Millennium Falcon collector's edition for some time now," he said.

"That's 300 bucks!" I knew it well, especially since Henry had spent the past three birthdays lobbying for it. His earmarked Lego catalogs had become regular fixtures throughout the house.

"How about the Imperial Dropship?" I bargained.

"That's chump change, sis. General Grievous's Starfighter?" Henry countered.

"How much is that one?"

"Sixty-six dollars," he said. "I'd say that's a deal, considering you're asking me to ignore the identity fraud operation you're running out of our house."

"Coming from a blackmailer, I'm sure you'll find a way to get over it." There goes a third of the money I'd saved for Europe. But, then again, I might not be going to Europe in the first place, and dealing with the issue at hand was definitely more important. "Fine! General Grievous's Starfighter. Deal?"

"Deal." We shook on it, and Henry disappeared upstairs gloating about his score.

When I stepped back outside, Julian was perched on his bike strapping on his helmet. My negotiation with Henry must have taken longer than I thought.

"I am so soddy," I said. "Henry can be—"

"It's no prob. I have to get going anyway. I just wanted to say hi. You go back to your gardening or whatever, and I'll see you soon," Julian said.

My face dropped at Julian's abrupt departure. Had he overheard me bargaining with Henry? Was he turned off by my frumpy weekend look? Was he coming to his senses and realizing he was way out of my league?

Julian seemed to sense my insecurity. "Really, it's okay. I have to pick up some things for my dad at the hardware store before they close. I'll text you later. Hopefully we can see each other next weekend, okay?"

"I would like zis very much," I said, relieved. I wasn't ready for this guy to be out of my life just yet. "Sank you for visit."

"No worries. See you later." I watched as Julian biked away, a sense of excitement filling me just knowing this beautiful boy was in my life. Once he was out of sight, I put my head in my hands and let the stress escape my body. One possible disaster had been narrowly averted. But somehow I knew the next one was lurking right around the corner.

7

"Janna, hurry up or you won't have time for breakfast before Molly gets here!" my mom called from downstairs.

"I'll be down in a sec!"

It was Monday morning, and I was sitting on my bed, surrounded by rejected outfits. I looked around at the clothes scattered everywhere. Talk about boring. I couldn't find a thing Janna Ika Ilka would find inspiring enough to wear. How could I possibly have spent my entire teenage existence dressed in such drab and predictable garb?

I glanced at the clock. Molly was picking me up in five minutes. I had to make something work here. I looked around again at my options. I was just going to have to make do with what I had, starting with . . . jeans. Everyone wears jeans, right? Even hip Europeans. I climbed into my hippest pair and started my search for a top. Black. The classic urban color. Those people in New York City are always wearing black everywhere they go, right? I scanned my choices and found a simple black T-shirt with three-quarter length sleeves and a ruffle at the bottom. A little last year, but it would have to do. Shoes. These had to make a statement. I got down on my knees and started rifling through the sea of shoes on the floor of my closet. I found a strappy platform shoe with a faux leopard-skin design I had worn, well, *never*, and slipped it on. I stood up and checked out my progress. Not bad. Plus, the shoe gave me another few inches, which was never a bad thing. Like a gambler in search of a missing lottery ticket, I frantically scrounged for the matching shoe, eventually finding it, but only after I'd broken into a full-fledged sweat.

Now we're getting somewhere, I thought as I looked in the mirror once more. But something was still missing. I needed some flair. You know, a little extra somethin' somethin'. Europeans were always wearing scarves and hats and whatnot, right? Tucked away under my keepsake boxes on the top shelf of my closet, I spotted a piece of funky fabric my aunt had brought back from a trip to Santa Fe. I pulled out the fabric, wrapped it around my neck twice, and tied it in a loose knot, letting the ends hang down along the front of my shirt. The olives and golds in the pattern contrasted nicely with my black shirt. My look was almost complete. I popped open my jewelry box and fished for a pair of never-been-worn, dangly, red agate earrings I had received as a birthday gift last year. Poking them through my neglected ear holes, I leaned back for one last review.

"Hallo," I said to the mirror. "I am Janna from Hungary. What do you sink of my outfit?" I stared hard at my reflection, waiting for a reply. When none came, I rolled my eyes at myself. Clearly I had lost it.

"Good morning, honey," Mom said when I walked into the kitchen a minute later. She was obviously trying but failing to act as if nothing was different about me.

"Hey, Mom. I'm running late. I'm just gonna grab a Pop-Tart and take it with me." I ignored the stares.

"Um, sis? Why are you wearing your bedspread for a tie?" Henry asked.

I looked at my mom in annoyance. Did she understand the torture I had to put up with on a daily basis in my very own home?

"Henry, leave your sister alone. I think she looks quite . . . nice," my mom said dubiously.

Luckily, the sound of Molly's horn beeping outside saved me from going on with this banal discussion.

"That's Molly . . . gotta run. *Viszlát!*" I said, using the Hungarian for good-bye.

As I stepped down off the porch, Emmett got out of Molly's car to switch to the backseat, doing a second take when he saw me but choosing to keep his mouth shut like any good friend suffering from an acute attack of disapproval would.

"Hey," I said as I slid into the front seat. "Happy Monday!"

"Happy Monday yourself," said Molly. She was unused to this level of cheer from me, especially at the start of the school week. She eyed me from head to toe before releasing the parking brake and pulling away. "Nice outfit." Her voice bore a subtle trace of sarcasm, but I chose to ignore it.

"You like? I just felt this urge to freshen up my look a bit, you know? I have to go shopping, though. I don't have anything decent in my closet."

"That's right. Damn those indecent clothes from Patagonia and the Gap. How dare they think they're worthy of being worn by you," Emmett said dramatically.

I laughed. I didn't mind being poked fun at today. In fact, for some reason, I had awoke with an optimism I hadn't felt in a long time. Nothing was going to change my mood—not even a pop quiz in physics (do these teachers not realize it's the end of the school year? Come on, people!), odd looks from classmates, and a blister the size of Mount Rainier on my little toe resulting from infrequent use of hip sandals, all of which happened before lunch.

In the caf, I waited until Emmett was out of earshot and Molly and I were sitting across from each other, picking at our lunch, before bringing up the topic of the new men in our lives.

"So, have you heard from Spence?"

"No." She sounded surprised I had even asked. "The requisite three days haven't passed yet. I am expecting to hear from him tonight, though," she said matter-of-factly. "Why? You haven't heard from Julian, have you?"

"Actually, yes." I hoped I didn't sound like I was gloating. "I tried calling you. Julian came by my house."

"He *what*?"

"Yeah, Julian stopped by my house yesterday. He just kind of showed up on his bike out of the blue."

Molly was clearly shocked. "What did you do? I mean, what happened?"

I relayed the story to Molly in great detail, secretly thrilled by her response. I suspected that Julian's surprise visit wasn't par for the course, but I was so inexperienced, I couldn't be sure.

"Wow, that's so weird," she finally said. "And great, I guess." Molly didn't exactly sound like she thought it was so great. Still, I knew she was happy for me, in her own way.

"You'll probably hear from Spence tonight," I said optimistically.

"I know I will." Molly shrugged off the conversation as she gathered her lunch trash onto her tray. She stood up. "Hey, I've gotta talk to Mr. Thorngate about something before class. I'll talk to you later?"

"But of course," I said in accent with a wink.

Molly had a dentist appointment in the afternoon, so I took the bus home from school. I began hobbling the four blocks from the bus stop to my house, anxious to get out of my ridiculous shoes and give my feet some much needed relief. I also wanted to try and wrap up my extra-credit paper for cultural studies. Ms. Kendall was being uncharacteristically agreeable and had told me that if I turned in my report by Wednesday, she would read it over the weekend and give me my grade by Monday. Since Monday also happened to be the cutoff for when Molly's mom had to confirm our flights, this was all the motivation I needed. Talk about coming down to the wire.

If it were possible, I was even more excited about the trip now that I was pretending to actually be from Europe. I was starting to love the way I felt when I was in character, and I had the feeling that traveling through Europe would give me more opportunities to tap into this more confident, more interesting Janna. Maybe Europeans would actually see me as a mysterious American? Wait a minute. Do Europeans even find Americans mysterious? No matter. The trip represented so much of what I wanted, I could barely stand it.

Visions of eating baguettes at outdoor cafés along the Champs-Élysées were swimming in my head when my cell rang. I grabbed my phone and smiled. Julian! I cleared my throat before answering.

"Hallo?"

"Hey, Janna, it's Julian."

"Hallo, Julian!"

"What's going on?"

"I am walking to house from zee bus stop," I said. "What goes on vis you?"

I heard Julian chuckle.

"What is eet? Why do you laugh?"

"Sorry. It's the accent. It's just so *cute.*"

"Oh, you sink so?" I said coyly. Um, hello. When exactly had I become an expert flirter? I almost felt possessed.

"Yes, I do think," he said. "Just like you."

I was at a loss for words. No guy had ever said anything remotely like this to me before.

"So, when can I see you again?"

"I don't know. Zis weekend?"

"Well, yeah, definitely this weekend, but how about before then? I have a rugby game on Wednesday. Do you wanna come? Wait a minute, do you know what rugby is? Do they play rugby in Hungary?"

Yikes. *Did* they play rugby in Hungary? I did a quick mental scan of the printouts Molly had given me on Hungarian leisure and recreational activities. My mind drew a blank, so I flipped a mental penny and chose heads. "Of course vee have rugby in Hungary!"

"Okay, cool. Just checking. I'll text you the info about my game. No pressure or anything. But it would be cool if you could come."

"Okay. I try." Was I ready to introduce Janna Ika Ilka to the student body of the Collins School? The idea of such a public outing made me extremely nervous.

By Wednesday morning I still hadn't decided whether or not to go. On the one hand, I wanted to see Julian. That was a given. I mean, the idea of watching him running around the rugby field all sweaty and strong sounded pretty good to me. I also thought it would be interesting to see him in his element, that it might shed more light on who he really was. And the more insight I could get, the better. While we'd had a great time on Friday night, and since then he'd called, texted, and even dropped by my house, I still wasn't sure why he liked me. Part of me was still worried he was just trying to score with the foreign chick. But I was more than open to being proven wrong.

The downside of attending the game was that the risks were high. Yes, Seattle was a big city, but it had a small-town feel. The odds of running into someone I knew at a high school sporting event were pretty high. Not that I wanted this facade to last forever, but I was just starting to embrace my inner renaissance woman. I wasn't ready to bid *viszlát* to her just yet.

The person I really wanted to get advice from about what to do was Emmett, but communication between the two of us had become increasingly awkward in the past week. I tried to bring it up last night after our rant, but I didn't get very far.

"So, is everything okay, Emm?" I had asked him.

"Yeah, why do you ask?"

"I don't know. You just seem kinda . . . distracted or something."

"Distracted how?"

"You know, you're, like, *distracted*. I mean, you haven't even asked me how things went with Julian on Friday night."

"Oh, I get it. I'm distracted because I don't feel the need to know every detail about your double life."

Where is this hostility coming from? "No, I'm just saying it's not like you, that's all. Usually you want to know everything that's going on with me."

"Sorry, Janna." He sounded sincere. "I've been swamped trying to finish up the yearbook design. Don't take it personally."

I accepted his excuse, but it was clear to me after that conversation that talk about Julian was off the table, even if it wasn't explicitly stated. I hated that I couldn't get his take on the whole situation, especially because it was a lot of what I was thinking about these days. It's almost as if something fundamental in my relationship with Emmett had changed, and I wasn't sure why. Was it just my charade? For now, I decided to take his word that things were okay and act like things were normal, even if it was without the usual intimacy.

Since I wasn't getting any guidance from Emmett, I had to rely on Molly when it came time to vote yea or nay on the rugby game. As it turned out, Molly didn't actually feel the need to engage in a discussion about it at all. Our conversation went something like this:

Me: I'm still not sure about whether or not I should go to Julian's rugby game today.

Molly: What do you mean you're not sure? We're going.

Me: We are?

Molly: Of course we're going. I already told Spence we'd
be there.

Me: You did?

Molly: Yeah, I thought I told you.

Me: No, you didn't. As far as I knew, I was still deciding.

Molly: Well, now you don't have to worry about deciding.
I did it for you.

I would get annoyed by Molly's habit of making decisions for me without consulting me, except the choices she
made on my behalf were usually ones I would have liked to
have made but didn't have the guts to. So, today, like every
other day, I accepted the fate she handed down.

"Why is it so important that we go to the rugby game?"
I asked Molly after she'd told me the plan.

"You know, it's not all about you, Janna. After you
told me about the game, I texted Spence and he said he
was playing too. So I told him we'd be there to cheer them
on." She threw her hands up in the air and pumped them
like she was holding giant pom-poms. "You know . . .
Rah! Rah!"

Of course. We were going to the rugby match so
Molly could scope on Spence. The fact that it was actually
Julian who had invited me and that I was risking certain

ridicule if my cover got blown were just minor details.

"What's happening with Spence, anyway?" Unless she had forgotten to tell me (unlikely), she never did receive a call from him on Monday night. I knew she must be wondering if she was losing her touch.

"I don't know. That's why we're going today—so I can find out. I figure he's just really busy with finals and everything. The end of the school year can be extremely stressful, you know." Molly was obviously trying to convince herself that Spence's aloofness had everything to do with being overscheduled and nothing to do with her.

I couldn't help but feel bad for her. When it came to guys, Molly liked being in control. She could write the handbook on the art of keeping guys waiting, wondering, and wanting more. So, I could only imagine her confusion at not knowing where she stood with Spence. And I could tell the way Spence was playing games with her just made her even more obsessed.

As much as I empathized with Molly, though, if I was going to spend the afternoon as a member of a two-person cheering squad, she needed to help me figure out how to get through the rugby match with my faux identity intact. As soon as she realized I had been swayed, she launched into strategic planning mode.

"Okay. Meet me after seventh period and we'll drive to

my house to get you ready." She was speaking in the hushed tones of a spy operative.

"But what about art?" Skipping out on class wasn't really my thing.

"Art schmart. Ms. Lenning won't even know we aren't there. She'll be too busy inappropriately hitting on the boys in class."

Molly had a point.

"Seriously. It's not a big deal. It's almost the end of the school year anyway. Everyone is so checked out at this place, we could get away with anything. Just be at my car by two fifteen. It will be fine," she said.

"All right." I shook my finger in her direction like a parent lecturing a small child. "But we'd better not get caught!"

"Sweetie, I'm not worried about it. And you shouldn't be either. If someone says something to you, just say you have a doctor's appointment. Trust me, no one's going to give you a hard time."

Once again, Molly was right. I could have paraded around the parking lot buck naked for all the attention I received when I walked out the front door two hours later. Molly was already in her car by the time I got there, diligently typing out a text message. A second later she hit send and looked up at me. "Hi!" She checked out my outfit and reached over to pull my hair out of my signature ponytail.

"Who were you texting?" I asked as she tried to style my hair. Apparently she'd forgotten that taming my waves was a losing battle.

"I was just letting Spence know we're coming. You know, so he can be all jocklike and testosterone-y and a macho show-off for me." She grinned.

"Do you seriously find testosterone-y attractive? Wait a minute. Is that even a word?"

"Totally! There's nothing better than having a guy show off for you. Which is why our being at the game is perfect. Julian and Spence will get to be all cool for us, and we'll get to be all girly and supportive and doting for them. Everyone wins!"

Hmmm. I definitely wasn't into the girly-doting thing. Sometimes I thought Molly needed her own MTV reality dating show.

"Why do you think Julian invited you in the first place? He's just trying to impress you so you'll like him more."

I wasn't so sure I agreed with Molly's explanation, but I did like the idea behind it. Because if Julian wanted me to like him, then that must mean he liked me.

"Okay, so here's the plan." She continued messing with my hair. "You're going to go to the match incognito."

"What do you mean *incognito*?"

"You know, just imagine you're like a celebrity who's going out to a club and doesn't want to be recognized. A pair of sunglasses, a cool hat, a little wardrobe change, and some makeup, and we'll be all set," she explained.

"Sunglasses? That's your grand plan?" Suddenly the nerves I'd managed to keep down since lunch started bubbling up again.

"Well, what did you expect on such short notice? Look, it's the best I can do. Besides—what are the chances that someone we know will even be there?"

"They're high enough," I said. "And what happens if we *do* see someone we know?"

"We'll have to come up with a code word or something. Something one of us says to the other to let them know we have to leave immediately. But it has to sound inconspicuous."

"How about 'The fat man walks alone?'" I suggested.

"Yeah, *that* won't raise any red flags." Molly rolled her eyes. "How about: 'I forgot to walk the dog!'"

"But you don't have a dog."

"I know I don't have a dog. I know *you* don't have a dog. But nobody *else* knows we don't have a dog. Anyway, we could always say we're walking a neighbor's dog who's out of town or something."

I shrugged my shoulders. "Okay, works for me. But just

so we're clear on the rules here: If we see *anyone* we know at the game—classmate, childhood friend, even the guy who works at 7-Eleven—we're out of there. The second that one of us spots a familiar face, we'll say, 'I forgot to walk the dog!' and the other person will immediately drop every-thing. Even if they're in the middle of a make-out session or whatever. Right?"

"Yeah, sure," Molly said.

I gave her a look.

"Yes! Right! Definitely!"

That settled, I once again put my faith in Molly, and we headed off to her house to get into disguise.

8

If you've never seen a rugby game, the best way to describe it is with this word: "carnage." Rugby involves running, throwing a ball, and tackling with complete and utter abandon. Kind of like football, but with much less protective gear. I'll be honest. Standing on the sidelines watching competitive sporting events wasn't really my thing. At least, it hadn't been my thing, up until now. Because now? I couldn't tear my eyes away from Julian. And not just because I was worried he might suffer a catastrophic injury and be left for dead on the field.

I'd only seen Julian three times before today (yes, I was counting). I wouldn't say I knew him well, yet I definitely thought I had a sense of the kind of guy he was—mellow, cordial, laid-back. Rugby? Definitely not mellow and cordial and laid-back. Watching Julian tear around the field in his muddy black shorts, black socks, shin guards, and crimson rugby shirt felt strange and exciting. I kept looking at him and the scene around me and asking myself, *How did I get here? Is this really my life?* The fact that Julian visually acknowledged me as soon as we arrived and even winked at me once in between plays was even more otherworldly.

I mean, seriously. How I went from Molly's plain-Jane sidekick with absolutely no romantic prospects to the potential object of this beautiful boy's attention in the span of two weeks was beyond me. No, I hadn't forgotten the most probable reason for his attention was that he thought I was someone else altogether. To be honest, I was actually starting to feel like I was that someone else anytime I interacted with Julian, kind of like how telling the same lie over and over again can eventually cause you to believe it yourself. But who's to say there wasn't a tiny smidgen of the real me that he actually liked?

As exciting as it was to watch the game, Molly's and my role of devoted spectators was to be short-lived. Following Molly's standard operating procedure, we had timed our arrival to correspond with the last few minutes of the game. This was both to ensure we didn't come across as overeager, as well as to get the guys wondering where we were so they'd be extra happy to see us.

Her plan just may have worked. As soon as the end-of-game whistle blew, Julian signaled he'd be right over. Which of course made my heart rate jump into high gear. I tried to stay relaxed while ignoring the stares we were getting from a group of girls standing near the bleachers. They were giving us that why-are-you-scamming-on-our-guys-go-back-to-your-own-school look.

Luckily, Julian and Spence didn't seem to notice or care, since they trotted over to us, lugging stuffed gym bags over their shoulders, as soon as the postgame huddle broke.

"Hey, guys," said Julian. "Glad you could make it!"

"Hello!" we said simultaneously, causing us to start laughing.

"What'd you think of the game?" Julian asked.

"It vas good," I replied. "You veddy good player!"

"Thanks," Julian said. "I'm glad you liked it."

You would have thought Spence was David Beckham by the way Molly put her hand on his arm and went into worship mode. "You were so great out there! And I can't believe how fast you are!"

Spence grunted something that sounded like thanks as he untwisted the cap on his VitaWater and downed the rest of the bottle.

"So, what are you up to now?" Julian asked. "You gals want to grab a bite?"

I could see Molly's eyes light up, but I had no intention of going out right now. Swinging by the game was one thing. A full-fledged night on the town was another. I wasn't mentally prepared to keep up appearances for the next three hours. If anything, I was just hoping to get out of this little excursion with my fake identity intact.

"Sounds like a great—"

"So soddy, we cannot!" I interjected.

Molly turned to me, half smiling, half gritting her teeth. "We can't? Why not?"

I racked my brain for a good excuse that didn't involve dog walking, since I needed to keep that one reserved for an actual emergency. "Remember? I must watch Henry tonight. My host parents have date." For once, having a pain-in-the-ass little brother worked in my favor.

Molly must have realized I wasn't going to change my mind. "Oh, *that's* right. But why don't we go out this weekend?" Molly said to Spence, giving him her very best look, batted eyelashes and all.

Whoa. Molly brought up another rendevous? Her modus operandi was to always let the guy do the asking, lest they decide you're not worth the challenge of pursuing.

When Spence didn't respond right away, Julian jumped in.

"We were just talking about that, right, Spence? I have a deejay gig on Friday, but how about Saturday? Are you guys free?"

"It just so happens that we are," Molly said. "Right, Janna?" She was trying to disguise her excitement by sounding übercasual.

I nodded.

"So, what should we do?" Molly asked.

"Do they have bowling in Hungary?" Julian asked me.

I acted confused, as if trying to remember the meaning of the word "bowling," while my cheeks flushed once again, my body's apparent response to the stress of possibly giving the wrong answer.

"You know . . . *bowling*," he said, pantomiming the act of picking up a heavy ball from the rack, slipping it over his fingers, and rolling it down an alley. "Ball. Pins. Lanes. Stinky shoes."

I laughed. "Ah yes, *bowling*. Yes, I know zis."

"Cool. Do you girls have ID? We could go to Attic in Capitol Hill . . . that way we could play pool, too, or do whatever," Julian said.

ID? The idea that I might ever need official documentation with my Hungarian name on it had never even crossed my mind. Of course, a fake ID wouldn't necessarily have my real or Hungarian name on it anyway—just thinking about it made my head hurt. I knew I couldn't handle the stress of keeping track of the identity details of three different people: myself, my Hungarian alter ego, and my fake-over-twenty-one-fake-Hungarian alter ego.

"No, soddy. No fake ID," I said. "We bowl somewhere else?"

"No ID? That sucks. We could probably find one for you," Spence suggested.

Argh. *Please just let it go*, I silently willed.

"That's all right," Julian said, as if sensing my stress. "We could go to West Seattle Bowl instead and then hang out in Alki or something." He was referring to a hip, little beach community on a peninsula that juts out into Elliott Bay.

I could tell by the expression on Spence's face that he was less than enthusiastic. "West Seattle? But that's—"

"I have to walk the dog!!" Molly shouted.

I froze, not daring to move, let alone breathe. I wasn't sure who Molly had spotted or where they were, but I was quite sure she wouldn't have used our exit line unless it was an urgent matter, since she was clearly enjoying basking in the glow of Spence's glistening sweat.

"What?" asked Spence.

"Oh yes!" I said with urgency. "Za dog!"

"What dog?" Julian asked in confusion.

I looked at Molly. Her eyes were wide with panic. She subtly glanced over my shoulder, indicating someone familiar was behind us. I freaked. Who was it? Were they approaching us? Was this the beginning of the end?

And then Molly proved that every penny spent on drama camps, improv workshops, and Broadway Bound was worth it.

"Her name's Sadie. I'm watching her for my neighbors while they're out of town," she said in a rush. She pulled out her cell phone and reacted with horror when she saw the time. "Oh no! She has diabetes! The dog, I mean. I have to give her an insulin shot every day at four thirty or she could die!"

Where does she come up with this stuff?

"Oh! Vee must go!" I said. I lowered my hat and peeked up at Julian. "Vee see you Saturday?"

"Uh, yeah . . . I'll text you the deets." He seemed to be flustered by our rushed exit.

"Okay, sweetie, we gotta go!" Molly sharply yanked me away by the hand. "Bye, guys . . . see you Saturday!" And then we bolted, heading off in the opposite direction of whoever it was she had recognized.

"Janna? Molly? The parking lot's that way!" Julian shouted. He was pointing behind him and looking awfully confused.

"Oh yes, we know! We just have to . . . get something . . ."
Molly turned and faked a smile. I held on to Molly for dear
life as our fast walk turned into a light jog. We circumvented
the entire field before hitting the parking lot. I breathed a
sigh of relief when we finally reached the safety of her car.
Though it was dirty, dented, and frequently stalled, I'd never
been so happy to see her little VW in my whole life.

"What happened? Who did you see?" I panted, finally
breaking my silence.

"Winona Ellis! She was coming right toward us! I *totally*
forgot she went to Collins."

"Winona who?"

"You know, Winona Ellis. From my old dance class?"

"No, actually, I *don't* know Winona Ellis. And Winona
Ellis doesn't know me! Damn, you scared the crap out of
me!" I was more than a little annoyed at the unnecessary
wringer Molly had just put me through.

"Well, sorry. I just saw her and panicked," Molly said
defensively. "Geez. Take it easy, Miss Paprika. I was just
trying to protect you."

"Sorry. I just got so freaked out." I closed my eyes and
rested my head on the cool glass of the passenger window.
"I don't know how much longer I can do this."

Molly must have sensed my spirit waning and her hopeful future with Spence at risk. So Molly did what she does

best. She rallied. "We said you only had to stick with it for two nights out, right? So Saturday night will be number two. After that, we'll come up with the perfect way to tell Julian the truth, okay? We'll figure it out. Trust me."

What choice did I really have at this point? "Okay." But telling Julian everything? The very thought of it made me queasy. So rather than dwell on nausea-inducing realities, I filed it away into the recesses of my mind and chose to focus on happier things.

"I *am* excited about Saturday night," I said.

"Yeah, definitely. It's going to be great. And, by the way, did you see the way Spence kept finding excuses to touch me back there?"

No, actually, I hadn't. The only thing I'd noticed was that Spence was acting a little too cool for us. But Molly didn't wait for my answer. "Saturday night will firm things up for me and Spence. I have a feeling he'll ask me to his prom, too. I bet their prom is amazing, don't you think? I heard the after party is on someone's yacht in Lake Washington." Molly's voice trailed off, no doubt caught up in visions of silk, wrist corsages, and limousines. I reached over and turned on KEXP, Seattle's indie and alternative rock station, which was playing Death Cab for Cutie, and we drove the rest of the way home without saying a word.

* * *

Emmett usually made the call for our nightly rant, so I gave him until 10:14 p.m. before I decided to stop waiting for the phone to ring and take matters into my own hands.

"Hey Ika Ilka, what's up?" Emmett said after a few rings. Ever since our movie date last week, he'd taken to calling me by my faux middle name. Affectionately, of course (or at least, I hoped).

"Not much. Is everything okay? I was waiting for you to call . . . it's way past ten."

"Sorry. I guess I got caught up in school stuff. I'm really crunching. Other than that, it's the same old same old," Emmett said halfheartedly.

"Oh, okay." For someone who generally thought of school as nothing more than a giant hormonal holding tank, Emmett's recent preoccupation with all things academic seemed a little odd. "So, do you want me to start, then?"

"Sure, why not."

"Okay. Here's me." I took a deep breath before launching in. "I think the main thing is that Molly's acting a little weird, like she doesn't understand that this whole situation with Julian is so incredibly stressful for me. Sometimes I just feel like I'm inconveniencing her with my petty little problems, even though my petty little problems are pretty much all her fault, you know? Somehow, whatever's happening with me always gets twisted all around until it's about Molly. What Molly *wants*, who Molly *likes*, how Molly *feels* . . ."

"I'm sorry . . . I know I'm breaking the rules here, but are you *serious*? You're just noticing this now?" Emmett was flabbergasted. "Molly's *always* only been about herself!"

"Well, yeah. I know she can be a little self-absorbed, but—"

"A *little*?" Emmett laughed like he was talking to a crazy person.

"Okay, wait a minute here. Whose turn is it, anyway? Geez, Louise. May I continue?"

"Sorry . . . my bad."

"How much time do I have left?"

"You've got about fifteen seconds."

"Okay. Now, where was I before I was so *rudely* interrupted," I said dramatically. "Oh, yeah. Well, I guess I said everything I have to say about Molly. Other things . . . um." I racked my brain to come up with something else to rant about. There must have been something—hormonal angst, out-of-touch parents, acne. But I came up empty.

"I don't know . . . I guess that's it."

"That's it?"

"Yes, that's it for me."

Emmett seemed surprised. "Why Janna Ika Ilka, I don't

believe you've ever not had enough crap to bitch and moan about to fill up sixty seconds."

He was right. But something about me was different. Despite the residual angst resulting from my frantic departure from Julian's rugby game, I felt light, excited, mischievous, confident, exotic, flirty . . . dare I say, *happy*. I was reflecting on these changes when Emmett interrupted my thoughts.

"Well, then, I guess it's my turn," Emmett said. "And me? I've got all *kinds* of crap I'm annoyed about. I've got yearbook crap, finals crap, Dad crap, Stepdad crap, and seasonal affective disorder crap. But the crappiest thing right now? My best friend seems to have vanished. And you know what? I kinda miss her."

Emmett's proclamation caught me off guard, but I let him finish.

"And it's not just that she's pretending to be someone that she's not. That would suck, but I could handle it because I'd know that she, my friend who I adore so much, was still in there somewhere. But now? I honestly don't even know who she is anymore. She's dressing differently, she's acting weird . . . she just doesn't resemble the person I care about so much. And that? That really blows."

Emmett ended his rant, his words hanging in the air like a skywriter's billowy message. My initial reaction was to feel attacked and defensive, but I tried to stop myself from getting too upset. Like Molly, Emmett had a flair for the dramatic. I knew better than to take Emmett's diatribe personally. I'd just chalk it up to his frustration with the situation. After all, I knew I hadn't changed. Yeah, I might have been dressing a little differently, but that was about it. For whatever reason, Emmett was making all this up in his head. I just needed to show him I was still the same Janna he knew so well.

"Are you done?" I asked him.

"Yeah, I think that about covers it."

"So, can I say something now?"

"Be my guest."

"Look, Emm. It's pretty obvious that you don't like the fact that I'm pretending to be from Hungary. And I get it, I really do. But you have to believe me when I say that I'm still the exact same person I was before the Starbucks incident. I still like eating entire boxes of Annie's Macaroni and Cheese in one sitting. I still have an annoying little brother who tortures me on a daily basis. I still have nightmares about beauty pageants and stage fright. And I still love going to see old movies with you. Which reminds me. *Charade* is playing this week." The classic Cary Grant and Audrey Hepburn thriller was one of my favorites. "Are we still on for tomorrow?"

Emmett chuckled. "Well, isn't that appropriate . . .
Charade. Although I can't think of a more fitting movie to
go see with you, unfortunately, I can't."

"Why not? Because of what happened last week? Look,
I told you I won't be in character when I'm with you anymore. It'll be just you and me . . . the real me. I promise!"

"No, really. I can't. The yearbook has to go to the
printer by Friday and I still have a kabillion things to do
before it's ready."

"Oh, well, maybe *Charade* will still be playing next
week." I was disappointed.

"Yeah, maybe."

Neither of us spoke for a few seconds, maybe because we
weren't sure where this left us.

"So, are we okay?" I finally asked.

"Yeah, we're okay." Emmett sounded convincing enough
that I believed him.

"Please just trust me, Emm. I know what I'm doing."
But even as I so confidently spoke those five little words,
part of me wasn't so sure.

9

I awoke Saturday morning to what was becoming an increasingly familiar sensation these days—nervous knots. But these knots felt different from the ones I had before the karaoke night or even showing up at Julian's rugby game. That anxiety had stemmed from the fear of the unknown, of being unsure about what would happen, of whether or not I could pull off what seemed like an impossible feat. After my past problems with performing, who could have predicted that acting would come so naturally to me?

But now? The nervous knots I had today? They were all about anticipation, pure and simple. Anticipation about what might happen tonight between Julian and me,

anticipation of how good it would feel to completely sur-
render myself to my alter ego, who, I had to admit, was
growing stronger and stronger every day. But there was one
more thing—something I'd been thinking about ever since
Julian brought his lovely soft lips so close to mine when
he kissed my cheeks. I was wondering—no, hoping—that
tonight I might get my first real kiss.

Don't get me wrong. I had been kissed before. There was
Cal Johnson, who kissed me at Samantha Greenberg's bat
mitzvah; Micah O'Brian, who slobbered on me after a particularly lame double date; and the handful of boys I kissed during an embarrassing game of spin the bottle at Ella Joslin's
birthday party in ninth grade. But these were nothing more
than the kind of awkward, closed-mouth-squishing-of-lips
kissing you do when you're not really into the person but feel
kissing is what you should be doing. I mean, let's be real—
inexperience and clumsiness isn't exactly a turn-on. But I had
the feeling tonight could be the night for the real thing.

Of course, there was still the small matter that I was
falling for a guy who thought I was an exchange student
from Hungary. I hadn't forgotten about that minor detail.
But rather than dwell on our unlikely beginnings, I'd chosen to follow Molly's advice and focus on what was happening with Julian right now. It was the best I could do
without losing my mind.

I did have occasional pangs of guilt about the whole thing, but when these happened, Molly was quick to put things in perspective for me. Because the truth was, as Molly and I had already discussed, Julian may not have even really liked me, or he might turn out to be a big, fat jerk. And if either of these things were the case, this all might end before I even had to tell him the truth. Therefore, why put myself through the drama of a painful confession if it wasn't necessary?

One thing I'd discovered in the past week was that I had an easier time suppressing my conscience when I actually *became* Janna Ika Ilka. Like when I dressed in my boho look or listened to Euro dance music or spoke in accent during routine interactions with strangers. I guess in some way embracing these characteristics made me feel like my alter ego wasn't so far off from the real thing.

And so that was why today I decided to get into character long before Molly and I met up with Julian and Spence at the bowling alley. While I was still lying in bed, I flipped through my Hungarian research binder, practicing a few key phrases I could throw into the mix tonight:

Megismételné, kérem? (Could you please say that again?)

Bocsánat! (I'm sorry!)

Köszönöm szépen. (Thank you very much.)

Nem értem. (I don't understand.)

And last but not least: *Hívja a rendőrséget!* (Call the police!)

Hopefully I wouldn't need that last one.

After brushing up on my Hungarian, I got dressed for the day. Before I could get to the good stuff tonight, I had to survive a family volunteer outing—one that I'd tried to get out of but couldn't, especially since I'd missed last weekend's. Plus, next Saturday I was signed up for booth duty all afternoon at the Regatta at Green Lake. The Regatta was an annual event where high schools from around the city descended on the park en masse for boat races and spectator festivities. It was also the site of my junior class's biggest fundraiser of the year, and Emmett, Molly, and I had all enlisted for the one to four shift.

Frankly, I would have preferred to stay home and veg out or go shopping with Molly, but instead found myself trying to scrounge up an outfit that not only helped me get into character but was also beach appropriate. I came up with a pair of oversized overalls, a ribbed tank with lace around the neck, and funky sneakers. Since accessories had recently become an established part of my new look, I searched for something to spice up my outfit, finally choosing my army-green cadet hat. Not bad.

Thankfully, my family ignored the fact that I was

dressed in anything other than the unofficial Seattle week-end uniform of Crocs, jeans, and fleece. Everyone except for Henry, of course.

"Now that's an interesting look," he said as I walked into the kitchen. I ignored him and grabbed a water bottle and proceeded to fill it up from the Brita.

"No, really. I mean it. The hat is a nice touch, sis."

"Ready to go, guys?" my dad asked.

"I'm ready, Dad," Henry said. "But I don't think Janna is. She looks really *Hungary* to me. Are you *Hungary*, Janna? Would you like something to eat so you're not so *Hungary* anymore?"

If looks could kill, Henry would have been six feet under by now. Instead, I ripped open an energy bar and rushed out the back door. "I'm ready, Dad! See you guys in the car!" I knew Henry was just messing with me, but still. As if what I was going through wasn't stressful enough without having to cohabitate with a master bully. Thankfully, my parents' favorite NPR radio show was playing in the car, so they put a ban on conversation, giving me a temporary respite from Henry's tormenting.

Today we were cleaning the beach at one of my favorite spots in the city, Discovery Park, and after winding down a steep drive, we parked the car and climbed over some large rocks to get to the beach, which lay at the base of a cliff. Above us, the park's well-known nature trails looped through woods and fields.

I abandoned my shoes by the car and spent the next three hours walking along the beach, picking up stray garbage that had been left behind by careless picnickers or washed ashore, happy to have the time to chill out and just be in nature.

Because it was low tide, the beach was dotted with shallow tide pools, and small sea anemones poked out of the sand like spiny chestnuts. Across the sound was Bainbridge Island, and beyond that, the snowcapped mountains of Olympic National Park peeked through a thin layer of clouds. Though I often dreamed of leaving Seattle behind for more worldly adventures, on days like today I couldn't imagine living anywhere else.

I managed to break free from the group for much of the time, giving me a chance to be alone with my thoughts while I made my way down the shoreline. I didn't realize how far I'd gone or how much time had passed until my mom came jogging down the beach telling me it was time to turn back. My mom took the opportunity to check in with me about school, boys . . . life, something I was used to her doing whenever we had rare one-on-one time.

"So, you and Molly have a double date tonight?"

"Yeah."

"Are these the same boys you went out with last weekend?"

"Yep." I really wasn't in the mood. I had a feeling my mom was disappointed that I hadn't had much interest in or luck with boys. She seemed to have this romanticized perspective of teen romance, and I wasn't quite living up to her vision.

"Where are you kids going?"

"We're going bowling. Some place in West Seattle. No biggie."

"Bowling! That sounds like fun!"

"Yeah, I guess so." Was she getting the hint yet that I wasn't feeling particularly chatty?

"And who is this boy you're going with? What's his name?"

"Julian." I couldn't hold back the smile that appeared when I said his name. Unfortunately, my mom took this as a sign she could probe further.

"Ah, so is this a nice boy, then? I can tell by the look on your face that you're smitten," she said.

Smitten? "I don't know . . . he's pretty cool, I guess."

"And does he feel the same way about you?"

I blushed as I thought about the possibility. "Yeah, I think so."

"That's wonderful! It's about time some boy took notice

of what an amazing girl you are and likes you for you. Ah . . . young love. Ain't it grand?" she sang. My mom put her arm around me and pulled me closer to her.

"Mom!" I said, wrenching out of her hold. "Can we please stop talking about this?" Better nip this little mother-daughter chat in the bud before things got really uncomfortable.

"Of course, sweetie." I could tell by the sound of her voice she didn't want to stop talking about it, but she acquiesced. All things considered, my mom was pretty good at respecting my privacy.

We walked in silence the rest of the way to the car, and as we padded along the beach, one thought kept repeating over and over in my head: *Is it possible that Julian could ever like me for me?*

We got home from the beach around three o'clock, sandy, sweaty, and slightly sunburned. Damn. Molly and I weren't meeting the guys until seven, which meant that the calm energy I'd gotten from the beach was replaced by nervousness in no time. I distracted myself by watching a *Real World* marathon on MTV, which actually worked for a while, mostly because, let's face it, those people had way more problems than I did.

I shut off the marathon by five thirty and jumped in the

shower. Clean, scrubbed, and if I do say so myself, smelling fine, I grabbed my oversized tote and stuffed it with a few essentials: two hats, one pair of jeans, four tops (I needed options, although I was hoping to borrow something from Molly's infinitely hipper wardrobe), "going out" shoes, makeup bag, purse, cell phone, pajamas, and toothbrush.

When my mom dropped me off at her house twenty minutes later, Molly's hair was set in Velcro curlers and she was putting on her eye makeup with the attention to detail of a debutante getting ready for her coming-out party. As I watched Molly construct her look, it became clear she was pulling out all the stops.

"Wow," I said once she was ready and gave me her best runway pose. "You look fantastic . . . as usual."

"Thanks! You don't think it's too much? I'm going for a blend of sex kitten and earthy girl."

"Well, I'll be honest—I'm not seeing a lot of the earthy girl, but either way I think you look great. What are you worried about, though? Spence was all over you last Friday night."

"I don't know," Molly said longingly. "I feel like things with Spence could go either way. There's something about him I can't quite put my finger on, like he's being elusive or something."

"Nice SAT word," I said.

Molly rolled her eyes at me. "Whatever. Anyway, tonight I'm going to seal the deal. Maybe even with more than a kiss."

I gave her a look of disapproval. "Slow down there, sex kitten. Let's just have a good time and hold off on any marriage proposals, or worse."

"Yes, dear."

"So, how about me?" I loosely grabbed Molly by the shoulders and scooted her a few steps to the right so I could pose in front of her full-length mirror. "Do I look all right?"

"You look great!" She critically scanned me up and down. "I'm definitely digging the hat look for you. It's the perfect touch."

"Thanks! I mean, *Köszönöm szépen.*"

"Wow! That sounded so real! You've been practicing?"

"A few phrases. You know, just in case."

"Wow, I'm impressed, Janna. You're really grabbing the bull by the horns on this one, especially considering, well, you know . . ."

"What?"

"Nothing. I'm just surprised about how much energy you're putting into this, since there's a chance it might not work out in the end."

My face fell.

"No, no! Forget I said anything. It's great! You look great . . . you sound great!" she said, trying to erase the words she had spoken. "Now let's go have a great time!"

I decided to push her painful comment aside for now. I did look great. And Julian was waiting for me, or at least for Janna Ika Ilka. And, for tonight, that would have to be enough.

10

When we arrived at West Seattle Bowl a half hour later, Julian and Spence already had a lane and were bowling away. We were late again, this time due to the combination of our unfamiliarity with West Seattle and an outdated GPS. Of course, I knew being fashionably late was most likely Molly's intention all along.

If I had been worried about whether or not we'd all be able to pick up where we left off last weekend without too much weirdness, I immediately realized my concerns were totally unwarranted.

"No fair! You had a chance to warm up," Molly said. I glanced up at the electronic scoreboard. Julian and Spence were in the last frame of a game, both racking up scores I'd never even come close to.

"Take all the time you need, Molly. I'll just sit back here and enjoy the show," Spence said slickly, leaning back along the seat and crossing his arms in front of him, a flirtatious smirk on his face.

Molly gladly took the bait and turned around, snagged a lightweight purple ball off the ball return, and did a comical butt wiggle for Spence's benefit.

I was embarrassed by Molly's performance, but I shook it off and focused on my own performance. Janna from America may have been horrified by Molly's desperate flirting, but Janna from Hungary would probably find it silly, characteristically American, and avant-garde. Most likely Janna from Hungary would go with the flow, so that's what I did.

"So, have you gone bowling since you've been in the U.S.?" Julian had just arrived back at our lane with sodas and a big basket of tortilla chips and was setting a bunch of little paper containers of salsas, chili peppers, and nacho cheese dip down on the table.

"Sank you!" I grabbed my Diet Coke and took a sip. "I have bowled, yes." I had made the decision before we arrived that, where I could, I would try to refrain from lying (other than the *big* lie, of course). In another ridiculous attempt at rationalization, I figured that if and when I did tell Julian the truth, the more honest I'd been with him about the little things, the less damage would be done.

"Oh, yeah? A bowler, huh?" My answer seemed to stir up a mock competitive spirit in Julian. "I bet you're a ringer for a group of underground Hungarian bowling hustlers or something, right?" He laughed. "I'm on to you."

I grinned, instantly put at ease by Julian's playful attitude.

"Well, let's get it on, then!" Julian stood up and clapped his hands together as if he were calling a huddle.

Molly and I traded in our fashionable footwear for multicolored, neon bowling shoes. Fortunately, we had planned our outfits in anticipation of this fact, so despite the scuffmarks and mismatched shoelaces, our overall looks still worked. And since both of us absolutely sucked at bowling, looking good was about all we had going for us.

We bowled one game, Julian being the superior bowler of the bunch and Spence a close second (I had a feeling there weren't many things these guys were bad at). Molly and I pretty much tied for last place, pitifully not even coming close to hitting the triple digits, despite the fact that Molly and I used the gutter guard usually reserved for toddlers and small children.

Despite our poor show at bowling, the date was going

fabulously. Julian and I were talking and laughing, and we teased each other between trips to the lane, while Molly and Spence effortlessly picked up where they'd left off last Friday. I had been a little unsure about where Spence stood, since he hadn't really made any effort to connect with Molly all week, but now they were stealing kisses and playful butt grabs at every opportunity. I was glad about the way things were working out for her—I knew she had pretty high hopes about tonight.

I had just come back from the bathroom when I saw Molly and Spence were putting on their street shoes and standing up to leave.

"Oh, hey, Janna! Spence and I are heading out."

"What?" Molly had assured me she wouldn't leave me tonight, but I should have known by her exuberant PDA with Spence that all bets were off. "But where do you go?"

"We're going to go to a party in Madison Park, I think. Right, Spence?"

"Yeah, I thought we'd stop by for a bit," Spence said.

Molly was clearly ignoring the look on my face. Otherwise, she would have known I was none too happy about this development. "It will be fine, Janna. Spence and I will take my car and Julian will drive you home. Right, Julian?" she said.

"Yes, ma'am." Julian turned to me. "We can stay here or we can go do something else . . . whatever you want to do."

It seemed as though everyone had already decided what was going to happen. Where was my vote?

"But I sleep at your home tonight, no?" I gave Molly my best confused-foreigner look, praying she'd snap into reality and change her mind.

"It's okay . . . we already worked it out. Julian's gonna bring you by my house later. And of course my mom is home, so even if you get there before I do, she'll let you in at any hour. If you need anything at all, just call me on my cell!" She already had her purse over her shoulder and one foot practically out the door. It was pretty clear that any protests at this point would be unceremoniously ignored.

Molly turned to Julian. "*Promise* you will take good care of my little foreign friend, okay?"

"Don't worry," Julian said. "She's in good hands."

While I knew he was right and, come to think of it, I actually *wanted* to be in his hands, this double date turned one-on-one wasn't what I had counted on. So, I asked myself, *What would Janna Ika Ilka do?* The answer was easy. Janna Ika Ilka would embrace the moment and not look back. Janna Ika Ilka would handle anything that came up with poise and grace and wit. Janna Ika Ilka would be the perfect date.

So, I surrendered to my reality and waved good-bye to Molly. "Have good time! See you later!"

As soon as they were gone, Julian turned to me.

"What do you say we get outta here, too? I'd love to show you some of my favorite spots in the city. Unless, of course, you want to try your luck at another game of bowling?"

Hmmm . . . let's see. Continue to heave a ten-pound ball toward a bunch of wooden pins or have a night out on the town with Julian.

"Vere do vee go?" I asked, already unlacing my shoes.

"I don't know . . . we could drive up by the market and walk around for a while, see where the night takes us?"

Julian looked at me with an excited smile. Seeing where the night took us sounded just great to me.

"Does it bother you that Molly left you like that?" Julian asked. We had just parked on a cobblestone street near Pike Place, a famous Seattle market known for its fresh flowers and fish-throwing vendors, and were strolling along the sidewalk, our footsteps the only thing breaking the silence. The merchants had long since shut down for the night, and the market was eerily deserted.

"Is okay. Zis not first time," I said.

"You mean she ditches you a lot? How did you two end

up being friends, anyway? You don't really seem like you have much in common."

I had figured this question might come up at some point, so I gave Julian my practiced answer about how Molly was one of the first friends I made in Seattle (true), and that she had taken me under her wing from the start (also true.) "Vee veddy different, but Molly is loyal friend. I also have good friend called Emmett. He always, how you say, have my back."

"Emmett, huh? Just a friend?"

I smiled at what sounded like a tinge of jealousy in his voice. "Yes. Definitely just friend."

But I wasn't the only one who had been ditched. I asked Julian what the deal was with Spence. To be honest, some of Spence's behavior definitely landed him in the "shady guy" category in my eyes, and the fact that he and Julian were such good friends made me wonder. You know, the whole guilt by association thing.

"Remember how I told you that I moved here when I was six? Well, back then I was pretty dorky-looking. I was this skinny little kid with wire-framed glasses, seriously crooked teeth, and really long hair . . . much longer than it is now. Oh yeah, and I had a lisp. Don't want to forget that charming little detail. I was exactly the kind of kid who was going to get the crap beat out of him, right? So on my first day of school, a bunch of older kids started messing with me during recess. And then all of a sudden Spence came along and totally saved my butt. Nobody ever messed with me after that. I'm still not exactly sure why he did it, but ever since then Spence has been like a surrogate brother to me. And then, when we were in middle school, his parents went through a really ugly divorce and he practically lived at my house. I guess you could say he's like family. I mean, I know Spence and I are very different. But he's still my bud, you know? He's always, how you say, 'got my back.'"

Julian's answer definitely put me at ease, at least as far as his choice of friends went. And I could tell it was important to him that I knew he wasn't like Spence. On top of that, I loved the image of Julian as a skinny kid with glasses and crooked teeth. Nice to know that even godlike creatures went through awkward phases. Of course, I'm sure that even back then Julian was still adorable.

We strolled along the market in silence for a few minutes, enjoying the unseasonably warm spring air and that wonderful feeling you get when it seems like you're the only people alive. As we neared the north end of the market, we ran into a small group of people huddled together, listening wide-eyed and alert to a woman telling them a story.

"Oh, this is so cool! Have you ever done the Market Ghost Tour?" asked Julian.

"Ghost Tour?" I wasn't acting. I had never heard of it.

"Yeah, supposedly Pike Place Market is one of the most haunted places in Seattle. So you can do tours of all the places ghosts have been seen in the market, and hear stories about different hauntings and stuff."

We stopped to listen to the end of the story about how the ghost of a man who'd died a violent death had been repeatedly captured in photographs on this very spot. Holy heebie-jeebies. Suddenly the abandoned market didn't seem quite as appealing as it had a minute ago.

Julian must have sensed that I was ever so slightly freaking out. "You okay?"

I laughed uncomfortably. "I okay. But can vee keep valking? Zis is creepy."

Julian laughed. "Sure. Hey, don't worry. Remember, I promised Molly you were in good hands with me. And I meant it." And then Julian grabbed my hand as we walked away. His hand felt big and strong, not to mention a little sweaty. To be holding on to it felt incredibly intimate and a little strange. In all honesty, I hadn't done a lot of hand-in-hand strolling before, and I wasn't quite sure what to do. Was I supposed to return his grip tightly or keep it loose and casual? Should I act like it wasn't a big deal or acknowledge it with a squeeze or meaningful look? Why hasn't anyone written a book about how to handle these situations?

Rather than continuing to wonder what to do, I decided that Janna Ika Ilka probably *had* held hands with boys before, many times. Consequently, tonight's holding hands should be approached as if it were as natural an event as crossing the street or brushing one's hair. So, I just relaxed, didn't overanalyze, and let myself feel safe in Julian's grasp.

We continued north to Victor Steinbrueck Park, a little patch of grass overlooking Elliot Bay. During the day, the park was bustling with street musicians, vendors, and tourists, but by dusk it was somewhat deserted, with the occasional homeless person or questionable element. My parents had always told me to steer clear, but tonight, holding Julian's hand, it felt fine. Come to think of it, I had a feeling I'd feel safe with Julian no matter where we were.

"God, this is a gorgeous city. I mean, look at that. Can you beat that view?" Julian asked.

We released hands and leaned against the railing, taking in the sight before us. The moonlight was reflecting off the calm water, and far in the distance the sky was still displaying shades of blue and orange despite the fact that the sun had already dropped below the Olympic Mountains and a dark cloud layer was moving in. We watched as two ferries passed each other in the bay, one heading toward the pier downtown and the other going to Bainbridge Island.

"Yes. Seattle ees beautiful," I said. "I really love eet here."

Julian suddenly turned to me with a look of adventure in his eyes. "Let's go on the ferry."

"Vat?"

"The ferry to Bainbridge. Let's go for a ride! It's only a half hour there and a half hour back, plus it's only like seven bucks."

I hesitated. My parents would definitely not be pleased if they knew I was taking the ferry to Bainbridge at night with some guy they'd never even met. What if something went wrong and we got stuck there for the night?

"Have you ever been on the ferry before?" he asked.

"No," I said without thinking. Why was I lying about this? I'd been on the ferry a ton of times, usually to visit my aunt who lived on the peninsula or to go antiquing in the town of Winslow.

"Then we have to do it. The ferry is one of my most favorite things in Seattle. And I'd love to do my most favorite thing with you."

Julian turned to me, his eyes full of promise. We stared at each other for a moment, my knees turning to jelly when I realized he might be leaning in for a kiss. Though I was half-relieved when he turned away to look back at the ferry, if I hadn't been dying to kiss him earlier, I certainly was now.

"Come on. If we hurry, we can get there in time to catch that ferry," he said, pointing to the incoming ferry approaching the terminal about ten blocks south of us.

Why not? I thought. *Janna Ika Ilka sees life as one big adventure, right?*

"Let's go!" I said.

We half walked, half ran, zigzagging our way down Western Avenue, past the Market parking lots and furniture galleries, under the Viaduct, and along the waterfront until we reached Pier 52. We ran up the steep ramp to the ticket booth, and an out-of-breath Julian shoved a twenty under the window.

"You'd better hurry . . . the ferry's about to leave," the woman behind the counter said with a surprising lack of urgency as she slid two tickets toward him.

We grabbed the tickets and scrambled up the walkway, our eyes on the deckhand who was about to cut off our only entry onto the boat.

"Keep it moving; we gotta go," he said. I'm pretty sure he enjoyed making us sweat it out.

Once we scooted onto the ferry, the deckhand closed the gate behind us, and as Julian led me up the stairs to the top deck, the ferry engines started to rumble. A moment later I realized we were already pulling away from the dock.

"It's pretty cold up here, but this is where the best

views are," Julian said. He was taking me to the very front of the boat, to the spot where I always stood when I took the ferry, no matter how cold and windy it was. "Will you be all right?"

"Yes, zis ees my favorite place on ferry," I said. *Whoops.* Better clarify, just to be safe. "I mean, on any ferry I ride."

"Cool. Me too." If Julian noticed my little hiccup, he didn't say anything. Instead, he moved to my right, shielding me from the wind as much as possible and tucking me under his arm. We stood there in silence for a while, hypnotized by the small whitecaps churning along the top of the water. I shivered slightly, but only partly from the cold. The other part? The closeness of Julian. Suddenly, I was aware of absolutely everything about his physical being. The weight of his arm, the feel of his long-sleeved shirt along the back of my neck, the hardness of his chest pressed up next to me, the smell of his breath as he turned to look at me.

Wait a minute. He was turning to look at me. He was close. He was . . .

Kissing me. Oh. My. God. The whipping of the wind, the sound of the engine, the motion of the boat, the feel of the cold . . . all of it vanished. Hell, we could have been on the International Space Station for as much as I knew. The only thing I could focus on were his incredibly soft lips on mine, thankful that I somehow knew how to respond. I can only figure that Janna Ika Ilka had a lot of experience kissing boys. If she hadn't been there, I probably would have passed out.

Our kiss was interrupted by the ferry captain announcing our imminent arrival at Bainbridge. (How long had we been kissing, anyway?) We broke free and gave each other a giddy, post-great-kiss smile, turning back to watch the way the captain gently steered the ferry next to the dock.

"I think we can just stay on board, since it doesn't cost anything to sail back to Seattle," Julian said.

"No, vee must get off boat first," I said. "Zen we reboard."

Damn. Strike two. The captain's voice came on a second later. "All passengers must disembark at Bainbridge Island. If you are returning to Seattle, please wait to reboard at the top of the ramp."

Julian looked at me like he'd never seen anyone with ESP before. "How did you know that?"

Yes, how *did* I know that? I thought fast, something which was becoming a survival strategy these days. "I sink I see sign at terminal in Seattle explain dis."

"Oh. Well, let's wait for everyone else to get off before we do. Then we'll be the first ones back on."

We waited a few minutes before heading downstairs and stepping off the boat. We stood in the cool, crisp air at the top of the plank until all the cars, bicyclists, and pas-sengers had disembarked. Though there was no chilly wind to contend with anymore, I suddenly found myself shaking with cold, the side effects of standing on deck for the past half hour.

Julian pulled me into a delicious, warm hug. "What do you say? Want to freeze on the deck some more or get the best seats in the house for the ride back and stay warm?"

"No to freeze. Yes to warm and seats," I said.

"You got it."

We stood like that until the reboard announcement, and Julian led me to the far end of the boat. We came upon several rows of large, comfortable, vinyl seats facing a huge window looking out at the water. Since we were the first ones aboard, we had our choice, so we snagged two seats in the middle of the front row. We sunk down and got cozy for the ride back, the dim fluorescent lighting making me feel tired and relaxed.

As the ferry started up and began its trip back across the bay, Julian held my hand comfortably while we talked about everything from our respective dysfunctional families to our favorite music. The more Julian talked, the more I realized we had a million things in common. It was down-right eerie. Julian was a world traveler. I *wanted* to be a world traveler (and was one for as much as he knew). Julian was a sugar freak. *I* was a sugar freak. Julian liked music. *I* liked music. Okay, I realize that last one wasn't a huge coincidence. I mean, who doesn't like music? But here's the thing—he was into all kinds of really obscure world music, something I had already gathered from the night I'd heard him deejay. And what do you know, I, too, had my own random musical tastes, some of which are international. For instance, we both loved cellist Yo-Yo Ma, and he's kind of international. What are the chances?

"Tell me something about yourself that I would never guess," Julian said. "I told you about my, how shall we say, awkward stage in elementary school when I was a lisp-talking, four-eyed freak with bad hair. I want to hear one of your stories."

As I thought about his question, I looked out the giant window in front of me. We were moving steadily across the bay, and the city, a beacon of tall buildings lit up against the now foggy night sky, was growing larger with each passing minute. I wasn't quite ready to break into a rousing rendition of "Born in the U.S.A." and 'fess up, but there was one story I had to tell Julian if he was to really know who I was.

"My mom vas a, how you say, beauty queen ven she was young."

"You mean she was in beauty pageants?"

I nodded. "Yes. And she vant me to be in pageants, too. Zis is somesing I do not vish to do. But ven I was little girl, she make me do many pageants. I hate zees pageants. Every time I say no to zem, but she keep putting me in. Zen, one pageant I had to do a, I sink za vord is talent, yeah?"

"Yeah, right. A lot of those pageants have talent competitions," Julian said. I could tell he was intrigued. "So, what was your talent?"

"I supposed to sing and dance," I said. I couldn't believe I was actually telling him this story. Every little agonizing detail was still so clear in my mind, it might as well have happened yesterday. My yellow sequined leotard. My sparkly baton. The cheesy prerecorded music that was meant to accompany my rendition of Frank Sinatra's "New York, New York." The way I opened my mouth to sing but nothing came out. The painful prompting from my mom offstage: "Come on Janna . . . *sing*!" The uncomfortable laughter that spread through the audience, apparently comprising heartless grown-ups who found paralyzing stage fright in a seven-year-old the height of entertainment.

"'New York, New York' in sequins with a baton?" Julian laughed. "I would have freaked out too!"

I was caught off guard by his laughter. Not many people knew this story, and the few who did, like Molly and Emmett, knew what a traumatizing memory it was. As a result, they tended to skirt around any and every discussion having to do with pageants, stages, performance anxiety, and the like. They knew my deepest insecurities, like the one that made me believe I was destined to continually fall flat on my face, were rooted in this one little pageant. Or, as my mom now refers to it, the pageant whose name shall not be spoken.

Julian must have noticed the pain in my eyes and realized as soon as he'd laughed that I didn't actually find it funny.

"Hey, I'm sorry, Janna. I didn't mean to laugh. I didn't realize it still upset you so much. Forgive me?"

I suddenly realized how ridiculous I must have seemed, making such a big deal out of something that had happened such a long time ago. I looked at Julian and immediately knew he wasn't trying to make me feel bad. So I decided I was okay with the fact that he found humor in my story. In fact, I didn't even feel offended.

"I sink zis is why I so shy and cautious." As soon as I said it, it struck me that I was describing a person Julian didn't actually know.

"You? I'm sorry, but did you or did you not do karaoke with me last week? I'd say whatever stage fright problems you've had in the past are no longer an issue, wouldn't you?"

Could Julian be right about me? I had noticed that

when I was being Janna Ika Ilka, I seemed to have a different way of looking at the world. But I was pretty sure the real me was still in there somewhere, lugging around all that unattractive baggage.

"And anyway, I wouldn't exactly call moving halfway around the world to be an exchange student a cautious move. In fact, I think it's pretty ballsy."

I shrugged my shoulders in agreement. I didn't feel like protesting, especially since he obviously saw me as someone I wasn't. No need to disappoint him tonight. Tonight, I just wanted to relish in Julian, relish in us. We both turned back toward the window again, and I leaned my head against his shoulder as he lightly caressed my hand. The last minutes of the boat ride passed by all too quickly. I was tired—exhausted, really—but I didn't want the night to end. Everything about it was so perfect, so magical.

We got off the ferry and started making our way back up to where the car was parked. With no ferry to catch, we slowed down our pace and held hands, peeking in store windows and talking about all the things we wanted to do together before I left Seattle. Despite the fact that I wasn't actually going anywhere, I almost felt a longing for the city, the need to experience adventures with Julian here before it was too late.

We were about halfway back to the car when the clouds we'd seen earlier made true on their promise and the rain started coming down.

"Here, come with me," Julian said. He pulled me over toward a corner deli and opened the door.

"Vat are vee doing?"

"It's raining out. I don't want you to get soaked."

"Oh, zee rain? No, no, it ees fine." But it was too late. Julian had already spotted the umbrellas and was pulling out his wallet.

A minute later we walked out of the deli and Julian opened up the umbrella. We huddled under it together, the perfect excuse to get close.

"But I sot people from Seattle no use umbrellas?" I asked him.

"Well, you're not from Seattle. And I certainly can't expect you to get all wet since I'm the one who dragged you down here in the first place."

I looked down and smiled. We walked for a while in silence, watching our feet take steps in unison, listening to the sound of the rain hitting the sidewalks. I started longing for the night we'd just spent together all over again. Typical me—missing something before it was even gone.

We made it back to the car and headed over to Molly's,

arriving there fifteen minutes later. We pulled in the drive-way and Julian turned off the ignition, unstrapped his seat belt, and turned to face me.

"I had an amazing time, Janna. Really. I think that was maybe the best time I've ever had going out with a girl." Damn. Did he know what he did to me when he looked at me with those gorgeous eyes?

"Me too." Coming from me, that probably didn't mean much, since I'd only been on, like, three dates. But he didn't need to know that.

"Listen. I know you're going back to Hungary soon. But I want to hang out with you as much as I can before that," he said. "I also wanted to talk to you about my prom."

My heart raced. Was he going to ask me to prom?

"I wish I could ask you to be my date, but I'm work-ing the prom as the deejay. I agreed to do it before I met you. I just wanted you to know that I'm not not asking you because I don't want you there. I was hoping we could meet up for the after party when I'm off duty."

"Zat sounds great."

Julian leaned in and put his hand under my chin to lift my face toward his, giving me one final fireworks-worthy kiss for the night.

"Sank you for tonight. I have wonderful time," I said after the kiss, my face in an obvious state of perma-grin.

I got out of the car and started up the walkway to Molly's house. I turned around one last time as Julian rolled down his window.

"*Viszlát!*" Julian said.

I laughed and waved. I wasn't the only one doing my homework. As Julian pulled away, I ran around back and quietly turned the handle of Molly's door, trying to rein in my joy and excitement so I didn't scream and wake everyone up the second I walked in the house. I couldn't wait to tell Molly about everything: the kisses, the ferry, the prom after party. Who could have known when I walked into her bedroom a minute later that I wouldn't be getting the welcome home party I'd been expecting?

11

"Where were you?!" Molly half whispered, half shouted when she realized I was home. I had walked into Molly's room a second earlier and was surprised to find her lightly sleeping in bed. In fact, I was surprised she was even home at all.

"Why? What time is it?" I had no clue as to how late it was.

"Why didn't you answer your phone?" she demanded angrily. "I tried calling you all night and you never picked up!"

"I'm sorry. I must have had my ringer turned off. Why? What happened?"

Molly sat up and flipped on the lamp by her bed. She

looked like hell. Even accounting for the fact that I'd just woken her up, her hair was disheveled and her eye makeup was all smudged like she'd been crying.

"What happened to you? Are you okay?" I asked. Overly dramatic or not, Molly looked more upset than I'd seen her in a long time.

"Spence is an asshole," she said.

"Why? What did he do?"

"He played me. Totally played me."

"What do you *mean*? Molly, tell me what's going on," I said.

She grabbed a tissue and blew her nose, then crumpled it up and tossed it in the general direction of the trash can across the room. I pulled up a pillow and gave her my undivided attention.

"So, he takes me to this party, right? It was in Madison Park at this really cool house. And it was totally packed. And I didn't know anyone, so of course I assumed Spence would be with me the whole time. I mean, he couldn't keep his hands off me tonight, right?"

"Yeah, I noticed."

"Anyway, so then he starts acting, I don't know . . . *different*. He would be all over me one second and the next he would totally ignore me and act like he was too cool to be seen with me. And then a minute later he'd be kissing me, and then he'd ignore me again. So I was like, what's going on with you? You bring me to this party with you and now you're being all weird? That's when I noticed this redheaded chick. I could totally tell by the way she was eyeing Spence that she was into him. And then I started to notice that the only time Spence would kiss me and be all affectionate was when this redhead came into the room. The second she was gone, he'd stop."

Hmmm. The problem was starting to become clear.

"So, finally I was like, who is that girl? And he told me it was nobody, just some girl from his school. And then, like a half hour later, I went to go to the bathroom, but there was a really long line, so halfway through I decided I could hold it, so I went back to find Spence. He was making out with the redhead! Like, full-on making out!"

Yikes.

"What, so he was just using you to make this other girl jealous?"

"Yeah. Can you believe he did this to me? Anyway, I kind of freaked out and just had to get out of there. So I just grabbed my purse and ran out of the party. I tried calling you a bunch of times. I was going to come pick you up, but you didn't even answer your phone, so I had to come home all by myself with no one to talk to."

"Oh my God. I'm so sorry, Molly," I said with empathy.

"What a total jerk!" I had a feeling Spence was sketchy but never would have guessed he'd pull such a lame move. "Did he know that you saw him?"

"I don't know, but I'm sure he figured it out when I never came back from the bathroom. I feel so humiliated! That redheaded chick can have him!"

"Wow. I still can't believe he did that to you."

"Well, at least now you can be done with this whole stupid foreign-exchange-student act."

I looked at Molly in confusion. "What do you mean?"

"What do you mean what do I mean? You're the one who wanted to stop doing this whole charade, anyway. So now you can end it. I mean, it's not like we're going to see them again after what happened tonight."

My confusion was starting to bleed over into annoyance. "Wait a minute. What does what happened between you and Spence have to do with me and Julian?" I asked.

Molly laughed at me in disbelief. "Are you *serious*? They're, like, best friends! What . . . are you saying you want to keep seeing Julian after what Spence did to me?"

This was not at all how I'd hoped to be ending my night, but the conversation had gone too far to turn back now. Yes, I knew my act couldn't last forever, but I wasn't quite ready to throw in the scarf yet. I liked being Janna Ika Ilka. And she definitely had way more fun than I did.

Whatever complications might lie down the road, I didn't want to give her up until I knew where things were headed with Julian. And I especially wasn't going to do it just because Molly was bullying me.

"I just don't understand what my relationship with Julian has to do with you and Spence! They're two totally different people! Julian isn't like Spence at all . . . he's actually a really great guy."

"I'm sorry, did you say your *relationship*? So now you're in a *relationship* with Julian? How can you possibly be in a relationship with someone who doesn't have a clue about who you really are?"

Ouch.

"There's really nothing to talk about, Janna. It all boils down to loyalty. If you're on my side, you can't be on Julian's side. It's that simple," Molly said coolly.

Molly had just found my last button and pushed it with all her might. "*Loyalty?* Who's the loyal friend here? Who's the one who would never dream of ditching her friend on a double date, no matter how miserable the guy she's stuck with is? Who's the one who is always there to listen to you go on and on about every guy who's broken your heart while you're too busy to even ask about me? Who's the one who went along with this stupid charade in the first place, even though it totally goes against everything I'm about?

And now, after all that, you're *still* trying to tell me what to do? Well, you know what, Molly? I'm done. I'm done being pushed around by you. You want to know whose side I'm on? I'm on *my* side. For once in my life, I'm going to make decisions for me!"

Whoa. Apparently I had a lot of built-up anger toward Molly. I could tell she was as surprised as I was because for once in her life she was actually speechless.

"Fine!" Molly finally shouted.

"Fine!" I shouted back. I grabbed a pillow and my overnight bag and stormed out of the room, my sights set on a living room couch far away from Molly and her ridiculous demands. A couch where I could dream about strolls in the market, romantic ferry rides, and kisses with Julian. Lord knows Molly and her agenda weren't going anywhere.

12

The sun poured in through the living room window Sunday morning, shining on the right half of my face until it was red and sweaty, officially prompting me to get up. Molly's mom walked into the room as I was folding the throw I had used for a blanket and straightening the pillows on the couch.

"Good morning, Janna!"

"Hi, Lisa." All my friends called each other's parents by their first names. Maybe it's a Seattle thing.

"Is everything okay between you and Molly?"

"Why do you ask?" I silently panicked. Had Molly told her mom about my Academy Award–winning performances over the past few weeks? I knew better than anyone that Molly had a nasty, vengeful streak when she felt she'd been wronged.

"Well, for one thing, she got up really early to go running at Green Lake which, as you know, isn't part of her typical sleep-until-eleven-on-the-weekend routine. And then there's the small matter that you spent the night out here on the couch," she said.

"Oh, it's nothing. We just had a little disagreement last night. It's no big deal." I was hoping she couldn't tell I was lying.

"All right, if you say so," she said. "Would you like some breakfast? I've got granola and yogurt and some fresh blueberries."

"No thank you. I have to get going. I have a lot of stuff to get done today," I said.

"Do you need a ride home?"

"That's okay. I'll grab the bus."

Lisa seemed to sense I wasn't up for small talk, so she padded upstairs. I gathered my things and stuffed them into my bag, heading out a few minutes later.

As I walked to the bus stop, my mind worked to try to make some sense of what exactly happened last night between Molly and me. Certainly this wasn't the first time Molly and I had gotten into a fight, but somehow this one felt more serious. But why? As I thought about the whole incident, it occurred to me how different Molly and I really were. On top of that, our friendship was unequal as all get out. I mean, if our friendship were a political ideology, it was a dictatorship, not a democracy. And in a dictatorship, only one person is in a position of power. In our case, it had always been Molly.

The electric bus quietly approached and pulled over for me. I climbed on and walked down the aisle until I found an empty double seat. I slid over to the window as the bus picked up speed.

While I was still superupset about the way Molly had tried to force her agenda on me last night, deep inside I knew it was my fault in the first place. I mean, in order to be a successful dictator, you've got to have people to govern. And I had all too willingly allowed myself to become Molly's loyal and unquestioning subject. So what did that say about me? Why had I always been so quick to put other people's wants, needs, and desires in front of my own? And what had happened all of a sudden that made me finally notice what was really going on with our friendship and take a stand?

I knew the answer to that last one. Janna Ika Ilka happened. And as I sat there, staring out the bus window, I had to wonder why it took me pretending to be someone else to figure out who I really was.

* * *

To say the next day at school was awkward would be an enormous understatement. Molly was an ice queen, the chill in the air nearly knocking me over anytime we came within ten feet of each other. Having Molly give me the cold shoulder would have been bad enough, but the taunting was pushing me to the brink of a breakdown. Specifically, while seated across the table from me at lunch, Molly offered to spare me the difficulty of confessing to Julian by telling him the truth herself. You know, because that's what loyal and good friends do for one another. I didn't think she'd go through with it, but with Molly one can never be too sure. Either way, the thought of Molly running to Julian and telling him the truth seriously stressed me out. Oh yeah, and then there's the fact that all communication between Molly and me was conducted without us actually addressing each other at all. Emmett was our reluctant mediator.

The afternoon was filled with more awkwardness, this time between Ms. Kendall and me when she called me up to her desk after cultural studies class.

"Ms. Papp. I have to say, I was very pleasantly surprised by your extra-credit report! You really put a lot of effort into it."

I nodded.

"Well, lucky for you it paid off. As long as you do well

on the final exam, I'd say you're in great shape to get a B in the class."

"Thanks," I said softly, grabbing the paper out of her hand.

"Thanks? That's it? I was expecting a little more enthusiasm. Wasn't this really important to you?"

"Yeah. Sorry. That's great news, really it is. And thanks for reading it over the weekend."

I folded my paper and stuck it in my bag as I trudged out of her classroom. Sure, I was glad I managed to eke out a B in my class, but today was the day Molly's mom had to confirm our plane tickets. And with the way we'd left things on Saturday night, I could only assume that the trip, at least for me, was off.

By the time Emmett drove me home from school that afternoon, I was feeling sick to my stomach. The giddy Julian crush feelings I was still experiencing were becoming increasingly overshadowed by the fact that the fight between Molly and me wasn't going to blow over anytime soon, and I was afraid of what she might do to make her point.

When we pulled up to my house, Emmett found a spot on the street and turned off the engine.

"All right Jan . . . seriously. I need to know everything. What's going on between you and Molly?" Emmett had been doing his best to be Switzerland, but neutrality wasn't his strong suit. And while in the past week he'd been increasingly distant, the fight between Molly and me actually seemed to revive my relationship with him a bit. Maybe he thought I was finally beginning to regret the charade Molly had pushed me into. Whatever the reason, I decided I needed his help.

"Everything's such a mess right now, Emm. Molly's mad at me because she got dumped by Spence, and she thinks that means I should dump Julian, too. She actually told me that if I was a loyal friend, then I would stop seeing Julian. And I'm just sick and tired of her always telling me what to do! It's like she thinks she can control my life, and since I finally stood up for myself and told her she can't, she's pissed off at me."

Emmett was listening thoughtfully, trying to make sense of the situation. "Okay. Let me see if I've got this right. Molly is mad at you because she can't make you stop seeing Julian. And the reason you don't want to stop seeing Julian is because Molly is telling you she wants you to? I'm confused," he said.

"No," I said. "I don't want to stop seeing Julian because"—I paused, my eyes filling with tears—"I like him. I mean, I really like him." I broke off, wiping my eyes with the sleeve of my jacket. I'd never cried over a boy before, but then again, I'd never felt this way about a boy before, either.

Emmett leaned his head back against the headrest and closed his eyes. He didn't say anything, so I kept talking.

"And now I don't know what to do. What if she really does tell Julian the truth about me? I don't think I could handle him finding out!" The tears were streaming down my face now, faster than my sleeve-wiping could possibly keep up. "I just wish I could make this whole mess go away. I mean, I know that if Julian had met me as just me, he wouldn't have been interested. But now, what's the point, anyway? There's no way he's going to like me once he knows the truth." I paused, waiting for Emmett to assure me I was wrong. He didn't. "Right?"

Emmett opened his eyes and looked at me. I could tell he was sad, too, because his eyes were full of hurt. Wow. I knew he was a good friend, but his ability to empathize was really amazing.

"Look," Emmett said slowly. "If you really like Julian, you have to tell him the truth."

"I know," I answered quietly. I took some slow breaths and blew my nose into a napkin I found on the floor of the car. "But how? How do I tell him the truth without him hating me?"

"I don't know if you can. But I do know that it's going to be worse if someone else does it for you. It should come from you and on your terms. Just be honest. That's the best you can do."

"What if you were Julian? Would you still like me if I told you what I did?"

Emmett didn't answer right away.

"I would definitely be pissed. And I would definitely feel used," he said. "I really don't know. I wish I could tell you that everything will be peachy keen and hunky-dory, but it really depends on Julian. Of course, if I were him, I would also know that you're an incredible person and that this little screwup was just a blip on an otherwise untarnished record of good deeds and thoughtfulness and general awesomeness."

I let a small chuckle slip out between sniffles.

"So, what are you going to do?" Emmett asked me.

I took a deep breath. Emmett was right. It was time for the charade to end. "I'm going to tell him," I said resolutely. "I don't know what I was thinking. Of course I have to tell him. And I have to tell him now. The longer I drag it out, the harder it's going to be."

Emmett nodded his head in agreement.

"And maybe he'll see how sorry I am and we'll still end up together, right?" I asked.

Emmett hesitated before answering carefully. "You'll find out soon enough."

I leaned over and gave Emmett a hug and a kiss on the cheek.

"Thanks, Emm. For listening. For understanding. For being my friend," I said. "You're the best."

"You are," he said. "The best, that is." He started up the car. "It's the right call, Janna. He needs to know who the real you is if you really want to see what's going on."

"Yeah, I know. But wait—what about the whole Molly situation?"

"Don't worry about Molly. I'll handle her. Anyway, she'll realize what a diva she's being soon enough, and then you guys will patch things up. Okay?"

"Okay, I guess so. I'll talk to you later." I grabbed my backpack and jumped out of his car. Emmett pulled away as I walked up the steps to my front door. A second later, my phone vibrated. I unzipped the small pocket in the front of my bag and pulled it out. It was a text. From Julian.

How's my favorite Hungarian girl today?

A flush of warm excitement coursed through my body just knowing Julian was thinking about me. I unlocked the front door and sat down on the love seat. It was time to engage in some digital flirting. Why not? I certainly wasn't going to tell him the truth via text message, right? I couldn't leave the boy hanging.

☺ Very good. U?

Great. When can I C U?

Don't you have picture of me on your cell?

LOL. R U always this funny?

☺ Yes.

Want to go to the Market w/me after school
    this week?

Yes. I wanted to go anywhere with Julian. Maybe that would be the perfect time to tell him the truth.

OK. Sounds nice.

Can't wait to C U.

Me 2.

TTYL.

Bye!

I clicked off my phone and leaned back in the sofa. What was I doing? *Digging a deeper hole for myself*, I thought. I sat up and grabbed my backpack, pulling out my extra-credit cultural studies paper. I flipped to the back page of the paper and read Ms. Kendall's note:

Janna, congratulations on putting together such a well-researched paper. I can tell that you took this

assignment to heart, and that's why I've given it an
A+. I hope this means your trip to Europe is back on!

I closed the paper and tossed it onto the floor. Too little
too late. Oh, well. Maybe not going to Europe this summer means spending more time with Julian. That is, if we
were still together. I closed my eyes and willed with all my
might for that to be true.

13

By Wednesday, things were no better. Between Molly and me, that is. And that sucked, because even though she may be a self-centered narcissist (as Emmett continued to remind me), she was still one of my best friends. Now that I was readying to level with Julian, I really could have used her advice.

Since turning to Molly wasn't an option, I kept a low profile, focusing on classes, avoiding Molly's hard stares, and allowing myself to enjoy being the continued recipient of Julian's attention, especially since I knew said attention was probably coming to an end, and fast.

Much to Emmett's obvious confusion and slight annoyance, I also continued to embody Janna Ika Ilka. No, I wasn't walking around Delmar High School speaking in a Hungarian accent, but I was still dressing like my alter ego. I figured I'd embrace the confidence and attitude that came along with my new look, at least until I had to say good-bye to Janna Ika Ilka for good.

"Have you told him yet?" Emmett asked Tuesday night after we had finished going through our respective rants. As had been the case over the past few days, my rant centered around Molly and Henry, the latter of whom was relentlessly trying to cash in on my situation by blackmailing me. He'd recently moved on from Legos and had begun negotiating for a cut of my allowance and pawning off the more undesirable chores. Why couldn't I have a brother who excelled in baseball or math instead of the fine art of extortion? At least once everything was out in the open, Henry would no longer have anything to hold over me.

But I digress. Going back to Emmett's question about telling Julian, I gave him a status update, aware that it would be met with disapproval. "Not yet. I'm going to see him tomorrow after school. I think I'm going to tell him then," I said.

"You *think*?"

"Let's just say I'm *planning* to tell him. I haven't completely figured out what I'm going to say yet. I'm still really scared of what's going to happen when he finds out."

"There's no easy way to do it, Jan. It's kind of like ripping off a Band-Aid. You just have to tear it fast and hard and hope you don't pull off too much skin."

"Thanks for the lovely visual," I said. "Look, I know you're right, Emm. I just feel like I'm going to puke whenever I think about it."

"It's not going to get any easier. In fact, the longer you wait, the harder it's going to be. I guarantee it."

And so that's why I decided to definitely tell Julian on Wednesday after school. I would just find the perfect opportunity and blurt it out. After much deliberation, I'd come up with the approach of, "What would you say if I told you I wasn't going back to Hungary next month after all?" thinking it might be a good place to start. You know, get him excited at the thought of me sticking around. Then I would simply explain why I was staying. Maybe the reason itself wouldn't even be such a big deal. Hey, maybe he'd be so glad he didn't have to say good-bye to me that he wouldn't even care about the whole deception thing. Yeah, right.

Julian and I had planned to meet by Rachel the pig, which is to say, the bronze pig statue that marks the main entrance of Pike Place Market. I'm not sure whether I showed up a few minutes early or Julian got there a few minutes late. It doesn't really matter. What does matter is that, in the five minutes I spent waiting for Julian, my resolve to tell him the truth slipped away. It's not that I was backing out altogether. Rather, after careful consideration, I had rationalized that I should wait for the universe to give me some sort of clear sign that it was the perfect moment to tell him. After all, timing is everything, right? And since the odds were stacked against me, having timing on my side would definitely better my chances of a positive outcome.

Now, some people might say the fact that I spotted one of my mom's best friends, Ms. Finchel, at the market might have been a sign that I *should* tell Julian everything. I, however, read it in a completely different way. To me, seeing Ms. Finchel's overprocessed mane of red hair moving toward me through the market stirred a fear in me I hadn't felt since the midnight showing of *The Exorcist* with Emmett last year. Furthermore, any lingering courage to tell Julian flew right out the window.

Up until the time I spotted Ms. Finchel, everything had been going great. Julian and I had been perusing the different tourist shops and artisan booths, inspecting the kitschy art, photographs, homemade jams, and other wares. We had watched the seafood vendors toss around gigantic fish, much to the delight of the throngs of vacationers, who followed up the theatrics with collective *oooohs* and *aaaaahs*.

The energy between Julian and I was light and playful. For the first time in my life I felt like I was actually half of a couple.

We had passed by the dozens of fresh-flower vendors and headed out of the market to check out the booths along Western Avenue when Ms. Finchel came into view. I wasn't sure if she had spotted me or not, but I couldn't afford to take any chances. The second I saw her, I dove into a giant pile of T-shirts in the booth to my right. I forgot, however, to tell Julian, and apparently he continued to walk a half block talking to air before realizing I wasn't next to him. By the time he found me, I was frantically rifling through T-shirts as though in a desperate search for the right color and size. I had pulled my hair out of my ponytail so it hung loosely and covered up most of my face.

"There you are! I didn't realize you wanted to look at these . . . cheesy T-shirts," Julian said.

Julian wasn't being judgmental. I looked up at the shirts on display. They were all images or sayings about cheese.

"Sorry," I said. "I, er, love cheese. I just vanted to look."

"That's cool." I could tell as he started flipping through the piles of shirts that he probably didn't think it was cool at all, but for whatever reason, he went along with it.

As I continued poring through piles of cheese shirts, I

stole a glance behind me and was relieved to see Ms. Finchel about to walk inside the market. Crisis averted.

Trying to simmer down the adrenaline coursing through my body, I stood up straight and suggested we move on.

"I done. I sink I don't get shirt."

"Really? Come on. Let me get you one. How about this?" Julian held up a T-shirt with a picture of a cowgirl on it lassoing a hunk of swiss. It said REAL GIRLS EAT CHEESE.

"No, zat's okay. Sank you."

"Come on, please? Think how cool you'll be walking around Budapest wearing this piece of art!" Ouch. The mention of Budapest jabbed me, reminding me of how I'd lamely chickened out of telling Julian the truth.

Julian held up another T-shirt, this one covered with cartoony pictures of different types of foods featuring cheese: Cheez Doodles, cheese bread, cheese fries, pizza, and so on. The saying was EVERYTHING'S BETTER WITH CHEESE.

I put my head down in embarrassment, but Julian took my lack of response as my way of saying yes. A minute later he'd handed over eight dollars and I had a new addition to my wardrobe.

"Come on, let's see it on you," Julian said, holding it up to me. What the heck. I didn't want to insult him. After all, this was the first present Julian had ever given me. It had meaning.

I slipped the shirt on over my black, long-sleeved T-shirt. "How does eet look?"

Julian stepped back and eyed me like he was a fashion critic. "Great. You'll be the envy of all your friends in Hungary."

There it was again. My lie staring me back in the face. As hard as it would be to tell him the truth, I wouldn't miss having this cloud of guilt hanging over my head, that was for sure. "Sank you," I said.

"My pleasure. A little something to remember me by."

After Julian dropped me off at home later, I walked in the door and saw my mom and brother had just sat down at the table for dinner. Dad was in Chicago.

"Hi, honey!" my mom called. "I was starting to get worried about you. Where were you?"

I peeked into the dining room. "Oh, just hanging out with Emmett," I lied.

"Hey, Janna. Crackers just called for you. They want their shirt back," Henry said. "Get it? Cheese and crackers?" Henry snorted.

I gave him a dirty look.

"Yes, that's an . . . interesting T-shirt, honey. Where did that come from?"

I pulled the shirt off over my head. "Nowhere. It's just a joke," I said, hoping she'd let it go. "I'll be down in a sec, okay? I just want to drop my things off in my room."

"All right honey. But hurry down . . . dinner's getting cold."

Grateful for a five-minute reprieve, I headed up to my room. I threw my things on the floor and sat down to quickly check my e-mail. A second later I got pinged. It was an IM from Emmett.

How'd it go?
Hey Emm.
Did you tell him?
Not yet.
Why not?
The universe told me not to. Long
    story.
When are you going to tell him?
IDK . . . This week.
You have to do it J.
I will. Promise. This week. Gotta run
    for dinner.
Okay. Talk to you tonight.

Thursday and Friday crawled by. Before my fight with Molly, I hadn't realized how much of my mental space was usually taken up with her drama and antics. As a result, I now found myself with way too much time on my hands to stress over the whole Julian situation. Julian and I had pretty much been in constant contact since Wednesday, though we couldn't see each other for the rest of the week since he had stuff going on after school and I wasn't allowed to go out after dinner on school nights. I probably could have pushed the 'rents a little on that one, but it just didn't seem like it was worth getting into it. Too many questions I didn't have the energy to answer.

Instead I was half looking forward to, half dreading Saturday night. Julian and I were going on the quintessential American date: dinner and a movie. At some point in there I had to find the perfect moment to come clean with him. That is, of course, unless the universe gave me more signs I couldn't ignore.

Friday night I was once again going over the scene in my mind—imagining the exact words I would say and how Julian would respond—while lying on my futon listening to music. In my most optimistic version, Julian would profess his love for me and say it didn't matter what country I was from, that we would take on the world together. Worst-case scenario? He'd tell me to take my goulash and shove it, never to speak to me again. I chose to focus on version one.

My visualization was interrupted by my cell. I looked at my clock: 10:00 p.m. Right on time. I grabbed the phone for my nightly rant.

"Yo, wassup!?" I said in a loud, obnoxious voice.

"Hello? Sorry, I must have dialed the wrong—"

Oops. It was Julian. Why was he calling me at ten o'clock on the dot? Should I hang up so maybe he'd think he dialed the wrong number? No . . . too risky.

"Julian? Oh, hallo!"

"Janna? Oh, it *is* you."

"Ah, yes! Soddy. My host brudder try to teach me slang!" I said with a chuckle. I surprised myself with how easily that little lie slipped out. And not in a good way.

Julian laughed. "I'd say you have it down. You sounded completely American just then."

I laughed nervously. "Yes, Henry practice vis me all night."

Julian seemed to buy my response. "I just wanted to check in about tomorrow. You're going to be at the Regatta, right?"

My eyes widened in fear. "Yes, I vill be zere. But you help friend move tomorrow, right?" Since every school in the city was participating in the Green Lake event, I had already confirmed Julian's plans for tomorrow to make sure I could still show up without having my worlds collide.

"Yeah, my cousin. What time are you finished? I was thinking I'd pick you up at your house around six."

"Zat is perfect. Zat gives me time to shower and get ready."

"Cool. Sounds like a plan. So, I'll see you tomorrow."

"See you tomorrow. Good night!"

I hung up the phone and let out a yell of frustration. These close calls were taking their toll. If the truth didn't come out soon, I was risking certain breakdown.

I jumped when the phone rang. Again. This time it was Emmett, who apologized for being late for our nightly rant. Again. I was in a pissy mood. Yes, I know I should have looked at the caller ID before answering the phone, but Emmett should have been on time. The way I saw it, my close call was pretty much all Emmett's fault.

"Don't blame this mess on me. I've been trying to help you get out of it. You're the one who keeps avoiding reality. Seriously, Janna, this is getting ridiculous," Emmett said.

"Stop judging me! I'm doing the best I can! I obviously need help!" I said desperately. I did need help. How was I going to go through with it?

"It seems to me like this whole idea of finding the right time to tell him isn't working for you, right?"

"I guess not."

"Then don't sit around and wait for the right time.

Call him up and see if he can meet you tomorrow morning for a coffee or a walk around the lake before the Regatta. Then, as soon as you see him, just tell him. Don't wait for the universe to give you a sign, don't wait until the perfect moment. Just tell him. 'I am not from Hungary.' They should be the first words out of your mouth. And don't tell him while you're speaking in accent, either. That would just be weird for everyone."

"But the moment I start talking without the accent, he's going to know."

"Exactly."

"That's not going to work anyway. Julian has something he has to do all day tomorrow."

"Well, maybe you can see him beforehand. I'm sure if you called him up and whispered sweet goulashes into his ear and asked him to meet you, he would."

Once again, Emmett was right. The time was now. I just had to bite the bullet.

"Okay. I'll do it." Wow. I actually said that with something that sounded like conviction.

"Great. I'll wait here while you get the ball rolling."

"What do you mean?"

"Call him on your land line and set up the meeting. I'll wait. It's called being held accountable. You'll thank me later."

Damn. Emmett wasn't messing around. But maybe being held accountable was exactly what I needed. "All right. Be back in a sec."

I set down my cell and opened the bedroom door, sneaking over into my parent's room to use their cordless phone. I quickly dialed Julian's number before I lost my nerve.

"Hello?"

"Hallo, Julian? Eet ees Janna."

"Hey, what's up? Everything still okay for tomorrow night?"

"Yes. But I have favor. Can you meet in za morning? Before you meet your cousin? I have somesing to talk vis you about."

"Yeah, okay, I guess so. I should be able to see you before I have to leave, but we'd have to meet by nine. Does that work?"

"Nine ees perfect. How about Starbucks, north of za lake?"

"Okay. I'll see you then." Julian hesitated. "Is everything okay, Janna?"

"Yes," I lied. "I just vant to talk."

"All right. I guess I'll see you in the morning, then."

"Sank you. Good night Julian," I said.

"G'night."

I sat down on my parent's bed and hung up the phone.

What had I just done? Was I going to regret making the call? Was there any way out of it? Why was Emmett pushing me so hard to set up the meeting? Would Emmett . . . oh shoot, *Emmett*. He was still on the phone in my bedroom. I ran back to my room and closed the door, scooping up my cell as I fell onto the bed.

"Hello?" I said.

"Yeah, I'm still here. So, did you do it?"

"I did it. We're meeting at nine."

"Perfect."

I sighed. "If you say so."

"It'll be okay Janna. By the time I see you tomorrow afternoon, this will all be over. Think of how relieved you'll be."

Yeah, relieved and single. "I know. You're right."

"I know I'm right. Hey, do you wanna head over to the park together tomorrow?"

"Sure. Is Molly still going?"

"I think so. Don't worry. I think she's starting to cool off. Maybe you guys can work things out tomorrow."

"I wouldn't count on it," I said. Yes, I missed her, but I was still feeling wronged and wasn't ready to make up just yet.

"Well, let's just see how things go tomorrow. We have to be there by one, by the way, so just call me when you're ready to leave. Then you can tell me how everything went with Julian."

"Okay. I'll talk to you tomorrow. Wish me luck."

"May the force be with you."

I looked at my clock: 10:11 p.m. In twelve hours Janna Ika Ilka would no longer be. In her place would be just plain old Janna. In twelve hours Julian and Janna might no longer be. The thought of losing Julian made me shudder. My life was a nuclear weapon that had just been armed by some clueless government official with the secret code. Operation Get Real was in motion, and there was no turning back.

14

Though I didn't have a fever, last night I did that whole half-sleep, half-hallucination thing where I tossed and turned and obsessed all night long. Since I was one hundred percent committed to telling Julian the whole story in the morning, I kept imagining what was about to unfold over and over and over again. Emmett was right . . . this was only going to get harder the longer I waited.

I awoke to the horrid beeping of my alarm at eight thirty, completely out of it, probably because I'd only gotten to sleep two hours earlier. The feeling of dread in my stomach didn't help matters much. Though I'd showered the night before, I decided that standing under a cascade of hot water for fifteen minutes might help shake the sleep and anxiety from my body. The anxiety clearly wasn't going anywhere, but at least I emerged from the shower slightly more awake. I walked into my bedroom just in time to hear my phone buzz that I had a message.

"Hey, Janna, it's Julian. Sorry to call last minute, but it looks like I can't meet this morning after all. My dad and I have to go to my cousin's place earlier than I thought. Hopefully we can talk about whatever you wanted to talk about at dinner before the movie? Sorry, but I'll see you tonight."

Even though I knew my fate was sealed, I'd be lying if I said I wasn't relieved at the last minute change of plans. I deleted the message and bent over, wrapping a towel around my wet hair, twisting it, and sticking the end under the back of the towel. I stood up, pulled my pajamas back on, and slid into my still-warm bed, mostly because it seemed like the best option at the time. *Well, some things are beyond my control*, I thought. *If that's not a sign from the universe, I don't know what is.* And then I closed my eyes and sank into a deep, dreamless sleep.

When I opened my eyes again, it was nearly twelve o'clock. And the only reason I knew that was because my brother started pounding on my bedroom door belting out the "Good Morning" song from *Singin' in the Rain*, a song my mom used to wake us up with when we were younger. Only, this morning Henry had replaced the original lyrics with his own. They sounded something like this: "Good morning, good morn-ning, you've slept in until noon, good morning, good morning, you goon." Cue laughter, exit stage left.

"Henry, leave your sister alone!" I heard my mom call from downstairs.

Noon? I slept until noon? I rolled over and looked at the clock, wiping the drool from the side of my mouth as I swung my feet around and sat up. I figured I'd better check in with Emmett about going over to the park together.

I turned on my cell and saw that Emmett had already texted me.

J. Ended up going to Regatta early to help out. See you soon.

Just as well. Despite my solid second sleep of the day, my head was still filled with cobwebs. Easing into the day seemed like a good plan to me.

May weather in Seattle had a habit of being extremely unpredictable, and more often than not, Regatta Saturday ended up being cool and rainy. But as I stepped outside the house to walk the mile and a half to the lake, I was psyched to look up at the sky and see not even a single cloud in sight. And though the air was slightly cool and breezy, the sun nicely warmed up my skin. It was a perfect spring day. A good omen, perhaps, for what was to come.

I left my iPod at home on purpose, enjoying the brisk walk to the park without the distraction of music. I didn't know if it was the weather or the walk or what, but somehow the sick feeling I'd had in my stomach in the morning had been replaced with a strange sense of calm. Somewhere between my phone call with Emmett last night and this moment, I must have surrendered to the inevitability of what was going to happen today. Even better, I had this weird feeling that everything was going to work out.

I had about three blocks to go when I felt my cell phone vibrate. I pulled it out of my backpack, continuing to walk while I switched it on.

Does Julian know the truth?

It was Molly. She hadn't contacted me directly since our fight a week ago. *Why was she asking me this question? What was she up to?* I debated whether or not to respond. The idea of getting into everything again with her over text didn't really jibe with the peaceful attitude I'd just embraced. But what if it was really important? Or what if it was another threat to tell Julian everything? What if by not answering her, I was going to push her to the brink of betrayal? Or worse, what if she'd already done the unthinkable?

I texted back:

Why are you asking?

It took a minute for her to respond.

Just tell me. It's important.

I unconsciously picked up my pace, feverishly texting as I continued to walk.

I'm telling him tonight. Why do you want to know?

I nervously held the phone, waiting for her answer. I made it nearly a full block and had just started down the shaded pathway toward the Delmar booth when she finally texted me back.

I think Emm just told him. Thought you should know.

What? I reread her message to make sure I didn't get it wrong. Emmett would never do that to me. Why was she messing with me like this? Besides, Julian wasn't even here today. He was helping his cousin move.

I was about to text Molly back but decided to go straight to the person being slandered. I speed-dialed Emmett, my fast walk turning into a jog as I made a beeline toward the booth. My heart was pounding. While Emmett's cell rang, I finally caught a glimpse of him. And then I stopped dead in my tracks.

Emmett and Julian were talking. Oh my God. Why were Emmett and Julian talking? Why was Emmett pulling out his wallet? What was he showing Julian?

"Janna!" Molly ran up to me.

I looked at her furiously. "What did you do!?"

"Me? I didn't do anything! I tried to warn you!"

"Then why is Julian here? Why did you have to go and ruin the best thing that's ever happened in my life? You had no right!" I knew Molly could be vindictive, but I never imagined she'd go this far.

"Janna, I swear to God it wasn't me. I didn't even know Julian was here until a few minutes ago—"

I didn't have time to listen to her lies anymore. I turned and started running toward the booth. Maybe I wasn't too late after all. Maybe I could still salvage this whole situation and get the happy ending I'd been praying for all week.

But when I saw the expression on Julian's face as he

spotted me, I knew there would be no happy ending. No happy ending at all. Clearly in no mood for conversation, Julian started walking away from the booth, away from me.

"Julian, vait! I can explain!" I shouted to him. *Why am I still talking in my accent?*

Julian turned around to face me. "Seriously? *Vait?* I cannot believe you've been lying to me this whole time! I can't believe what an idiot I was to fall for it!" He was red-faced, his expression a mixture of anger and hurt.

"I'm so sorry, I didn't mean to—"

"You didn't mean to *what?* Lie to me for the past month? Oh yeah, you just 'accidentally' pretended to be from Hungary. Oops! You know what, Janna, if that even is your name . . . just . . . just . . ." Unable to even get the words out, Julian put his hands up in defeat and stormed off.

"Please, Julian . . ." My voice trailed off.

"Just let him go, Jan," Emmett said.

My eyes filled with tears. "What happened? Why did Molly tell him to come here? Why would she do this to me?"

I started crying hard now, my hands flailing helplessly to wipe away the sudden rush of tears. Emmett came over to me and pulled me into a tight hug. I collapsed against him, thankful for the dry shirt to soak up my blubbering and his strong chest to steady me.

"I don't think Molly told him to come here, Janna. I think he just showed up. He said something about finishing early." Thank God, Emmett was being supercalm, the rock I needed.

"But I don't understand. Why did she have to tell him the truth? What right did she have to do that?"

Emmett didn't say anything for a minute. He stroked the back of my hair lightly as I cried. The situation seemed overwhelmingly hopeless. I kept flashing to the look in Julian's eyes when he glared at me. It bordered on hatred. Could he really hate me? Was I a fool to think I ever had a chance of things working out?

"It wasn't Molly, Janna. It was me." Emmett spoke so quietly I wasn't sure I heard him right.

"What?" I sniffled.

"I'm the one who told Julian. I'm so sorry. It was an accident."

I abruptly stopped crying, wrenching myself from his embrace. "What? *You* told him? How could you? Why would you?!" I was yelling now, my sadness from a moment earlier replaced with a rage I hadn't known before.

"I didn't mean to do it, Janna," Emmett said defensively.

"What do you mean you didn't *mean* to do it? I told you I was going to tell him. Now you've ruined everything!" Emmett grabbed me by the arm and led me away from the booth, which to passersby was probably starting to resemble the set of *The Jerry Springer Show*.

"Look, I told you it was an accident!" Emmett was mad now too. "I thought you already told him! You promised me you were going to tell him this morning!"

"It doesn't matter what I promised! You should have kept your big mouth shut!"

Emmett was pissed, but he lowered his voice and spoke to me in an almost-too-calm voice. "Of course. You're right. I should have just lied to him, right? I mean, what's the big deal? What's one more lie on top of everything you did?"

I closed my eyes and clenched my fists. "You're twisting everything around! You know I didn't mean to do this."

"Oh, so your lying to Julian for the past few weeks *has* been one big accident?" There was nothing I hated more than being the target of Emmett's sarcastic cuts. "But then again, who am I to talk? I've been acting out a charade too. In fact, I've been lying to you for years."

I stopped seething long enough to turn toward Emmett.

"What are you talking about?"

Emmett looked away and put his hands on his hips, hanging his head. He stood like this for a minute before turning around to face me.

"I'm talking about the fact that I've been in love with you for as long as I can remember," Emmett said. "That's right, Janna. All this time you've been pretending to be another person just so someone would like you, I've been pretending to be your best friend even though I wanted us to be something more."

My heart ached at hearing the words come from his mouth. I felt the anger in my body soften. He looked so vulnerable.

"Emm," I said softly. I reached out to grab his hand, but he yanked it away.

"Crazy, isn't it? Of course, now that I've told you what I've been hiding for so long, I don't think it's even true anymore. I mean, had I known you had the potential to be so selfish and self-absorbed, there's no way I ever would have fallen for you in the first place." His eyes were red, his voice shaky.

Okay, that one hurt. "Emm," I tried again.

"I think Julian had the right idea. I've had enough of the new Janna." Emmett walked away without another word. And just like that, I was alone. Despite the thousands of people milling about, there I was, standing on scattered pine needles underneath a fir tree, more alone than I'd ever been in my life.

15

To be honest, I don't remember much of the walk home from the Regatta. I was a giant, twisted-up ball of emotions, and my mind was frantically trying to make sense of everything that had just happened. I was so utterly exhausted by the time I got home that I may as well have just returned to base camp after summitting Mount Everest.

Thank God my family was at the boat show in Lake Union, so I had the house all to myself. Having to interact with anyone right now would be tantamount to torture. I went up to my bedroom, kicked off my shoes, pulled down my blinds, and crawled into bed. My eyes were swollen and red, and my brain had gone into a sleeping mode of sorts, not unlike the way a computer does after a few minutes of sitting idle. But that was fine with me. I didn't want to think anymore. I just wanted to shut out the world and sleep. Thankfully, my body didn't put up a fight.

I'm not sure how long I slept before my mom came into my room. I vaguely remember her trying to rouse me from bed, but I was so out of it, she must have decided I was sick or something. After a few minutes of sitting on the edge of my bed, she put the back of her hand on my forehead as if checking for a fever and then quietly slipped out of my room.

The next time I woke up it was still daylight, but my stomach was growling with hunger. Confused, I sat up to look at the clock: 9:43 a.m. Holy crap. It was morning? Next to my clock was a glass of water and a plate with some crackers on it, a sign that my mom really did think I was ill. No need to correct her—at least this way she'd keep my brother at bay and give me some space. I got out of bed and peeked into the hallway to assess the family status. I wasn't ready to face the world yet.

The house was still, so I tiptoed down the stairs, carefully skipping the middle step that creaked loudly, and quietly made my way to the kitchen. I breathed a sigh of relief when I noticed the car wasn't in the driveway and found a note from my mom saying they'd gone to Henry's baseball game in Columbia City.

I poured myself a giant bowl of granola and padded into the living room, where I spent the next four hours sprawled on the couch watching HGTV, QVC, and fly-fishing, which was about as deep as I could go with my TV programming today. God forbid I inadvertently stumble upon *Ella Enchanted* or some other romantic comedy I'd seen a zillion times. I would be reduced to a pile of soggy tissues in a matter of minutes.

I only got up from the couch three times—once to use the bathroom, once to see if we had any Annie's Macaroni & Cheese in the house (we didn't), and once because my cell rang. Well, that last time I didn't so much get up from the couch as I bolted. Despite my better judgment, I was hoping against hope that it was Julian calling to say he'd forgiven me and could he come over right now to patch things up. Of course it wasn't Julian. It was just Molly. In fact, I realized she'd called me more than a half-dozen times since yesterday afternoon, a fact that made me roll my eyes with annoyance. Even if she hadn't been the one to actually tell Julian the truth, as far as I was concerned, things between us were exactly where we'd left off after our fight last week. My guess? She probably found some sick pleasure in my public outing. Or maybe she was happy she wasn't alone now in having been dumped.

After watching three couples increase the value of their homes through kitchen renovations, learning the proper line casting method when fly-fishing for striped bass, and seeing the potted plant that doubles as a litter box fly off the shelves for the low, low price of $39.95, I decided I'd better head back upstairs, since the 'rents and sib would probably be home any minute. I wasn't sure how long they'd buy my whole sick act, but I was more than willing to find out.

I lay down in bed, trying in vain to read a novel I'd gotten for Christmas, but I kept scanning the same sentence over and over again, so I tossed the book on the floor and closed my eyes. What the hell. Might as well sleep the rest of the day away, right? It was better than dwelling on the sorry state of affairs my life had become.

A minute after I closed my eyes, there was a light tapping on my door. I assumed it was my mom, since I thought I'd heard the car pull up into the driveway a few minutes earlier.

"Come in," I said, doing my best deathbed impression.

The door cracked open and a hand slid through it. The hand was holding something white, and was waving it back and forth to draw my attention.

"Peace, peace! I come in peace!"

Molly.

"Will you accept my peace offering?" Molly pushed the door open wider, and she timidly poked her head into the room. She looked as sheepish as I'd ever seen her. Humility . . . a new look for her. She wore it well. "I hope you don't mind . . . I used the garden rock key to let myself in."

I slowly sat up in bed, not saying a word. I wasn't ready to talk yet. But considering how alone in the universe I was feeling at this particular moment, I decided I might as well listen to what she had to say.

Molly took my lack of objection as an invitation to enter my room and sit down on the bed. She put her hand on my leg and looked me square in the eye.

"Look, Janna, I'm sorry," she said. "I know I was a total, selfish jerk to you last week. I was so upset about what Spence did to me that I couldn't think about anything else."

Nice opening line. If apologizing were an Olympic sport, I'd say Molly's performance thus far would have rated her a score in the high eights, low nines. But I still wasn't ready to forgive and forget just yet. We Scorpios can be stubborn like that.

"Of *course* you had the right to keep seeing Julian. I totally get it. I mean, I probably would have done the exact same thing myself."

Probably?

"I think I thought it would be easier for me to deal with what Spence did if you were going through it with me, you know? And to be honest, over the past few weeks, you haven't really been yourself. I mean, I know you were pretending to be from Hungary, but even when you weren't in character you've been kind of different, like more outgoing and stuff. I think I was weirded out that you were getting so much attention, since that's the role I usually play. I didn't know how to handle it."

Where was all this depth and insight coming from? Could it be that Molly was actually evolving?

"But I get it," she continued. "I was being a jerk and you were just sticking up for yourself. Which, by the way, you did pretty well, considering it's never really been your thing. But then, yesterday, when I realized you actually thought I would have screwed you over by telling Julian, I got really freaked out. Because even if we're fighting about something, I would never do something like that. Did you honestly think I would do something that awful?"

I didn't answer. But the truth was, now that I wasn't in the heat of the moment, no, I didn't.

"Geez, Janna, I would die if I ever lost you as a friend. If you want to have a big personality or be more outgoing or wear questionable shoes . . . *whatever* . . . I can handle it!"

Molly was wearing me down. I mean, she did seem really genuine, and on top of that, she'd addressed all of my gripes without me having to even say a word.

"Do you think you can forgive me?" Molly held up the white piece of paper that she'd been waving in the doorway earlier. It was an envelope with my name written on the outside in her mom's handwriting. "Come on . . . what do you say? You and me? Paris? London? Madrid? You're not going to miss out on the trip of a lifetime just because I can be such an insensitive dope, are you?"

I gave a slight smile, the first one that had escaped my lips in more than twenty-four hours. I snatched the envelope out of her hand and opened it up to peek at the airline ticket safely ensconced inside.

"I was *really* mad at you," I said, softening. "You were being totally unfair."

"I know. I really am sorry, Janna. From now on, I'm going to be as loyal as one of the Three Musketeers, even if there are only two of us."

I felt a wave of relief. Making up with Molly was the first sign that things in my life might eventually go back to normal, or whatever normal looked like these days.

"It's okay, Molly. I accept your apology. And I'm sorry I accused you like that. I was clearly freaking out." I felt lighter as soon as I said the words. "And by the way, I'm not interested in having a big personality or getting lots of attention. That kind of stuff just gets me in trouble." I leaned over, and we shared a nice, long hug. But as we were about to pull apart, she gave me an extra squeeze for good measure and I burst into tears.

Molly leaned back to look at me. "Oh, baby. What's wrong? I thought we just made up?"

I started crying even harder now, grabbing a tissue from the side of my bed and burying my face in it.

"Oh. *Julian*," she said.

She was a quick study, that Molly.

"And *Emmett*," she added.

"Yes," I whimpered. "Everything's so screwed up."

Never one to back down from a crisis, Molly swung into take-charge mode. She gently lifted the wet hair matted to my cheek and relocated it behind my ear before speaking. "Don't worry, Janna. We'll figure everything out, okay? I give you my word. I got you into this mess, and I promise you we'll find a way to get you out of it, okay?"

I let out a few last, desperate soblike gasps before reining in the tears.

"Have you talked to Emm?" I asked quietly. I was almost afraid to know the answer.

"Yeah. He called me last night."

"Did he tell you what he told me?"

"You mean about him being in love with you? Yes. But, Jan, that wasn't really news to me. Or probably anyone else, for that matter."

"Well, it was to me," I said. "And now that he put the *L* word out there, nothing will ever be the same between us again. I mean, seriously. There's no way we can ever go back to being the way we were! Plus, you should have seen how angry he was at me for everything that went down with Julian." Mentioning Julian's name made me hurt all over again, and I burst into a whole new set of tears. "And Julian totally hates me!" I sobbed.

"Just slow down, Janna. Let's take things one at a time, okay? Let's start with Emmett. Things with Emmett are going to be fine. You just need to give him a chance to get over himself. I mean, he's gotta be feeling superembarrassed and humiliated."

"And guilty, too, I hope," I added.

"Well, I don't know about guilty, but he definitely feels bad. It really was an accident, you know."

"What exactly happened, then?" I wanted to know every little detail of Saturday's events. Maybe I'd find some glimmer of hope in the retelling of the story.

"Emmett said that Julian came up to him and started asking about you. And the whole time Julian was talking to him—I don't know if it was because of something

Julian said or what—Emmett totally assumed that you had already told Julian everything. And Emm was so surprised at how well Julian was handling the whole situation, that he said something like that. Something like, 'Wow, so you're really okay with Janna's whole fake Hungarian act.' Anyway, as soon as he saw the look on Julian's face, he realized that Julian didn't actually know the truth. But by then it was too late. Julian started asking him what he was talking about, and, well, you know Emmett. He can't lie to save his life. So the truth just kinda came out."

I closed my eyes and shook my head. Julian must have been so caught off guard. Not that there was a good way to find out you've been lied to, but if there was one, this wasn't it.

"So, then what was it that Emmett pulled out of his wallet to show Julian?"

"Oh, yeah. I guess Julian didn't believe Emmett and he started getting annoyed and called Emm a liar. Which, as you know, is something Emm doesn't take to very kindly. So, to prove he was telling the truth, he showed Julian a picture of the three of us at Disneyland together from that trip we took in eighth grade."

"Ugh." I hung my head down in shame. I was busted, and how.

"Yeah," Molly said empathetically. "That kind of put

the last nail in the coffin. And I think that's when you came up to them and, well, you know the rest."

"I just can't believe that it's done, that Julian and I are over." I stared out the window numbly.

"I know this sucks. But today will be the worst day. Trust me, I've been through this before," Molly said.

I gave her a glare to let her know that what I'd had with Julian was not a little Molly-esque fling.

"Okay, maybe not exactly this but, still, breakups that sucked. You'll feel a little better tomorrow, and a little better the day after that. That's the way it works. Anyway, maybe it's not as bad as you think. Maybe you could write him an e-mail or something, apologizing and telling him how you feel?"

I didn't let Molly know that I'd already drafted nearly a dozen e-mails to Julian in my head, but hadn't had the guts to follow through. How could I even begin to put into words how sorry I was?

"I have an idea . . . why don't we trash your fake Facebook profile and create a new and improved one for the real Janna?" Molly was trying to switch gears and refocus my attention. It was a classic distraction ploy, but I was too tapped out to protest. Molly booted up my computer and logged on to my Facebook account. I couldn't help but notice that my fake profile had one fewer friend. Hard not to notice, really, considering it only had three friends to start with. I wasn't surprised—who could blame Julian for unfriending me? He was probably trying to erase all evidence I had ever existed.

"Say good-bye to Janna Ika Ilka!" Molly said as she clicked Delete Profile. And just like that, all digital traces of my alter ego were gone. I couldn't help but feel a pang of sadness. Yes, Janna Ika Ilka had seriously messed up my life, but there was a certain quality she'd brought to it that I was going to miss.

Talk about having an identity crisis. As I sat there looking at the new profile Molly had whipped up for me in no time, the one that was supposed to represent the real me, I had to wonder who the real me was and how she fit in to the world. Did Emmett love the real me or the me he had built up in his head? Did Julian love the fake me? Did he hate the real me? Or was there some part of the real me that he might be able to love someday, too?

Only time would tell.

16

When you're a zombie, you can walk and talk and eat and sleep, but you don't actually give a crap about any of these activities. Your face remains expressionless, your emotions buttoned up. You are the undead—going through the motions without actually feeling anything at all.

The reason I know this so well is because that's exactly how I felt the week after Operation Get Real blew up in my face. The only thing that got me through the day after Molly left my house was her promise that Monday would be better. But when Monday rolled around, I had a hard time distinguishing between levels of miserableness from the day before. Tuesday I felt maybe five-thousandths of a percent better, but that flipped to ten percent worse after getting up the nerve to send Julian a text message:

Hi Julian. Are you okay? Can we talk? I'm so sorry.

And getting this response:

No. No. Whatever.

By Wednesday, I was feeling mighty proud of myself because not only had I showered, but I also managed to look in the mirror before I left for school. What I saw in the reflection wasn't very comforting, but that's a whole other *Oprah*.

I still hadn't spoken to Emmett; actually, I hadn't even seen him. I'm not sure if he was staying home sick or coming to school in disguise or what. I was, however, sensitive to the fact that he might be feeling embarrassed, so I gave him space and didn't pelt him with phone calls and texts. But that didn't mean I was going to let him out of my life without a fight, especially now that I understood the circumstances behind his telling Julian the truth. Actually, I felt terrible for being such a jerk to him. I should have known he would never do anything to purposefully hurt me.

I decided to follow Molly's advice (this was actually *good* advice) and try to get through this whole messed-up situation by tackling one thing at a time. And by Wednesday, I realized the issue I needed to tackle first was fixing my friendship with Emmett. So I waited until ten o'clock on the nose and dialed his number. And then the phone rang. And rang. And rang.

Eventually, Emmett picked up. He sounded like crap.

"Hello?"

I nervously cleared my throat. "Hey, Emm, it's me."

Long sigh. "I *know* it's you."

Attitude, yes, but at least he answered knowing it was me calling. "I, um, was wondering if we might be able to do our nightly rant."

Silence.

"We don't even have to really talk if you don't want to. We could just do our rant and then hang up. What do you say?"

"I guess so," he said unenthusiastically.

"Great. Can I go first?"

"Be my guest."

"Okay. Here's me." I took a deep breath before diving in. "I'm so angry at myself because I really screwed things up with the guy who means everything to me. And I can't believe what I've put this person through. It was totally uncalled for that I got so angry at the Regatta and accused this person of doing something terrible. And now I just miss him so much and it's weird and horrible and depressing to not be able to talk to him whenever I want to about everything. I have no one to rant to, no one to tell me I look fabulous, no one to kick me in the butt when I need it, and no one to tell me how to fix everything I've screwed up. I'm terrified I won't be able to find a way to make things right with this person, and I can't imagine my life without him in it. All I really want to do is apologize and take back every offensive thing I did and said." I paused. "I'm talking about *you*, you know."

"You went over by seven seconds," he said flatly.

"Sorry."

"It's my turn."

"Okay, go ahead."

Emmett sighed again. "Well, it's a strange coincidence, but I, too, am missing my best friend. And I'm really pissed at myself for doing something so stupid that I know must have hurt her badly. And since I've pretty much dedicated my life to protecting this person, hurting her is the last thing I ever wanted to do. I also really hate sneaking around school, ducking behind lockers and hallways just to avoid seeing this person. In part, because it's freakin' hard to do. But, mostly, because I've been so afraid that she hates me." He paused. "And *that* I don't think I could stand."

He stopped talking for a few seconds. "Anything else?" I asked.

"Is there anything left to say?"

"Yes, actually. I have more to say. I don't hate you, Emm. I could never hate you in a million years. I'm so sorry for doing this to you, for putting you in this ridiculous position. Molly told me what happened on Saturday, and I want you to know that I would never want you, or expect you, to lie for me. I seriously don't know what happened to me at the Regatta. It's like, when I realized Julian knew the truth, I just kind of lost it."

"Well, I can understand why. When you think the person you love is gone for good, it makes you do pretty crazy things."

The *L* word hung in the air for a few seconds, and neither of us said a word. But if we were going to salvage our friendship, I knew we had to go there, big, hairy, and uncomfortable or not.

"So, um, Emm? About that."

"About what?" He paused. "Oh, you mean *that?*"

"Yeah, *that.*"

"You mean that little thing about me telling you I was in love with you?"

"Yeah, that." God, was this hard. "You should have told me."

"I thought I did."

"Yeah, on Saturday. I'm talking about before we were in the middle of a screaming match. Don't take this the wrong way, but it wasn't the best timing, you know?"

"I know, but I've felt that way for so long, I didn't even know how to think about bringing it up anymore. I think I just got used to ignoring the way I felt when it came to you and me, since I was pretty sure if I ever did say anything about it, I'd find out you don't feel the same way."

Again the silence.

"Do you?" he asked. "Feel the same way?"

I'd thought about this a lot since last Saturday. I mean, I trusted Emmett more than anyone, and he was the one person who had always been there for me. Emmett knew all my dark, creepy secrets, yet he still managed to like me (love me, even!). And then there was the fact that he was absolutely adorable. But despite all the items I could check off in the good-boyfriend-material column, I couldn't make myself feel that extra something I had with Julian. It just wasn't there.

"You have no idea how much I wish I did feel the same way, Emmett. You are the perfect guy. You are. And I do love you more than anything—"

"—but not like that," he said, finishing my thought.

"But not like that," I repeated.

We were quiet again.

"So, where does this leave us?" I asked.

"It leaves us as friends," he said. "Just like we were before. But better."

"Better how?"

"Better because I'm going to stop hoping for it to be something more. From now on I'm going to accept that we aren't ever going to be together like that, and that's okay. Actually, I think I kind of built up in my mind what I thought we should be. The truth is, I love what we have as friends. Maybe that's all we're supposed to be anyway."

I smiled.

"That's not to say that should you ever change your mind and decide you *do* want to be more than friends, you shouldn't let me know . . ."

"Emm . . . ," I said.

"Just kidding," he said. "Kind of."

I laughed. For the first time since Saturday, I knew things were going to be okay. "So, we're good?"

"Yeah, we're good."

Thursday felt better, at least compared with earlier in the week when Emmett and I weren't talking. My friendship stresses no longer a factor in the internal turmoil that had racked my body over the past week, I had actually managed to get a decent night's sleep Wednesday night.

That's not to say I still wasn't suffering from acute hole-in-the-heart syndrome. I felt like the definition of the word "heartbreak," like everyone who laid eyes on me could take one look at my face and know exactly what was going on inside. I was still clinging to Molly's promise that things would get a little better each day. Any day now would be great with me.

When the final bell rang at the close of yet another meaningless day of school (not because of my bad attitude, but because it seemed both the student body and the teachers were already suffering from a severe case of summer-itis), I grabbed my stuff out of my locker and walked down the hallway toward the front doors. I had told Emmett earlier that I wasn't up for our weekly movie, mostly because a solo sulking session at home suited my mood better than a screening of *Invasion of the Body Snatchers*.

But as soon as I walked out of the building, I heard what sounded like Molly's horn. Snapped out of my daze, I looked up and saw Emmett and Molly pulling around in her little car, flagging me down.

"Janna!" Molly shouted out the window. "Come with us!"

They stopped right in front of me, and Emmett jumped out and got into the back.

"What? What is it?" I had been looking forward to what had by now become a daily postschool pity party. And it was one party that didn't require any other guests.

"Just get in," Molly said.

"But why? What are we doing?"

"What happened to the spontaneous Janna I came to love over the past few weeks? Get in the car, girl! We're going to my house. That's it."

"That's it?"

"That's it."

"But I was really in the mood to go home and—"

"Yeah, yeah, we know, be sad, mope around, listen to cheesy love songs, watch *Atonement* over and over again, blah, blah blah. Just get in the car, would you?" said Emmett.

Reluctantly, I slid into the front seat, shoving my bag between my feet before pulling the car door closed. Having successfully made her pickup, Molly peeled out of the parking lot and headed toward her house.

"Will somebody *please* tell me what's going on?" Yes, I was happy to have my friends back, but I was still incredibly fragile. I wasn't up for any of Molly's usual shenanigans.

"Just relax, Janna. It's all good. We'll talk about it when we get home, okay?" Molly said.

"Fine. Whatever." I leaned my head back against the

headrest and listlessly stared out the window. I studied the faces on people we passed by, noticed how they seemed engaged with life. There was something so unzombielike about them. Would I ever look that way again?

"Come on, sweetie. Let's go inside." We'd just pulled into Molly's narrow driveway and squeezed out of the car. Once inside the house, Molly hooked us up with some trail mix and water and we went into her living room, where I fell into the big comfy chair built for two.

"Okay. I'm here. What's so important?" I asked wearily. I appreciated their efforts to cheer me up, I really did. But frankly, I didn't want to do anything but sleep and wait for time to pass so this heartache would go away.

"I have a plan to help you get Julian back," Molly said, her eyes shimmering with hope like she'd just told me she'd discovered the cure for cancer.

"A plan?" I shook my head. "I don't think I can handle another one of your 'plans' right now. No offense."

"Just hear her out, Janna," Emmett said.

I looked at Emmett, surprised. "You're actually going along with this?"

"It's a good plan, Jan. In fact, I'd even give it the Emmett seal of approval," he replied.

I eyed Emmett suspiciously. Since when was he so interested in helping me get back my guy? Hmmm . . . get back my guy. Was there a chance in hell? Apparently they thought so.

"All right, I'm listening," I said. Might as well hear them out.

Molly leaned forward on the couch. "Okay. Now. I think we'd all agree that in order to get Julian back, you're going to have to do something, you know, *big*. Something that makes a statement. Something that says, 'I love you and you know you love me, too.' Right?"

"Big *how*? Big like charging in on a white horse and sweeping him off his feet? My life isn't a romance movie, you know."

"Bigger," she said.

"Bigger?" I said.

"Bigger," Molly and Emmett said simultaneously.

"Like what?"

"I've got just one word for you . . . prom."

"Prom?"

"Prom," they both said in unison.

"Enough! Somebody just tell me the plan already!"

"We're going to crash the Collins junior prom on Saturday night. We already know Julian will definitely be there, since he's deejaying it," she said.

"Crashing Julian's prom? *That's* your big idea?" I was still waiting for the really big part that would be so brilliant that Julian would forgive all and come running back to me.

"It's more than just crashing the prom, Janna. It's about putting everything on the line and doing something crazy to let someone know how important they are to you. It's about making a complete fool of yourself for love," Emmett said.

"Easy, Mr. Romance. As I just told you, my life is *not* a teen romance movie. Things don't always work out happily ever after in real life."

"I know," Emmett said. "Believe me." His look let me know he was still feeling his own heartache. I was pretty impressed he was sticking to his word, though, and focusing on just being my friend. "But I also know this. You need to tell Julian how you feel or you'll never know what you could have had. And maybe when Julian sees the lengths you'll go to for him, he'll give you another chance."

I played with a piece of loose thread I'd pulled off my T-shirt, twirling it around my pinkie while I thought about their idea.

"But how would we get in? How would it all work?" I asked.

"You let us worry about getting in. Spence owes me, *big* time, and I'm going to collect," Molly said.

"And I'll make sure Julian is where you need him to be and that he's open to hearing you," said Emmett.

"All you have to do is figure out what you want to say and how you want to say it," Molly said.

I crinkled my eyebrows together in a scowl. "You really think this could work?"

"Totally!" Molly answered enthusiastically.

"Not you," I said to her. *"You."* I pointed to Emmett.

"Yes. I really think it could work. Look. What do you have to lose? Besides. You? Janna? The original one? You're pretty freaking amazing. And I know it sounds all cliché and everything, but it's true—if Julian can't see how great you are, then he's probably not the guy for you anyway, right?"

I shrugged my shoulders in agreement. "I guess so."

"So, what do you think? Can I put the plan in motion?" Molly asked.

I hesitated. Would I be able to go through with it? Could I come up with the perfect thing to say and do that would, as Emmett said, put it all on the line? I looked up at Molly and Emmett, both of whom were staring at me with the expectancy of children waiting for a puppy on Christmas morning.

I let out a long sigh. Emmett was right. What *did* I have to lose? "Okay," I said. "I'm in."

Molly let out a whoop of excitement, clapping her hands. "This is going to be so awesome, Janna!"

Awesome? Doubtful. Humiliating? Probably. But how much worse could things get between Julian and me at this point? At the very least, I owed it to him, to me, and to Janna Ika Ilka to give our love one more shot.

17

"Are you ready?" Molly asked me.

Definitely not. "As ready as I'll ever be."

Emmett put his hand on my shoulder comfortingly. "Got your music?"

I patted my bag and felt the outline of the CD inside, nodding my head nervously.

Molly, Emmett, and I were outside the yacht club where Julian's prom was being held, circling around the parking lot looking for a spot. We found one in the last row, and Molly pulled in, cracking open the windows a smidge so we wouldn't fog up the windows before turning off the ignition. We sat there in silence, listening to the muffled sound of music coming from inside the club. Julian's music.

Julian was in there, right now. I couldn't wait to see him. I was terrified to see him.

"I can't do this." Rapid heart rate. Shortness of breath. Queasiness. *Is this what having a heart attack feels like?*

"You *can* do it," Molly said. "We're here for you. You're not going to be alone."

"I know."

Molly looked at the clock on her dashboard. "We've gotta go. Spence is meeting us at the side door in two minutes."

"I still can't believe he went along with this," Emmett said.

"Yeah, me too. Are you sure he didn't say anything to Julian?" I asked.

"Yeah. For as much as a jerk as he was to me, he has this savior complex thing when it comes to Julian. And he said Julian's been miserable since he found out about you. When I told Spence how you felt and what you wanted to do, he agreed. The fact that I gave him the guilt trip of a lifetime for what he did to me didn't hurt," Molly explained.

I remembered Julian's story about Spence sticking up for him when he was little. I guess he was still doing it today.

We got out of the car and made our way across the damp parking lot. The air was thick with clouds, but the rain had tapered off for now. We hurried toward the door like we were on a covert mission. We were half the gang from Scooby-Doo . . . Emmett as Shaggy, Molly as Daphne, and me as Velma, of course, minus the glasses and kneesocks. Instead, I was wearing a long black skirt, heels, and a T-shirt covered with cheesy foods. Not my best look, but I was hoping it would at least get Julian's attention.

We ran up to the door and Molly gently rapped on it three times. Nothing. She knocked again.

"Where is he?! He promised he would—"

"I'm right here." Spence propped open the door, looking dapper in a black tux.

"Oh, hi. Thanks." Without thinking, Molly gave him a smile, then quickly erased it once she remembered what he'd done to her.

"No problem," he said. He looked at me and my outfit with confusion before turning to Molly and smiling. "You look very nice tonight," he said to her.

She gently pushed him on the shoulder. "Focus. We're here for Janna and Julian. That's it."

"Hey, hey, take it easy. We're all on the same team here, right?" he said.

Molly glared at him impatiently.

"Damn, okay, girl. I get it." He pointed to the stairs at the far end of the room. "The ballroom is up there. Julian's finishing his set in five minutes, and they'll be announcing the prom king and queen five minutes after that. Whatever you need to do, I would do it in between. There's already a mic set up onstage."

"What do you think Julian's going to do once he goes on his break?" Molly asked.

"I don't know . . . take a piss, maybe?" Spence answered.

"That won't work. We need him in the room," Molly said. "Can you keep him there?"

"Yeah, I guess so. I could tell him that I need to talk to him about—"

"Can I go with you? I want to be there with him when Janna does her thing," Emmett said.

Spence looked at Emmett as if he'd just noticed he was there. "Who are you?"

"I'm Emmett. I'm with them. I'm the, uh, one from the Regatta."

"Oh yeah, I heard about you. I'm not so sure he'd be into seeing you, dude."

"I'm just here to apologize. And to make sure that he hears what Janna has to say."

"All right, I guess that's okay. Look we gotta move. His set's going to be over in a minute." Spence gave us a serious look. "Don't screw this up."

I felt the color drain from my face. This was it. We

scrambled across the room and up the stairs into the grand ballroom, where the Collins prom was in full swing. I looked onstage and spotted Julian off to the side at his booth. He was rocking with the beat of the music, completely focused on the control he had over the room. I felt like I'd just been punched in the chest at the very sight of him. I wanted him back. Bad. More than anything I'd ever wanted before.

"Okay, guys. We're moving. Good luck!" Molly said. She grabbed my hand as we snaked our way through the crowds along the far wall of the room. We reached the foot of the stage on the opposite side from where Julian was and huddled together.

"Okay," Molly said. "As soon as Julian gets off the stage, we'll go. You head straight for the mic, and I'll go put your CD in, okay? I'll give you a thumbs-up sign when I'm ready."

"I can't do this!" My voice was laced with panic.

Molly grabbed me by both shoulders and looked at me hard, eye to eye, her face the epitome of determination. "You *can* do this," she said slowly. "I promise you . . . you can do this. And if you need to, pretend you're Janna Ika Ilka while you're up there. Remember her? Janna Ika Ilka could do anything."

I closed my eyes and breathed, summoning the spirit

of my alter ego. It's true. She'd never let me down before. I hoped tonight would be no different. I opened my eyes with a new conviction.

"Okay. I'm ready."

Suddenly Julian's voice came through the speakers. "All right all you Collins juniors. I'm signing out for a bit, but don't go anywhere. Your prom king and queen will be announced in just five minutes!"

Julian took off his headphones and put on some background music before snagging his bottle of water and jumping off the stage. I turned to Molly. She was crouched at the base of the stairs, watching Julian work his way through the crowd, waiting for Emmett and Spence to intercept him. A minute later she turned around and motioned for me to follow her.

"Come on!" she said with urgency.

I was on automatic pilot now. I wordlessly followed her up the stairs and across the stage, stopping when I reached the microphone while she ran ahead and put my CD into Julian's player. She looked at me one last time, giving me the thumbs-up sign. I flashed it back, and she pushed play.

Up until this point, no one had even noticed I was on the stage. And when the first few bars of Frank Sinatra's "New York, New York" began playing over the sound system, I still wasn't noticed. But when I opened my mouth to sing the first line? People noticed . . . big time. I wish I could say it was because of my melodic singing voice, but that would be a lie. In fact, I'm not sure which was worse—the shriek of feedback emanating from the microphone or the painful sound of my off-key warbling. I do know that every, and I mean every, eye in the place was on me. I managed to get out two more lines before I started to freeze up.

The full-on stage fright took hold when I realized the spirit of my alter ego was no longer with me. And in her place was a seven-year-old girl in a yellow, sequined leotard, desperate to be anywhere but onstage. The hundreds of teenagers staring at me were my mocking audience, first eyeing me with silent confusion and shock (as in, what *is* that horrible sound?) before their murmurs of laughter began to fill the room. I opened my mouth to sing the fourth line, but no sound came out. Oh my God. Holy stage fright. What the *hell* was I doing up here?

I looked at Molly in complete distress, wide-eyed and in straight-up panic mode.

"You can do it, Janna!" She would make a fantastic stage mom someday.

I turned back to the audience. I needed to see Julian. Needed to see the look in his eyes. The accompaniment barreled on as I scanned the crowd. Where was he? Was he listening? Could he see me?

Finally I spotted him toward the back of the room near the bar. Spence and Emmett were with him, and he was just standing there, looking at me, no real emotion on his face that I could read: happy or sad. Instead, his face bore a blank stare, not unlike the one I had worked so hard to patent.

"Julian," I said into the microphone in my Hungarian accent. Then I remembered that Janna Ika Ilka wasn't here anymore. I was on my own. That's the way it had to be.

"I mean . . . *Julian.*" This time I used my real voice.

Molly abruptly switched off the music, its absence filled by my trembling soliloquy.

"I . . . I . . . I . . . wanted to tell you how sorry I am." I paused. I had rehearsed what I wanted to say over and over again, but the words temporarily left me. I looked at Molly again. She mouthed a message to me: *You can do it.*

I turned back to Julian and the roomful of people. Everyone was frozen now, staring at me, waiting to see what would come next. Maybe my stage fright had given them a case of audience fright? Hard to tell.

"I . . . um . . ." *Come on, Janna! Get it together. This is it. Your big chance. Your time to do something big to get him back. Your time to be foolish. Be foolish!* "I never meant to do that to you. It's not who I am." Suddenly the script I'd rehearsed started coming back to me, and I gained more confidence, the words coming faster.

"I may not be Janna Ika Ilka from Hungary. But I do still suck at bowling. I do still love standing on the front deck of a ferry, no matter how cold it is. I do still think Yo-Yo Ma rules." I paused. "And I do like you. A lot. I think you're pretty much the greatest guy I've ever met. And I'm so sorry for everything. I really am. I'd take it all back if I could, except then I wouldn't have met you. So I can't take it back. I can only say I'm sorry."

"Get a room!" some obnoxious guy in a powder-blue tux yelled in my general direction. "Nice shirt!" someone else yelled. I looked down at my cheese T-shirt. A fool for love or not, I knew I'd pretty much just made a complete ass of myself. I looked back at Julian to see if I could gauge anything, get a sense of how he was feeling. But no could do. Especially since he was no longer even standing there.

The guy in the blue tux started yelling again. "Hey, cheese girl, get off the stage!"

"Yeah, quit ruining our prom!" I was pretty sure that last comment came from one of the chicks Molly and I had seen at the rugby game, probably a prom queen hopeful who wanted to find out if she'd won or not.

Of course, in classic Janna style, I just stood there, frozen. I had figured out what to wear, what to sing, and what to say, but I had never figured out an exit strategy. This was probably because I was operating under the delusion (fueled by Molly and Emmett's belief) that following my declaration of love, Julian would come running up, sweep me into his arms, and carry me offstage where we'd spend the rest of the night making out. Okay, maybe the part about carrying me offstage was unrealistic, but I thought I had a real shot at the rest.

I hadn't planned on what to do if Julian didn't go for the making out option, though. If he actually disappeared and didn't even acknowledge my gesture. Thankfully, true to her word, Molly was there for me. She swooped across the stage and looped her arm around mine, whipping me into the wings offstage and out of the line of fire.

"Let's go!" I cried. The anxiety and fear and humiliation combined to push me over the emotional edge. I wanted to curl up into a very small ball and hide away in a corner somewhere far, far away. Possibly as far as Hungary.

Molly shoved her keys into my hands. "Here. Go wait in the car. I'll find Emmett and meet you there." Before Molly left, she turned around to look at my sobbing self and gave me a powerful hug. "You were amazing out there, Janna. You did it. You. Janna Papp. All by yourself. See? There must be some of Janna Ika Ilka in you after all."

I let out a little laugh while continuing to cry. Molly ran off, and I ducked out the stage door, immediately finding myself alone on a loading dock. In the pouring rain, no less. I squealed as I realized I had no raincoat, no umbrella, and no idea where the car was. I jumped down from the loading dock and scoured the parking lot, finally stumbling upon Molly's car after a good ten minutes. By the time I managed to climb in, I was completely drenched. I reached around in the backseat in search of a towel, but only came up with a pair of socks. They appeared to be clean, so I unfolded them and tried to dry my face, which was pretty much impossible since the tears were still flowing freely. I wrung out my hair with my other hand.

A moment later there was a light rapping on the window. I shoved the key in the ignition so I could roll down the window a crack. It was Emmett.

"Get in!" I shouted.

"Is Molly in the car?"

"No! She was looking for you!"

"Damn. Okay. I'll go find her. Be right back." The windows were already so fogged I could barely make out Emmett's outline as he disappeared into the dark, rainy night. Sitting in the car waiting, I replayed the scene that had unfolded inside over and over again in my mind, shaking my head vigorously as I continued to cry.

I still couldn't believe I had actually done it. And the weird thing was, even though I was embarrassed, humiliated, and definitely did not get the guy, there was just the tiniest part of me that felt something like pride. Not proud of my singing or anything like that. But proud of the fact that I had faced my ultimate fear—standing onstage and putting myself out there to be ridiculed—and survived. Maybe Molly was right. Maybe Janna Ika Ilka wasn't as far off from who I was after all?

There was a light rapping at my window again.

"Did you find her, Emm?" I sniffled as I rolled down the window a crack.

"Find who?"

I looked up. "Julian!"

"Hi, Janna," he said. "That *is* your real name, isn't it?"

I didn't know whether to laugh or cry even harder. "Yes. That's my name." I looked at him, his gorgeous light eyes piercing right through me, raindrops dripping off his hair, lips glistening.

"Are you okay?" he asked me. "That was a pretty wackadoodle thing you did in there."

I looked down and nodded, then looked back into his eyes. "Are *you* okay?"

"No, not really."

I nodded again. Of course he wasn't okay. What an insensitive thing for me to ask after everything I—

"I'm not okay because I'm getting soaked out here. Can I please come in?"

"Oh my God, I'm so sorry. Of course!" I rolled up the window and slid over into the driver's side. Julian climbed into the car, and in an instant his energy, his very presence, made me weak all over. I wanted to kiss and hug him so badly. Having him so near to me and not being able to even reach over and grab his hand was torturous. But I needed to know where he stood. I'd put it all on the line. Whether or not we had a future was up to him.

Julian let out a big sigh. I wasn't a fan of sighing. It was so hard to know what the sigh meant. I wasn't sure if this one was a why-did-you-crash-my-prom-and-embarrass-me-in-front-of-all-my-friends sigh or an I-thought-I-made-it-clear-that-I-didn't-want-to-see-you-again sigh? Of course, maybe, just maybe, it was an I-can't-live-without-you-slash-you-complete-me sigh. These were the things I was thinking about when Julian spoke up.

"So, you *like* me?"

I sniffed and blotted my eyes with the sock. "Yeah. I like you. A lot."

"And is impersonating foreigners how you pick up all your boyfriends, or was I just special?"

I couldn't tell if he was trying to make a joke or not. I also noted the use of the word "boyfriend," which sounded so delicious coming from his mouth, especially because that meant he had thought of me as his girlfriend, at one time, anyway. I decided his question was my cue. It was time for the whole truth to come out.

"It wasn't like that. It really did just kind of happen. I mean, I was just making a joke to Molly, and then you came up to us, and then Molly said that I was an exchange student, and, I don't know why . . . I just went along with it. I didn't tell you right away because I figured that if you thought I was from Seattle, you would never have given me a second look. I mean, I'm not exactly a guy magnet. I didn't expect you to actually like me, didn't expect, you know"—I looked at him deeply and motioned my hand back and forth as if displaying the invisible field of energy between us—"*this*. I didn't know I was going to . . . fall for you. Not that what I did would have been okay even if I didn't like you, but falling for you just made everything so much more complicated. And then I didn't know how to tell you. The more I got to know you, the more I liked you. And the more I liked you, the more I didn't know how to tell you. And I just kept digging a deeper and deeper hole until I didn't know what to do. I'm so sorry you found out the way you did. I was going to tell you last Saturday morning. That's why I called you and asked you to meet me for coffee."

"Yeah, I figured that out after the fact," he said. He had been listening to me intently as I explained the whole situation. Now he turned to look out the window, as if the drops of rain streaming down the outside of the window held the answer to the big question: Where do we go from here?

By then my crying had pretty much stopped. Having the whole truth out there was actually an incredibly freeing feeling. There were no longer any obstacles, any deceptions, any great secrets to hide. Of course, I knew this probably meant there was no Janna and Julian relationship, either. It was time to find out.

"Julian," I said. "I know you probably still hate me and don't want to see me anymore, and I understand. You have a right to feel that way. I really just want you to know that I'm sorry and that I never meant to do anything to hurt you."

He turned around slowly to look at me. Was that a slight smile in his eyes? "But what if I do want to see you again?"

I swallowed hard. Had I heard him right? "Do you . . . I mean . . . could you ever . . . I mean, do you think we could try—"

Julian leaned over and shut me up with a kiss square on the mouth. He reached around and pulled me close to him, brushing my damp hair back as he continued to kiss all the fear, tension, and embarrassment out of my body.

We kissed with passion and excitement and possibility for a long, long time, my heart bursting with emotion. When we finally came up for air, my body had been reduced to a pile of Jell-O. I'm quite sure I would have miserably failed a drunk driving test . . . there was no way I could have possibly walked in a straight line, let alone stood without swaying. Luckily, I didn't have to.

"So, you still like me?" I said with a dopey grin on my face.

"Yes, Janna from Seattle. I still like you."

I smiled.

Julian turned sideways to face me and leaned back against his seat. He grabbed my hand and held it in both of his. "I *was* really mad about what you did. I felt like you had totally played me for a fool. But this week, not seeing you or talking to you . . . I *really* missed you. Yes, the reason you got my attention in the first place was your accent. That and the fact that you were different. I like different. But what I came to like was you, accent or not. And so, even though I was so pissed off, I got to thinking that maybe the fact that you weren't Hungarian was actually okay with me, especially if it meant you weren't going anywhere anytime soon. You're not, right? Moving to Hungary, I mean."

"No!" I laughed. "I am going to Europe with Molly for a few weeks at the end of June, but that's it. I swear."

"Good." He leaned over and gave me another kiss. "Anyway, after thinking about everything, I was actually planning on coming over to your house tomorrow to see if we could work things out."

"You were?"

He nodded his head.

"You mean I didn't have to go through with this whole 'New York, New York' pageant re-enactment humiliation thing to prove my love to you?"

"No, I guess not. But don't feel bad . . . I mean, think of how much more exciting you made my prom!" Julian laughed.

My face turned red in embarrassment. He was right. I was that crazy girl people would tell stories about for years to come. "About that. I'm so sorry if I embarrassed you. I didn't realize until just now that you might get a lot of abuse for having the freaky girlfriend in the cheese shirt crash your prom and sing bad karaoke."

"Don't be. I'm not really concerned about what my fellow classmates think of me. Besides, while they're all in there celebrating the prom king and queen, I've got my own pageant queen right here."

We laughed and kissed again.

"Speaking of which, we should probably go back inside and find your friends."

Oh, yeah. Molly and Emmett were still in there somewhere. What had happened to them? "Okay. But do me a favor? Don't leave me when we get inside. There's some guy in an ugly blue tux who is kinda freaking me out."

Julian laughed. "Don't worry. It'll be you and me in there, together. And if anyone gives us a hard time, we'll just sic Spence on them."

We got out of the car and slushed our way through the parking lot puddles, arm in arm. I think it had stopped raining. I can't really be sure. All I knew was that Julian and I were together. I'd gotten my happy ending after all.

When we got into the ballroom, the lights were low, and a slow song was playing. We scanned the crowd for Spence, Molly, and Emmett. We eventually spotted Molly and Spence on the dance floor, dancing. Together. How long had we been out there? Had hell really frozen over?

We walked up to them, and I tapped Molly on the shoulder. She turned around and burst into a huge grin when she saw me and Julian together, most likely also noticing my lipstick was smeared off and I had that dazed look in my eyes she is all too familiar with. She squealed in delight and roughly pulled me into a hug.

"I knew it! Emmett and I went out to check on you a while ago and we saw you guys in the car, so we left you alone to work things out," she explained. She looked back and forth between Julian and me. "So, is everything okay?"

I smiled my goofy smile again and leaned my head against Julian's shoulder.

"See, Spence, I told you so!" She gave him a high five.

"What's going on here?" Julian asked Spence suspiciously, motioning back and forth between him and Molly.

"Nothing's going on. We're just dancing," Spence said.

"Spence gave me a very nice and very genuine apology. And I decided that if I was expecting you to forgive Janna, then I should be able to forgive Spence for being such a jerk. But that doesn't mean anything's ever gonna happen between us again." She turned to Spence and pointed at him. "Got it?"

He laughed and put his hands up in the air like he was being held up. "Easy. I got it."

I looked around the room. Someone was still missing from this picture. "Where is Emmett?" I asked.

Molly pointed up onstage. There he was, manning Julian's deejay booth. There was a pretty girl leaned up against the booth, giving Emmett all her attention.

"And who's that?" I asked, pointing at the girl.

"Chelsey Thoms," Julian and Spence said simultaneously. They looked at each other and chuckled.

"Why are you laughing? Is she okay? Because I'm very protective of Emmett, you know," I said.

"No, no, she's great. She's actually a really cool and interesting girl. Lots of guys in school would kill to go out with her, but she's just never been into anyone here."

My face broke into a grin. If anyone deserved to find a cool, beautiful, interesting girl, it was Emmett. Just then he looked down and saw me standing there with Julian. He gave me a genuine smile, one that said he was truly happy for me. That, and he was very much enjoying hanging out with Chelsey Thoms. He held up his index finger as if to say *hold on* as the current song faded out.

From the very first note, I knew exactly which song was next. A huge smile spread across my face as I turned back around to Julian, who was smiling, too, memories of our first date bubbling to the surface.

"May I have this dance?" Julian held out his hand to me.

"But of course," I said. I put my hand in his, and he pulled me close as we moved together to the opening of "(I've Had) The Time of My Life" from *Dirty Dancing*. Even when the music picked up a few bars later, we stayed close, alone in our own little world, happy to be starting over.

"You know, I think this song should be our anthem," Julian said softly into my ear.

"You think so?" I laughed. I did love the song.

"Definitely. It was while I was singing this song with you at karaoke that I first realized I could really like you."

223

I smiled. "But that was Janna from Hungary doing karaoke with you. I don't know if Janna from Seattle can pull it off. Is that okay?"

"Are you kidding me? After your rousing rendition of 'New York, New York' tonight?" he laughed. "I'd say Janna from Seattle can pull off anything she wants to. In fact, between the singing and the cheese shirt, I'd say you're the perfect girl for me. I told you I like different, right?"

I laughed as I looked down at my outfit again.

"I do have one request, though."

"What's that?"

"Next time, can you do it with the baton? Just for me? Please? I promise I won't laugh. In fact, I can pretty much guarantee that you'll be happy with the outcome."

I looked up at Julian and smiled, melting into his arms. Everything I'd been through in the past month—the impersonating, the angst, the friendship ups and downs, the karaoke—had been worth it. And in the end, I not only got the guy. I got me, Janna Papp, better than I'd ever been before.

Cupidity

For Richard

1

Flies buzzed around the Dumpster in the alley, and the late-summer heat was brutal even in the shade. Laura Sweeney swatted a mosquito away from her arm and pushed her glasses back up her cute but sweaty nose. Her friend Taryn sat across from her on the benches behind the Dairy Queen, and both were dressed in the blue polyester uniforms of the DQ.

In time-honored lunch break tradition, they weren't eating food from their own establishment; Taryn had just returned with goodies from the 7-Eleven across the street. She gave Laura her chocolate milk and beef jerky, while she opened up a big straw that was full of pink sugar. *Mmmm, lunch.*

"How much do I owe you?" Laura pulled a garish red and yellow wallet from her pocket and handed Taryn a few bucks. The plastic corners were tattered from wear, but the heroic figure of a woman warrior still graced the shiny cover.

Taryn laughed out loud and nearly spit up her sipping sugar. "When are you getting rid of your Xena wallet?" she asked in amazement.

"As soon as I give up the Hercules lunch box," answered Laura proudly. "And speaking of my mythology obsession—I read the most beautiful love story last night. It was about a wood nymph named Egeria, who fell in love with a mortal king named Numa Pompilius." Laura got a wistful look in her eyes, and she took off her glasses. The weeds in the alley didn't look so bad blurry.

"When the king died," she went on, "Egeria was so sad that she couldn't stop crying. Nobody could comfort her, and she wouldn't leave the spot in the woods where they always met. The goddess Diana took pity on Egeria and turned her into water. Her legs became an eternal spring, and her torso shot up into the sky!"

"Wait a minute, hold on," said Taryn, tossing her thick black hair. "The dude dies, and the girl cries so hard that she gets turned into a *fountain*?"

With a sniff, Laura nodded. "That's right."

"And you call that a great love story?" scoffed Taryn. "I'm sorry, but when my boyfriend dies, I don't want to be turned into a fountain. I want to find another guy with a nicer car."

"Well, Egeria wasn't a *girl*," replied Laura defensively. "She was a wood nymph. They used to meet every night in a sacred grove, and she gave him good advice on how to govern his people. They *really* loved each other. I've got the book in my car, if you want to see—"

Taryn reached out, grabbed Laura's arm, and forced Laura back onto the bench. "Girl, you need to get out of these fairy tales and into a reality show. In a week, you're going to be a senior in high school, and have you ever been kissed?"

"Well, of course," said Laura, bristling. "There was that party when we played spin-the-bottle."

"In fifth grade!" snapped Taryn. "Laura, you're pretty—in a bookish kind of way—and there have to be guys who would crawl after you. What about Peter?"

"Peter Yarmench?" asked Laura with a laugh. "Oh, I've known him since we were in kindergarten. He's not my type."

"What *is* your type?" asked Taryn suspiciously.

Laura hugged her beef jerky and smiled dreamily. "Jake Mattson."

Her friend snorted a laugh. "Right, the most popular boy in school. He's *everyone's* type. Can't you aim a little lower than that?"

With a pout, Laura thought about all the boys who really appealed to her, and she came up with another name. "Cody Kenyon. I like *him*."

"The baddest boy in school," muttered Taryn. "I have a hard time seeing you with a bad-boy skater dude."

Laura squared her shoulders and smiled mischievously at her friend. "Is that right? Well, I'm going to surprise you this year. I'm for sure going to have a boyfriend, and it's going to be whoever I want!"

"Those guys won't even talk to us," said Taryn bitterly. "You need a cheerleader outfit in a size four."

Laura's shoulders slumped and she sat back on the cold cement bench. "Not my style, huh?"

"You're top pick for valedictorian," said Taryn, waving her sugar straw around. "Stick to your own crew—you know, the other valedictorian types."

Laura frowned and put her glasses back on. "Does it always have to be like this? We can never look outside of our usual circle? What if I want something . . . else?"

"Girl, you've got to try *one* boy before you can try them all," said Taryn with a sniff.

Suddenly the back door of the Dairy Queen opened,

and a greasy-haired teen stuck his head out. Allen was also wearing a blue polyester uniform, but he had a name badge, which neither one of them had.

"Hey, princesses," he snarled, "your lunch break was over five minutes ago. I need you to get back to work."

Taryn shot a nasty glance at Allen. "We're expanding our minds by talking about Roman mythology. Do you know anything about that?"

"Heck no," he snapped. "I just know this afternoon is going to be hotter than Hades! We need to inventory before the rush, so hurry up." He ducked back inside, banging the door shut behind him.

Laura chuckled. "'Hotter than Hades.' He knows about mythology, and he doesn't even know he knows. These aren't just fairy tales, Taryn—people worshipped these gods for thousands of years."

"Well, now they worship the mean green," said her friend, rising to her full five-foot-one stature. "That's why we have to work. Come on, back to the custard pits."

With determination, Laura grabbed her chocolate milk and stood up. *This year is going to be different,* she told herself. *I'm going to make sure it is.*

A week later, it was still hotter than Hades, but the school year began as scheduled. As the first warning bell rang, students streamed into the main door and through the halls of Fimbrey High School in Denton, Ohio, looking for new lockers and old friends. Laura Sweeney had picked out a strategic spot next to the central stairwell, where she could catch sight of everyone going up and down and passing through.

Fimbrey High School didn't require uniforms, but everyone was dressed in a uniform anyway. She picked them out as they walked past: the jocks and preppies in their stylish clothes; the goths and skaters in black shirts, chains, and carefully torn jeans; the homeboys with their super low-rider baggy pants, and the nerdy types, who were the only ones actually obeying the school's dress code.

Laura was a senior this year, which meant that she should be one of the goddesses of the school, but she didn't feel like a goddess. Maybe the sophomores looked up to her, but nobody her own age did, unless they envied future valedictorians. She was carefully showing a little midriff, because she was skinny enough to pull it off. But she didn't show enough skin to get in trouble.

Suddenly the crowd parted, and she could see all heads turning toward a tall, striking blond boy wearing a letter jacket, even though it was way too hot for a jacket. It didn't matter, because Jake Mattson didn't sweat unless he wanted to. Laura moved her glasses farther down her nose—she didn't want to steam them up. She read about Greek gods all the time, but here was one in person. Finally a senior, Jake Mattson really *was* king of the school. Even his girlfriend, Megan Rawlins, looked up to him, although the head cheerleader looked down at everyone else.

Megan got to walk beside Jake, acknowledging the greetings from their chosen subjects and ignoring the stares of the peons. The heavenly couple got a snarl from Emma Langdon, a goth chick who wore more eye shadow, piercings, and studs than ten other girls combined. Her cadre of goth-activists snarled along with her, but Jake Mattson ignored the purple-hair crowd. Not everyone was going to like the king, but that didn't change the fact that he still *was* the king.

The skater punks had their own hero, and he made an entrance, too. Looking like the underworld god Pluto with his shaggy raven hair, skintight T-shirt, and studded jeans, Cody Kenyon strolled down the hallway. Now it was Emma's turn to stare dreamily as the dark lord walked past, carrying his scarred skateboard over his shoulder like a weapon. Curvy little Chelsea Williams hurried after him; clearly, Cody was cool enough to be acceptable even to her popular crowd. Cody gave Chelsea a sneering smile and wrapped his arms around her waist.

Laura wanted to step forward and say something to Jake or Cody, but her feet seemed to be rooted to the spot. Still her mouth was working, and she had once helped Jake with his trigonometry. So she worked up her courage and had lifted her hand to wave hello when a voice boomed behind her.

"Hey, Laura!"

That broke the spell, and she whirled around to see Peter Yarmench, a skinny guy with wavy red hair and numerous freckles. He beamed at her as the royal couple glided past, taking her moment of bravery with them.

"Oh, hi, Peter," she answered, trying to muster some cheer. "How are you?"

"I'm great!" he answered, sounding impossibly cheerful. "I thought school would never start."

And that's why you're so not one of the cool kids, thought Laura. "Yeah, well, here we are again."

"Hey, I called you a bunch of times last week, but you never returned my calls." Peter looked like her puppy when he got caught going through the garbage. She realized it wasn't his fault she was grumpy about school starting this year . . . with *no* romance.

Laura looked away. "Well, I was working really hard down at the DQ." That was a lame answer, she thought, but at least it was partially true.

"Hey, let's see your schedule," he said cheerfully. "Do we have any classes together?"

She fished around in her new planner for her schedule, but she already knew the answer. They would have at least half of their classes together, even though Fimbrey was a big high school with almost two thousand students. For some reason, she and Peter had been joined at the hip ever since first grade, and the scheduling gods never kept them far apart. Of course, they usually took the same advanced classes, and they were competing to be valedictorian.

He grinned as he studied her schedule. "Wow! We've got second period, third period, fifth period, and seventh period. That's amazing!"

"Isn't it?" she replied, mustering a smile. "Who would have thought?"

"I'm looking forward to this year," said Peter with a crooked smile. She peered up at him, thinking he had gotten taller over the summer. "Did they give you a new locker?" he asked.

"Yes, in the old wing by the music room," she answered. "That's good, maybe I won't get trampled."

"Hey, mine's there too!"

The last warning bell rang, and even the slouching homeboys began to hurry a bit toward their first class. Peter looked worriedly at his watch and began to shuffle off. "See you in advanced calculus. Hey, Laura, it's going to be a great year."

She nodded. "I hope so."

Perhaps it was going to be a great year, but it started out like every other year of high school. Laura Sweeney attended all her classes on time and met her new teachers—all of whom were overjoyed to have such a well-regarded student in class. She saw Peter several more times that day, and she ate lunch with Taryn and all her friends from her regular group. She never did work up the courage to talk to Jake Mattson or Cody Kenyon or any of the other boys she didn't already know.

At home, her mom asked her, "How was your day?" and she gave the usual polite but vague answers. She wasn't going to share the fact that the only boy she had had the courage to talk to was Peter Yarmench. Her dad gave her the standard lecture about how this year she had to work harder than ever to keep up her grades, although she knew that her future place at Ohio State was secure. It was only a matter of whether she would be the valedictorian and get some extra scholarship money. Her future looked safe, humdrum, steady as she goes: no excitement, no worries, no big question marks.

And Laura was no closer to getting a boyfriend.

Being the first day of school, there was hardly any homework, so Laura went to her bedroom after dinner to read one of her mythology books. It started to rain, and the warm drops beat a steady rhythm against her window as she read. Although Laura knew the story well, she thrilled at the tale of Pygmalion and Galatea.

Pygmalion was a famous sculptor who created a statue of a woman that was so beautiful that he could love no real woman. When he asked Aphrodite, whom the Romans called Venus, to find him a living mate as beautiful as his creation, the goddess could find none. Taking pity on the lonely sculptor, Aphrodite breathed life into his fantastic statue, and it turned into flesh and blood. Pygmalion named his beloved Galatea, and they married and were deliriously happy for the rest of their lives.

Why can't I have that? thought Laura bitterly. *Why isn't there a perfect boy out there for me? Someone I really like.*

In anguish, she lifted her head and shouted to the rainy sky, "Jupiter, send me a boyfriend!"

A crack of thunder startled her, and she looked around, feeling a slight chill. Her dog, Chloe, suddenly ran into the room and jumped on the bed, cowering in her arms like she always did when there was loud thunder. Chloe was not a very brave mutt, despite having been named after a brave heroine in mythology.

Laura laughed and scratched her puppy's head. "If only real life were as simple as these fables," she lamented, "but it's so not."

Outside the rain started to fall harder, and the thunder growled a low reply.

"Mercury! Mister Mercury, wake up!" The desk clerk of the Mount Olympus Retirement Home in Tarzana, California, gently shook the elderly man awake. Mercury was sitting in a wheelchair, his head completely bald except for tufts of white hair around his ears. He was dressed in an undershirt, plaid shorts, and white shoes. A little drool was running from the side of his mouth, and he wiped it on the back of his hand, which was covered with brown age spots. Mercury wasn't just old, he was ancient, and he could be forgiven for moving a little slowly. At four thousand years old, any movement at all was a good thing.

"What?" he rasped. "What is it, Randolph? Time for my nectar?"

"No, no!" exclaimed the desk clerk, a little man with a pencil-thin mustache. He waved a slip of paper in the air. "You got a *message*!"

"A message?" growled Mercury, blinking fully awake. "I haven't gotten a message since . . . what century is this?"

"The twenty-first," answered Randolph.

"My, how time flies." The messenger god blinked fully awake and cast rheumy eyes upon the mortal, who was still a young man, only sixty years old. "You say it was in my *special* box?"

The clerk nodded excitedly. "I didn't open it up—do you want me to?"

"Yes, read it," said the elderly god, sitting up in his chair. They were on the veranda of Mercury's room in the retirement home, and it was a very nice room, if a little old-fashioned. A pair of silver winged slippers hung on the wall, and dusty statues of his family rested on half columns.

The desk clerk tore through the envelope and opened the letter. "It's from a certain Laura Ann Sweeney of Denton, Ohio. It says, 'Jupiter, send me a boyfriend!'"

Mercury bolted upright in his wheelchair. "What? A mortal actually made a plea to Jupiter to find her a boyfriend?"

"That's what it says here," answered Randolph. "Do you want me to throw it away?"

"No, no!" answered the elder. "This is a Heroic Task, and this Laura Sweeney appealed directly to Jupiter, king of the gods! We can't ignore it. Where are the others?"

"Some of them are out by the pool."

"And the big guy?"

Randolph looked over his shoulder. "Jupiter is in the sauna. Do you want me to tell the others?"

"No way. This is *my* job," insisted Mercury. "I'm the messenger god."

"I'll push you out," offered Randolph.

Mercury brushed him off. "No, get me my walker . . . and my winged slippers." As the desk clerk hurried inside to fetch the articles, the elderly god rose uncertainly to his feet. "How long has it been since anyone appealed to the gods?" he mused. "Don't they know we're retired?"

"Semiretired," corrected Randolph when he returned with the winged slippers and the chrome two-wheeled walker. "You still have a lot of Heroic Deeds left in you!"

"Yes," said Mercury, lifting his chin, which was covered in the stubble of a snow-white beard. "We used to find True Love for mortals all the time. In fact, often we put on disguises and supplied all the love they needed by ourselves." He chuckled with some fond ancient memories.

Randolph placed the walker and the slippers in front of the aged god and stood back. Mercury gripped the arms of the walker to steady himself as he slipped his wrinkled feet into the magical winged footwear. "There, that's better."

A moment later the desk clerk stumbled backward in awe and alarm, because the centuries began to melt away, revealing an elderly but handsome god. After a while, he didn't look a day over two thousand, though he still had most of his aches and pains.

Gripping the message from Laura Sweeney in his hand, Mercury used his walker to shuffle out to the pool area. On the West Coast, the sun was just beginning to go down, and a soft golden glow suffused the blue pool and the marble pillars that surrounded the water. A warm breeze brought the smell of nectar mixed with Metamucil.

As Mercury approached the swimming pool, he heard the whining voice of Juno, Jupiter's wife. "I told Venus, 'I can't possibly have another lift and tuck,'" she complained, "'or my armpits will be under my ears.'"

Diana nodded, although the elderly goddess of the hunt seemed to be half-listening as she painted her toenails with a long peacock feather. Half a dozen of the graceful birds wandered the grounds, and they outnumbered the gods in attendance. Fat Apollo grumbled under his breath when his foe, Vulcan, made a good shot on the shuffleboard court. In the pool, Neptune splashed around, trying to climb aboard an inflatable raft, but slipping off each time.

None of them noticed the messenger until he had shuffled up right in front of them. "Mercury!" exclaimed Vulcan with surprise. The misshapen god of the forge limped toward him and glanced at his winged feet. "What are you all dressed up for?"

"This!" he crowed, waving the slip of paper in the air. "A mortal has beseeched Jupiter for help. It is a matter of True Love . . . a Heroic Task."

Apollo wheezed. "Are you sure we didn't get that message by mistake?"

"How many Jupiters are there?" asked Mercury.

"Just one," came a raspy voice, and they all turned to see their frail leader, wearing a white terry-cloth robe that seemed to blend in with his long white beard. "Or two, if you count the planet Jupiter. Did we get any royalties from all those planets they named after us? Not a drachma."

Mercury bowed to the elder with the long white beard. "Sire, a mortal has pleaded for your help. Just like the old days—a quest for True Love!" Breathlessly, he told their leader everything he knew about Laura Sweeney and her search for the perfect romance.

"We must handle this correctly," said Jupiter excitedly. His flip-flops smacked the soles of his feet as he paced beside the pool, and he tugged thoughtfully on his flowing beard. "We can't take any chances—we must assign this delicate task to the right hero."

"You mean Venus?" asked Diana, who was always a bit ditzy.

"No! No! Spare us!" cried all the gods at once, jumping to their feet with alarm. "Not Venus!"

Everyone glanced at Vulcan, the brilliant but ungainly god of invention. After all, Venus had wronged him the most. "My ex-wife? You'd be crazy!" he answered. "The less she knows about this, the better."

"Don't worry," said Jupiter, with a wave of his bony hand. "I do not intend to involve Venus, even though this would be easy work for her. Out of spite, she would thwart this mortal because she asked *me* first."

"Her son," suggested Mercury. "Cupid could perform this deed for you."

That brought another scowl to the king's cracked lips. "Yes, matters of love are in his domain, but that cherub is a mercenary and will exact a stiff price."

"Get a grip, husband," said Juno. "If not Venus or Cupid, who will help this maiden? You? Mars? Who?"

Jupiter looked around at the elderly gods gathered beside the sparkling pool and shook his head. "Where is Cupid?"

Apollo pointed over his shoulder and sneered. "At this

hour, he likes to hang with mortals at Pinkie's Pool Parlor."

"I might have known." Jupiter heaved a sigh and cast his eyes at Mercury, who was still holding the request from Laura Sweeney in his hand. "Mercury, shall we go fetch him?"

"I have my winged shoes on, don't I?" answered the messenger god with a sniff.

Jupiter snapped his fingers. "Apollo, summon your chariot. But the black limo, not the Hummer."

Twenty minutes later Jupiter and Mercury hobbled into a pit so dank and obscure that Mercury had to light his magic torch just to look around. A rat scurried off along the brown and yellow baseboards, chirping angrily at them, and a putrid draft brought the foul odor of cheap cigar smoke and the aged dust of pool chalk. A maze of dark, rectangular tables confronted the gods, and from somewhere in the bowels of Pinkie's Pool Parlor came a burst of raucous laughter.

Jupiter sneezed, rattling his crown around atop his snowy white mane of hair. He wiped his nose with his long beard and growled, "That mold is playing Hades with my allergies. I say, Mercury, remind me why we're doing this?"

"Laura Sweeney wants a boyfriend, and she appealed

directly to you." The frail god clicked his winged slippers and stuck out his chin importantly. "I told everyone about it, and they think we need this heroic task to give our existence a little purpose."

Jupiter groaned and rubbed his rheumy eyes. "Yes, but to bring Cupid out of retirement? I don't know. The world doesn't need him anymore—they have chat rooms!"

Mercury shuffled forward and prodded his old associate in the ribs with a bony elbow. Chuckling, he suggested, "Maybe the mortals need a little more of that old bolt of lightning. You know, that insane, short-circuit jolt that Cupid's arrow used to bring them. We could watch it all in the reflecting pool."

Jupiter nodded and squared his scrawny shoulders. "Lightning bolts," he repeated, as if reminding himself of the mission. With determination, the two elders moved into the dark pathways between the felt-covered slabs of slate. After negotiating the maze, they reached a small circle of light in the far corner, where four men were huddled around a pool table.

Holding court and waving a cigar in the air was Cupid, and his gravelly voice cut through the clack of balls and drone of conversation. The aged cherub, wearing a pith helmet, multipocketed field vest, and stylish hunting clothes, looked ready to go on safari.

His three scurvy companions spotted the aged visitors first, and one brute looked up and laughed. "Who are you guys? Man, the homeless soup kitchen is four doors down."

"We're not lost," said Mercury indignantly. "We're here to talk to your friend." He and the king of the gods turned their attention to the short, squat player with the big cigar.

"I told you guys to leave me alone," said Cupid, while he studied his shot and avoided looking at them. "I'll join the association of retired people when I'm ready, and not before!"

That joke brought a chuckle from the other players, but they scowled when neither Jupiter nor Mercury found it amusing. "Yeah, make an appointment," growled one of the men. "He's busy right now."

As if to prove it, four-foot-tall Cupid stood on his tiptoes, bent over the rail of the pool table, and made a respectable shot, sinking the four-ball in the side pocket.

"You can only stay here if you rent a table," said the smallest of the three mortals, a weasel in a striped suit. "And that costs twenty bucks . . . each." His friends tried to keep a straight face, but two of them laughed.

Jupiter scowled and scratched his long beard. "We really need to talk to Cue here. That is what you call him . . . Cue?"

The diminutive god sank another ball and laughed. "What else would they call me? I'm a pool player. We've got no business together, Old Man. That partnership closed shop . . . long ago."

"One of our old customers," said Jupiter in a hoarse whisper, "has just asked for our help."

That revelation caused Cupid to miscue and awkwardly strike the white ball, sending it on a pathetic spin that avoided every other ball on the table. "Hey!" growled one of the mortals. "You spoiled Cue's shot, and I've got five hundred bucks riding on him! You guys need to get out of here, and I mean *right now.*"

The big human hiked up his jeans and moved threateningly toward the frail elders. "Manny, wait a second," called Cupid, trying to warn his associate.

Jupiter lifted his hand and made a fist, and the entire building began to shake as if besieged by an earthquake. As dust and pieces of plaster rained down on the players, Manny backed up, and his two friends shouted and ran for the exit. Jupiter lowered his hand, having made his point, and the building stopped shaking.

"Whoa!" exclaimed Manny, his mouth agape. "That must've been a five or six on the Richter Scale!" He looked at Cupid and waved his arm. "Let's get out of here, Cue!"

"You go," answered the cherub, chomping on his cigar. "I'll protect these two old codgers."

"Don't wait too long," urged Mercury with a pained grimace. "My bones are aching . . . I feel another one coming on."

The man ducked, looked around furtively, then dashed for the exit. When the door opened, a ray of sunshine invaded the darkness of the pool hall for a moment, then the gloom rushed back. Marooned in a pool of golden light, the three ancient gods stood, waiting.

Shorter than the others and technically a cherub, Cupid still looked young enough to be taken for a mortal. He waved his cigar around the gloom, dispensing smoke like smelly incense. "Okay, you guys have my attention. Who asked for what?"

Excitedly Mercury explained about Laura Sweeney beseeching Jupiter to find her a boyfriend. "A true heroic task!" exclaimed the messenger god, who enjoyed explaining matters. "And we figured you would be the perfect one to help this teenager in Denton, Ohio."

The cherub chuckled. "Did you try my mom yet?"

Jupiter turned as pale as his beard at that question. "Uh, no. She's still upset about that thing between you and Psyche."

"Ah, Psyche," mused Cupid with a wistful smile. "The

only woman I ever really loved. You and my mom should not meddle in other people's love lives. That's my job!"

"That's why you're the perfect one for this heroic quest," insisted Mercury, trying to steer the conversation back on track. "Please tell us you'll do it . . . for our reputation."

Cupid shook his head and chomped on his cigar. "I'm not sure about coming out of retirement, Big Guy. Look at me—I haven't strung a bow in years, I'm a little out of shape, and I don't know squat about modern teenagers. For the last two hundred years, I've only seen the insides of pool halls and casinos. I'd have to get into Laura Sweeney's life and get to know her in order to pick the right love for her. That's a lot of work."

"All right," muttered Jupiter with a scowl. "I know something you want. I'll give you back the power to be invisible, even though you misused it."

The fat cherub whirled around, sputtering. "You never should have taken it away from me! When I'm invisible, my job is a slam dunk, but nooooo! You had to run me out of business, you meddling old geezer!"

"We all ran out of business at the same time," insisted Jupiter as he leaned over the pool table, looking all of his four thousand years despite the terry-cloth robe he wore elegantly. "Laura Sweeney is a true fan of ours, or we wouldn't know of her plight. Help her, Cupid, not me. In return, I will give you the cloak you once wore."

"Which my father made for me," muttered Cupid. The cherub blew cigar smoke from the side of his mouth and watched it curl upward into the ancient stains on the ceiling. "How is dear old dad?"

Mercury cleared his throat to show his discomfort with the subject, because no one really knew who Cupid's father was. Plodding Vulcan was as likely a candidate as most of the other gods and half the mortal world, but the Olympians had a hard time imagining wayward Cupid as his son. Nevertheless, Vulcan had been Venus's husband at the time, and so they behaved as father and son.

The messenger god could see that Jupiter was tongue-tied at the question, and he answered impatiently, "Your sire is excited by this deed, as we all are. He says he can help you with a disguise."

"A disguise?" echoed Cupid, breaking into a mischievous laugh. "Yes, Vulcan can work wonders with his special clay. To get *me* into high school, this will have to be a very special disguise."

Mercury felt a sudden chill on his spine. He had always considered Cupid to be one of the more unstable demigods, and it didn't surprise him that he was still a favorite of the mortals. *He has to be half-mortal,* thought Mercury with a sniff of disdain. *This bargain is going to be trouble, but the pact has been made.*

The king of the gods and the grizzled cherub, who had once been young and lovely when known by the name Eros, gripped each other by the forearm. Overhead the clear California skies growled with an unexpected burst of thunder.

Several days later, Mercury and Jupiter were sent e-mail messages to meet Vulcan by the swimming pool at midnight. Since this was past the bedtime of most of the elderly gods at Mount Olympus, the two cronies had the shimmering water hole to themselves. Or so they thought. When Mercury caught sight of a slender figure breaking the surface of the illuminated water, he grabbed Jupiter's frail forearm.

"Who's that swimming in our pool?" asked Mercury with indignation. "Another rotten neighborhood kid, I suppose." Jupiter shrugged, and both of them squinted into the darkness.

When the mysterious swimmer emerged from the water and climbed up the ladder, Mercury gasped. Even in the suffused light from the pool, he could see it was a maiden of unearthly beauty. After tossing back her glistening blond hair, she wrapped a silky robe around her body and strode toward them. Jupiter gripped the messenger god's forearm, trying to steady himself.

The girl was young, and her beauty was brought down to earth by a wide-eyed innocence and appealing trust. "Hello, my lords," she said with a lilting voice and a graceful curtsey. "My master will arrive any second, and he is eager to see you."

"And Cupid arrived at Vulcan's laboratory, as planned?" asked Jupiter.

"I believe so, because Vulcan has been occupied," answered the fair maiden.

He must be sorely occupied to leave you alone, thought Mercury. The messenger god wanted to say something witty to this marvelous creature, but he was as tongue-tied as a mortal. A shuffling of footsteps could be heard on the walkway, and he turned to see the slow arrival of the god of invention, Vulcan.

"Hello, Brother!" called Jupiter as the hunched, deformed immortal hobbled toward them. "We were just being entertained by, uh . . . by your lovely assistant. What is her name?"

"I haven't named her yet," replied Vulcan, making it sound as if such details were a bother. Mercury cringed, because there were often disastrous results when Vulcan fabricated a female. He shivered at the memory of Pandora, who had let her wicked curiosity ruin the world. This time, he hoped, Vulcan's art would have less drastic effects.

Jupiter finally said, "I had hoped to find Cupid here."

"That is no problem," said Vulcan with a wink at his fair assistant.

The girl chuckled, her voice sounding like wind chimes; then she punched the frail god in the ribs and nearly doubled him over. "I *am* Cupid, you old sot."

Jupiter groaned and peered at her in amazement. Mercury felt his stomach knot and shrivel, because no good could come of this ruse. "Nice disguise, huh?" asked Cupid, turning about and giving them a good look at the rest of "her" godly figure.

Mercury gulped. "I think, uh . . . you had better be very careful in that disguise."

"I'm the god of love," sniffed Cupid. "I know my business."

Vulcan wagged a crooked finger at her. "Remember what I told you—this maiden disguise is only good for twenty-five days. On midnight of the twenty-fifth day, the clay will dissolve, leaving you with your regular appearance."

"You worry too much," said Cupid with a charming shake of her hips. "Twenty-five days will be plenty of time to handle this job. Now where's my bow? You refurbished it, right?"

"Yes, yes," answered Vulcan wearily. "New string, fewer jewels, and pearl inlay. I still couldn't make it look like a modern bow, but it no longer looks like a one-string harp. And your arrows have all been refletched."

"Good." The blond enchantress moved close to Jupiter and batted her lashes at him as her dazzling blue eyes drilled into his. "Jupiter, from you I need a nice purse full of credit cards, car keys, and other useful goodies. I'll need a few days to set this up—I'll start school next Monday." She frowned, and a cloud crossed her precious face. "Uh-oh, do I have to deal with . . . feminine products?"

As if appeasing a bratty child, Vulcan sighed. "No, Cupid. We figured you couldn't handle such matters with any maturity. Hence, twenty-five days."

"Oh good. Fine. That's plenty of time anyway," said the lovely cherub with a confident smile. "Laura Sweeney, you are about to get some serious love in your life."

3

"Have you seen her?" came frantic whispers in the hallway of Fimbrey High School. Boys were gathering in tight-knit groups all over the place. "You've got to see her. She's off the hook!"

"Who? Who are you talking about?" came the eager replies.

"The new girl!" hissed one of the guys. "She's got it goin' on."

"And she just moved here," added another one. "No ties, no baggage . . . She doesn't know a soul!"

Laura and Taryn waded through the crowded hallway, and every guy they passed seemed to be extolling the charms of the new girl. Laura had seen this phenomenon before, of course. The New Girl or New Boy was one of the few elements of surprise that could perk up what would otherwise be the ordinary high school day.

"The new girl . . . the new girl . . . ," mimicked Taryn. "There's nine hundred girls in this school, but the boys see us every day, so we're invisible. Then comes some new chick they haven't been staring at since first grade, and they're drooling all over themselves!"

"She'll be exotic for a day," said Laura, "but by tomorrow they'll stick her into one of the normal groups. She'll be the 'old girl' then. We should try to catch a glimpse before she turns into one of us."

Taryn reached out a hand to stop her friend, and her eyes darted behind them. "We may have a chance," she whispered. "Here comes the Welcoming Committee, and they look none too happy about the competition."

Laura turned to see Megan and Chelsea leading a mob of about ten irate popular girls. Down the hallway they marched with fierce determination in their eyes, and Taryn grabbed Laura's arm and dragged her into the procession.

After a moment, Chelsea looked back at Laura and Taryn, and her eyes blinked with surprise. "What are you trailing along for?" she asked. "You haven't got boyfriends to protect."

"Protect from what?" asked Laura, playing innocent.

Taryn laughed. "Don't tell me Cody is sniffing around this new girl?"

A little too quickly, Chelsea snapped, "Of course not."

Taryn gave Laura a wink, and they both quickened their step to keep up with the swarm of enraged cheerleaders. Led by Megan, the mob swept down the corridor until they spotted their target—a bunch of boys huddled around a tiny figure in front of a locker. Laura recognized Jake Mattson, Cody Kenyon, and half a dozen other popular seniors, but she couldn't get a good look at the object of their attention. All she caught was a shimmer of blond hair.

Laura also unexpectedly glimpsed a familiar face on a gangly body, hovering back a few feet but using his height to check out the attraction. A second later, as if hearing her footsteps in the crowded hallway, Peter Yarmench turned and glanced directly at Laura. But before she could say anything, she was distracted by an audible female growl.

Like a heat-seeking missile, Megan Rawlins zoomed toward Jake and the dazed crowd of boys. Sensing danger, the ones on the outside scattered to let Jake and Cody take the brunt of the attack. Megan's steely glare said it all: She was still the school's reigning queen, and she wasn't giving it up easily.

For the first time, Laura got a good look at the new girl. *Whoa,* she thought, *she's drop-dead, movie-star gorgeous!*

As the other girls had the same revelation, they skidded to a stop. In the presence of this petite but shapely hottie, dressed in the latest couture threads and showing off abs of steel, they were stunned. To her credit, Megan somehow went on with her mission.

"Jake," she said, putting sweet daggers around his name, "you were supposed to meet me outside biology."

"Uh, yeah . . . right . . . s-sorry," he stammered, reluctantly tearing his attention away from the fresh face smiling sweetly at him. "But we were just making our new arrival feel comfortable. She doesn't know anybody at Fimbrey."

"Oh, that's too bad," said Megan, doing her best to look unimpressed by the stunning beauty in front of her. "We'll make sure that she learns everything she needs to know to get along here at Fimbrey."

"What's your name?" asked Chelsea, sounding as if she hoped the new girl would at least have an ugly name.

The girl thought for a moment, flipped her perfect hair, and answered, "Cupidity. You know, like Charity or Felicity."

"Or Stupidity," joked Megan, getting an uneasy laugh from her girlfriends.

For the first time, Cupidity looked a bit annoyed, and her dazzling blue eyes narrowed at Megan. "That's not very nice," she remarked.

Megan crossed her arms and shot a cutting glare at the newcomer. "I'll tell you what's not very nice—moving in on somebody else's territory!" She grabbed Jake's arm possessively and held him tightly, even though he shrugged uncomfortably.

"We were only talking!" he protested.

Megan ignored his defense, never taking her steely eyes off the competition. "Cupidity, you've got to decide whether you're with the program or against it. One word of advice: Pick your friends very carefully."

Cupidity looked thoroughly confused by Megan's veiled threats. "Uh, I just want to make friends," she answered with pert innocence. "That's the only program I'm with."

Chelsea sniffed and turned to leave, grabbing Cody Kenyon's arm. "Are you coming, baby?"

As the closest thing the cool crowd had to a bad boy, Cody had more latitude to break the rules. "I'm leaving, but not with you," he told her. Until five minutes ago, Chelsea had been the great love of his skater-boy life, but now he ditched her with a sneer. With all this attention around, he had a large audience—including the new girl—and he squared his black-clad shoulders and sauntered coolly into the crowd.

Chelsea broke into tears, and her friends gathered around to comfort her. This bad vibe, along with a warning bell, seemed to signal the end of the hallway confrontation. Everyone headed off in different directions, and Taryn waved good-bye too as she hurried off to class. For some reason, Laura hung back to study the petite force that had just invaded the school, even when the bells warned her that she would be late.

She was fascinated by anyone who stood up to Megan, Chelsea, and the other queen bees, and Cupidity had done so without even breaking a sweat. As the newcomer peered into her locker, Laura felt a shadow pass them. She turned to see Megan, who had returned.

"Oh, you two are hanging together," said Megan with a sneer and a laugh. "I might have known. Just what this school needs—another brain!" Megan ambled her way down the hall, waving her hall pass and turning her back to them.

Cupidity reached into her locker and pulled out a small bow and arrow, which she aimed at Megan's back.

"Whoa there!" exclaimed Laura, jumping between Cupidity and her target. She quickly grabbed the bow and stuffed it back inside the locker, whispering, "What's the matter with you? You can't bring *weapons* to school!"

"It's just a little bow," protested Cupidity. "When I use it, there's hardly any blood."

"Do you want to get kicked out your first day of school?"

Laura sighed and slammed the locker door shut. "Now promise me you won't go waving any more weapons around."

"It's really a bad idea?" asked Cupidity innocently.

"Yes, a very bad idea," said Laura. "Where did you go to school before this . . . Middle-earth?"

"I was, uh . . . homeschooled," answered the newcomer. "Private tutors all the way."

"Lucky you," said Laura. This girl was definitely odd, but Laura sensed that she was honestly confused and overwhelmed, despite all the attention from the guys. So she held out her hand. "I'm Laura Sweeney."

At that simple declaration, the girl's blue eyes widened like hubcaps on a Hummer. "Laura Sweeney! I was hoping to meet you!" She eagerly shook her outstretched hand.

Laura smiled, but asked suspiciously, "Me? Why did you want to meet *me*?"

"Uh, because," stammered Cupidity with a frown, "I heard you, uh, could help me with my grades."

"It's your first day. How bad can your grades be?"

"I had lots of tutors, remember." Cupidity smiled hopefully. "I have a good feeling about you, Laura. So many people want to be my friend, because . . . well, I'm gorgeous. But you seem down to earth, like there's more to you than the usual boy-crazy teenagers. Of course, I often have lots of boys hanging around."

Laura shrugged. "Yeah, and you certainly haven't made many friends among the other girls here. You weren't really going to shoot Megan Rawlins with a bow and arrow, were you?"

Cupidity gave a lilting laugh. "Oh, no, that's just my way of taking out frustration. My therapist told me to do symbolic acts like that. I wasn't going to hurt her, honest." She looked around the empty hallway. "So are we late to class?"

"Very," answered Laura glumly. "At least you have an excuse, being new. We'd better stop by the office and get a hall pass."

"Oh, thank you," said Cupidity, granting her insta-friend a sparkling grin. "We're going to be super close, I can tell!"

Laura shook her head, wondering if this would be a blessing or a curse.

After school, the boys were still falling down steps to get a good look at Cupidity. She was totally surrounded. Even Cody and Jake had ditched their former loves to follow the new girl around. To her credit, Cupidity didn't play favorites with them or anyone else; she was unfailingly friendly to everyone she met. Even a few of the girls seemed to be warming to her, but Megan and Chelsea were nowhere to be seen in the crowd on the edge of the parking lot.

Laura watched from a safe distance, although she was supposedly going home with Cupidity after school. That was going to stun everyone when they saw her stroll off with the hot new chick, but Laura had mixed feelings about her fast friendship with the newcomer. For one thing, she was carrying Cupidity's duffel bag, and she could feel the distinct outline of her bow and the sharp tips of her arrows, which could get them both into a lot of trouble.

That's ironic, thought Laura, *a girl named Cupidity being into archery, even if it is only symbolic.* She shrugged and decided, *Probably no one but me would get that.*

Laura felt a familiar presence hovering behind her, and she turned to see Peter Yarmench staring over the top of her head. "Hey, Laura, do you think you could maybe introduce me to your friend?" he asked. "Maybe when there aren't four hundred other guys around."

"You too?" she remarked with a sigh. "Well, I don't really know how long she and I will be hanging out, but I'll try. You might have to get at the end of the line, and it's a long line."

"Oh, come on, don't count me out," said Peter. "She likes you, so maybe she likes the brainy type. She smiled at me in the lunchroom. Besides, after this summer, I'm not as shy as I used to be."

Laura turned around expecting to find him staring at Cupidity and her admirers, but instead he was gazing at her with a mysterious smile. He quickly glanced away, though, and shifted on his feet, looking as shy as ever. "Anyway," he went on, "if you two want to form a study group or anything, call me."

"I think she could definitely teach us a few things," said Laura. "So tell me, what about this summer?"

Peter smiled enigmatically. "Oh, up at the lake, when my folks and I were at the cottage."

"You met someone?"

"*Two* someones," he answered with a smile. "You know, it's a lot different to meet a girl *outside* of high school, when you don't have all those years of history. You're just *you*. You know what I mean?"

"Yes," Laura answered with a wistful nod. "A fresh start."

"That must be what it's like for Cupidity to start over here," said Peter. Again he peered over Laura's head at the new star of Fimbrey High. "Hey, she's coming this way! She waved to us!"

"I hope so, I've got her stuff." Laura waved back and hefted the duffel bag.

Jake Mattson broke off from the others, proudly waving a slip of paper in the air. "I'll call you later, Cupidity!" he shouted, loudly enough for everyone to hear.

Peter licked his fingers and tried to stick down a cowlick at the crown of his head. "Will you introduce me to her, please?"

"Okay."

Laura tried to introduce her old friend to her new friend, but everyone was talking at once and moving off toward their cars, rushing to escape from school.

Peter said something, and Cupidity grinned and answered, "Cool to meet you, too, Peter. Any friend of Laura's is one of mine, too."

"Hey, Sweeney!" shouted a voice from the crowd; it sounded like Chelsea. "We'll remember the way you turned on us!"

What does that mean? Laura whirled around, trying to find the source of the shout. Maybe she had misunderstood, because it was noisy in the parking lot. With her heart beating faster, Laura darted ahead of her friend. "Where are we going?" she asked with concern.

"Right here." Cupidity halted at a sleek yellow convertible, which looked brand-new. In fact, it still had dealer's plates on the back, as if it had just come from the showroom. The crowd of stragglers came to a stop and stared as she and Cupidity climbed into the beautiful car. This was not the type of vehicle people in Denton, Ohio, drove, and Laura guessed that it was Italian, maybe a Ferrari or a Lamborghini.

She didn't usually attract attention, so Laura felt funny with half the school watching her as she drove off with her new friend. She hoped Taryn, Peter, and the others understood, but *somebody* had to take this exotic creature under their wing. Cupidity couldn't be left entirely to the mercy of Cody, Jake, and every other boy in school. At least one girl had to befriend her.

No good deed goes unpunished, thought Laura. *It's taken me twelve years, but I've finally made enemies of Megan, Chelsea, and the whole clique.*

Tires squealing, Cupidity roared out of the parking lot, cutting in front of several other cars and barely missing the gate and the crossing guard. Laura sank into her seat, but the top was down and everybody could still see her, especially the old crossing guard, who was yelling his head off. "Hey, this is a school zone," he reminded the driver.

"Well, duh!" answered Cupidity, then turned to face Laura. "So the first day of school was fun. How do you think I did?"

"How did you do?" asked Laura with surprise. "You mesmerized half the school and made the other half furious at you. Do you know what effect you have on guys?"

Cupidity smiled. "I've always been lucky at love. My birthday is Valentine's Day."

"Why does that not surprise me?" said Laura, shaking

her head. "You know, Jake and Cody and some of those guys had girlfriends . . . before you came."

"I know their kind," scoffed Cupidity. "I've seen them a million times—heroes already posing for their statues. They're too in love with themselves to really be in love with anyone else, but they're the most fun to mess with."

Laura peered curiously at her new friend, thinking that she had a weird way of talking, but that she'd certainly make senior year interesting.

"We're here!" announced Cupidity, pulling the yellow sports car into the driveway of an elegant apartment complex. "I thought it would be best to live close to school."

Laura breathed a sigh of relief, because she had been certain that Cupidity would live in a huge mansion. These were nice apartments, but still apartments. The new girl parked the car, grabbed her duffel bag, and jumped out, while Laura grabbed her backpack and followed meekly. A few seconds later, they walked into a fantastic apartment that looked freshly painted and was furnished with all new stuff. In fact, Laura could still smell the paint, and she saw a price tag on one of the lamps.

"You really did just move here, didn't you?" asked Laura, looking for a place to sit. All of the couches and chairs were elegant leather and appeared as if they hadn't even been sat on yet. She finally picked a big armchair, and dropping into it felt as if she were oozing into a vat of butter.

"How come you moved to Denton?" asked Laura. "Did one of your parents get transferred?"

"My parents aren't here," announced Cupidity as she went to the refrigerator. "I live alone. Do you want a soda?"

It wasn't easy to bolt upright in the cushy leather chair, but Laura managed to sit up. "Did you say you live alone? *By yourself?*"

"Yeah," answered Cupidity as she returned with two sodas. "I don't see the need for parents; they just get in the way."

Through her brave smile, it seemed that a tear welled in the corner of a dazzling blue eye. Laura looked at her friend with concern and asked, "Is something the matter?"

Cupidity nodded and lowered her voice to answer, "Parents have always been a sore subject with me. My mother was a party girl, and I haven't seen my father in a while. They have money, of course, and I've had the best of everything. Now a rich uncle looks after me and rents me this place. You won't tell the school board, will you, that I live alone?"

"No, of course not!" Laura laughed nervously. The idea of a high school student living like an adult was exciting but also somewhat frightening. Then again, Cupidity seemed mature beyond her years, and she looked as if she could take care of herself. Maybe she would shoot any intruders with her bow and arrow.

Laura leaned forward, choosing her words carefully. There was no way to ask this politely, so she just came out with it. "Cupidity, you know you could be friends with *any* of the girls at school, including all the really popular ones. Why would you choose to be friends with *me?*"

"Lacking a little self-esteem, are we?" asked her hostess with a sympathetic smile. "I don't see *you* hanging out with Megan and Chelsea and their herd of water buffaloes. Who can blame you? It's mentally tiring being around that many snobs. Besides, there's only room in the school for one queen, and Megan just got dethroned."

"Totally," answered Laura. "You can be the new ruler of Fimbrey High."

"Me?" scoffed Cupidity. "Not me . . . *you!*"

"*Me?*" squeaked Laura. "You just met me, but haven't you realized yet that I'm not exactly the Homecoming Queen type?"

"But you like that type of guy, don't you?" asked Cupidity with a sly wink. "Which one do you really want? Jake? Cody? That other boy you introduced me to—Peter? You can take your pick."

Laura gulped in embarrassment. "Now you're making

fun of me. I don't have a boyfriend, and Jake and Cody are way out of my league."

"That's why you have *me* around, to give you a little help. Why don't we try them out first, and then decide."

The telephone suddenly rang, making Laura jump. Cupidity gave a merry laugh and said, "That should be Jake calling . . . right on cue."

She picked up the cordless phone from the coffee table and said, "Hello?" After a moment, she smirked. "Yeah, I knew it was you, Jake. Of course I want to go out with you . . . tomorrow night."

While Cupidity chatted, Laura was relieved to have a second to think about what she'd been saying. Why was the new girl so intent on hooking her up and making her "queen"? It was kinda sweet, but definitely bizarre.

As if she were reading Laura's mind, Cupidity winked again at her and said into the phone, "But I want to double-date, Jake. I want my friend, Laura Sweeney, to go with us."

Now Laura jumped to her feet and waved her hands, but Cupidity ignored her. "I don't care who it is," she said, "you know all the guys. Pick one Laura would like—a hot date!"

Laura circled the couch and felt like pulling her hair out. True, her new friend was just trying to do her a favor, but being on a double date with Jake Mattson was going to be seriously bizarre. Cupidity laughed softly at something

Jake said. Apparently Jake was so smitten that he had agreed to go on a double date with one of the dorks. It was hard to believe.

When Cupidity finally hung up the phone, Laura just stared at her. "Why did you do that?"

"To get to know Jake better," answered Cupidity with a flip of her blond hair. "Don't you want to get to know Jake better?"

"Yeah, but . . . umm, I have parents, and they might not want me to go out on a Tuesday night." Laura began to pace again. Dating wasn't a common occurrence for her, especially not with Jake Mattson. In truth, her parents wouldn't mind at all if she went on a double date—they would probably open a bottle of champagne!

"Face it, Laura," said Cupidity, "from now on, your life is going to have a little romance in it." She laughed happily, as if enjoying a private joke.

Laura could only shake her head and wonder what she had gotten herself into. Cupidity was a trip, and she definitely had that wonderful new-girl quality of having no preconceptions. *For some reason, she thinks boys should be chasing me,* thought Laura, *and I hate to discourage that idea.*

4

Cupidity's second day at Fimbrey was a bit more sane, because the novelty had worn off . . . a little. Cupidity picked Laura up in her shiny convertible and took her to school, where Cody Kenyon met them in the parking lot. It had gotten around at the speed of light that Cupidity was going out with Jake Mattson, which had scared off most of the other boys, but not the bad-boy skater dude.

Cody strode right up to the car and asked, "Cupidity, what's this I hear about you going out with Jake Mattson? Dude, that's scraping the bottom of the barrel."

The newcomer laughed. "Oh, is it? Not all the girls around here think so. Besides, it's only *one* date, and I have lots of nights open."

Cody's eyes sparkled, even while Laura rolled her eyes. He came closer to Cupidity and whispered, "Oh, so we could like . . . meet up another time?"

Cupidity shrugged and gave him an enigmatic smile. She hadn't promised him anything, thought Laura, but he looked as if he had won the lottery. She pointed into the distance, and they all turned to see Jake coming, followed by another guy. Cody nodded and flung his skateboard to the pavement; he jumped on while it was still moving and careened off between the cars.

"Silly, aren't they?" said Cupidity, giving Laura a sly smile. "Are you sure you want one?"

Laura gulped, unsure what her new friend meant by that. *Is it that apparent that I want a boyfriend? Does she think she's doing me a favor?*

"Oh, it's your friend, too!" Cupidity waved to the boys walking toward them, and Laura adjusted her glasses to get a good look. She had to blink twice, because it looked like Peter Yarmench hurrying to keep up with Jake Mattson. They seemed to be walking together.

Laura wrinkled her nose into a puzzled expression and turned to Cupidity. "I don't get it—Peter and Jake?"

The boys were only a few feet away, and Laura marveled that Peter was taller than Jake and only a little skinnier. Her old friend was dressed in his best impression of a preppy, and she almost laughed out loud.

Jake pouted at Cupidity and asked, "Hey, who were you talking to?"

"Anybody I want," she answered cheerfully. "Don't act like you own me, Jake. Come 'ere. I want to talk with you a sec." She motioned coyly for him to follow her, and he did, leaving Laura and Peter alone.

Peter looked only slightly less confused than she did, and he finally said, "You know I'm your date tonight, right?"

Laura tried not to slap her head and say, "D'oh!" Instead she mustered a smile and answered, "I didn't know it would be *you*. Listen, Peter, this wasn't *my* idea. I didn't want to go on a date with Cupidity and Jake."

"Why not?" asked Peter with surprise. "This is great! All of a sudden, you're best friends with the hottest girl in school, and *Jake Mattson* calls me up and wants a favor. We just jumped about three rungs on the social ladder, and I don't know how we did it. But I don't think we should complain about it." He smiled slightly. "Besides, I think you can suffer through one date with me."

"That's not what I meant." Laura caught Peter looking past her at Cupidity and Jake, who were huddled close together near the hood of her car. "You like her too, don't you?"

"Well, uh . . . what's not to like?" stammered Peter.

"She's beautiful and funny, and there's something different about her. I know you like Jake—you always have." Peter laughed, and Laura had to laugh along with him at their ridiculous plight.

"Okay," she admitted, "us going out with the beautiful people is kind of funny. I guess we should enjoy it while it lasts."

"Which may not be long," whispered Peter.

"Why not?"

He pointed to a group of girls lurking near the hedges that ran along the parking lot. "Megan Rawlins, Chelsea Williams, and their crew are spying on us," explained Peter. "Well, maybe not *us* . . . more like Jake and Cupidity."

Laura sighed. "And when they get their revenge, it won't be funny, will it?"

"So let's enjoy it while it lasts," suggested Peter with a smile. "And let's agree to always stay friends, no matter what happens."

With relief, Laura nodded, and it was great to feel that she had at least one ally in this crazy adventure. She heard footsteps and she turned to see that Cupidity and Jake had rejoined them.

"We were just deciding what to do on our date tonight," said Cupidity, flipping her blond hair. Laura noticed that she did that a lot—and that it usually caused the boys' jaws to drop. "I hope you don't mind if I picked something."

"No, sure, anything you want!" said Peter quickly.

Jake looked down and cleared his throat. "I wanted to go bowling or maybe to a movie, but Cupidity wanted to do something a little different."

"Like what?" asked Laura hesitantly.

"Archery," answered Jake, looking puzzled.

"It's fun!" insisted Cupidity. "I know a great little place where they rent bows. You'll all be hitting the bull's-eye in no time."

"Archery!" exclaimed Peter, faking enthusiasm, or maybe he really was enthusiastic about doing any activity with Cupidity. "We'll be like the elves in *Lord of the Rings*!"

"Whatever." Jake rolled his eyes, but he looked resigned to following Cupidity's orders along with the rest of them. Then again, she hadn't really done anything the three of them should complain about.

Laura peered curiously at her petite friend. "You're really into bows and arrows, aren't you?"

"You never know when you gotta hunt big game," she answered with a wink.

That night Peter came to Laura's house to officially pick her up for the date, and her parents made themselves scarce. All they requested was a ten-thirty curfew, being a school night, and then the parental units disappeared. Peter hemmed and hawed but smiled a lot and seemed to be enjoying this unexpected fling with the old king and the new queen of the popular crowd.

"And Jake says that maybe I can be the manager of the basketball team," bragged Peter proudly. "He says he can swing it with the coach, him being the star of the team and all."

Laura tried not to roll her eyes, because she was sure that Jake would have promised Peter anything to make this date happen. Now that it was happening, they were both expendable, but she didn't tell him that. Instead she grabbed his arm and convinced herself to have fun on this date, no matter what happened.

Descending the steps, Laura gasped when she caught sight of the dazzling couple in the glow of a streetlamp. Cupidity had let Jake drive the convertible, and he was basking in glory with the sleek sports car and beautiful blond under his apparent command. Cupidity and Jake both had glistening hair that was wind-blown and electrified from the night air, and their cheeks bore a rosy glow. *They look like the costars of a teen chick flick,* thought Laura glumly. *How can I have a chance with Jake?*

Cupidity squealed and waved at her, and Laura was cheered by the fact that her newest friend was still acting like her best friend. But it also made her think of Taryn, which brought a twinge of guilt. Laura plastered a smile onto her face, especially for Jake, and she and Peter climbed into the open backseat of the convertible. With Peter's long legs, it was cramped back there, and their limbs pressed against each other no matter how much they shifted around.

When the car roared off, Laura forgot all the cramped seating in the rush of wind. She had spent half an hour fixing her hair, which was a long time for her, and the wind blew it into a tumbleweed shape in a few seconds. By the time they reached the next stop sign, Laura had severe convertible hair, while Cupidity and Jake still possessed perfect locks.

Peter looked at her and tried not to laugh. His wavy red hair was now wild, but it was still kind of cute. "Tell me it will be dark at this place," whispered Laura, trying to corral her unruly locks with a hair band. "Wherever we're going."

He shrugged. "Archery—that's all I know. I don't think Jake plans to stay there long. He has other ideas."

"I bet he does." Laura worried that those in the front seat would hear them, but she could barely hear Peter in the fast-moving convertible. Cupidity yelled something over her shoulder, and her words were completely lost in the blast of wind. Still it was fun being outside, under the stars, *on a date!*

Jake said something that made Cupidity laugh, and she pointed off to the right. A moment later, they turned down a rather lonely country road, and Laura and Peter exchanged puzzled glances. If she didn't know how avidly Cupidity wanted to do archery, Laura would have thought they were headed down this deserted road in order to reenact a 1950s make-out movie and go "parking." Peter laughed nervously and tugged at the collar of his shirt, and Laura was glad to see another car following them.

After driving through a stand of dark trees, they passed a high metal fence that had some weird murals on it—crossed sabers, rifles, and bows. Behind the fence, the lights were so bright that Laura wondered if the place was a junkyard. Seconds later, they slowed in front of a large gate and a sign that read, WAR GAMES COMBAT CAMP.

As they crunched along slowly on the gravel, she heard Jake say, "Yeah, I came here once to play paintball."

"I've heard of it," Laura admitted, but she had always thought it was a front for some illegal militia.

Even though Jake had been here before, he didn't seem anxious to drive in until Cupidity ordered him. "Go on in, you silly," she insisted. "They won't bite."

Peter looked at Laura and gulped, and they both managed a nervous smile. "I don't want to wound anybody on our first date," said Laura.

"Me neither," squeaked Peter. "Cupidity, you'll show us what to do, right?"

"Oh, sure," she answered eagerly. "It's like really simple—be careful where you shoot, and don't shoot unless you're prepared to accept the consequences."

"What consequences?" asked Jake with a sneer. "I always hit what I'm aiming at."

"Me too," answered Cupidity with a saucy smile.

When the purring sports car rumbled onto the spacious grounds, Laura saw why they needed so many lights. At least a dozen pretend soldiers in camouflage fatigues were running around a paintball field that looked like a sparse junkyard. Here and there sat old vehicles, large shipping crates, stacks of tires, and other found objects that gave the participants cover as they lumbered around. Laura could hear the metallic thuds of the paintball guns, and she heard the cries of outrage when someone was hit and had to leave the game.

The archery range wasn't nearly as large, and it was kind of crude, with the bull's-eye targets mounted on bales of hay in the distance. There was also a regular shooting gallery, which was dark at this late hour, and a driving range where four golfers were hooking balls into a great stretch of dirt. Whoever owned this acreage was making the most of it, considering that it was nothing but a lot of dirt, a few trees, and some old junk.

Cupidity leaped out of the car and ran to an old wooden building, where two men were lounging on the porch. Like males everywhere, they jumped to attention when she approached, and they seemed to know her. She showed them her ornate bow, and one of them marveled over it, while the other went to fetch some regular bows. Meanwhile, she nocked one of her own arrows, and tested the tautness of the string.

Jake killed the engine in the convertible and turned to the passengers in the backseat. "I know this is a funky place," he whispered. "Don't worry, we're not going to stay here any longer than we have to . . . unless she wants to take a walk in the woods. I'd be up for that. How about you guys?"

"You lead, and we'll follow," answered Peter meekly. Laura just shrugged and tried to look game for anything. In truth, she wanted to see Cupidity shoot her precious bow and arrow more than she wanted to walk in the ominous woods. Looking at this surreal scene, Laura thought that it might not be such a bad thing that she never "dated." Dates were like reality TV shows—some of them were just determined to go wrong.

"Come on, guys!" called Cupidity as she motioned them over to the archery range. One of the workers traipsed along to show them how to nock an arrow and shoot a bow, but it wasn't difficult. The long ones required lots of strength, but the compound bow mostly required concentration, cool nerves, and good aim. Laura found out she was pretty good with it, and she surprised herself by enjoying the archery contest.

At one point, Jake scored last out of the four of them, and Laura saw the ugly competitive side of her Greek god. He challenged them to another round and forced Laura and Peter to use regular long bows, as he did. Laura couldn't muster the strength to be very accurate with the old-fashioned weapon, and she finished dead last. She didn't know for sure, but it appeared as if Peter threw the match to Jake and let him finish second. As usual, Cupidity whipped all of them with her peculiar harp-shaped bow.

In fact, Cupidity was a deadly shot, and she peppered her targets on the old bale of hay. Her arrows weren't always bull's-eyes, but she was in the general vicinity, unlike the rest of them, who kept sailing arrows into the bushes. After every round, Cupidity carefully collected her spent arrows, and Laura got the impression that they were as rare as her bow.

The girl's skills were so amazing that she collected a small crowd of onlookers, mostly paintballers just getting off the field. A few of them hung back in the shadows, watching from a distance, and Cupidity put on a show for them. Jake tried again to beat her and only made a fool of himself.

As they walked through the muddy parking lot, Jake muttered darkly about going bowling the next time. It was clear that he didn't like to be shown up by anyone, not even the remarkable Cupidity. Laura wasn't sure that there would be a next time with Jake and Cupidity. Despite looking gorgeous together, they didn't seem to have much chemistry, or much in common.

Laura smiled at Peter and gripped his hand, and he gave her a gentle squeeze. *Peter would make a low-maintenance boyfriend,* she decided, *unlike Jake, who would be a royal pain.*

Without warning, two paintballers jumped out of the shadows and fired a barrage of colorful orbs at Cupidity. Bright green and purple gobs exploded all over her clothes like neon spaghetti sauce. A paintball caught Laura in the shoulder and splattered purple paint on her glasses. She yelped, because it stung. Cupidity tried to dodge the attack, but there was no place to run—several messy shots found their mark. Jake dove for cover behind a car, while Peter jumped in front of Laura and stopped two more projectiles intended for her. But they weren't shooting at the boys.

Since the ambushers wore protective masks and army

fatigues, it was impossible to make out their faces, but Laura recognized their malicious giggles. When they shot paint all over the beautiful yellow convertible, she knew it had to be Megan and Chelsea. Still shrieking with laughter, the attackers dashed between parked cars, and Jake staggered to his feet and chased after them.

Peter caught Laura in his arms and stared wildly at her. "Are you all right? I'll strangle those stupid morons!" With a grimace, he bit off even angrier words.

"I'm okay," muttered Laura, massaging her sore shoulder. She looked past Peter to see Cupidity lifting her bow with an arrow nocked and ready. The petite archer swiveled slowly as she followed a moving target in the parking lot, then she let her missile fly into the darkness.

"No!" shouted Laura a second too late. A distant figure whimpered and sprawled on the ground, but it was hard to see if the arrow had struck her or if she had just tripped.

"What are you doing?" demanded Peter, whirling on Cupidity. "Okay, what they did was bad, but you can't shoot *arrows* at them! You'll get arrested—we'll *all* get arrested."

Cupidity studied Peter as if seeing him for the first time. "You'll do," she said, nodding. Then she nocked another arrow to her bow, drew back the string, and shot Peter at point-blank range.

"No!" cried Laura once again. She rushed forward, but an invisible shock wave slammed into her, sending her reeling back on her heels. With a gasp, Laura felt her legs weaken beneath her, and she tumbled into the mud.

5

I'm having a really awful nightmare, thought Laura from the hazy depths of a brain fog, *because there's Megan sobbing over Peter's bloody body. No, he's not really covered in blood, unless blood is neon green.*

Laura vaguely remembered something about paint and a battle. She had been involved too, because her shoulder hurt and there was purple paint on her face and glasses. Jake was yelling and stomping around, and a couple of people had gathered to watch the spectacle.

What a stupid dream, she thought.

"Oh, my precious! Oh, Peter!" wailed Megan, who in this dream was dressed like a soldier. The cheerleader bent over the red-haired, paint-covered boy and shook him as if trying to bring him back from the dead. "I didn't mean to hurt you! I would *never* hurt you!"

"What are you talking about?" demanded Jake, who was also in this dream. He shook his fists at both Megan and Chelsea. "You shot paintballs at us! You totally meant to hurt us. You're psychos!"

"Well, she shot arrows at us!" exclaimed Chelsea, pointing an accusatory finger at Cupidity.

Cupidity smiled innocently beneath several coats of contrasting paint, and she pointed to her multicolored hair. "Do I look like I started this? And look what you did to my car! I ought to have you arrested for that alone."

Now Laura stirred from her stupor, because something had a hint of reality. *Of course, reality is often mixed up in dreams,* she told herself. *Look, there's Megan kissing the paint off Peter's face while sobbing pathetically. They're both real people, yet this would never happen in real life.*

Laura relaxed, knowing she was still in a dream. A stranger, someone who seemed to work in this park place, stepped forward and said, "Okay, do you want me to call the police? What about an ambulance for them?"

He pointed to Peter, who had Megan draped all over him, sobbing fitfully. Suddenly Peter reached up and grabbed her butt.

"Well, I think he's still alive," said Cupidity.

"Hey, that's *my* girlfriend!" snapped Jake.

"Megan . . . Megan!" breathed Peter. He opened his eyes and saw Megan only inches away. From the grin that spread across his face, it looked as if Peter had died and gone to heaven. Sobbing for joy, they embraced.

Laura giggled dazedly. *What a crazy dream.*

"Teenagers!" growled the old stranger, waving his hand at them. "All of you, get out of here before the sheriff comes by. And you two girls—" He pointed to Megan and Chelsea. "Don't ever come back."

Megan was oblivious to anything but Peter Yarmench, and she grunted as she helped him to his feet. They were instantly besieged by Jake and Chelsea, who didn't look very happy.

Laura felt strong hands under her armpits, and she turned to see Cupidity deftly lifting her to her feet. In doing so, Cupidity smeared paint all over Laura's back, and it felt cold and sticky in the night air.

"Don't wake me up," muttered Laura. "I'm having a weird dream."

Cupidity laughed. "Come on, Sleeping Beauty, let's get out of here before the old man calls the cops." She peered across the parking lot and called, "Jake!"

Jake was pointing his finger and yelling at Megan and Peter. After a few moments, Chelsea joined in, shrieking at her best friend, but the cheerleader and the gangly geek were lost in each other's embrace. They looked like drowning victims clinging to life preservers.

As the small crowd drifted away, Jake walked back over to Laura and Cupidity shaking his head. "Dude, I don't get it. She hit him with a couple of paintballs, and now he's like her long-lost love."

"Don't worry," said Laura blissfully, "it's all a dream, it's not real."

Jake stared at her. "Hello! Get a grip, will you? Your date just ditched *you* for *my* girlfriend!"

"I thought you and Megan were over," said Cupidity, folding her arms. "What's the deal, Jake?"

"Hey, it's just a shock, that's all," he answered, turning away from them. When he caught sight of Peter and Megan again, he scowled.

Laura smiled at Jake's discomfort until she saw Chelsea headed their way. The curvy, dark-haired beauty looked frumpy in her army fatigues, and she pouted under her bulky mask. "Can I get a ride with you guys?" she pleaded. "Those two lovebirds don't even know I exist."

"It's just a dream," answered Laura confidently. "Don't sweat it."

"It's no dream," said Cupidity gravely. "Peter and Megan have found each other, and we should be happy for them. Wake up and smell the love connection." She reached out and pinched Laura's arm.

"Ow!" exclaimed Laura, as everything came into focus. Jake Mattson was standing before her, looking miserable. In the distance, Jake's longtime girlfriend, Megan, was making out with the unlikely Peter Yarmench. And Chelsea's stunned, crestfallen expression only verified this bizarre turn of events. The only person who looked contented was Cupidity. But then again, she barely knew these people.

Memories suddenly flooded back, and Laura stammered, "D-did you shoot Peter with an arrow?"

Cupidity laughed. "Does he look like he's been shot with an arrow? I told you, I use my bow symbolically, so I don't really get angry with people. It's working, isn't it?" she asked as she flipped her paint-covered hair. "I got the worst of this prank, and I'm not angry. So the rest of you, chill out."

"Chill out?" said Jake in confusion. "You must've gotten hit in the head by those stupid paintballs. That's a cheerleader over there with the king of the dorks!"

"Hey!" said Laura angrily, "Peter is my friend."

Chelsea broke into tears and sobbed pitifully as she climbed out of her paintball gear, which she had worn over her regular clothes. "What's going on? First Cody leaves me, and now I lose my best friend! This is so unfair!"

"Cheer up!" chirped Cupidity, clapping her hands together like a cheerleader. "It's a school night, and we'll all get home in time to make our parents happy. Who cares if we have a little paint on us?"

Chelsea sniffed and grabbed the new girl's paint-smeared arm. "I'm sorry about everything, Cupidity. We followed you here, and it wasn't until we saw that we could rent paintball stuff that we decided to tag you." She looked wistfully over her shoulder. "I didn't think Megan would get so weirded out over it."

"Forget it," insisted Cupidity, happily leading the way to her car. "Get in the car, and don't worry about getting paint on the seats."

"This is why I hate archery," grumbled Jake. He pointed back into the shadows. "Yarmench, I'm not done with you yet!"

No answer came from the funky complex of trees and shooting ranges, and the lights over the paintball field suddenly blinked out, leaving them in deep shadows. One by one, the uniformed figures disappeared into the darkness, and Laura shivered with a feeling of unease.

She wanted to call after Peter and tell him to get back where he belonged, but she had resisted others doing that to her. Peter had found something unusual, and why should she begrudge him that? Maybe Megan was playing him along to get even with Jake, but her concern for Peter had looked genuine. She wasn't that good an actress.

What exactly happened to me? Laura asked herself, but her memories remained vague. Starting with the paintball pummeling, she wasn't sure what she'd experienced, only that something had hit her. *An invisible force?* Or maybe it was just the splatter of a paintball. One thing was certain—this wasn't her typical Tuesday night.

When Laura reached the car, Chelsea was in the backseat, still babbling and crying. "I can't believe it! This is totally whack. Jake, what will we do for the Homecoming Dance? If I don't go with Cody, and you don't go with Megan . . . well, that makes everything totally whacked out! Who will be the king and queen?"

Laura had to resist rolling her eyes as she got in the car next to Chelsea.

"When is this dance?" asked Cupidity with another flip of her paint-splattered hair.

"It's a formal. Early in October," whined Chelsea. "Like three weeks from now."

"Who cares?" muttered Jake. He pounded a beefy fist into his palm. "That geek is going to have some explaining to do."

Laura looked over her shoulder, searching the parking

lot for Peter. It was just sinking in that her date had been taken away by the future Homecoming Queen, and she was going home without even getting a kiss. Not that she necessarily *wanted* one from Peter, but still. This was a terrible first date!

Cupidity hummed as she started the car engine. When she moved in her paint-covered clothes, she made squishy sounds on the seat. "Ah, it felt good to shoot again," she remarked.

"What are you talking about?" said Jake, who stared in amazement at his cheerful date. "Tonight was a bust."

"Depends on how you look at it," answered Cupidity. "For example, you'll never have to worry about Megan bugging you again." She laughed softly as Jake scowled.

Laura glanced over her shoulder again, but Peter was gone.

"How could she turn Peter into a love zombie?" asked Taryn with a disdainful sniff. She and Laura were standing at the back of the lunch line, watching Peter Yarmench and Megan Rawlins near the front of the line. The moonstruck couple were gazing at each other so intently that the line had stopped moving. In one day, Peter and Megan had become one of those insufferable, inseparable couples who cling to each other all day long. Finally somebody yelled at them, and they moved a few steps, still gazing at each other with goo-goo eyes.

"You were there—what happened?" asked Taryn.

Laura shook her head. "I was there, but I have no idea what happened. Megan hit him with a couple of paintballs, and he passed out. She felt really bad about it, and then she was thrilled when he woke up. They've been like this ever since."

"Ew!" exclaimed Taryn, wrinkling her nose. "Whoever thought getting hit by paintballs could be so romantic?"

"Yep." Laura nodded glumly and looked around the crowded cafeteria. She was trying to find Cupidity, who had disappeared shortly after they arrived at school that morning. Last night had been a blur, and now that Laura was clearheaded, she had questions for the new girl.

She found Taryn staring at her with pity. "What?" asked Laura.

"It's just that . . . you go on a date for the first time in like forever, and you lose your date to Megan Rawlins," said Taryn. "That's raw. What are you going to do about it?"

"Do about it?" snapped Laura. "Do you want me to steal him away from Megan? Look at them! I've never seen Peter look at anything like that . . . except maybe pepperoni pizza."

Taryn lowered her voice to add, "They say that Jake Mattson is going to do something about it after school."

"Where did you hear that?"

"Oh, just around." Taryn smiled slyly. "So, will there be any more double dates with Cupidity?"

"I don't know if I can stand the excitement," admitted Laura. "Look, I have to find her. I don't want Peter to get hurt. Catch you later." She rushed out of the lunch line, accepting the fact that she wouldn't get anything to eat.

Laura prowled the cafeteria, then wandered the halls, looking for Cupidity. She finally decided to check outside in the parking lot. Although students weren't allowed to leave campus during lunch, Cupidity tended to follow her own rules.

She finally found her new friend sitting on the hood of her convertible, which was sparkling clean again. Cupidity was talking to an unlikely person, Emma Langdon, and the goth leader with the spiky black hair was nodding at something she said. Emma handed Cupidity a piece of paper, and they both studied it for a moment. When Laura approached, Emma tucked the paper back in her jacket and gave the valedictorian a smirk.

"I heard you had quite a date last night," Emma said.

"Yeah," answered Laura, "it was more fun shooting at the targets than *being* the targets."

"Man, if I were you, I would so get even with them!" vowed Emma, pounding her fist into her palm. "Those snots think they can get away with anything, and now Megan has ripped off a new boyfriend from the brainiac bunch."

"Yeah," answered Laura, bowing her head and wanting to change the subject. "What else were you two talking about?"

"The usual," answered Cupidity. "Boys."

Emma blushed behind her mask of heavy eye shadow and pale foundation and pointed toward Cupidity. "You'll keep it quiet, right?"

"Don't worry," said Cupidity. "I have great respect for love and secrets. Let me handle it."

Emma glanced at Laura and muttered, "Your friend's okay. Sorry everyone's on your case about her. See ya." With a wave, Emma swaggered across the parking lot as if she owned it.

"You know, I kind of like her," said Cupidity. "She reminds me of my mother—smoldering and intense."

"Where have you been hiding all morning?" asked Laura, wringing her hands. She was nervous for Peter's safety, but she didn't want to jump in about that and look like she was freaking out.

Cupidity admired her reflection in her windshield. "After I dropped you off, I left."

"What? You ditched all your morning classes?" asked Laura in amazement.

"Well, I had to get my car cleaned," answered Cupidity, affectionately slapping the hood of her prized vehicle.

"But your parents—" Laura bit her lip, because she remembered that Cupidity was self-sufficient, no untidy parents around. Although she looked young and fresh, who could tell for sure that she was a high school student? Maybe she was a cop or a con artist or something.

"I'm getting paranoid," blurted Laura.

Cupidity shrugged and patted her on the back. "Well, it comes with the territory. You should have thought of that before—" The blond girl stopped in mid-sentence and started searching through her purse. "What did I do with my cell phone? I hate those things."

"Before what?" demanded Laura, certain she was going to say more.

"Totally nothing," replied Cupidity with a flip of her hair. "Emma was showing me a photo of a boy she likes, as if I didn't know. She wants me to arrange a double date for *her*—can you believe? But I don't think that guy is right for her. She needs to get out of her rut."

"Like Peter did?" asked Laura, wringing her hands again. "What's happening? My life has been turned upside down, and I don't know what happened. Everything seems so crazy . . . ever since I've been hanging out with you."

"Don't blame all your problems on *me*," responded

Cupidity with a sniff. "If you liked Peter, why didn't you grab him? You had plenty of opportunity."

Laura's shoulders slumped. She thought about denying it, but she had a feeling her friend was dead on. "Yeah, you're right," she muttered, "I'm hopeless with boys. But at least I'm not the only one who's confused. I mean, who would have thought Megan Rawlins even knew Peter was alive?"

"Maybe Megan has always liked him," answered Cupidity with a shrug, "and when he got hurt, something snapped in her brain. Love is crazy like that. Okay, so we've crossed off Peter and Jake. Now, who do you *really* like? Cody?"

"Oh, I don't know anymore," said Laura in exasperation. "One thing for sure, I don't want to see Jake do something to hurt Peter. Have you heard the rumors? Can you reason with that Neanderthal?"

"Did you ever try to reason with a Neanderthal?" asked Cupidity with a chuckle. "Never mind. If it gets out of hand, I'll deal with him. Come on, let's try to find him."

The halls were crowded with kids rushing to class after lunch, or rushing to the next lunch period. Laura and Cupidity searched until they were both late, but they didn't find Jake. Several of his friends claimed not to have seen him, and it looked as if he was trying to avoid Cupidity at all costs.

The afternoon crawled by, and Laura could only stare at the clock and feel helpless. *We won't be able to find Jake before he finds Peter,* she thought with dread. *And how could we stop him, anyway?*

When the final bell rang and the kids stampeded into the hallways, there was a feeling of electricity in the air. Someone had stolen Jake Mattson's girlfriend, and it was way too weird a someone to just let it go. It was causing ripples in the smooth pools of high school status.

Laura got caught up in the flow of the crowd heading out of the building, all of them looking for Jake or the love zombies, Megan and Peter. Laura also searched for Cupidity, with no luck, but she managed to hook up with Taryn and a few other friends.

A crowd was gathering at the far corner of the school parking lot, and Laura sprinted ahead of Taryn and Ashley to see what was going on. A group of students had surrounded Megan and Peter, pestering them with questions about their newfound love. The happy couple, meanwhile, seemed lost in their own world, content to just gaze into each other's eyes.

The group parted as Jake muscled through to join in the questioning. He shrugged off two of his friends who were trying to stop him, because they knew how jealous Jake could be. Apparently, so did Megan, who clung to Peter for support. Laura could see fire in Peter's green eyes—she knew he would defend himself and Megan. But it didn't make her feel much better.

The crowd had taken a few steps away from Laura, too, and she realized that she stood apart. Most of the students had heard about what happened the night before, so they expected some kind of reaction from her, too. *I'm the other wronged party,* she thought with a sinking feeling. *At least that's what they all think.*

"How long has this been going on?" yelled Jake. "Have you two been fooling around behind my back?"

"Of course not," said Peter, trying to sound calm. But then he took his hand from Megan's waist and balled it into a fist. "You know, you dumped her, remember."

Jake puffed out his chest beneath his tight polo shirt. "Are you kidding? That wasn't serious—how can I be serious about Cupidity? It was just a misunderstanding between me and Megan, and you jumped in like the loser you are!"

"He's not a loser," countered Megan. "He's wonderful! *You're* the loser!"

Jake roared and took another step closer, fists flailing. But Megan stood her ground and bravely warded off the attack. Jake tried to reach around her, but she blocked his every move; the best he could do was to give Peter a symbolic shove and back off. Peter staggered but stayed on his feet.

Now the crowd was into it, egging them on. Laura couldn't get over how ridiculous the whole scene was. And she finally ran into the middle, the mob roaring their approval. "Hey, I was there last night too!" she yelled at Jake. "Peter was *my* date, so I got dumped the same as you." Then, realizing how pathetic that sounded, she took a deep breath. "Look, you were clearly with Cupidity last night, so stop whining about it."

Jake scowled. "Your friend Cupidity is a skank, a tease . . . and a nutcase on top of it!" The crowd tittered with uneasy laughter at this Jerry Springer moment.

Suddenly the group shifted, and a dazed-looking Emma Langdon muscled her way through. She looked like a person dying of thirst who has suddenly seen a lake. "Jake!" she croaked, holding out a trembling hand.

Along with everyone else, Laura was watching Emma's dramatic entrance, but she still caught a flash of reflected light in the corner of her eye. Someone grunted, and she whirled around to see Jake stagger forward, as a gust of wind pushed her back a step. The preppy king swayed to and fro and looked as if he would pass out, but Emma Langdon rushed in to catch him.

From back near the school building, a loud authoritative voice boomed, "What's going on over there? Break it up now."

Everyone realized that the show was over and scattered quickly toward their cars. Taryn tugged on Laura's sleeve and urged her to move, but she had to hang back for a moment. She could see Emma kneeling beside a dazed Jake Mattson, comforting him. *What happened to him?* wondered Laura. She hadn't seen anything hit him, only that vague flash, but maybe Megan had struck him from behind.

The vice principal was bounding across the lot toward the disbanding group, and Taryn pulled harder on her sleeve. "Come on!"

Laura let Taryn lead her away, just as Cupidity's car shot by, tires squealing. As the rear end fishtailed, the yellow convertible made a sensational U-turn to stop right next to Jake and Emma. Cupidity waved them into her car and sped away while the vice principal yelled.

Students were piling into cars and zooming off in different directions, and Laura had no time to think about what had just happened. When she reached the sidewalk, she saw Megan and Peter in the distance, strolling hand in hand as if nothing had happened. They looked blissful, not even mortified by the fact that they didn't have a car. Laura slowed down and shook her head, thinking that Megan probably hadn't walked home since grade school.

Why do I care so much? she thought. *Could I actually be jealous?* The happy couple definitely grated on Laura. She could understand how Peter deserved some good luck in love, but Megan Rawlins? The cheerleader *always* had good luck. Still, being around Peter made her seem more normal, more mellow, almost fading into the background at times. Megan had given up ruling the popular crowd in order to obsess on Peter, which was an improvement, she guessed.

Laura turned to look for Taryn and spotted her trailing by several strides. "I'll see you later!" she called. "I've got to talk to someone."

6

Greasy smoke from the barbecue wafted through the back patio of the Mount Olympus Retirement Home. While most of the gods and goddesses lounged by the pool, sipping nectar, three of them stood in the shadows of the patio. They gazed solemnly at a shallow bowl made from the finest black porcelain. Filled with water, it stood on a pedestal, and smoke seemed to gather around the gaunt figures of Mercury, Jupiter, and Vulcan.

Mercury stood to the king's right, but Vulcan shook his bushy head and limped away from the pedestal. "I don't see a darn thing."

"Give it a minute," said Mercury. "It's a miratorium, not a TV."

"There!" croaked Jupiter, pointing into the bowl. In the flickering glow of the bug zappers, Jupiter and Mercury stared at the shimmering portal of blackness.

After a moment, Mercury saw Cupid, in his sultry guise of young maiden, shoot his magical bow in an evening encounter and again in a large parking lot during the day. The elder god felt an emotional tug on his immortal heart, and he could sense the undying love of the two couples Cupid had united. However, he knew from the shimmering vision in the bowl that Laura Sweeney remained unfulfilled.

"*Twice* he has used his powers," remarked Jupiter with a frown on his droopy face.

"Twice?" asked Vulcan curiously.

"But not to aid Laura Sweeney," added Mercury.

Vulcan scowled. "Ack, what is that irresponsible imp doing? I swear, that boy can't be given the simplest task. Those high school students don't need Cupid—they have raging hormones!"

"Maybe you made his disguise too good," remarked Mercury with a disdainful raised eyebrow. "Looking like he does, that cherub could be having too much fun."

Jupiter lowered his bushy eyebrows at the messenger god. "Merc, do you know what I'm thinking?"

The god looked down at his winged slippers and sighed. "You want me to go to Ohio to check up on him . . .

or her. What about asking for help from Venus?"

"No!" shouted Vulcan and Jupiter at the same time, and they glanced at one another with suspicion.

"If we alert Venus, the cure could be worse than the bite," said Jupiter. "And perhaps we're worried about nothing. All I'm asking you to do, Brother, is take a firsthand look at the situation."

"Will you need a disguise?" asked Vulcan. "Perhaps you could be a dog? Kids like them."

Mercury gave him an imperious scowl. "A dog? I think not. Besides, I couldn't disguise myself from Cupid—he's too clever. But I will have to assume an identity that will get me close to him. Perhaps you could take a few centuries off my face."

"Heh, heh!" laughed Vulcan with a wheeze. "You won't look a day over sixty."

Laura tiptoed down the sidewalk, trying not to make any noise as she snuck up on Peter and Megan, who were talking in a low, intimate whisper. She wanted to make it look as if she had just stumbled on them, not that she was following them. From Peter, she wanted to find out how it felt to fall madly in love, and why she couldn't bring herself to do it. From Megan, she wanted to know how she could throw away twelve years of class consciousness in one brave kiss.

Secretly, Laura also wanted to make sure Megan was genuine and that she wasn't pulling the ultimate punk on Peter. Even thinking about such a prospect made her furious, and Laura gritted her teeth as she strode forward. Lost in imagined anger, she accidentally tripped over a crack in the sidewalk and stumbled forward, plowing into Megan's back.

"Hey!" shouted the shapely girl, whirling around with fists raised. "You want a piece of me too?"

"Whoa!" said Laura, jumping back, trying to wipe the envy and anger off her face. "I didn't mean anything—I just fell forward. I was the one stopping the stupid fight, remember?"

Megan dropped her hands a little, but she still looked suspicious.

Laura glanced from Peter to Megan and twisted her hands as she said, "Look, other people are being weird, but I'm not trying to be. I mean, I don't care that you two are together. Peter, I'm *glad* you've got a girlfriend . . . even if it's not someone I would ever guess."

"What's that supposed to mean?" asked Megan, lifting her fists again. Laura recoiled a few more steps, because she could see how Megan's possessive side had probably driven Jake crazy. It didn't seem to have the same effect on Peter . . . yet.

In fact, Peter took in the whole awkward exchange with a dimwitted smile. "Hey, you two, there's no point in anyone fighting. They'll all get used to us being together. They'll *have* to." With that, he threw a gangly arm around Megan and pulled her close to him.

At the overt show of affection, Megan gave Laura a triumphant sneer. "Yeah, they'll have to get used to us being together, whether they like it or not. Any other questions, Laura?"

About a thousand, she thought, stunned. But she could only manage to blurt, "When did you two . . . when did you realize you were in love?"

That question brought puzzled expressions to both of their faces, and the love zombies looked curiously at each other. "Well, I always thought Megan was the hottest, the coolest, the most—"

"Okay, I get the picture," replied Laura, cutting him off. "What about you, Megan? When did you know?"

The dark-haired beauty shook her head as if it was an incredibly stupid question. "I guess . . . I have always liked him. Yeah, that's it—from the time I was in kindergarten, I liked Peter!"

"Then how come you never talked to him before our date last night?" asked Laura sweetly.

Megan bristled once again. "Hey, that's none of your

business, and I don't even think it's true." She turned and batted her eyelashes at her beloved. "Sweetie, I must have talked to you lots of times before that night . . . didn't I?"

Peter scrunched his face, thinking hard. He finally smiled and said, "Yes, you asked me for a pencil once in fifth grade."

"No, seriously," said Megan, looking troubled. "I feel as if I've always loved you, but I was afraid to express it. Then when I saw you lying there . . . in the mud and the paint, knowing that *I* put you there . . . my heartstrings just snapped."

Laura nodded with understanding, because she had actually seen that happen. Peter had looked pretty pathetic, but there was still something wrong with this picture.

"I don't think *you* knocked him out," said Laura with a frown. "I can't remember exactly what happened, but Cupidity did hit you with an arrow, didn't she?"

"Right!" Megan snorted sarcastically. "That cow couldn't hit the broad side of the principal with her stupid bow. I tripped over something, or somebody pushed me—I can't remember."

"Hey, I think we all hit our heads out there," said Peter, "so what does it matter? It was a dumb stunt, but it worked out great—for us." He gave Megan another insufferable hug.

"Sweetie, it wasn't a dumb stunt," protested Megan softly, staring up at Peter with puppy-dog eyes. "It started out really funny, and I thought we improvised it like champs. We totally didn't know what we were going to do to Jake and Stupidity. Excuse me, Cupidity."

Laura opened her mouth to defend her absent friend, but she really couldn't think of any reason to absolve Cupidity. She had shot an arrow at Megan and pointed one at Peter. Clearly neither one of them had holes in them, but they were stupid in love. *Cupidity and stupidity,* she thought, *they do seem to go together.*

She looked somberly at Peter and said from her heart, "I feel like I'm missing something here, but I'm happy that you're happy. You've got to be better for Megan than that jerk Jake could ever be, and I hope she appreciates you."

Megan sneered. "What I'd appreciate, Laura, is if you left us alone. I know he used to be one of your friends, but now he's all mine."

"Hey, babe, that's a little harsh, isn't it?" asked Peter. "I didn't agree to give up all my friends for you."

Megan put her hands on her hips and stared at him. "Come on, you hardly *have* any friends. I've got enough friends for both of us, so you don't need this loser."

"I'm glad to see you haven't changed all that much," cracked Laura as she turned and strode away.

She got only a few steps down the sidewalk before Peter caught up to her and grabbed her arm. "Laura, please!" he begged. "Stop and talk to me! She didn't mean it."

Laura stopped long enough to look back at Megan, whose eyes were shooting laser beams at her. "She meant it," hissed Laura. "But maybe she's right. Maybe she *is* all you need. Why would you need me or any of your old friends if you have the Homecoming Queen?" She yanked her arm out of his grip and dashed down the sidewalk.

"Laura!" Peter called after her, his voice filled with confusion and guilt. But Laura didn't stop again. She didn't want him to see her crying.

Laura's run eventually mellowed into a walk, and she called her parents to say she would be late. It was unusually cool for an early autumn afternoon, and she kept going for miles, letting the cool bracing air shake her into reality. She hated to admit it, but even Megan was right—she had to accept what had happened even if she couldn't explain it. And Peter was still Peter—though clearly a bizarre in-love version of himself.

Laura sniffed glumly but held her head up as she walked. One good thing had come from talking to Megan—she realized that the girl hadn't changed. If anything, being in love with Peter had made her more nasty and controlling than before, only now it was directed at one person instead of her hand-picked group. It was Megan and Peter in a very exclusive club: them against the whole school. *Maybe love doesn't turn you into a different person or a better person,* she decided, *just a more obsessed person.*

Laura scowled, because outside of their classes she knew she'd never see Peter alone anymore. *But why do I want to see Peter at all?* she asked herself. *I never thought about him like this before Megan came along. Cupidity is right—there are lots of other boys out there. I can certainly find one of my own. After all, love* is *in the air.*

Though she was walking a roundabout route, Laura realized she was heading toward Cupidity's apartment. She was going to ask the new girl for advice and find out what she had seen in the parking lot or heard from Emma and Jake in the car. Maybe Emma had told Cupidity what had freaked her out so much during the fight. It was truly amazing that Cupidity had rescued Jake like that after all the unkind things he said about her, but she was a big-hearted person.

The more Laura thought about it, the more she realized that Emma and Jake must have been freaked out at the same time—maybe by the same thing. They had not really been *together* after the fight, they were just frozen in the same spot. Laura laughed at herself for thinking the pair could ever have been together in any other way.

As she rounded the high wall of hedges that separated the sidewalk from Cupidity's apartment complex, Laura heard giggling. It wasn't little kids, because one of them had a very deep voice. Then she heard the unmistakable clatter of a skateboard, and she realized it was just skaters, probably middle schoolers. She kept walking and turned the corner to approach the guardhouse, where there was actually a guard. For Denton, Ohio, these were very swank apartments.

Suddenly she heard a cry of alarm, and a skateboard shot across her path. It rumbled across the road and skittered to a stop against the curb, as a car had to squeal its brakes to keep from hitting it. "Oh, you silly!" cried a voice. "That's not how you do it!"

A darkly dressed figure with pale skin skipped across the driveway and retrieved the skateboard, while the driver looked on with annoyance. Laughing, smiling—even giggling!— Emma Langdon grabbed the board and rushed back to her friend, who Laura was shocked to see was Jake Mattson.

"Let me try it again," said Jake, taking the board from her. "What do you call that move you do? An ollie?"

Emma giggled again. "First, dude, you've just got to learn to keep your balance. Maybe you're a goofy foot—try leading with your left foot."

"Emma?" asked Laura with amazement. "Jake?"

"Hi!" called Emma. They both smiled at Laura as if the goth chick giving the preppy king a boarding lesson was the most natural thing on earth. "Okay, Jake, try it again with your left foot, more perpendicular to the board. Hold your hands out to keep your balance."

Jake gamefully leaped on the board and promptly fell off again, but he laughed as he landed in a pile of dirt. "Hey, this is hard! I'll never knock skater dudes again."

"You'd better not," said Emma, giving him a warm smile. "I'm going to get you a skateboard for your birthday. When is that?"

"Not until March," Jake answered sadly.

"Then I'll get you one just for being sweet." Emma unleashed a mushy smile on Jake, and he gazed at his pale gothic princess with a goofy grin.

Laura rubbed her eyes, certain she was seeing things. Before now, these two hadn't simply ignored each other as Peter and Megan had, they'd actively *hated* each other. To see them acting cozy and sharing a skateboarding lesson was even more shocking than seeing Peter and Megan together. Once this became common knowledge in school, all the social classes would be flipped upside down.

Flapping her lips, Laura only managed to stammer, "Is . . . is Cupidity at home?"

"Yeah," said Jake, turning his dazzling blue eyes to Laura. "I apologized to her, and I'd like to apologize to you, too, for acting like a jerk. Not that I *am* a jerk—I just act like one sometimes."

Emma beamed with pride. "That was a wonderful apology, Jakey, and she knows you meant it. Dude, we've got to thank Laura for hooking us up with Cupidity. Both of you have been really cool about *everything,* and Jake and I want to triple-date with you. Don't we, Jakey?"

"Uh-huh." He nodded as if he had heard her, but he was too busy casting love-smitten goo-goo eyes to understand anything but the basics.

"To triple-date, I have to find a boyfriend," Laura reminded them. "I'm apparently the only one who can't find one."

"Maybe you're just looking in the wrong place," said Emma, grabbing Jake and pulling him possessively to her ample side. He almost drooled on her thick eye makeup. "Walk on the wild side," suggested Emma as she hugged her preppy prize, whose polo shirt was now dirty and untucked. "Think outside the box."

Laura wagged her finger at the unusual couple. "You two are so outside the box you're in . . . a tetrahedron."

"We'll find you a date for Homecoming," insisted Jake, and he sounded as if he meant it.

"No, thanks!" answered Laura with dread. "I'm still recovering from the last date you arranged for me. I, uh . . . I'll talk to Cupidity." Laura staggered away, thinking that the world had to be coming to an end.

She could accept that a girl might find Peter attractive, and that it might even be someone as unlikely as Megan Rawlins. But Emma Langdon and Jake Mattson pawing each other? This had really gone beyond the laws of physics, romance, and high school order. *Not that I should care,* thought Laura with a frown. *I don't have any claim on Jake. In fact, I wouldn't want that jerk, but Emma should want him even less.* It didn't matter that Jake was now dishing out apologies like a sensitive New Age guy—he still had acted like such a jerk. Megan hadn't really changed, and neither had he. But *something* had happened to them.

Cupidity . . . bow and arrows. Laura's fevered imagination seized on a ludicrous explanation for these two unlikely romances. Cupidity had shot her arrows that fateful night when Megan and Peter fell for each other. . . .

No, it's too insane to think that Cupidity is some kind of modern-day Cupid, Laura decided. *I've got to keep my imagination in check. It's got to be a coincidence that her name is Cupidity. Come to think of it, it's a wonder there aren't more girls with that name. It's kinda pretty.*

Then again, this thing between Emma and Jake was

too far beyond normal to have any earthly explanation. But Cupidity hadn't shown up until it was all over. Or had she?

Laura marched up the steps toward Cupidity's apartment, determined to get some answers. She rang the doorbell, and the blond girl answered it wearing a towel, her hair all wet from the shower. A cell phone was stuck in her ear, and she motioned Laura inside her luxurious apartment without ever stopping her conversation.

"Yes, yes, Cody, I know I owe you a date!" she said with a knowing wink at Laura. "Well, I've found that going out on school nights is not such a hot idea, so why don't we wait until Friday? It's only a couple of nights away. But I won't go with you unless I can double-date with Laura Sweeney. You've got friends who would like her, I'm sure. So find one."

Laura waved her hands, trying to get out of the double-date trap, but Cupidity ignored her. "Just find somebody by Friday, and we'll hang! Later, Cody."

With a satisfied grin on her face, the blond girl turned off the phone and beamed at her best friend. "It's all set for Friday night—don't make any plans. Hang on a second while I get dressed."

"Wait!" Laura tried to protest the arranged date, but Cupidity rushed off to her bedroom. Laura twiddled her thumbs for a few minutes until Cupidity reappeared in jeans and a T-shirt. Laura marveled at how perfect the fresh-faced girl looked without any makeup.

"Don't worry," insisted Cupidity, "we're going to get you a solid date for the Homecoming Dance. Someone who will make you happy and treat you right."

"And just how are you going to do this?" blurted Laura. "How are you putting these weird couples together? And come to think of it, why?"

"What do you mean?" asked Cupidity with a forced laugh. "People double-date all the time, it's no big deal."

"No, that's not a big deal," agreed Laura. "But Peter and Megan going together? And now Emma and Jake—that's like the Alien dating the Predator! They couldn't stand to be in the same school before this, and now they're best buddies? It's not natural."

"Love is always natural," insisted Cupidity. "It's just surprising sometimes. Out of all the people I know, I didn't think *you* would complain about people crossing social barriers to go out with each other."

Laura shook her head and tried to corral her scattered thoughts. "I'm not complaining about it—I'm just trying to figure out how it happened! I saw you pick up Jake and Emma in your car after the fight. Are you saying that you had *nothing* to do with their romance?"

Cupidity shrugged. "Well, I gave Emma the same

advice I gave you—to get out of your rut. If you can't win at eight ball, switch to nine ball."

"What?" asked Laura, puzzled. "What did you do to . . ."

"What do you think I did to them?" scoffed Cupidity, putting her hands on her slender hips.

Laura's mouth opened, but the ridiculous words froze on her tongue. She couldn't accuse this cute, ditzy new girl of being some kind of relative of Cupid's—the whole idea was absurd. Instead she asked lamely, "How did you get your first name?"

The blond girl shrugged and tried to look disinterested. "What excuse do parents need for crazy names anymore? They wanted something like Felicity or Charity, so they picked Cupidity."

"Have you ever looked up the meaning of cupidity? It means 'greed, desire, wanting something that doesn't belong to you.'"

"And your point?" asked Cupidity, her blue eyes narrowing with anger. "What's your deal, Laura? Do you want to be in love, or don't you? Do you want my help, or do you want to stumble along in the weeds, getting nowhere? Now you've seen that people *can* find love when they open themselves up to it. If they keep themselves all scrunched and uptight, like you, it ain't gonna happen."

Feeling sufficiently sidetracked, Laura sighed. Once

again, it had all come back around to her and her deficiencies, which didn't seem quite fair. Whatever she was going through, it didn't explain these two strange romances, which had exploded right after the arrival of the strange new girl.

With a sympathetic grin Cupidity reached out and patted Laura's shoulder. "Don't worry, it'll happen for you. Look, you seem to think I can work some magic, so why not give me a chance to help? Cody's pretty desperate to go out with me; let's see what kind of dude he scrounges up for you. We know he can't go back to Peter, so it's got to be someone different."

Her pleading smile was so sincere that Laura felt herself giving in. "Okay, whatever. But I'm gonna watch Emma and Jake."

"Do that. Maybe you'll learn something," answered Cupidity. "If you see them, tell them they can keep my skateboard. I'm going to bed early."

"That's *your* skateboard?" asked Laura with surprise.

Cupidity shrugged. "When in Rome, do as the Romans. I'll see you tomorrow." The beautiful blond girl sauntered into the living room, where she grabbed a fat cigar from the mantel and calmly lit it. Puffing away, Cupidity disappeared into the kitchen, leaving Laura to show herself out.

Ew, thought Laura with a lump in her stomach, *she*

smokes cigars! And what does she mean by, "When in Rome do as the Romans"?

The perplexed teenager stepped into the bracing fall air; it was almost dark, and lights twinkled in the bare trees of the apartment complex. If Emma and Jake were still playing with their skateboard, they were awfully quiet about it. As Laura walked down the sidewalk toward the street, she could hear the echo of another pair of footsteps. She looked up to see a slender, well-dressed man with a cane ambling toward her.

He tipped his homburg hat and gave her a crinkled smile, and she had the feeling that he was very old, and very sweet. His wing-tipped shoes paused in mid-step, and he asked, "Miss, may I bother you for directions?"

"Of course," she answered, happy to help the man.

He looked puzzled as he waved his cane at the different buildings in the complex. "I'm looking for apartment C-17, but I'm not sure which one—"

"C-17?" said Laura with excitement. "Isn't that where Cupidity lives?"

The old man's face brightened. "Why, do you know Cupidity? You wouldn't by any chance be Laura Sweeney?"

"Yes!" she answered. "But how do you know my name?"

The elder chuckled. "Oh, Cupidity has spoken of you. She says that you've been a very good friend in her new school situation. I must go and surprise her." The old man shuffled off.

"Excuse me," said Laura, "who . . . who are you?"

"Oh, I'm Cupidity's father," he answered with another crinkled grin. "It's been some time since I've seen her."

Laura stepped forward and lowered her voice. "Listen, you may smell cigar smoke in her apartment, but that wasn't her. It was the . . . dishwasher repairman."

The elder's smile looked pained as he replied, "I know Cupidity smokes cigars. That's one bad habit we'll be sure to break. Anything else I should know about my lovely daughter?"

For a moment Laura considered telling him about the bow and arrows at school, but decided against it. Instead she chirped, "She's, uh . . . she's quite a girl."

"Yes," answered the old man doubtfully. "A girl . . . to warm any father's heart. Thank you for your help, Laura. I'm sure we'll see you again soon." He tipped his hat and ambled down the sidewalk, relying on his cane.

He must've been about fifty years old when she was born, thought Laura, but she wiped that thought out of her mind. *So Cupidity has a real father,* she mused. *That rules out any crazy idea about her being Cupid's evil spawn.*

With a sigh Laura hurried into the street and down the sidewalk, anxious to get home in time for dinner.

7

The next morning Laura lingered in bed, not really wanting to go to school, which was unusual for her. After her mother had to call her three times to get up, Mom sweetened the deal by telling Laura that she could take the car. Knowing she would be driving herself and not depending on Cupidity for a ride was enough to get Laura crawling out of bed.

Still Laura moved so slowly that she was nearly late to school. Pulling the white grandma-style sedan into the parking lot, she grabbed her books and dashed toward the main doors. She thought she had avoided most of the gossip and hoopla, but then Taryn ambushed her right inside.

"Did you hear? Did anyone tell you?!" she shrieked as

she grabbed Laura's arm. "Emma and Jake are . . . together!"

"I know," muttered Laura.

"Like *together* together. They're holding hands!" exclaimed Taryn.

"I heard they exchanged notes!" whispered Ashley, who grabbed Laura's other arm. "In the middle of the hallway!"

"I know, I know," repeated Laura as she tried to muscle her way through her friends. The whole corridor was abuzz.

Taryn shook her head and grumbled, "Jake's gotta be punkin' her out. It's a goof."

"No goof," answered Laura. "Think back, Taryn. I told you about this on the phone yesterday. It was after the fight."

"Crazy!" blurted Taryn. "You did! You're like . . . psychic!"

Ashley frowned in worry. "You know, my dad says they're putting too much fluoride in the water. Maybe it's causing us all to go crazy."

Laura sighed. "Tell your dad to give me a web address— I'm looking for an explanation." She charged ahead and ran into a muscular body looming in her path. He was dressed in really baggy pants and had multiple bandannas tied to his bag and his clothes. "Oh, sorry, Chester!" said Laura with a gulp.

Chester was one of the toughest guys in the school, but

he jumped back in embarrassment and looked past her. "Excuse me. Uh, Taryn, can I talk to you?"

"Sure, Chester," she answered, walking up to the looming presence, a curious look on her face. "You have chemistry before I do, so the test is whatever—"

"It's not about chemistry," he replied, gazing down at her with extreme earnestness. "It's about the Homecoming Dance."

Whoa! thought Laura. *Where did that come from?* Before she could hear more, Ashley grabbed her arm and dragged her away.

"Did you hear that?" she whispered. "Chester is asking Taryn to Homecoming. I *know* it's the fluoride!"

"No," answered Laura in a daze. "It's just the end of high school as we know it."

The warning bell went off, and the crowd in the hallway began to dissipate. On instinct, Laura wanted to hang back to see what was happening with Taryn. But she knew that it was a Homecoming invite, and she didn't want to get in the way—even if it was from as unlikely a source as Chester. Still, she thought curiously, she could chalk up one more unlikely match in this romantic dimensional distortion they were all suffering at Fimbrey High.

Before third period Laura met up with Cupidity outside biology class. The new girl looked a bit subdued and was dressed more demurely than usual; her belly button hardly showed at all, as befitted a teenager who had an actual parent at home. "Hey, I met your dad last night," said Laura. "You didn't tell me he was visiting you."

"Yeah," grumbled Cupidity. "I didn't know he was going to pop up. Quite a kidder, my dad—always likes a surprise. Look, we've got to get you fixed up. Have you seen Cody today?"

"I don't exactly travel in Cody's circle," admitted Laura with a puzzled expression. "But I usually see him by now, and I haven't."

"I think he cut school today," muttered Cupidity. "He probably heard about Jake and Emma, and he didn't want the competition for attention. I didn't know Emma and Jake would turn out to be such a high profile pairing."

Laura nodded sagely, while she tried to figure Cupidity out. "Yes, they sorta took the spotlight off Peter and Megan, who are even weirder if you think about it. Before you got involved in these people's lives, you didn't know them very well."

"Hey, I didn't make any of these people what they are," said Cupidity, sounding defensive. "Jake drooled on me before I pushed a single button—he can act like such a sleaze. Emma Langdon is tough enough to actually stand up to that big head of his. Maybe it will work out."

"Yeah, okay," admitted Laura, bowing her head. "They did look pretty happy together when I saw them yesterday."

Cupidity winked at her, suddenly full of the old spirit. "Don't worry so much. You just be ready for our double date tomorrow night."

Laura tried not to shiver, although another double date sounded more like a threat than a good time. Somehow she summoned the courage to smile and say with a sigh, "I'll be there."

By lunchtime Laura was moping through the hallways, trying to ignore the gossip and the buzz. Were two people falling for each other really worth all this excitement? The fact that it was Jake Mattson had a lot to do with it. She couldn't wrap her brain around any more surprises or unusual romances, so Laura tried not to talk to anyone. As she climbed down the central staircase, headed to her locker, she didn't realize someone was walking beside her until he spoke.

"I've got to talk to you," he said.

Laura lurched to a stop and stared at Peter Yarmench. He immediately bolted two steps ahead of her, as if he feared she would escape to the bottom floor. She could still turn around and run back upstairs, but she was too surprised to move.

"Where's your girlfriend?" asked Laura snidely. She instantly regretted her snippety tone, but it was already out.

"I ditched her," whispered Peter with a smile. "It wasn't easy, but I had a decoy lure her to the computer lab."

"Is that really a healthy relationship," asked Laura, "when you have to sneak around just to talk to an old friend?"

"No, it's not okay," he admitted, casting his troubled eyes downward and showing her a shock of unruly red hair. "I don't really understand this thing with Megan. It's . . . a little scary."

"Yeah, you look scared all right," said Laura, laying on the sarcasm. "She's Miss Popularity—isn't that what you wanted?"

He shook his head and lifted his startled green eyes to peer into hers, and he seemed to beg for understanding. "You know, it's really weird. I like . . . love Megan and all, and I mean, it's great having a girlfriend. But I really miss you. I mean, I miss us hanging around. You know?"

"I don't think Megan misses me," replied Laura. "And you can't be giving me the 'I just want to be friends' speech, because that's all we ever were—friends."

"I know." His shoulders slumped.

"Besides, you've got a girlfriend," she insisted, "and she

obviously doesn't want to share you—even with your old friends."

Peter held out his hand and touched her forearm, and a chill flew up Laura's shoulder. It reminded her of the night she was knocked out, the night Peter had woken up in Megan's arms. "I don't want to lose you," he said in a husky voice. "For some weird reason, falling in love with Megan has opened my eyes . . . and made me realize . . . well, how much I need you around."

Laura couldn't speak, there was such a knot in her throat. She didn't realize how badly she had wanted to hear this, but Peter's timing couldn't be worse. "Okay," she blurted, "so break up with Megan!"

"I can't *do* that." He grimaced and balled his hands into fists, as if he was being torn apart by internal conflicts. She felt sympathy for him, but she also hated him at the same time.

"Call me when you can," Laura muttered. "And lose the dramatics—they don't work."

She hurried down the stairs, trying to lose herself in the lunch crowd. *He wants two girlfriends,* she thought angrily. *Peter is just like Jake and Cody and all the rest of them—just in love with himself!*

After school Mercury sat in Cupidity's yellow convertible, waiting for the cherub-in-disguise to exit the school. He finally spotted her, surrounded by other teenagers, all of them yakking. Who could possibly be listening when they all talked at once? Nevertheless, Mercury was impressed by how many friends Cupidity seemed to have, and there was one handsome lad, dressed in black leather and silver chains, who would have commanded attention among the gods themselves. He even gave Cupidity a kiss on the cheek.

Before Cupidity reached her car, she bid her friends adieu, although several of them stared curiously at her "father." Mercury tipped his hat politely.

Cupidity gave him a smug smile as she climbed into the driver's seat. "See, I told you they all liked me, and I've got everything under control. Seriously, Mercury, you don't have to hang around here." She started the car engine with a loud *vroom*, and the fumes made Mercury wrinkle his nose.

"They've accepted you, but that doesn't mean you've done the job," said the elderly god with a sniff. "So far, you've paired up other mortals, but not Laura Sweeney."

"They were just warm-ups," insisted Cupidity as she backed the sports car out of its parking space. "I told you I was out of practice. Besides, we're talking about two lousy couples. That's nothing for me—in the old days, I'd do two pairs before breakfast."

"I've met Laura Sweeney," said the elder, "and it doesn't seem that it would be difficult to make a match for her."

The young lady laughed. "Ah, you don't know Laura that well. Outside she seems normal, but inside she's a fruit loop."

She motioned to a gang of students who clogged the sidewalk. "Most of them are ruled by their hormones, but Laura still depends on her brain. Makes it very difficult to get just the right match for her. Sure, I could pair her up with anyone—even you—but would she be happy?"

Mercury shrugged. "Who can guarantee a mortal happiness?"

"Hey, I've only had a few days to get to know her," said the cherub as her car careened around the corner, tires squealing. "You all agreed that I should have some time to get to know her, so let me do my job! Tell Jupiter and those worried old ladies that all will be well. I've planned a double date for tomorrow night, and I'm sure the arrows will be flying."

"Do you have someone picked out for her?" asked Mercury.

"Yes, Cody Kenyon. Maybe you saw him—black leather jacket, spiked hair, Elvis sneer."

"Oh, yes," answered elder with a knowing smile. "I approve."

"Well, good. So leave me the Hades alone!" Cupidity pulled to a stop and looked at the messenger god. "Can I take you to the airport?"

"Why can't I stick around?" asked Mercury, sounding hurt.

"Parents just get in the way." Cupidity stared pointedly at him. "Airport?"

"You just want to be able to smoke cigars again," muttered the god.

"Well, duh!" Cupidity scowled. "Listen, I'll be back at Mount Olympus when the job is done. You won't be missing anything."

"Remember, your disguise doesn't last forever," warned the god.

"I've got two more weeks!" scoffed the beautiful cherub. "I'll be out of here long before that, believe me."

Mercury sat stiffly in his seat. "Well, I was able to go to the office and fill out some paperwork for you. Perhaps you need me."

"That's good they got to see a parent," allowed Cupidity. "But I don't really *need* a parent—I'm three thousand years old! Come on, Merc, I took a couple extra shots as a warm-up, but now I'm ready to get down to business. You can see that everything is fine here."

"Okay, take me to the airport," grumbled Mercury. "We won't watch you or nag you—we'll just trust you."

"Good idea!" chirped Cupidity as the yellow convertible jumped the curb and headed off down the boulevard.

* * *

Right behind them came a white sedan driven by a pre-occupied Laura Sweeney. "Wasn't that Cupidity's car?" asked Taryn from the passenger seat. "She has the coolest car."

"Huh? Oh, yeah, I guess so," muttered Laura. In truth, she was still so miserable over Peter that she could barely concentrate on driving.

"She had an old guy with her," Taryn pointed out.

"That's her father." Laura brought the car to a stop at the corner and tried to snap out of her daze. "Listen, I'm going to the library. Where am I taking you?"

"To cloud nine," answered Taryn dreamily as she hugged her books to her chest. "Can you believe it? I've got a date for Homecoming!"

"Congratulations," answered Laura, trying to muster a smile. "Chester the Homeboy—who would have thought he was crushing on you?"

"Well, I catch him looking at me a lot in class," answered Taryn, "but I thought he was trying to copy off my paper." She laughed so joyfully that Laura couldn't stay jealous of her old friend's new relationship.

"Are you two going out this weekend?" asked Laura.

Taryn nodded gravely. "Yes, we're going to a rap concert. What do you wear to a rap concert?"

"I'm sure you can wear almost anything. Chester will look out for you."

They drove a bit farther in silence, Taryn gazing wistfully out the window and Laura trying to concentrate on the road. As they turned down the street to Taryn's house, Taryn said, "I know we made fun of Peter and Megan, then Jake and Emma, but I don't think Chester would have asked me out if they hadn't broken the ice."

"Probably not," admitted Laura. "Anarchy in the high school social order is a good thing." She pulled to a stop in front of Taryn's house. "Here you are—cloud nine."

Laura's friend squeezed her arm and looked sympathetically at her. "Don't worry, Laura, we'll get you a date too. Now all the boys in school are up for grabs—not just the ones you're *supposed* to date."

Laura mustered a smile, but that thought wasn't very comforting. Now she could be turned down by *any* guy in school. Taryn jumped out of the car and ran toward her house, no doubt anxious to spread the news about her date. Trying to be happy for her friend, Laura sniffed back her conflicting emotions and waved good-bye as she pulled away from the curb.

Since she had the car, she decided to drive downtown to the big library, where they had all kinds of old and rare books that weren't allowed to be taken out of the building.

Laura wasn't sure exactly what she was looking for, just some general research into the supernatural aspects of love. Cupidity might be a regular girl with a regular father, but *some* kind of love bug had infected the kids at Fimbrey. Maybe there was another explanation.

At the library Laura's footsteps echoed down the marble staircase and into the cavernous main chamber. A cold draft swirled around her, and she smelled the musty odor of old paper, fabric, glue, and dust—books. A door creaked somewhere in the old building, and she felt a chill. It almost felt as if these ancient tomes didn't want to give up their secrets. Maybe this was a stupid waste of time, but Laura felt as if she had to do something. It was research or go crazy.

She dove into the card catalog and computer listings and grabbed all the books she could find off the regular shelves. An hour of looking through them didn't really give her anything that she thought was pertinent to the love epidemic.

So Laura culled through the listings of rare and fragile books, which were kept in a special room and not allowed to leave the library. Clutching her requests, she found a librarian, an older woman in a business suit with flaming red hair, and gave her the slips of paper.

"Love spells, love potions, love candles, fortune-telling," said the old librarian, reading the subjects she had requested.

When she was finished, the old woman clicked her tongue and gave Laura a sympathetic smile. "You know, dearie, those love spells don't work. Why don't you try the personal ads, like I do."

"Personal ads?" said Laura with a nervous laugh. "I'm a little young for those." She didn't add that the librarian looked a little *old* for personal ads. "I'm really doing this for a school project. If you've got any books about Cupid or Venus, that would be good too. I've read all the mythology books on the shelf."

"Hmmmm," said the librarian, sounding impressed. She gave Laura a wink. "I'll bring you all the good stuff, but they don't have many pictures."

Laura laughed nervously. "That's fine. I don't need pictures . . . I have a good imagination."

"Give me a few minutes." The old woman tottered away, but she didn't return for almost half an hour. Laura had almost given up on her when she finally wheeled in a cart full of books, most of them old and tattered.

"You want the good stuff, right?" she said with a chuckle. "I hope you're not going anywhere for a while."

Laura sighed. "No, I'm not. No place else to go."

Laura Sweeney read and skimmed until the words on the yellowed pages blurred and the windows darkened except for pools of light from the streetlamps. A fierce wind kicked up, and branches scraped against the windows. The history of love, famous lovers, love spats, love spells and potions, and gobs of myths about love spilled from the books. Ghostly love, true love, tragic love, unspoken love, and lots of variations were discussed at length, sometimes with statistics. Laura learned more than she wanted to know about some topics, but she didn't find anything that would explain what was happening to the kids at Fimbrey High.

In all the morass of words and images, there were plenty of stories about Cupid and his mother, Venus. Laura's eyes were drooping as she leafed through one musty volume of Roman mythology, which she had read before. Normally she could lose herself for hours in a book like this, but her energy and hope were waning.

Suddenly Laura's bleary eyes landed on a picture of an old Roman fresco that had been uncovered in the ruins of Pompeii, Italy. The ancient image stopped her cold, and she blinked in amazement at the painting of Cupid and his mother. The youthful cherub wore long blond hair, making his face look an awful lot like Cupidity's. But that wasn't what startled Laura—it was the bow and arrow in his hands. The weapon looked remarkably similar to Cupidity's bow, down to its harp shape and ornate workmanship.

"What the—?" she muttered, rubbing her eyes. "That can't be."

"Did you say something, dearie?" asked the old librarian.

Gripping the book, Laura jumped excitedly to her feet. "Can you make me a photocopy of this page?"

"As long as the pages aren't too brittle," answered the librarian. The old woman grunted when Laura handed her the heavy tome, and she peered at the page with curiosity. "*That's* what you were looking for . . . a picture of Cupid and Venus?"

"It's perfect for what I need," answered Laura with a forced smile. *And that's to discover the truth about Cupidity,* she decided, *which I will do tomorrow night when I get a closer look at her bow. I have to find out whether I'm crazy or the rest of the world is.*

8

Smart Cody, thought Laura the moment she opened her front door and saw her date for Friday evening. Cody had enlisted a guy from another high school but of the same tribe as himself—a scruffy, handsome skater dude with spiky, dyed-auburn hair. Laura was reminded of Peter, who had real red hair, but she quickly put that image out of her mind.

"Laura Sweeney, this is my bud Rip Durkens," offered Cody, sounding like the perfect host. Cupidity stood on the step behind her date, looking pleased at his show of good manners. "Rip's a senior, too," added Cody. "He goes to the charter school down at the mall."

"Hi," said the scrawny skater, giving her a wry smile.

"I didn't know what to expect, but Cody never steers me wrong." He was charming, especially for someone who was trying to act tough, and Laura was definitely attracted to him.

Down, girl, she told herself. *You have no idea if Rip even wants to be on this date, or how long it's going to last. So just enjoy it for what it is.*

"Cupidity never steers me wrong either," lied Laura, trying to fit in with the theme of the evening. As she stepped out of the house, she yelled back, "Bye! We're leaving now!"

Nobody answered, because her parents were hiding again. The four students walked slowly to the car, and Laura asked, "So what's the plan? Burgers and a movie?" That's what they had talked about earlier, and she hoped it would be a somewhat normal date.

"Burgers, for sure," answered Cody, "then we've got a couple of parties to go to. And maybe we'll end up at Cupidity's place for a private party."

Hmmmm, thought Laura, not certain she liked the sound of that. "Is your dad home?" she asked Cupidity.

"No," Cupidity answered with a flip of her perfect blond hair. "Daddy Dearest went back to California last night. He just wanted to make sure I was settled in."

Cody laughed appreciatively and turned to his friend.

"Rip, can you believe it? Cupidity lives alone. No parents around."

"Niiice," replied Rip, casting a sidelong glance at Laura, who tried not to appear too sultry. "Cody and me are going to get a place, as soon as we graduate."

"Shouldn't college or a job come first?" asked Cupidity as they reached her car. Even though the air was getting chilly, she still had the top down.

"Ahh, we'll be on the pro skateboard circuit by then," answered Rip confidently. "You should see us on the half-pipe."

While they talked about their fantastic future, Laura walked to the rear of the car. She felt her back pocket to make sure she still had the picture of Cupid and his bow. "Cupidity," she called. "I've got this heavy purse—do you think I could throw it in your trunk?"

"Sure," Cupidity replied. Pulling a lever under the dashboard, she popped the trunk lid while she made conversation with the boys.

While they were occupied, Laura looked inside the trunk and saw the duffel bag she knew so well. Even though no archery was planned for tonight's date, Cupidity had still brought her bow and arrows with her, which was rather suspicious. Knowing this wasn't the right time to get nosy, Laura dropped her purse into the trunk and shut the lid.

Rip gallantly held the car door open for her with one hand while he pulled the front seat forward with the other. Laura could've jumped into the backseat, but this was nicer. As Laura climbed in, she began to worry about what Cupidity might have planned for them this evening. If she really was a female Cupid, then she was like a god. She could strike without warning, and Laura might find herself crazy in love with a wild skater boy by the end of the night. The prospect of turning into a love zombie, like Peter and Megan, made her shiver.

Suddenly frightened, Laura almost bolted from the car, but Cupidity started the engine and roared away from the curb, tires squealing. Cody laughed merrily at her reckless driving, and Laura buckled her seat belt. She felt a wiry arm around her shoulder, because Rip was already getting friendly. He didn't even need to be hit by a magic arrow.

"So what are you into?" Rip asked her. "What do you like to do in your spare time?"

"Well," she mused, "I had a job at the Dairy Queen, but I quit that when school started. I like to read."

"Read?" echoed Rip, as if he had never heard of such a thing. "Like what, magazines?"

"Greco-Roman mythology," she answered hesitantly.

Cupidity laughed and said, "Yeah, Laura is really into that stuff—all those silly gods and goddesses."

That remark ticked Laura off, and she decided to give Cupidity a little test. When they stopped at a traffic light, she said, "There are some great love stories in mythology, like Cupid and Psyche. Psyche was the most beautiful woman in the world, and Venus got jealous of her. So she sent her son, Cupid, to make Psyche fall in love with a monster, but instead Cupid fell in love with Psyche. But he was so short and funny-looking that Psyche ran away from him."

"Funny-looking?" scoffed Cupidity. "She never saw him—Cupid was invisible. It was all her stupid sisters!"

Cody gave his date a quizzical stare. "Oh, so you're an expert, too. But look at your name!" He laughed as if he was the first one who had ever made the connection.

Cupidity chuckled uneasily and glanced back at Laura. "I'm no expert . . . but I happen to know that story." As the light changed, she peeled away from the line.

They drove to the Gaslight, a 1950s-style diner where the waitresses wore poodle skirts and beehive wigs. It was a good enough place to get a burger, and Laura ate while Cody and Rip told stories about each other's exploits on skateboards, snowboards, and rollerblades. They were a mutual admiration society, and they were both ready to go pro, by their assessment.

All through dinner, Laura caught Cupidity gazing curiously at her, as if measuring her for an arrow. When Laura mouthed the word "What?" Cupidity shook her head and looked away. Even though her father had left, his visit still seemed to be having an effect on Cupidity. Tonight the new girl seemed uncertain, troubled, and just as real as anyone, and Laura began to feel guilty for thinking such bizarre thoughts about her.

I'm crazy, thought Laura. *She's just trying to do me a favor, and I'm so suspicious of her. How can I be so ungrateful?*

While the boys were laughing at each other's stories, Laura reached over and touched Cupidity's arm. "Hey, cheer up. I'm having a great time. I want to thank you for doing this."

Cupidity brightened. "Are you really? Good, I was beginning to think that it was all for nothing. You *do* want a boyfriend, don't you?"

"Yes, but it's got to be the right one," answered Laura. "Any dude off the street . . . I could do that myself."

"Am I 'any dude off the street'?" asked Rip with a chuckle. "What are you guys talking about?"

"Blind dates," answered Laura, lifting her glass of soda. "I'm all for blind dates. Here's to blind dates!" She hefted her drink in a toast, and everyone joined her.

"To blind dates!" they echoed.

"And you are not 'any dude off the street,'" Laura told Rip, shooting him what she hoped was a sexy look over the top of her glasses. He seemed appreciative, and he set down his burger to reach for her hand. It was a greasy grip, but Laura didn't yank her hand away. She had to get through this date as gracefully as possible and stop worrying about Cupidity.

After dinner, they jumped back into the convertible and took off, this time with Cody driving. It was so cold in the backseat that Laura welcomed the extra warmth when Rip sat close and put his arm around her. At one point he tried to kiss her, but Cupidity turned around and interrupted them. Laura couldn't tell if that was on purpose or not, but she was too cold to do anything but cuddle with Rip.

After a while they found themselves cruising the rust-belt outskirts of town, where abandoned factories, rusty grain silos, and run-down warehouses stood. Every window was broken in these dark derelicts of lost industry, and weeds grew on the railroad tracks that ran along the rear of the buildings. This sure wasn't the movies, thought Laura, and she wondered what kind of party could be happening out here in the boondocks.

Only one parking lot in the deserted district had any cars in it, and Cody pulled in there and parked on lumpy, cracked asphalt. With the top down, Laura could hear the muffled thumping of rock music coming from somewhere nearby, but it was drowned out by the chilly wind. She was thankful just to be arriving in civilization where there might be heat, and she almost jumped out of the car before Rip opened the door for her. He held the door like a perfect gentleman, and Cody rushed to do the same for Cupidity.

The guys smiled knowingly at each other, and Laura glanced at her buddy, who gave her a wink. *Cupidity's in charge here,* she told herself, *not these two smug boys.*

"This is a skater rave," explained Cody, putting his arm around Cupidity's tiny waist. "I think you'll have a good time, but you might have to do some skating."

"Skating?" asked Laura uneasily. "What kind of skating?"

"Skateboard skating," answered Rip as if that explained it all. "It keeps the old people away."

"You'd be surprised at what some old people can do," remarked Cupidity.

"Like what?" asked Cody doubtfully.

She laughed as if remembering something funny. "At this retirement home I know, they race their wheelchairs down the stairs. And they dive off the top floor into the swimming pool."

"Cool," said Cody in admiration. "And where do these crazy old dudes live?"

"In Los Angeles," answered Cupidity. "Where I used to live."

"That must be a blast," mused Rip, "living in L.A. and going surfing every day. Did you ever surf, Cupidity?"

"No, mostly I played pool and smoked cigars," she answered with a glance at Laura.

"That's my girl!" exclaimed Cody with a laugh. He gripped her tightly around the waist, making it difficult for them to walk very quickly across the pitted parking lot. Rip held Laura's hand, which was welcome, because her hands were freezing.

They circled around to the rear of the building, where a couple of skaters were standing in the shadows. The grimy warehouse had to be three stories high, and a row of windows across the top were all broken. The muffled music seemed to be coming from deep underground, and a strange smell wafted from the aged railroad tracks in the rear. They walked toward a pair of metal doors that were set at a sloping angle in the brick wall. Farther away a door opened, and a gang of giggling girls staggered out on their high heels.

The doormen approached the foursome, shining a flashlight in their faces. "Cody! Rip!" they shouted when they recognized the guys. They exchanged skaters' handshakes and punched each other in the shoulders like old friends.

"Dudes, you have picked a primo night to party with

us!" said the bigger of the two guards. "We're grindin' it tonight."

"Cool," said Rip. "You got a band or a sound system?"

"Sound system," answered the other doorman. "Like normally we would have to charge you five bucks each, but hot chicks like these two are always free." They couldn't take their eyes off Cupidity.

The new girl winked at Laura and said, "It's good to be hot."

Laura shivered, and her teeth chattered. "I don't feel hot at the moment."

"Here's your ten," said Cody, taking a crumpled bill from his pocket and paying for Rip, too. "The party's on me."

Cupidity gave him a grateful smile. "Thanks, sweetie, but we're not going to get busted here, are we?"

"Can't promise that, but you are going to skate to get in," said the smaller doorman. His partner pulled open the metal doors and revealed a long chute that led down into darkness and the din of a party. With a gulp, Laura realized that it was an old coal chute descending to the furnace room, probably long abandoned.

She laughed nervously. "I can't slide down there, I'll get all dirty. I'll take the door."

"You're not sliding." The big doorman pointed to what looked like a pile of lumber, but it was really a pile of old skateboards. Laura saw one of the girls teeter over to the pile and add a board to it. "Everybody skates down, especially first-timers," he explained. "It doesn't matter how hot you are."

Rip put a comforting hand on her shoulder. "There's like air mattresses and pillows down there. I'll go first and look out for you, and you just go down on your knees."

"On my knees?" she asked doubtfully, glad she had worn jeans.

"Come on!" called Cupidity, grabbing a battered old skateboard and heading for the door. Without a moment's hesitation, she knelt on the skateboard and pushed herself down the old metal chute, which rattled under the small wheels. Her delighted squeals pierced the night.

Cody took a board and hurtled down the chute in a crouch, and Rip was right behind him. He gave Laura an encouraging smile and a wave before he plunged into the darkness. Shivering more than ever, she grabbed a skateboard and noted the smirks on the doormen's faces.

"If I have to go to the hospital," she said, "I want to go to Mid City General."

"That's our favorite," answered the shorter one.

With a gulp, Laura edged toward the door and the dark chute. Once she got close, she realized that there was light and gaiety at the other end, along with many mattresses, which Rip was busy arranging for her. It was probably only twenty feet and not as steep as she feared; there was no sense putting it off.

"Xena!" she shouted as she had when she was a little girl, flinging her knees onto the skateboard and shooting into space.

Immediately she knew she was in trouble, as the wheels ground and squealed on the old sheet of metal. Certain she was going to fall off, Laura gripped the front of the board with her hands and screamed. The wild ride reminded her of sledding, which also scared her. Before she could catch her breath, she flew into space and landed in a comforting cloud of old mattresses, followed by Rip's strong arms.

For no good reason, he needed to fall onto the mattress with her and grab her shivering torso. Rip nuzzled her and gave her a brief kiss, which warmed her up at once. "You all right?" he asked with concern.

I'm good enough to kiss, she thought happily. Instead she smiled and said, "Can I get up and make sure I'm in one piece?"

"Oh, you're in one piece," he said, giving her body an extra squeeze. "What are you drinking?"

"Something legal," she answered.

Rip slid off her and vanished into the crowd, which was barely lit by a few strobes and some hokey discotheque lights. Pools of light and people were scattered throughout the huge basement, especially around the disc jockey and his sound system, but there didn't seem to be any good reason to light this dingy space. With all the smoke, it would be hard to see anyway.

Against the wall was a stairwell, which led to the exit they had seen before, and it was well marked by a sign. Some brawny straight-faced guys looked as if they were on security, but the crowd wasn't fighting. It wasn't as warm as Laura had hoped, but the crush of bodies and promise of dancing gave her some hope.

Cupidity bumped into her and shouted over the music, "Hey, princess, what do you think?"

Laura looked around at the funky surroundings and loud revelers and answered, "I just realized, skaters wear more corporate logos than anybody."

"No, I meant the *boys!*" said Cupidity, looking a bit frustrated. "Do you like Cody?"

Laura narrowed her eyes suspiciously at the new girl. "Why are you always trying to give me your dates? I have one of my own, and he can't keep his hands off me."

"Good," said Cupidity with a sigh. "So you like him and things are clicking. I was . . . I was asking about Cody for me, of course. I think he should ask me to Homecoming, even though I can't go."

"Why can't you go?"

"Well, I've got to go out of town that weekend," she answered. "Some family business in L.A.—it can't be changed. I may have to leave suddenly, so if you see that I'm gone, don't worry about it."

Laura tried not to look concerned about this information, because Cupidity was Cupidity. Still it got her thinking about her mission to compare her friend's fancy bow with the one Cupid had in Pompeii. Maybe she was all wrong about the girl's matchmaking skills, but she had to put her mind at ease.

"Homecoming is still a long shot," complained Laura. "Skater dudes aren't known for going to Homecoming."

Cupidity flipped her golden tresses and laughed. "Don't worry about that—these skater dudes will go to Homecoming and be happy about it."

Muscling through the rowdy crowd came Cody and Rip, carrying cans of some high-caffeine, high-energy drink. Rip also balanced a bowl full of potato chips on his head. The girls relieved them of their burdens, and they stepped away from the coal chute as more partygoers dropped in.

"Hey, I found a place to sit down!" announced Cody, yelling over the din.

"Where?" asked Laura doubtfully. She didn't see any furniture, not even a folding chair.

"On those mattresses on the floor, against the wall," replied Cody. "Come on!"

Carrying all their supplies, they trekked across the run-down warehouse basement until they reached a very shadowy, bad-smelling corner, where partyers lay sprawled about in odd positions. *This is the make-out place,* Laura realized, *and maybe the restroom, too.*

She pushed her drink back into Rip's hands and said, "I like this song! Don't you want to dance?"

Numbly he nodded his head, and Laura grabbed Cupidity's hand and pulled her back toward the masses. "Come on, we've got to shake some booty!"

"Yeah, thanks!" replied Cupidity as if she was glad to be rescued. Once they got to the dance floor, the new girl shed her coat and began to shake everything she had, which was a lot. To a frenzied song by some angry band, Cupidity gyrated wildly until she had every boy in the warehouse drooling over her. The girls glared at the stunning show-off, except for a few who were stomping along with the boys.

Cody was entranced by Cupidity's performance, and Rip watched his friend's date while he tried to talk to a third girl. Nobody was watching Laura, and she realized that this would be a good time to slip out to the car to inspect Cupidity's bow. She danced her way against the flow of the crowd until she made it to the stairway. Then Laura ran upward without even looking back.

The cool night air smelled wonderful after the smoke and odd odors below. The two skater doormen gave her a look as she walked past, but they were occupied with new arrivals. Laura dashed over the muddy, uneven parking lot until she reached Cupidity's yellow convertible, which stood out like a lighthouse. Earlier in the evening, she had seen Cupidity pull a lever under the dashboard to open the trunk of her car, which was a trusting way to secure it when she left the top down. But Cupidity didn't seem to be bothered by the things that bothered other people.

It took a bit of searching, but Laura managed to find all the levers—for the gas, the front hood, and the trunk. She stole a glance around to make sure nobody was watching her, and she saw nothing but silent cars in the unlit parking lot. With a rush of adrenaline, Laura popped the trunk and scrambled to the back of the sports car to see what she could find.

The courtesy light in the trunk came on, and there was her purse, right beside Cupidity's duffel bag. Laura reached for the bag to make sure it contained the precious bow and arrows, and she could feel the slender, carved lines of the aged weapon. It had to be specially made for someone so short. With trembling hands, she unzipped the bag and reached inside to pull out the bow. Laura had held the bag itself before, but she had touched the bow only once, briefly, on the first day when Cupidity had pulled it out of her locker.

She was going to use it even then, thought Laura with a shudder. *I should have seen it at the time, but who expects the supernatural in Denton, Ohio?*

Even as she drew the bow out of the duffel bag, she knew it was not just a curved piece of wood with the string already taut, ready for immediate use. No, this was an ancient artifact that had been painted many times, including very recently. It was now light brown, trying to look like a normal child's bow, but she could easily tell that it had once been gilded in gold, painted in gleaming white enamel, and encrusted with jewels. She didn't even need to take the photocopied picture out of her pocket to tell.

This is Cupid's bow, only Cupid is a girl. When did that happen?

An owl hooted somewhere overhead, probably from the broken windows of the deserted warehouse's top floor. Taking a deep breath, Laura reached back into the bag for the next piece of the puzzle. As soon as her fingers touched an arrow, it seemed to spring into her grasp as if eager to be unleashed.

She slowly lifted the old-fashioned missile from the bag and marveled at its intricate design and workmanship. The arrow tip was gleaming and sharp, but it seemed to be made of moonbeams that passed right through her fingers. The feathers of the fletching were as long and delicate as an eyelash, yet as stiff as a knife blade; they bristled from the shaft in vibrant colors, like the light beams from a prism.

Her hands trembled, yet her recent archery lesson came back to her as she lifted the bow and nocked the arrow to the string. The night wind sent a primitive feeling of power coursing through her veins, as if she were the greatest hunter in the world. Laura could imagine herself on the prowl, stalking the elusive prey—man and woman. Involuntarily, she drew back the arrow, and the bowstring tightened. Her arms tingled as if a current had suddenly connected through them, and her muscles ached to unleash the magical missile.

"No!" shouted a voice. Laura was startled and whirled in the direction of the sound just as she lost her grip on the shaft. The arrow flew straight from her hands and into Cupidity's heaving chest.

"Urrgh!" exclaimed Cupidity with a groan, and she staggered backward from the impact.

"They're not real arrows!" cried Laura, who was suddenly hysterical with the fear that she might have hurt

Cupidity. "The points aren't real!" She reached into the duffel bag to pull out another arrow, and she pointed it toward Cupidity, who was still staggering about.

"What are you doing? You psycho!" yelled a male voice. Cody charged between them, as angry as a young bull. All he could see was Cupidity flailing her arms helplessly, while her crazy friend pointed a bow and arrow at her.

"Give me that!" ordered Cody, lunging for the weapon. Laura flinched and poked him in the wrist with the arrow tip, and the arrow disappeared. "Ow!" he cried, recoiling as if from a shock.

While Cupidity crawled on the ground in the dirty parking lot, Cody began to twitch and gurgle. Laura gasped and watched in horror as his face went through a multitude of changes—disbelief, a flare of anger, followed by a puzzled expression as if he had forgotten where he was. A moment later, the dark lord of the skaters looked as if he would burst into tears.

"Cupidity!" he wailed.

9

Laura felt as if *she* was the one who'd been shot with an arrow in that dingy parking lot outside the skaters' rave. She didn't really start breathing again until she was sure that Cupidity and Cody were not seriously hurt by her careless missiles. Then she remembered that physical injury wasn't the real danger from Cupidity's arrows.

When Cody spotted Cupidity, he rushed to her side and gently picked her up from the ground, all the while kissing her like a puppy who was glad to see his master. "Are you all right? Are you hurt?" he asked worriedly. "Oh no, you skinned your knee!"

"It's nothing," she rasped, holding on to his arm for support. When she looked into his eyes, Cupidity broke into a dazed but ecstatic smile. "I couldn't be better . . . no way."

Laura nervously approached them, wringing her hands. "Uh, Cupidity," she asked, "do you know what happened to you?"

"What happened to me?" she repeated, looking as if her brain had been fried. All Cupidity could manage to do was hang on to Cody's arm, although both of them were swaying uncertainly on their feet. "I found my skater punk dude," she muttered, "that's what happened to me."

"Uh, yeah, for sure," agreed Cody. His trademark sneer completely gone, he gazed fondly at the petite blond. "I found my very own goddess tonight, and I'll never leave her side."

"Oh no." Laura groaned and covered her eyes.

"Codykins," asked Cupidity, batting her eyelashes at him, "will you go with me to the Homecoming Dance?"

"Whatever you want, Cupie Doll." They hugged each other blissfully.

"This is too much," murmured Laura, starting to panic. The ornate bow was still in her hand, and she waved it like a life preserver. "Cupidity, look at this bow! Don't you remember what you used to do with it?"

"Archery practice," answered the girl with a nod, then she snuggled into Cody's armpit. "I'm giving up archery."

"Don't you know what your name means?" asked Laura, begging her to come to her senses. Although she had never admitted to being Cupid, the new girl didn't seem to be putting on an act. She had been honestly smitten with her own dumb love bolt, just like Emma and Jake . . . Megan and Peter . . . and how many others!

"How do you reverse the spell?" Laura pleaded.

Cupidity just giggled and hugged Cody. "You're crazy, girl. I don't care that you got into my trunk and messed with my bow, I just didn't want you to hurt anyone. You don't need to come up with a wacky story to explain it."

"You're *Cupid*!" shrieked Laura. "Don't you know who Cupid is?"

"Sure, we know who Cupid is," answered Cody, "one of Santa's reindeers."

"That's so true!" chirped Cupidity, hugging him tighter. "You're so smart, Codykins! Let's go back inside and find one of those mattresses."

"Good idea," answered the skater dude, looking as if he had been brainwashed.

Laura wanted to scream, but instead she tried a desperate ruse. "I've got a terrible headache—can we end the date early and go home?"

"No," they answered in unison, turning their backs on her. Looking like the most darling, devoted couple,

Cupidity and Cody ambled arm in arm back to the party.

"Oh, you idiot!" Laura yelled at herself. "What have you done?" She threw the magic bow back into the trunk as if it were a live snake, then grabbed her purse and slammed the trunk shut.

Maybe Cupidity is just pretending to have amnesia, Laura told herself. *Maybe she's only punking me in order to stick to her lame cover story. But I shot her with one of her own arrows and pricked Cody a moment later—it's got to have had some effect! The two of them are exactly like the other Stepford Lovebirds.*

Laura stomped around the darkened parking lot, trying to forget the distant laughter and music, because she had to think. There were two possible explanations. One was that the Roman god Cupid was real, that she was living as a teenage girl in Denton, Ohio, and that she had just gotten amnesia. The other possibility was that Laura Sweeney was insane. At this point, she wasn't sure which explanation she preferred.

I might need proof, she told herself. Laura looked around to make sure that Cupidity and Cody had gone and left her by herself in the parking lot. That alone was suspicious behavior, because normally Cupidity wouldn't leave her bow and arrows for Laura to use again. She had rushed out here to stop Laura from handling the bow, and now she was willing to just walk away from it. That didn't seem likely.

For the second time that night Laura reached under the dashboard and pulled the lever to open the trunk. Gingerly she grabbed the bow and put it back into the duffel bag, making sure not to touch any of the arrows. After shooting the bow, Laura was sure it had powerful magic—so powerful that Cupid didn't have to be the one using it.

I could have the power of Cupid, she realized. *But I don't want it, especially if I might make as many bad decisions as Cupidity has. Look at the ridiculous couple I just created!* she thought in despair. *No, this is too much power for any teenager to have. But then again, what if I need proof?*

Despite her misgivings Laura again grabbed the duffel bag, stealing Cupidity's bow and arrows. She looked around and slammed the trunk lid shut before scurrying into the darkness.

As she walked back to the road, Laura pulled her cell phone out of her purse and dialed a taxicab company. Normally she would have called a friend, like Taryn, but Taryn was out with Chester tonight. Plus she didn't want to have to explain carrying a large duffel bag on a blind date, or what had happened on that blind date. Love was still in the air, like the flu, and Laura felt bad about making the epidemic worse.

Laura gave the taxi company her general location, then checked to make sure she had enough money to get home.

I'll figure it out, she told herself. *I'll do* something *to correct this.*

In time, headlights cruised down the road, coming toward her, and she recognized the slow-moving vehicle as her taxi. Laura waved it down and bounded into the backseat, anxious to get out of there. As she clutched the precious duffel bag to her chest, she realized that magical weapons could turn their bearers evil or insane. She knew she was taking a terrible chance keeping the bow and arrows, but it was a great relief to know the truth, especially about Peter Yarmench.

It's not Peter's fault that he's in love with Megan—he's under a spell, in the clutches of her undeserved affection. I have to save him!

Laura worried all night about what had happened and what to do, and by morning she was bleary-eyed and confused. She had almost convinced herself that she had to be crazy— no bow and arrow could make normal people fall madly in love with people they hated. Although it seemed that was exactly what had happened, especially with Jake and Emma. But then again, hate and love were similar, she had always been told, and maybe she had just let Peter be stolen by Megan. Only one person could really solve this mystery and tell her the truth: Cupidity.

So by eight o'clock Saturday morning Laura was waiting at the door of Cupidity's apartment, stomping her foot. She had already rung the doorbell twice, and then she heard stumbling sounds from inside. Laura was about to ring the doorbell a third time when it finally creaked open; looking disheveled and sleepy, Cupidity peered out through the slit.

"Laura," she croaked. "What are you doing here? There isn't school on Saturday, is there?"

"No." Laura pushed her glasses up her nose and tried to stay calm. "Can I come in and talk to you for a moment?" When the other girl seemed hesitant, Laura added, "It's an emergency."

"Oh, emergency," muttered Cupidity as she opened the door. "Hey, what happened to you last night? You disappeared on us!"

"Remember me telling you I didn't feel well?" answered Laura. "Well, I went home early. Besides, you didn't need me."

Cupidity smiled wistfully and scratched her ribs through her silky nightgown. "No, we sure didn't need you. What a dreamy night."

"You and Cody—" Laura wiggled her fingers instead of saying more.

"Me and Cody did what?" asked Cupidity, sounding offended. "He was a perfect gentleman—more or less . . ."

She strode into her living room and began to pick up various bits of trash. When she found the cigars on the mantel, she wrinkled her nose and touched them as if they were bugs.

"Ew! Where did these come from?" The blond girl marched into the kitchen and threw the cigars into the trash.

"Wait a second," said Laura. "You were smoking those cigars last time I was here."

"As if!" shrieked Cupidity, sounding totally offended. "My dad must have left them here. What's going on with you, Laura? You didn't make any sense last night either."

Laura stared intently at her friend and begged, "Please remember what happened last night. You're forgetting something important. You left the rave, came outside to your car, and found me holding your bow. You shouted at me to stop—do you remember that?"

"Yeah," she answered doubtfully. "Sure, I remember it. But mostly I remember Cody." A blissful look swept across her innocent face.

"I know we can't forget Cody," said Laura, trying not to get frustrated, "but that wasn't on your mind when you shouted at me. You didn't want me to hold your bow . . . because . . . because?"

"Because I didn't want you to hurt Cody." Cupidity

smiled sweetly at the thought of her beloved. "He's so smart and cute."

Laura rubbed her face, knocking her glasses askew. "All right. Let's back up a bit. Where did you say you grew up?"

Cupidity scowled. "What are you, my guidance counselor? I get asked questions all week long in school, and now I have to answer questions on Saturday?"

"You don't know where you grew up," declared Laura, "because you have amnesia. Last night you lost your memory."

"That's ridiculous," scoffed Cupidity. "I know *you*—I know my friends . . . and my boyfriend. And I know how you ditched poor Rip last night. Poor boy was heartbroken. Those skaters are like really sensitive, you know."

Laura sputtered with disbelief. "You've known all of us for a whole week! Do you remember your old friends, before you moved here?"

"I told you . . . I was homeschooled!" Cupidity folded her arms and stomped into the living room. "I don't care about my past, anyway. My life begins *now* . . . now that I've found Cody."

Laura followed her friend across the room, waving her arms. "But you've got to care, because that proves that you've lost your memory. The bow and arrows—don't you know what they *do*?"

"I don't care about the stupid bow," replied Cupidity.

"You can keep it—you're the one obsessed with it!" When the phone rang, she dashed toward the device as if she already knew who it was.

"Hello, Codykins!" she cooed, slumping into an over-stuffed chair. "Yes, I've been longing to hear your voice! Laura is over here now, and she's being a real grump. She doesn't even *care* that she devastated poor Rip last night. And she keeps asking me all kinds of weird questions about my past. Do you care about my past?"

She giggled and curled into a cute ball. "I didn't think so." After a moment, Cupidity looked up at her guest and said, "This is private stuff, Laura. Good-bye. And don't bring the bow and arrows to school anymore, like you did before. You'll get us in trouble."

While Laura clenched her fists and her mouth, Cupidity went right on babbling to her boyfriend. After a moment, her conversation degenerated into gooey baby talk, and Laura had to flee from the apartment. She climbed back into her mom's car and pounded her fists on the steering wheel.

I can't help any of them, she despaired. *They're doomed to mindless, pointless love.* From her misery, Laura thought of another friend who might be more helpful than Cupidity had been. She scrounged around in her purse for her cell phone and dialed Taryn's number.

"Good morning!" said an incredibly bright, cheerful voice.

"Taryn?" asked Laura uncertainly. "Is that you?"

"Well, of course it's me," she chirped. "I had a great time on my date last night. First of all, I wore my new tank top, the blue one—"

"Listen, I'd really love to hear this," lied Laura, "but I'm driving and I've only got a moment. Can I get a phone number from you and then call you back?"

"Hey, how was your date last night?" asked Taryn, oblivious to everything but love. "Did you hook up?"

"Yeah, he kissed me," said Laura, glad she could tell the truth. "Listen, what's the name of that psychic you once told me about? The Conjure Woman, you called her."

"Oooh," breathed Taryn, sounding impressed. "The one with the love spells? Are you that serious about someone? I want to warn you, Laura, once you get involved in that stuff, you may not be able to get out. It can backfire on you too."

"No kidding," said Laura sharply. "The number, please?"

"I'm looking! Madame Luisa is her name, or something like that." Taryn breathed a triumphant sigh. "Ah, here's the number."

As she rattled it off, Laura wrote it down on a slip of paper. She was uncertain whether she would have the courage to call the Conjure Woman, but she had to get help from somewhere. "Thanks," she answered glumly.

"Are you sure about this?" asked Taryn, "I didn't figure you to believe in love spells and stuff."

"Well, some things have changed my mind lately," admitted Laura. "What are you doing tonight?"

"Going out with Chester again," answered Taryn in a dreamy tone of voice. "And you?"

Laura shook her head. "I'm not sure yet, but I'll call you back later. I *do* want to hear about your date, really."

"Yeah," answered Taryn, "and since you're hunting for love potions, I want to hear about your date too."

Laura said good-bye and clicked off her cell phone. She stared at the number in her lap, wondering if she had the courage to call it. But doing nothing meant leaving things exactly the way they were, and that was unacceptable.

With determination Laura dialed the number. Nervously she tapped her steering wheel as the phone rang. Finally a sleepy voice answered, "Hello."

"Hello, I'm looking for Madame Luisa," she began.

"Well, you found her . . . at an ungodly time of the morning, I might add. What can I do for you?"

Laura gulped. "I need to see you."

"I can give you an appointment next Wednesday—"

"No!" exclaimed Laura. "I need to see you today!"

She heard a low grumble. "I'm booked up all day, from ten o'clock on."

"It's not even nine o'clock yet," said Laura. "Please! I'm desperate."

"Aren't they all?" muttered the sleepy Conjure Woman. "Do you have my address?"

"No, but I'm ready to write it down."

"Bring forty bucks with you too," added Madame Luisa.

Laura didn't know what to expect from the Conjure Woman's home, but she was still a little surprised to find a typical split-level ranch house in a nice part of town. Of course there weren't any steamy swamps in Denton, Ohio, so it might be hard to find a shack surrounded by gators and lightning bugs. Running around in the front yard were three little kids, wearing bath towels as if they were capes, and Laura had to dodge them on her way to the front door.

The door opened before she reached it, and Laura found herself confronted by a very tall woman with dusky skin but bright blond hair. She was dressed in jeans, a T-shirt, and a long cardigan sweater with a chain around her waist.

Madame Luisa looked surprised at the sight of her visitor. "You're a teenager? What problem can you have, being young and cute?"

"Plenty," answered Laura. "May I come in?"

"Sure, my consulting room is in the back. I've got a pot of tea brewing." Leading the way, the statuesque woman led her customer through a neat living room, down a long hallway, and into a bedroom in the back of the house. Looking around, Laura felt better, because this room was very atmospheric, with walls bedecked in religious symbols, candles, and artwork from around the world.

"You have all the bases covered," said Laura in amazement. She didn't add that Cupidity's bow would fit right in with the clutter of artifacts on the walls.

Madame Luisa shrugged. "You never know. Normally in a case like yours, I recommend Blue Succory. It makes a wonderful love potion—you can blow the powder up his nose or put it in his underwear, next to his skin."

Laura sat solemnly at the table and chose her words carefully. "That's not my problem. I'm looking for an anti-love potion."

The Conjure Woman sat at the table, scratching her blond hair. She gazed curiously at the girl and asked, "You want to get rid of a guy, right? I've got something you can put in your bath water—make you smell like a week-old fish."

"Ah, it's not something for me," said Laura carefully. "I can make people fall in love with each other, I just can't make them fall out of love."

"Is that right?" growled the tall woman, sitting back in her chair and looking very skeptical. "If you could really do that, then you'd ride up here in a limousine."

Laura leaned forward and narrowed her eyes at the Conjure Woman, hoping to convince her how serious she was. "If I can prove it to you, will you help me?"

Madame Luisa scowled. "How are you going to do that?"

Laura took a deep breath, then blurted, "You must have couples that you're supposed to get together. So give me one—their names, addresses, and stuff—and I'll make sure they hook up. I'll do your job for you, but just this once and with a pair who really deserve to be together."

"Whoa," replied Madame Luisa, looking impressed. "You seem to have confidence in this skill of yours. Okay, I'm going to give you a file, and you're going to fix them up."

She rose from her chair and walked to a closet, took a key from the chain around her waist, and unlocked the door. Madame Luisa disappeared inside the closet, but her voice boomed, "Honey, it's not fair that you know all about me—where I live, what my kids look like—and I don't know nothin' about you. Giving you this file, I'm putting a lot of faith in you . . ."

"I'll give you my address and phone number," offered Laura.

"There's pen and paper by the teapot."

Laura dutifully wrote down her details, wondering whether Madame Luisa was for real. She didn't want to put powder into people's underwear, and she really doubted if that would help. But she had made the offer, and she had wisely kept quiet about Cupidity's bow.

The Conjure Woman stepped out of the closet holding a file folder, and she carefully locked the door behind her. "Okay, your assignment is to put these two oldsters together," she said, tossing the folder onto the table. "She's rich, and she's my client. They're truly in love, but he won't marry her because he's proud about money and his independence. Otherwise, they'd be hitched. So you really only have to work on him."

"They'll both be completely smitten by tomorrow," Laura promised grimly. She opened the folder to find photos and extensive notes about one of the wealthiest and most famous women in town, Dorothy Planchett. "Wow, she has trouble finding a husband?"

"No, she's got him going, but he just has issues," said Madame Luisa. "You think you can wipe them out?"

Laura closed the folder and rose to her feet. "Mr. Barclay won't know what hit him. I'm going to do you this favor to prove that what I say is true. But in return you need to promise me that you will show me how to make people fall *out* of love."

The Conjure Woman picked up the paper with Laura's information. "Hey, I'm good for it. I didn't charge you the usual forty bucks, did I, Laura Sweeney?"

"No," she answered, moving toward the door, "but I need more than a discount—I need help."

Madame Luisa didn't say anything as she escorted Laura Sweeney outside to her car, and the cautious girl locked the file folder in her trunk. The Conjure Woman didn't entirely believe her story, but she knew when people were sincere—and desperate. The girl believed she could conjure love spells, even if she couldn't.

As soon as Laura drove away, Luisa pulled a cell phone out of her sweater pocket and dialed a number. "Arnie, it's me. Get your notebook, because I've got a job for you. I want you to tail somebody for me."

10

Laura felt like a stalker. Not only that, but she was armed with what looked like a deadly weapon. Thinking about how shady she must look, she crouched in the hedges running along the parking lot of the Institute for the Blind in downtown Denton. She had checked the social calendar in the newspaper and found that Mrs. Dorothy Planchett was attending a fund-raiser for the institute that night, and Mr. Roger Barclay was also scheduled to attend.

It was nearly ten o'clock at night, and the event had started at six. Well-dressed people were beginning to leave, and her chance was coming—but so was an attack of the nerves. Shooting Cupidity and Cody in the parking lot had been an accident, but deliberately turning this powerful love spell on two strangers was difficult. It didn't really help to know that one of them had asked for it.

What if I miss? thought Laura. *I'm not half the archer Cupidity is.* She thought about waiting for the couple at Dorothy Planchett's mansion, but the place was a fortress with a high brick wall. Plus she had no guarantee that they would be going back there after the fund-raiser. It was here and now—this might be her only chance. At least the bow was a silent weapon.

The night was dark with no moon, but the parking lot was brightly lit and Laura could see clearly. But then again, so could everyone else. What if she was caught? Not everyone coming out of the institute was blind. And in fact, the lovebirds might be with other people.

Wait a minute, she told herself, *I don't actually have to shoot them with the arrows. I only had to poke Cody with one by accident, and that worked.* She had a feeling that the second arrow would find its mark without much trouble, because love gathered momentum once it was launched.

Laura was distracted by a burst of laughter, and she turned to see six elegantly dressed attendees emerge from the institute. Catching her breath, she lifted her binoculars and watched them amble down the walkway to the parking lot, talking and laughing. She instantly recognized her quarry, that distinguished older couple Dorothy Planchett and Roger Barclay. How was she going to do this? The parking lot was starting to get crowded with people.

If I'm not careful, I'm gonna end up in jail, Laura thought ruefully. She realized that every time Cupidity shot her little bow, there had always been a distraction. The paintball attack, the fight between Jake and Peter—that's why she didn't get caught. Laura worked her way through the bushes, braving the thorns and stickers until she reached the other side. Then she screamed as loudly as she could.

That stopped the partygoers in their tracks, and they shouted and pointed. To make sure, Laura grabbed the bushes and shook them as she screamed again. Dorothy and Roger hurried over to check it out, while Laura dashed around the end of the hedgerow in order to flank them. While they were searching the bushes, she hoped to catch them from behind.

Laura was reaching into the duffel bag to grab the bow and arrow when she ran right into a chubby security guard. "What is going on?" he asked her nervously. "I heard a scream!"

"Robbers!" she answered, clutching the duffel bag to her chest. "They tried to steal my purse, then they hauled somebody else into the bushes. There they are!" Laura pointed to the two dark figures forty feet away, crawling among the hedges.

Looking jittery, the security officer drew his club. "I'll fix them. You wait here!"

She didn't wait there but followed the guard at a discreet distance. She saw him grab the distinguished older man and threaten him with his club, while Dorothy Planchett began to argue and point at the bushes.

There was no more time to think about it. Laura grabbed her bow and arrow and let the duffel bag fall to the ground. While everyone was busy talking at once, she nocked the arrow to the string, pulled it back, took careful aim at Mrs. Planchett, and let fly. The arrow streaked through the darkness into the clutch of people, and she heard a loud yelp.

Before she had any more time to think about it, Laura grabbed another arrow and nocked it to the bow. Now people were looking around, trying to figure out what was happening. The security guard walked back toward her, waving his hands, and she cut loose with the second arrow. It was intended for Roger Barclay, but the brave security guard jumped in front of the arrow and took it in the chest.

"Oops," said Laura, quickly jumping into the bushes and ducking out of sight.

She didn't have to worry about the security guard anymore, because he staggered for a few steps, then keeled over onto his stomach. Dorothy Planchett ran to comfort the fallen guard, and she slumped over him and cried, the same way Megan had wailed over Peter. Roger Barclay just stood around, looking confused.

There was great commotion, someone went to call an ambulance, and the parking lot was soon full of concerned people. In due time, it became clear that nobody was really hurt, but Dorothy Planchett was distraught over the security guard. While the rich widow fussed and fawned over the dazed man, Laura tried to sneak away.

"Thanks," said a voice in the darkness. "You just made my richest client fall in love with a nobody half her age."

Laura skidded to a stop as Madame Luisa stepped out of the shadows, staring grimly at her. There was a seedy man lurking behind her, wearing a dark suit and a Panama hat.

"Madame Luisa!" said Laura with a start. "What are you doing here?"

"Came to see how you work your miracles," answered the Conjure Woman, stepping toward her. "You're not impressive, but that little archery set sure is."

Laura clutched the duffel bag protectively. "I . . . I don't know what you're talking about."

"I'm a big strong woman, and you're just a little slip of a girl," said Madame Luisa with a sly smile. "What's to keep me from just *taking* it from you?"

"Nothing," replied Laura evenly. "But I warn you . . . this bow is cursed. Your own love life will nose-dive, and you may totally freak out—like the person I stole it from. She doesn't even know who she is."

The imposing woman narrowed her eyes and gazed deeply into Laura's soul. The girl felt herself tremble as the Conjure Woman studied her, but she had been honest, and so she was able to stand her ground.

"Bless me, child, you're telling the truth," said Luisa, her voice barely a whisper. "You're right, it is bad juju to steal an item of power. I just wouldn't feel right about doing that."

Laura breathed a sigh of relief. "Oh, good. Then you'll help me reverse the spell?"

"I wouldn't feel right about it," said Madame Luisa, "but my friend Arnie doesn't care so much." She snapped her fingers, and her henchman rushed forward and tried to grab the duffel bag out of Laura's hands.

Laura struggled and managed to hang on, even though she was tossed around the parking lot like an old rag. Finally she let out the same piercing scream she had used earlier, only now it really was a plea for help. "Robbers! Robbers!" she shouted.

Her cries attracted attention, and three onlookers started walking toward them. "Arnie, let's get out of here!" hissed Madame Luisa. "She'll let her guard down eventually." With a malevolent glare at Laura, the Conjure

Woman slipped away into the darkness, followed by her hired thug.

"This magic stuff really sucks," muttered Laura as she shoved the duffel bag into the bushes. When the partygoers reached her, she pointed after the fleeing figures. "They took my purse. Please get it back!"

"Absolutely," said one of the men, charging after the fleeing pair. Another followed him, and the third man looked at Laura with concern.

"Are you all right?" he asked. "What the heck is going on here?"

"Purse thieves," she answered breathlessly. "They hit us all at once. Better get after them!"

"Okay." The man nodded and took off, and Laura dragged the duffel bag out of the bushes and dashed in the other direction. She was so scared and upset that she didn't stop running until she was almost home.

Oh, what am I going to do? thought Laura desperately. *Peter is in love with that stuck-up Megan. Cupidity is so gaga over Cody that she's forgotten who she is. Jake the jock is madly in love with über-Goth Emma, which has thrown the entire social order of the school out of whack. The Conjure Woman is trying to steal the bow from me. I just made the wrong couple fall crazy in love, and I still don't have a date for the Homecoming Dance!*

Only one thing was certain, Laura decided grimly: Cupidity's bow and arrows were the real deal.

Monday at school was awful, because it seemed as if everybody was part of a blissfully happy twosome except for Laura. Plus all day long she imagined that Madame Luisa and her evil henchman were stalking her, trying to find the magic bow. It wasn't there—it was in Laura's locker with a brand-new combination lock, but that wasn't very comforting. Not only did she have a weapon at school, but any moron could break into a locker. It happened every day.

Also, it seemed that the entire school was in the throes of preparation for Homecoming, only two weeks away. Fimbrey was a basketball school, and the football team was often mediocre. Still it was a big deal when they came home to play after their road trips to Marion and Mansfield, and the Homecoming Dance was as big as the spring formal. Watching all of her friends, from Taryn to Cupidity, making big plans for the dance made Laura even more depressed.

But it was Cupidity who delivered the final blow. With Cody lurking only a few feet behind her, she ambushed Laura in the hallway after lunch. "Sweeney, I have to talk to you," said Cupidity importantly.

Laura stopped and forced a smile as she turned around. "Yes?"

The petite blond crossed her arms and looked quite stern. "Cody and I agree—we don't want you around anymore in the Cupidity group."

"Because you're a nut!" added Cody from the cheap seats.

Laura's mouth hung open. "The Cupidity group? Sounds like an online dating company. Are you saying you don't want to be friends with me anymore?"

"That's right," answered Cupidity, "and you've got to stay away from my other friends, like Jake, Megan, and Peter."

"What?" asked Laura, aghast. "That's ridiculous! I haven't done anything to any of you."

Well, except for accidentally hook you up with Cody, Laura thought. *But she's deliberately pulled the same trick on lots of people, only she doesn't remember.*

"There's just something weird about you," said Cupidity. "The way you like that bow and arrows . . . and all those old Roman gods."

"*Me?*" responded Laura in amazement. "You say *I'm* weird, when you can't even remember what you were doing a week ago? And the bow and arrows belong to *you!*"

"Yeah," said Cupidity with a puzzled expression, "I can't remember why I bought those things. But anyway, you need to be more normal again before you can hang with us."

Laura rolled her eyes. "Whatever. If you only knew how abnormal *you* are."

"Hey, who are you calling abnormal?" snapped Cody, swaggering up to Laura. "That's my woman you're talking about . . . and the future Homecoming Queen. Maybe the future Mrs. Cody Kenyon."

Laura tried not to cringe. After all, it wasn't entirely his fault he was goofy in love. "I hope you'll be very happy," she said, although she was plotting how to break them up. "But you can't tell me who to be friends with."

"We'll see about that," said Cupidity with a sniff. She whirled on her heel and marched away, while Cody gave Laura his trademark sneer.

Laura went through the rest of the day in a blur. She felt that the whole school was looking at her, pointing her out as the girl who was condemned by Cupidity. Taryn and her old buds were friendly to her, but they only wanted to talk about boys, the dance, and boys. Laura was fed up with romance; it seemed like a fever that had affected all their minds.

The funk lasted all day until she caught sight of Peter Yarmench, waiting for her after her last class. Laura looked around to make sure that Megan and Cupidity weren't going to ambush her, but they didn't seem to be around. The hallway was crowded, and Peter was standing in an alcove by the drinking fountain.

Laura tried to act cheerful as she approached him. "Hi!"

"Hi," he answered, looking down as if he were embarrassed. "I heard about what Cupidity said to you, and I think she's really out of line."

"Thanks," answered Laura, smiling for real.

"So what if you're a little whacko," said Peter. "We all get that way sometimes."

Laura frowned. "How am I whacko?"

"Well, you stole Cupidity's bow and arrows and made her out to be a nutcase," answered Peter. "And you ditched three people in the middle of a double date."

"I remember that you once ditched *me* on a double date," said Laura, glowering at him. "There's a lot more to this than you understand, Peter."

He leaned against the wall and smiled. "And Taryn told me that you went to see some kind of witch doctor . . . the Conjure Woman?"

"That loudmouth," muttered Laura. "Forget about my problems. Look around you, Peter. Look at yourself. You've never dated anyone in this school before, and now you're dating the head cheerleader. The Prince of the Preppies is going out with the Queen of the Goths. Homeboys are dating geeks, skaters are with debutantes—it's all messed up. Not that it's entirely bad, but do you ever remember high school being like this?"

"It's kind of nice," said Peter. "Everyone is getting a date to the dance."

Laura winced, and Peter instantly regretted his remark. "No, I mean, there's you . . . you still have time. Oh, Laura, I'm sorry. Listen, I'll talk to some of the guys and—"

"No!" she yelled, backing away from him. "No more matchmaking!" Unsure why she was so mad at him—when it wasn't *his* fault—Laura turned and scurried away from her old friend.

"Laura!" he called after her, but she didn't stop.

As if this day could be any more wonderful, Laura found a police car parked in her driveway when she reached home. Instantly she lifted the duffel bag and clutched it tightly to her chest; she could almost feel the tingle of danger coming from the magic bow, and she knew it was threatened. As she slowly walked toward the front door, it opened, and her father escorted a uniformed police officer out.

"I think that's all we need," said the officer, closing her notebook.

"Oh, here's my daughter," said Ed Sweeney, pointing to Laura. "The house is okay, honey, but it's quite a mess. We had a break-in."

"Oh no!" exclaimed Laura. She tried to look more surprised than she felt. "Did they . . . did they take anything?"

"Oddly, not much," answered her father with a puzzled expression. "Some of your mom's jewelry had been lying out, and they took that, but they left a lot of electronics and appliances and stuff."

The police officer gazed suspiciously at Laura. "It looks like they tossed your bedroom worse than the others. Do you have any idea what they were searching for?"

"No!" She gave a nervous laugh.

"What's in the bag?" asked the officer.

"Just my books . . . and a prop for the school play." Laura began to open the bag.

"That's all right," said her father, looking a bit annoyed with the police officer. "My daughter is a straight-A student who's never been in any kind of trouble. She can't have anything to do with this."

"All right," said the officer. "Take an inventory, then let me and your insurance company know exactly what they took. You might want to put in a burglar alarm when you fix that broken window in back."

"We probably will," he agreed. "Thanks for coming so quickly, Officer."

"That's my job." The police officer tipped her hat and returned to her patrol car.

In shock, Laura watched the officer drive away, and her father put his arm around her shoulders. "Hon, don't let the questions bother you—it's not your fault. We've got lots of cleaning up to do. Why don't you start with your bedroom, and I'll work downstairs."

But it is *my fault,* Laura wanted to shout. *I have a magical bow, and villains are trying to steal it!* She wanted to tell her father the truth so badly, but she knew she would have to use the bow in order to prove it. And she didn't want to do that again.

"I don't feel very well," she said, already planning to stay home tomorrow to protect the precious bow.

He frowned. "Seeing your room won't make you feel any better."

Glumly Laura climbed the stairs and stepped cautiously into her bedroom. When she saw the ripped pillows, torn mattress, overturned dressers, broken lamps, and scattered papers, she began to cry. Her most private possessions were scattered all over the floor, and she felt violated. It didn't bring any comfort that she still had the object they were looking for, because the bow had done nothing but make her life miserable.

I ought to just give it to them, she reflected. But Laura couldn't stand to think what Madame Luisa would do with such a powerful weapon. It made her shiver with fright.

I ought to destroy it, she thought. She could burn the stupid bow in the fireplace, but she worried that she needed it to reverse the spells. Besides, it was an artifact from a magical time three thousand years ago, and destroying it was like destroying one of the wonders of the universe.

Unsure what to do, Laura sat on her shredded bed and cried.

11

Laura Sweeney didn't go to school for a week. Since she almost never missed school unless she was deathly ill, her parents barely questioned it. After a while they took her to the doctor, and he couldn't find much wrong with her. But there was a low-grade fever going around, and Laura was careful to keep the thermometer no higher than a hundred when she heated it on the lightbulb.

There was a lot of straightening to do at the house, and workers came to fix the window and measure for a burglar alarm, which would be installed next week. Still Laura didn't feel entirely safe sitting home all alone while her mom and dad were at work. She did more cleaning than a sick person really ought to do, and maybe that was another reason her parents didn't complain. Her mom made sure she got her schoolwork assignments from her friends.

Taryn came over often, but she was depressing with her talk of Chester, the Homecoming Dance, and the dresses they were all going to wear. Laura tried to act enthusiastic for her friend, but she was afraid she didn't fake it very well. She kept hoping and dreading that Peter would come over to visit, but he never did.

According to Taryn, Megan was keeping a short leash on Peter, especially after it became known that he had talked to Laura in the hallway. He had also broken Cupidity's edict not to socialize with Laura, and Cupidity and Megan were best buds now. Laura considered just leaving the mismatched couples alone, but she felt personally responsible for Cupidity. Plus she didn't believe Peter was happy with Megan, and he seemed honestly torn.

The question is, can I battle the perfect cheerleader to win Peter's heart—even when they share a love spell? Laura didn't know the answer, and it was easier lying in bed thinking than taking any kind of action.

What kept her alert was the certainty that Madame Luisa and Arnie were out there somewhere, waiting for her to let down her guard. Twice in one day she thought she saw a white van cruising slowly past her house, and her phone rang with constant hang-ups.

By Thursday she had decided that sitting in the house, guarding the Cupidity Stupidity bow, was driving her crazy. And it wasn't doing anyone any good. *I've got to do something,* she realized. *The dance is only eight days away.*

It was time to stop being scared and go back on the offensive. No one else knew about the magical weapon, except Cupidity, who had forgotten what she knew about it. *How can I free the love zombies?* Laura wondered. *Who could help me?*

Cupidity's father, came the answer. Although she had met him only once, she had a feeling that he knew more about his strange daughter than he had let on. But how could she contact him when he lived in California? Maybe there was a phone number or an address in Cupidity's apartment.

Laura collected all the arrows she had hidden around the house and put them into the duffel bag with the bow. Carrying her prize, she headed outside. She didn't have a car, so she had to walk to Cupidity's apartment—but she had plenty of energy for that. The new girl would be in school this time of day, and Laura would have to break into her apartment. She wondered if she would have the courage to do so.

After half an hour of brisk walking, taking alleys and side streets, Laura stood outside Cupidity's luxury apartment complex. In the middle of a chilly September afternoon, most of the residents were at work or school. Dried leaves skittered across the sidewalk, and the trees waved their bare, skeletal branches at the slate sky.

The gloom matched Laura's mood, and she nearly turned away from Cupidity's door. If she had to break in she might get into more trouble. Then she decided that more trouble was barely possible, so Laura took a deep breath and tried to buck up her own spirits.

Come on, girl, you've dreamed all your life about the great heroes and fools in Greco-Roman mythology, and now it's happening in real life! Think of this as a play starring you. The only problem is, you don't know whether it's a tragedy or a comedy. . . .

On impulse, she reached for the doorknob and turned it, and the door creaked open. Laura jerked in surprise, but she knew that lots of people in Denton left their front doors unlocked. Plus Cupidity was a ditz—and getting ditzier every lovesick minute. She hefted her duffel bag, pushed open the door, and stepped into the empty apartment.

"Whoa," muttered Laura. The place had none of the elegance she had seen before. Now it looked like a teenager's bedroom, with posters of rock stars, Mardi Gras beads, stickers, and other knickknacks covering the walls. Notes and papers lay scattered across the floor, and dirty plates and fast-food wrappers covered the tables. It was obvious that Cupidity had stopped keeping house after getting amnesia.

As she kicked a mass of papers out of her way, her spirits sank. There was no way she was going to find anything helpful in this mess. If she wanted to be nasty, Laura figured she could always turn Cupidity over to the authorities as a minor living alone, but that would only cause trouble. It certainly wouldn't do anything to free Peter and the others, and it wouldn't free her from the burden of what was in the duffel bag.

Laura heard shuffling behind her, and she realized that she wasn't alone. She was about to reach into the bag for her weapon when a voice said, "That won't be necessary, Laura."

She whirled around and saw Cupidity's dapper but frail father, looking rather disgusted at his surroundings. "Apparently we both came to the simultaneous conclusion that something had to be done," he said, removing an elegant silk glove from his hand.

Laura stammered, "I, uh . . . do you know . . . there's something in this bag. How much do you know about your daughter?"

"Too much." The elderly man gave her a sour frown and looked down at the duffel bag in her hands. "Do you know you're the first mortal to have used that bow? And you say it's been working for you?"

In shock, she nodded.

"Remarkable. All these years, we never really needed

that obnoxious cherub. I'm not his father, and I couldn't tell you who is." The elder held out his ungloved hand. "My name is Mercury, the messenger god."

Laura felt herself swooning, and she looked down at his elegant wing-tipped shoes. Like ghostly banners, real wings seem to sprout from his heels, and Laura fell backward. His outstretched hand caught her, and his strength was effortless as he steadied her.

"You're . . . you're a Roman god?" she asked, sounding more doubtful than she felt.

He sighed. "I know you haven't seen many shrines to me lately, but I used to be quite the rage."

"And you're not Cupidity's dad?"

"Cupidity is Cupid in disguise," he answered with a frown. "And now he's madly in love with a skater boy, thanks to you."

Laura's face brightened with hope. "Is this like old Greek dramas where the god shows up to fix things? *Deus ex machina?*"

"No!" he snapped. "This is reality. I suppose I could take that bow from you and make matters worse—like you did—but I can't fix love problems."

"Who can?" asked Laura desperately.

"Cupid's mother," said the god, thin-lipped. "Venus."

Laura moved toward the door. "Well then, let's go get

her. Come on! You're the messenger god—send her a message!"

Mercury lifted his white eyebrows. "It won't be that easy. Venus doesn't live with the rest of us. She can be difficult to approach, and frankly, none of the gods want to deal with her. *You* will have to approach her."

"Me?" asked Laura in shock. "That doesn't seem very fair. Isn't she your sister or something?"

Mercury pursed his lips and replied, "It is eminently fair since it was you who involved the gods in the first place. Don't you remember calling on Jupiter to bring you a boyfriend?"

Laura racked her brain and finally remembered back to that rainy night after the first day of school. She gasped. "Whoa there! I said that one night, yes, but I thought it was like a . . . rhetorical request."

"Well, we didn't take it that way," sniffed Mercury. "We're very passé, not a lot of people believe in us anymore. Not like the olden days when Julius Caesar's battle cry was 'Venus Victrix!' He never would have gotten so far without her help. Ah well, I guess this Cupidity affair just proves that we're old and useless."

"That's a little harsh," replied Laura, touching the old man's arm. She blinked at him in realization. "You mean, you sent Cupid in disguise to help *me* get a boyfriend?"

Mercury sighed. "Yes, Cupid wanted to get to know you as a friend . . . to know who was best for you."

"Wow," murmured Laura, "he sure screwed up."

The old man grabbed the duffel bag and shook it angrily. "You didn't help matters by piercing Cupid with one of his own arrows! Since you started this, you must end it. You must be the one to come to Los Angeles and approach Venus."

Laura gulped and pushed back her glasses. "How tough can that be?"

"Let's put it this way," said Mercury, "Venus has tamed all her boyfriends, including the Minotaur. And she doesn't know anything about Cupid's assignment, because we were afraid to tell her."

"Uh-oh." Laura began to wring her hands. "You know, I can't just like . . . fly off to Los Angeles. I have a mom and dad, and these two creeps are trying to steal Cupid's bow."

"I'll take care of them," promised Mercury as he handed her back the duffel bag with the precious cargo. "You have the power to distract your parents. They won't even remember they have a daughter." He pointed to the duffel bag.

Laura felt the curve of the bow in her hand and winced in disgust. "Use it on my own parents?"

"It's for a good cause," said Mercury, "and you don't have much time."

"What do you mean, I don't have much time?"

The elegant elder paced the floor, kicking the wrappers and papers with his wingtips. "Cupid will soon lose his disguise—no more Cupidity. I see he's been partying as usual."

"Probably more than usual," answered Laura, "considering who he's with. Will changing back cure his amnesia?"

Mercury shook his head. "I don't know, but his disguise lasts only twenty-five days. It is over at midnight a week from tomorrow."

Laura's eyes widened in horror. "That's the night of the Homecoming Dance, and she'll be there with Cody. *He'll* be there . . . whatever. You're right, I don't have much time."

"We will have to find Venus first," said Mercury with a sigh, "and I will have to get approval for all of this from Jupiter. I don't see how he can turn down a brave mortal who is willing to seek Venus on his behalf." The dapper god looked intently at her. "You are willing, aren't you?"

Laura nodded, unable to speak. *I do seem to be the starstruck heroine of this drama,* she thought. *And somehow I've become the fill-in Cupid while the real one is out sick.*

Mercury lifted a well-manicured finger. "Be ready at midnight Saturday night, and I'll come for you. I can't do much about love, but I'm fairly good at transportation. Don't worry about luggage, we'll supply what you need.

Bring the bow, as having that will get Venus's attention."

Mercury gave Laura a wrinkled smile. "Do take care of your parents first—try giving them a *romantic* gift, if you know what I mean. I'll see you Saturday night."

He tipped his hat and strolled out the front door, as Laura gripped the bow through the heavy nylon of the bag. Now all of her questions had been answered; like the heroes of most Greek tragedy, she was in the middle of a mess of her own making. Numbly Laura walked toward the door and decided, *I've got one more place to go.*

Through binoculars Laura could watch all the happy couples filing out of Fimbrey High School from her hiding spot behind a telephone pole on the far side of the parking lot. Despite the distance, she could see Megan and Peter, holding hands and joking with Cupidity and Cody. Behind them came Emma and Jake; Jake was wearing dark gray instead of his usual pastel collared shirts, and Emma had on a cardigan sweater.

Laura lowered the binoculars and rubbed her eyes, but she soon went back to spying. It was getting colder, and Cupidity had actually pulled the top up on her convertible. The golden couples didn't linger long in the chilly parking lot, but she could imagine them making plans to meet later. Peter looked happy with his cheerleader, although she caught him glancing over his shoulder in her direction. She knew he couldn't see her, but it was still eerie.

Finally Laura spotted the person she really wanted to see—Taryn, accompanied by her man, Chester. Were they genuine, or had they been smitten, too, by the magical arrows? It was impossible to tell fake Cupid love from real love, although it was clear that some social barriers had broken down. She had the means to break down more of them—think of the havoc she could wreak among this crowd of unsuspecting students.

Laura found that she was gripping the bow through the nylon of the duffel bag. She took her hands off the curved weapon and let it fall back into the bag, and the impulse to shoot it went away. *It's hard to have power and not abuse it,* she thought.

Fortunately, Chester and Taryn were walking downtown, where Chester had to do some youth program as part of his probation, and Laura was able to ambush them on the sidewalk, away from prying eyes. Gripping the duffel bag, Laura dashed across the sidewalk. "Taryn, can I talk to you?" she asked.

"Oh, Laura!" said her friend happily. She took off her backpack and unzipped it. "I was going to come over to your house later this afternoon. I've got the assignments in calculus and English—"

Laura held out a hand to stop her. "Just hang on to them for me." She smiled at the hulking boy, whose brawny arm engulfed Taryn's shoulders. "Chester, can I talk to her alone for just a second? I promise, I won't keep her long."

"Sure," he said, nodding and stepping away. "I heard you been sick. How ya feelin'?"

"Terrible," she answered, mustering a smile. "But I'm happy for the two of you guys."

"Thanks." Chester spotted one of his buddies and waved to him. "You know, Laura, if you need a date to that dance—"

Wincing, she responded, "I appreciate the offer, but I think I'm going to be out of town."

When Chester finally turned his back to them and lumbered toward his friends, Taryn asked, "What's the matter with you? You don't look sick. Insane maybe, but not sick."

"I'm not sick," Laura admitted, "and I am going out of town for a few days. I want you to cover for me."

Taryn stared at her. "How?"

"It won't be difficult," explained Laura. "As far as the school goes, I'm already absent. There's a good chance my parents will never call you to check on me, but if they do, just say I'll call them later. They'll forget all about it."

Taryn looked skeptical. "Are we talking about *your* parents? You didn't trade them in for Cupidity's parents, did you?"

Laura looked intently at her friend and held her hand. "Just trust me on this. It's all going to be okay."

"*What's* going to be okay?" asked Taryn in frustration. "Where are you going? For how long? *Why?*"

"I don't know," admitted Laura. "But it's urgent that I go, believe me." Desperately, she began to back away from her best friend. "I'll call your cell phone."

Worriedly, Taryn followed her. "Are you in some kind of trouble? Does this have anything to do with the Conjure Woman?"

"Stay away from her!" warned Laura. She gripped her duffel bag and hurried off down the street.

Five minutes before midnight on Saturday, Laura stood in her parents' bedroom, silhouetted in the light from the hallway. The Sweeneys were snoring a few feet away, blissfully unaware that their loving daughter was aiming a bow and arrow at them. *This is too easy,* she thought.

Before she plunged two people who'd been married for twenty-two years into passionate love, Laura made sure they would find her handwritten note on the vanity. The note "reminded" them that she was spending a few days at Taryn's house to catch up on her schoolwork before going back to school. She doubted if they would spend much time worrying about her after she fixed them.

Holding her breath as she always did, Laura shot a love sticker into the first sleeping figure. Her mom groaned softly from the wound as Laura rummaged in the duffel bag for a second arrow. She had never stopped to count the arrows, but it seemed as if there was always one at hand when she needed it. Before the groaning could wake her dad, she stuck him with an arrow too. Now they were moaning in unison, and she sure wanted to be out of the bedroom before they woke up.

As she walked down the stairs she saw a dapper man in a homburg standing at the bottom of the staircase. The elderly god tipped his hat as she approached. "Ready to go, Miss Sweeney?"

"I guess so," she answered doubtfully. "I'm just wearing this sweater and jeans, but you said I didn't need a lot of clothes. What about a toothbrush?"

"You've got the bow, that's all the luggage you need." Mercury snapped his fingers, and the living room of the Sweeney home was filled with two massive, sparkling wheels. As Laura stared in amazement the colorful apparition solidified into a gleaming chariot encrusted with jewels and golden inlay. The reins glowed like rays of the sun, and they stretched from the shining coach to two winged horses. The ghostly steeds pranced on the carpet, anxious to be going, and Laura staggered on her feet.

Mercury grabbed her elbow and steadied her. With a smile he said, "To begin with, Cupidity was on a quest. Now it's *you* on the quest. So I figured you should go in style. Welcome aboard Apollo's chariot—the original one."

The elegant god helped her onto the gleaming coach, and the ethereal steeds snorted their approval. Laura felt the vehicle shifting under her feet, as if it were real, and she gripped her duffel bag and the rail for support. Mercury took his place beside her, and he picked up the golden reins. Laura panicked, thinking they were about to slam into the wall. But this magical conveyance had gotten into the house, so there must be a way to get it out.

"Hang on!" said Mercury, snapping the reins. At once the horses reared and the carriage took off, zipping through the front wall of the house as if it weren't there. As a lonely bell tower chimed midnight in the town of Denton, Ohio, Apollo's twinkling chariot rose above the rooftops and shot into the stars.

Laura stirred from a very deep sleep, and she felt the soft contours of her bed and the warmth of her blankets wrapping her like a cocoon. *Oh, what a crazy, delirious dream,* she thought. *One for the record books, no doubt inspired by reading too much mythology.*

In her rococo nightmare, Cupid had come to Fimbrey as a high school student, and Peter was dating Megan! Everything was turned upside down. *I'll have to cut out the Roman gods for a while,* she decided, *at least after eating a whole pizza.*

Her stomach felt tied in knots, and her memory was very cloudy. Laura wondered what time it was, and she noted that it was dark in her bedroom. She couldn't see a thing, but she could hear the drone of traffic outside. That meant it had to be later than it seemed, because she didn't normally hear much traffic in the middle of the night.

The days are growing shorter, thought Laura as she sat up in bed and rubbed her eyes. She looked for her slippers on the floor by her bed but couldn't find them, and that's when she decided to turn on the light. Her hand fumbled for the lamp on her nightstand, because it wasn't where it was supposed to be. Her fingers finally found the knob near the base and twisted it, and the room was illuminated.

"Whaaa!" she screamed when she saw unfamiliar paintings and luxurious chaise longues. Laura dove back under the covers and pulled them around her shivering body, until she realized she was still wearing her clothes. The sweater, the jeans, the strange bedroom . . . and the duffel bag on the floor.

Whoa! she thought, sitting up again, *it isn't a dream!* She looked more closely at the room and realized that the French doors led to a balcony, and beyond that there was a huge, sprawling city. It was lit up like the glowing chariot . . . the one from her dream.

A door whispered open, and she turned to see an elegant older man, who nodded to her. "I'm glad to see you're awake."

"Mercury!" she exclaimed with a gasp.

"And still have your mind," he added. "You passed out on the way here. I thought we were going to lose you over Kansas."

She blinked at him. "How long have I been asleep?"

"We left Ohio early Sunday morning, and it's now Monday morning," he answered. "Over twenty-four hours you've slept. I'm sorry, I had forgotten what effect travel by sky chariot has on mortals. As I told you, we're rather rusty at this."

"It's okay," she answered numbly. "I remember it all now . . . we've got to find Venus."

"We'll try." Mercury sighed and sat in one of the luxurious chairs. "I looked in the miratorium—do you know what that is?"

Laura nodded. "Like a crystal ball, only it's a bowl of water."

"Yes," he answered, "but Venus knows how to cloud the image. I thought I saw a hotel, which is why I brought you here. This is a hotel in Beverly Hills where she often stays when she's recovering from plastic surgery or liposuction."

"Liposuction?" asked Laura with distaste. "What is she, like three thousand years old?"

Mercury rolled his eyes. "Yes, and she needs lots of help to keep looking beautiful. I thought we might get lucky, but she's not here."

"Who would know where she is?"

The dapper god gazed at his manicured fingers for a moment and seemed to be thinking. "There are a few she trusts . . . her posse, as you would call it."

"Let's find them." Laura started toward the door, energized by her determination to set things right.

Mercury cleared his throat, and the girl stopped in midstride, knowing it was going to be bad news. "There's just one problem," said the god. "Her posse is all satyrs."

"Satyrs?" she asked with a squeak in her voice. "You mean . . . like randy goatmen?"

"Yes," he answered gravely. "Randy goatmen, and age hasn't tempered them much. Dionysius and Cupid also hang with her, when they feel like it."

With a groan the elder rose to his feet. "Perhaps we should check all the hotels in Los Angeles first."

"Oh, come on, it can't be that bad," insisted Laura. "The posse, I mean."

"Venus has some local haunts we should check," said Mercury. "I'm certain about the hotel I saw in my vision, but I don't know which one it is."

When Laura started out the door, he gripped her arm and pointed to the duffel bag. "Don't forget the bow and arrows—that's your passport into my world."

* * *

For two days Laura Sweeney and Mercury roamed Los Angeles in a Rolls-Royce limousine piloted by a burly driver named Lar. Laura recalled that Roman households often had their own domestic gods, who were called the Lares, and she wondered if Lar was one of them. She had a lot of time to ponder this question, since they visited every plastic surgeon, luxury spa, private club, and fancy hotel in town. But they found no sign of Venus under any of her pseudonyms.

Laura's senses were blown by all the wonders she had seen in the city—museums to massage parlors—but they weren't getting any closer to their goal. Nobody had seen Venus, who had several human guises and identities. After questioning so many people, Laura felt as if she were part of some surreal TV cop show. As they cruised a street north of town, night began to fall on another day of frustration.

They stopped at a busy corner on a main boulevard, and Mercury leaned over to whisper something to their driver. Yawning, Laura gazed out the window and saw what looked like a pleasant residence hotel on the corner. The sign read MOUNT OLYMPUS RETIREMENT HOME.

She chuckled and pointed. "Look, there's a place we ought to check, Mount Olympus."

"Venus never visits the old gang," answered Lar sadly.

Realization dawned on Laura as her gaze traveled from

the driver to the messenger god. "Is that where you live? Now I remember—Cupidity said something about a retirement home."

"Yes, that's our home," answered the elder, sounding tired and frail.

"Can I see it, and meet the rest of you?"

Mercury gave her a crinkled smile. "No, you don't want to meet us. You should think of us as we exist in the old books and stories, not as we are now. Our time is past, and this fiasco only proves it."

Laura suddenly felt very sorry for the aged immortal and his forgotten kind, who had only wanted to do a favor for a girl they didn't even know. "You're so close to home, why don't you spend the night here?" she suggested. "And tell me where to find the satyrs, because time is running out."

The elder nodded thoughtfully. "I suppose it is the moment when you prove yourself. If you're successful and find Venus, tell Lar to call me. I would go with you, but the leader of the satyrs is Pan, who is my son. We don't speak anymore, I'm afraid."

"Oh," said Laura sympathetically. "I hope I'm still speaking to my parents after this."

Mercury assured her, "While you continue the search, I'll go back to Ohio and make sure you aren't missed."

"Excuse me, sir," said Lar, "but I heard on Dionysius's

grapevine that the gang is at Pinkie's Pool Parlor, looking for Cupid."

"All right, take her there, Lar," said Mercury. "She'll have better luck with them than I would. I'm going home."

"Very good, sir." Lar parked the limousine in front of the retirement home and rushed to open the passenger door for Mercury.

"Pinkie's Pool Parlor?" asked Laura hesitantly.

"That's where we would be looking for Cue," answered Lar with a smile.

"Tell Pan . . . tell him I'm sorry I wasn't a better father," said Mercury hesitantly. "His mother and I had too many differences. See you tomorrow, I hope." Lar helped the frail god out of the Rolls-Royce and escorted him to the door.

A moment later the chauffeur returned and said, "That was very noble of you, my lady, to let him rest. He's always cared more for humans than any of the rest of them. Just hold your own with the satyrs, my lady, and don't take any guff."

Laura nodded, with a sick feeling in her stomach. When she pressed the button and rolled down the window, the odor of salt, sea foam, and hibiscus invaded her senses. Giant cypress and pine trees waving in the cool evening wind told Laura that the landscape was changing. Through her haze of disappointment she realized that she was on a fantastic adventure, carrying a magical weapon. Someday they would make movies about her!

I'd settle for a date to Homecoming, she decided, just before falling asleep in the gently rocking vehicle.

Laura awoke when the heavy car bounced over a rut in the road, and she bolted upright with a start. She looked around to see a drab street that was barely lit by a few orange streetlights. Most of the storefronts were empty, but a few showed signs of life, especially the flickering neon that spelled out PINKIE'S POOL PARLOR. A fleet of big-hog motorcycles were parked in front of the establishment. In the driver's seat, Lar hummed softly to himself as if nothing was amiss.

She gulped. "That's where we're going?"

"Where *you're* going," he answered. "I'm going to stay out here, unless I hear you scream."

"Satyrs?" she muttered fearfully. "Open the trunk and let me get my bow."

"That's the spirit!" answered Lar, sounding relieved. He popped the trunk lid, and Laura climbed into the breezy night. This grungy patch of urban blight hardly seemed like cheerful southern California anymore, but she didn't think they had driven that far. Laura grabbed the familiar duffel bag and slammed the trunk shut.

Even before she got to the door, she heard raucous male laughter and loud rock music. When she opened the door, the music became louder and sounded very foreign, with lots of flutes and bongo drums. With a start, she realized that it was *live* music, being played by what looked like a country and western band. On stage were several shaggy cowboys, wearing cowboy boots and chaps. Two of them were playing pan pipes—reeds of different lengths tied together—two played drums, and the fifth played a ukulele.

They were wrapped up in their playing, so Laura strode down between the pool tables until she was close enough that they had to see her. That was when she noticed that the musicians weren't wearing chaps over their cowboy boots— those were gigantic hooves at the ends of their hairy legs!

They gave the song a rollicking finish, then set down their instruments and stared at Laura. One satyr smiled, and his mischievous green eyes twinkled. A dark one seemed to lick his lips, and another one lifted a mug and toasted her. She quickly reached into the duffel bag and took out the bow and arrows. *I have to show them, anyway,* she decided.

The one with the green eyes laughed. "Oh, look, isn't that cute. She's come with a darling little weapon!"

The satyr rose to his hooves and stalked toward her. His

tight T-shirt didn't do much to hide his silver-gray pelt, and she could see that his upper torso was well muscled. Below the waist, he was a goat. "I'm sorry, dearie, but you missed the party," he said with a bow. "However, visitors like you are always welcome."

The other satyrs laughed and stared lustfully at her, and Laura lifted the bow and took aim at each one in turn. The elder creature kept circling her, and he said, "That toy is not going to hurt us."

"I think it will," answered Laura with determination. "It's *Cupid's* bow, and I know how to use it!"

That brought the silver-haired satyr to a halt, and it made the others stop laughing. "Don't come any closer, but take a good look at it," ordered Laura, thrusting the bow into the light over a pool table. The weapon tingled in her hands as if it were especially eager to inflict love misery on these creatures of the woods and the cue stick.

"By Hades, that *is* his bow," said a drummer, who still had some dark hair in his pelt. "Pan, be careful there. I like you, but not *that* much."

"Understood," said the gray beard. "Why should I believe any of this?"

Laura lifted her chin and blurted, "Because I've been hanging out with your father. Nice fellow, great dresser—dig those wingtips. Hey, he's sorry he wasn't a better father to you, but I guess he couldn't get along with your mother." She wanted to ask what species his mother was, but she dared not.

The satyr blinked at her in amazement and acted as if he had just been shot with Cupid's arrow. After a moment, he scratched one of the horns that poked up through his silvery mane and asked, "Is Cupid in danger?"

"Yes, he's in Denton, Ohio!" she answered, as if that explained it all.

As the satyrs muttered among themselves in a language she couldn't understand, Laura lessened her tension on the bowstring. "Listen, Cupid is not in physical danger, but he has amnesia. He's not in his right mind."

"Oh!" roared the satyr with the ukelele. "Then he's perfectly normal." One drummer laughed, but Pan did not.

"Would I have his bow if he was normal?" asked Laura in desperation. "Listen, I only want to know where Venus is. Tell me where to find her, and I'll go away."

"Ah," said Pan, stroking his belly as he stepped to her right, "we can't give away our friend's position to the enemy, now can we?"

She lifted the bow, pulled back the string, and took aim at his sculpted but hairy chest. "Take one more step, and you'll be a monogamous satyr. I've already done Cupidity, and I can take care of you, too."

"Who did you say?" asked Pan, halting his effort to outflank her. "Who's Cupidity?"

"Cupid . . . now that she's a girl. Vulcan put her in a disguise—a really hot disguise."

"Oooh, gossip!" they cried. "Tell! Do tell!"

At their delighted smirks, Laura sighed. "All right, settle down, and I'll tell you the whole story. But no satyr stuff near me. Okay?"

As soon as Pan had heard Laura's story, including parts where he laughed hysterically, he jumped to his feet and rallied his band of satyrs. "Everybody! Listen up—get your leathers on. We're taking a cross-country bike ride!"

"Yahoo!" cheered the satyrs, stomping around on their big hooves in the empty poolroom. "I want the three-wheeler!" cried one of them, dashing out of the encampment.

"Wait a minute!" yelled Laura, "Are we talking motorcycles? I don't want to go on a cross-anything ride—"

"Do you want to find Venus?" asked Pan, cutting her off. He lowered his voice to add, "I know where she'll be on Friday, but I can't tell a mortal like you. Still, if I feel like going on a trip and inviting you along, who's to know? It was an accident, right? If we leave now, we can make it by Friday, and I think we'll end up close to Ohio."

Laura gnawed her lower lip. "Finding her on Friday will be cutting it awfully close to the dance."

"Just think how much time you'll save having us with you." The silver-haired satyr winked at her and added, "When we put our leathers on, we'll look like any regular motorcycle gang. Don't we clean up real nice, boys?"

"Yeah! Sure do!" growled the randy goatmen.

"All right," relented Laura. If they didn't know where Venus was until Friday, she had time to kill . . . if she could trust them.

Ignoring her, the crew of five satyrs began to don over-sized boots, leather pants, leather jackets, bandannas, and scuffed helmets. Soon they were transformed into an especially scruffy gang of motorcyclists.

They gave Laura a helmet and her own sleek leathers, which fit perfectly. After she strapped the bow to her back, she looked at herself in the bathroom mirror, thinking, *I actually look hot for once in my life.*

"Let's ride!" yelled Pan, heading for the door. Whooping and hollering, his gang of satyrs stumbled after him. They leaped on their big hogs, and started the engines with lusty roars and clouds of greasy smoke.

Pan turned to Laura and pointed to the rest of the banana seat behind him, then held out his hand.

I agreed to do this—no excuses, she thought. With a terrified squeak, Laura grabbed his hand and climbed onto the back of the big two-wheeler.

"Hold on!" shouted Lar, the chauffeur. He dashed in front of the motorcycles, waving his hands. "You boys will behave yourselves with Miss Sweeney, I hope!"

"She's under my father's protection," declared Pan. He zipped up his aged leather jacket, which was covered in road rash, and added, "She'll be safer with us than with you and Pops. You don't know the kind of place we're going."

Laura shouted doubtfully, "I'll be fine!"

"I'll get word to Mercury," answered Lar.

Pan revved his engine until it sounded like Jupiter's thunder, and the chauffeur scurried out of the way. When the satyr waved his arm, the growl of engines reached a fevered pitch. Laura heard the click of the gears, and she gripped Pan's waist as the chopper flew off the curb and shot into the night.

13

"Yes, yes, Mr. Sweeney, this is Taryn's father," said Mercury, who was seated in an unmarked, high-tech van parked across the street from Taryn's house. He and his crew of expensive minions were intercepting any calls between the two households, although so far there had only been two. "I know I don't sound like myself, but I have a cold." The god gave a polite cough.

On the other end of the line, Edward Sweeney stammered, "It's . . . it's just that we haven't seen our daughter since last Saturday or Sunday. I'm not sure when." He added quickly, "I've been very busy."

"I'm sure you have," answered Mercury with only a

trace of sarcasm. "I can tell you that Laura has been a total delight to me and—"

He paused to look at a technician, who read off a computer screen, "Melissa."

"Melissa," said Mercury. "Yes, Melissa really likes Laura, who is a delightful houseguest. I think Taryn has brought her up to speed on her schoolwork, and she'll return home at the end of the week. Now, don't you worry about Laura . . . just get back to those pressing matters of yours. Good-bye."

"Good-bye." As Ed Sweeney's voice faded away, Mercury heard him plead, "Honey, wait until I get off the phone!"

The messenger god sighed and took off the headset. "Well, that should hold them for a while. It's Wednesday night, only two days to go. I think you gentlemen can spare me for a while." He started to open the door of the van.

"Boss, do you want us to drive you somewhere?" asked the technician.

"No, I can walk there," he replied. "It's something I have to do alone."

Grabbing his cane, the elder got out of the van and walked gingerly down the damp sidewalk. It was October, and the chill winds of Janus were in the air. He longed for the warm, sun-kissed shores of California, Greece, or Italy, but he had promised to help Laura Sweeney. It was probably hopeless to appeal to Venus, but Laura had been able to move the gods to action before.

Mercury had also returned to Denton because he felt a responsibility to Cupid. They had sent the inept cherub on this quest, knowing that meddling in the affairs of mortals was dangerous. This was another instance where they should have minded their own business instead of getting caught up in crazy schemes. Whether Venus made it or not, Mercury felt obligated to be there at the dance . . . when it would all unravel.

Unless he could persuade Cupidity not to go.

By the time the aged god reached her apartment complex, night had fallen in all its dark glory upon the quiet Ohio town. Autumn had arrived, and it felt like olden times knowing there was a fall festival coming on Friday. Now was the time to shelter the harvest and loved ones to make ready for the icy grip of winter.

Mercury walked slowly up the steps to Cupidity's door, and he could hear laughter and raucous music coming from within. *Her neighbors must love her,* he thought sarcastically. Since it was technically his abode, he didn't knock; he just barged in.

He caught Cupidity and Cody kissing, or maybe they were dancing, in the middle of the heavily littered living room. Rock music was blaring so loudly that they couldn't hear him come in, but a gust of wind entered with the messenger god.

"Cupidity, look at this mess!" he yelled at her. "You haven't been doing your chores."

She pulled away from Cody and looked sheepishly at him. "No, I suppose I haven't been. Why the visit, Dad?"

"Because I ought to live here," he answered. "With you. How can I desert my only child . . . and miss out on you growing up?"

Cody shifted uncomfortably on his feet. "Excuse me, Mister, uh . . . Cupidity's dad, but I can look after your daughter for you. I'm over here every minute."

"Yes, you're all over her," muttered the angry "father," slamming the door behind him. "Young lady, because you've made the house such a mess—while entertaining boys without my permission—I'm going to ground you! You can't go anywhere until . . . Saturday."

"No!" she shrieked. "The Homecoming Dance is Friday. I've got my dress, my date . . . we're going with a bunch of people. You can't do this to me, Papa!"

"Please, Mister, have a heart," insisted Cody. "We'll clean it up, we'll start right now. Hey, Cupie, where's the number for that maid service?"

"You'll be leaving right now, Mr. Kenyon," insisted Mercury, mustering all the strength he had and shoving the handsome lad toward the door. "You've had it your own way, but now Daddy's home."

Thankfully, the boy was too dazed to resist, and Mercury managed to shove him outside and lock the door behind him. Cody cursed and beat on the door a few times, while Cupidity pouted. Mercury caught his breath, because the disguised cherub was truly the masterwork of Vulcan's art. It was a pity that this dazzling creature was not going to last until the end of the week.

"This . . . this is the worst thing you've ever done!" wailed Cupidity.

"Oh, come on," said her fake father sternly. "I've grounded you lots of times, and you never carried on like this."

She gazed at him with a troubled frown, and he knew that Laura had been right—the cherub had truly lost all memory, except for the cover story that went with the disguise, which she thought was real.

"This feels worse," complained the petite blond, stamping her foot on the hamburger wrappers. "I want to be Homecoming Queen more than anything I've ever wanted in my whole life! Come on, Papa, you can't just pop into my life and stop me."

"I can try," he vowed.

More pounding shook the door, and Cody's forlorn voice shouted, "I'll call you later, Cupie!"

"I love you, Codykins!" she cried in anguish.

The satyrs never got tired. They could go for twenty-four hours, day and night, never stopping . . . just riding those big two-wheelers down the interstate. It was a good thing Laura was young and had already gotten lots of sleep in her youthful life, because she didn't get any sleep on their mad dash across the country. She took some solace from the fact that they were headed in the right direction and got closer to Ohio with every blurred mile.

The pain set in only when she got off the banana seat and tried to walk after hours frozen in place behind Pan. She made the motorcyclists stop as often as she could without being a nuisance, because she knew time was running out.

It was late on Friday afternoon when they stopped someplace in Indiana. The town looked so much like Ohio that she got homesick, although she didn't remember the hotel chain. Why had they stopped at this podunk hotel? Laura couldn't shake the thought that maybe the satyrs were taking her for a ride—figuratively as well as literally. Maybe there was no Venus at the end of the road, just a Homecoming Dance to which she wasn't invited.

She looked up to see Pan walking toward her with a

big smile on his face. "We're here," he said proudly.

"Here?" she asked, glancing at the tree-lined street in the quiet midwestern town, much like the one she had left. "Venus is *here*?"

The silver-haired satyr pointed to the nondescript, midsized hotel. "It's Friday, so she'll check in sometime tonight. Come, I'll show you."

He took off his battered helmet, and she gasped. "Listen, you'd better put that back on—I can see your horns."

"It doesn't matter here." The satyr waved to her and strode toward the hotel, walking with a swagger in his specially designed boots.

Laura groaned as she stretched her stiff legs, but she managed to follow him into the hotel. After the elegant L.A. hotels and spas she had visited, this couldn't be where Venus was hanging out. No way was this mediocre roadside inn the grand hotel in Mercury's vision.

When they stepped into the lobby, she saw why Pan was unconcerned about his horns. Everyone had pointed ears, hairy feet, medieval dress, bad wigs, and light-sabers. Laura shivered. "What is this? Another dimension?"

Pan lowered his head and laughed. "This is a science fiction convention. They're fun for us, because we can be 'in costume.' Venus likes to attend these events . . . posing as herself."

He strode into the hotel lobby and grabbed a rather large woman clad in furs and chain mail. "Hello there, beautiful!" growled the satyr.

"Oh, honey, I remember those horns!" She laughed, running her fingers through his mane of silvery hair. "What are you supposed to be?"

"A randy goatman," answered Laura, stepping up beside them.

The chubby girl in lion skins giggled. "And you know, he looks just like one! He should enter the masquerade."

Laura looked pointedly at Pan. "Listen, before you ditch me, where do I find her?"

"She'll be dressed like a Greek goddess," the satyr answered. "Don't worry, when it comes to being noticed, Venus makes Narcissus look like Medusa."

"I want to see the art exhibit!" said another satyr, galloping in on his hooves. In a few moments, the satyr motorcycle gang was absorbed into the costumed swarm of fantasy and science fiction fans.

With a sigh, Laura adjusted her glasses and looked down at the skintight black leather outfit she was wearing. She didn't look like she was from Middle-earth, but she was dressed more bizarrely than usual. Maybe she would fit in after all.

"Have you seen Venus?" she asked every fan she bumped into.

"Not yet," came the answer. "Try the gamers' room."

She checked there and found no Venus, so she asked again, "Have you seen Venus?"

"Try the video room." Laura went up to the ballroom level and searched all the meeting rooms. For the next two hours, she searched every public corner of the hotel, and they finally made her buy a membership to the convention and wear a badge. A few people asked her what was in her duffel bag, and she claimed it was just her luggage.

Although they were dressed oddly, the people at the science fiction convention were extremely friendly. Most of them seemed to know Venus, and they said she came to this con every year. But she wasn't exactly punctual.

Laura roamed through the dealer's room, looking at the collectible toys, fantasy jewelry, movie posters, and old books. A friendly security guard came up and told her that she couldn't carry her bag into this room. Instead of checking it, she just took out the bow and quiver of arrows and wore them on her back. Laura didn't look much different than scores of fans who were wearing fanciful weapons.

She saw many mythical and marvelous characters, including the satyrs, who winked slyly at her, but no flamboyant goddess. At nine o'clock, she sat down in the hotel lobby to wait, figuring that Venus had to come this way to check in.

At this very moment, she mused, *the Homecoming football game is going on at Fimbrey High.* Laura was sad that it was her senior year, her last Homecoming, and she couldn't be there. The way things were going, she wasn't going to make the dance either.

Mercury sat in the living room of Cupidity's recently cleaned apartment, listening to the drone of the football game on the radio. Except for that noise, it was too quiet down the hallway near Cupidity's bedroom. He got up to investigate when he heard the door open, and he caught sight of a blond figure in a bathrobe dashing down the hall into the bathroom. All right, Cupidity was accounted for.

He hadn't seen his so-called daughter much since he had put her on restriction. Had she really been his daughter, Mercury might have felt bad about that, but he couldn't feel bad about punishing a deranged cherub.

Something seemed to happen in the football game, because he heard a shriek of delight. The messenger god sat back in his chair, thinking that Cupidity didn't understand football. She didn't know a halfback from a hunchback, so what was she cheering about?

Mercury rose to his feet again and hobbled down the

hall. As soon as he did, Cupidity again bolted out of her bedroom and into the bathroom. He didn't get a good look at her, because she moved like a track star.

He stopped at the bathroom door and asked, "Darling, are you all right?"

"Don't come in," she said in a muffled voice, covered by a sneeze. He didn't go in, but he marched down to her bedroom and went in there. The first thing Mercury did was look in her closet, where she had kept the gown she intended to wear to the dance. It was gone!

The anxious god heard the crackling sound of static, and he found a small black-and-white TV set hidden under her pillow. It was a security monitor, and the image showed the chair in which he had been sitting. They had been spying on him with a hidden camera! The window was also open several inches.

Those lousy teenagers, he thought, *they're worse than Harpies!*

Mercury didn't know who was in his bathroom, but he doubted whether it was Cupidity. This time he banged loudly on the bathroom door and shouted. "How long has she been gone?"

"Achooo!" came the response. "I can't hear you—the hair dryer is going!"

"You've been caught! I know Cupidity is gone. Now open up!"

Slowly the door creaked open, and a sheepish blond-haired girl stuck her head out. "Oh, please," she begged, "the dance meant so much to her. Let her go!"

"She's already there, isn't she?" muttered Mercury. "What's your name?"

"Chelsea," answered the chastened teen. "I just wanted to do her a favor . . . help her out. Everybody loves Cupidity—she's like the spirit of the school!"

"Yeah," grumbled the elder, "she's always been the life of the party. Did she go out the window, and was a car waiting for her?"

Chelsea nodded. "Cody brought me here, and we switched places. Don't be mad—they're like really in love!"

"I know." Mercury glanced at his watch and saw that it was ten o'clock. He scowled and started for the door. "Come on, I'll have my driver take us to the dance."

"It's going to be a madhouse at school," warned Chelsea, tossing away the robe to reveal that she was fully dressed. "The game is almost over."

"That's for sure," said Mercury with a sigh.

Laura was actually dozing in a big overstuffed chair in the corner of the hotel lobby when a fresh babble of voices woke her up. She bolted upright, angry at herself for sleeping on the job, when she saw a mass of people swarm through the front door. At the center of this maelstrom was a tall, elegant woman in a cream-colored, diaphanous gown that swept behind her like a superhero's cape.

Members of her entourage descended on the check-in desk and the con desk, and it was obvious that a personage had arrived.

"Hello, Yoda! Hello, Captain Picard!" the raven-haired beauty called out to people. Even though the lobby was already crowded with fans, it got twice as crammed as people pressed forward to greet the new arrival. Many of them called her by name: "Venus."

Laura took a deep breath and rose from the comfy chair. She moved the magical bow from her back to her front to make it easier to see, then she marched into the crush of people. As she got closer to her quarry, she could tell that Venus was of uncertain age, one of those well-preserved women somewhere between forty and four thousand years old.

"Venus!" she called.

"And who are you supposed to be?" asked the goddess snidely. "Lara Croft?"

People swarmed around them, but Laura pressed forward. "I'm trying to be Cupid."

"You don't look anything like Cupid," replied Venus with a scowl. She waved over Laura's head. "Gandalf, good to see you!"

"What about this bow?" asked Laura, holding up the weapon. "It's Cupid's bow!"

At first Venus rolled her eyes, then she narrowed them and took a closer look at the willowy weapon. "That's a good copy, but you still have a lousy costume."

Someone handed the dark-haired woman a convention badge that read VENUS, and she carefully pinned it to her gown. "Who's got my room key?" she demanded.

"Right here!" said a member of her entourage, handing her a small envelope. When Venus and her crew began to make their way out of the lobby, Laura doggedly followed her.

"Venus!" she called. "Pan and his gang brought me here on their motorcycles . . . all the way from Pinkie's!"

Despite being caught up in the flow of people through the lobby, Venus stopped dead in her tracks. The goddess of love turned and cast a suspicious gaze at Laura. "You're beginning to annoy me."

"I just want five minutes of your time," promised the girl. "To tell you about what happened to Cupid."

Venus sniffed in disdain. "You obviously have me confused with someone who cares. I'm here to have fun. Be fun, or be gone!" The goddess gave her a dismissive wave and walked on.

The rejection plunged Laura into despair, and she again

felt like a stalker as she followed Venus from one part of the convention to another. She could always use Cupid's bow to get her attention, but she couldn't risk getting into trouble with the law or security. Every room seemed to have a giant clock in it, and time was ticking off. It was almost ten thirty.

As the evening wore on, Venus and most of the revelers found their way to the hotel ballroom, where a Regency Dance was in progress. Laura watched glumly as people costumed in velvet finery from the court of England two centuries ago dipped and curtsied to baroque music from a string quartet. To Laura, it looked like elegant square dancing, with much touching of fingertips.

Laughing gaily, Venus joined the lines of courtly dancers, and she knew the archaic steps better than any of them. Watching them and thinking about the Homecoming Dance only depressed Laura. Time was running out, and she had to talk to the love goddess. She noticed that the participants were thrown together for a few seconds here and there, when they could converse.

So Laura took the plunge and jumped into the stately dance. She smiled a lot and tried to master the steps while she waited to come in contact with Venus. More people from the audience joined in, and all of them were in the wrong costumes, too.

She was finally paired with Venus in the fingertip touching. "Oh, you again," said the goddess with a sneer. They curtsied and stepped back and forth in time to the music.

Laura laughed. "I've got a funny joke—I promise! There was this old cherub who smoked cigars, and Vulcan turned him into a hot teenage girl to go back to high school. Have you heard this one?"

"No," said Venus doubtfully, her stunning blue eyes peering at Laura.

In a rush, Laura blurted out the rest. "Cupidity is the hottest thing in high school, but her stupid friend shoots her with her own bow and arrow. How silly! Now Cupidity is in love with a skater boy and doesn't know who she really is."

Venus threw back her head and roared with laughter. "That *is* funny!"

The teen grabbed her hand and dragged her out of the line of dancers. "It gets even better," promised Laura. "At midnight tonight, Cupidity will turn back into this cherub, but who knows if she'll get her memory back."

"Who cares?" snapped Venus, pulling her arm away from the leather-clad biker chick. "It's every god for himself."

"Oh, please," begged Laura, giving up any pretense,

"help me! Cupidity will be right in the middle of getting crowned Homecoming Queen, and a good friend of mine is in love with the wrong girl. And—and—" Breathlessly she tried to collect her thoughts before the goddess fled from the ballroom.

Venus frowned and said, "Wait a minute; they're crowning a queen of this dance, and it's going to be Cupid?"

Laura's eyes widened, and she realized the chink in Venus's armor. "You mean Cupidity," said the mortal, "that's who she is now. She's the most gorgeous female on the planet, and she's also madly in love—from her own stupid arrows. So she's got that glow thing working. At our Homecoming Dance, we always crown the most beautiful woman in the world as queen. That could only be Cupidity."

"More gorgeous than *me?*" asked Venus with astonishment.

Laura pondered the question. "That would be hard to say, unless I saw the two of you standing together." Laura looked up at the clock over the door. "We could still make it to the festival by midnight. It's only ten forty-five now, and it's right next door in Ohio."

"Ohio?" asked the goddess thoughtfully. "Yes, but Indiana is in the Central Time Zone, and Ohio is in the Eastern Time Zone. It's an hour later in Ohio—it's a quarter till midnight."

"Oh no!" sputtered Laura, grabbing her wrist. "We've got to rush, we've got to go!"

"Let me call my brother," said Venus, reaching under her gown and pulling out a cell phone.

14

After fighting horrendous traffic, crazed football fans, and a person selling tickets who didn't want to let him in, Mercury finally entered the high school gymnasium. It was just as chaotic inside as out, and he could hardly believe this Homecoming event had been organized by adults. On stage, a rock band blasted music that made his teeth hurt, but the laughter and conversation threatened to drown out the band. Strobe lights, fog machines, and balloons didn't do anything to help his vision or his mood.

There were hordes of kids, mostly standing around in large packs and doing precious little dancing. It was so dark that he wondered why any of them had bothered with the fancy outfits they were wearing. The gangly boys looked ridiculous in suits and tuxedos, although some of the young ladies looked fetching in their gowns. None of the girls were quite as delectable as Cupidity, but he couldn't find the cherub anywhere.

Of course Chelsea had deserted him as soon as they entered the place, and she had probably run off to warn Cupidity that he was there. *Patience,* he told himself, *I'll find her.* After all, the gymnasium was massive, and the students washed back and forth across the floor like the tide.

Mercury was dressed well enough to fit in with this exuberant crowd, as long as he kept to the shadows. He stalked the refreshment tables, looking for Cupidity but not finding her. He returned to the entrance, where the couples were having their pictures taken under a harvest archway of squashes, corn, and pinecones.

The elder asked nicely for Cupidity but was told that she and Cody had gotten their pictures taken earlier. Every couple was automatically entered for King and Queen, but the votes were already counted by now. As Laura Sweeney had told him, there were a great many mismatched couples at the dance, possibly more victims of Cupid's troublesome arrows.

The god of punctuality checked his watch and saw that it was ten minutes until midnight. With any luck,

Cupidity would be hiding from him when the hour struck, and everyone would be spared having to witness her transformation. How would they ever explain that away? He could affect mortals' minds but only on a small scale, not a gymnasium crammed with hundreds of people.

Wincing from the noise, he looked around, realizing that Laura was not going to return with Venus in time to help matters. Well, that had been a long shot, anyway. Such a mess as this was bound to end in disaster. With any luck, maybe it would only be a small-scale disaster.

The gruesome song ended with a discordant chord that made Mercury grit his teeth. In the silence that followed, he tried to collect his thoughts, but a loud drumroll shattered the brief calm.

"Fimbrey rocks!" shouted the lead singer to raucous applause. "Students of Fimbrey High, it's almost midnight—are you having a good time?"

"Yeah!" they bellowed back.

"To announce the Homecoming King and Queen, here is your principal, Denise Waterbury!" The singer stepped back to allow a middle-aged woman to take the microphone, and the crowd began to press closer to get a better look. Spotlights bathed the stage, showing that the principal was dressed in a proper business suit, bringing a touch of class to the chaotic proceedings.

The principal beamed with pride. "Students of Fimbrey High," she began, "this year's attendance at the Homecoming Dance is almost double last year's attendance. It's wonderful! I've seen so many faces I've never seen before at any of our events, although I do see you in my office from time to time."

There was polite laughter, and the principal went on, "I am truly pleased by the diversity I've seen tonight. In fact, the last few weeks. I know we've had a few strange incidents around school, but overall problems have been down. And our football team scored a touchdown tonight and only lost by ten points. Let's give them a big hand!"

When that got scattered boos, Mrs. Waterbury plunged on. "So let me announce our Homecoming King and Queen. We counted all the votes, but we hardly needed to. It was a landslide! You know them as a perfectly darling couple, and it's hard to believe that one of them came to our school just a few weeks ago. I can't imagine Fimbrey without her. Our Homecoming Queen—Cupidity Larraine!"

The audience applauded wildly as the stunning, fairhaired beauty sauntered toward the microphone. The lights caught her sparkling skintight gown and her shimmering skin and hair. She looked unreal—an apparition concocted by gods. Mercury could understand how all of these people had been fooled, all of them except Laura Sweeney.

"And the Homecoming King," announced the principal, "Cody Kenyon!"

Dressed in an Edwardian tux and looking impossibly rakish, the skateboarder strode onto the stage to wild applause. Mercury had to admit, his brooding dark looks contrasted nicely with Cupidity's sunny appeal. Who could deny that they were the King and Queen of this rowdy lot of mortals?

A gaggle of girls and a mob of boys rushed forward to clamp crowns on their heads, and Cupidity giggled into the microphone. The petite blond had to stand on tiptoes to reach the device, and every male in the audience stood on tiptoes to watch her.

"This is such an honor!" she yelled to much cheering and stomping. "You could have picked Megan and Peter, or Emma and Jake . . . or so many others. Kisses!" She promptly took time out in her speech to blow kisses at her beaming friends.

Mercury's watch buzzed, and he groaned as he turned off the alarm. *Already midnight,* he thought ruefully.

Cupidity sniffed back a big tear, and it sounded like a goose honking. "I never thought I would be welcomed so warmly in my new school," she declared in a hoarse voice. "It makes me forget about all the other places I've ever lived . . . wherever they were! Here I've found true love and friendship. I see you, Papa!"

She waved directly at Mercury, and he tried not to cringe. "Kiss her!" shouted the crowd. "Kiss her, Cody!"

This was apparently a rite that everybody eagerly awaited, and Cody wasn't going to disappoint. He scooped Cupidity up in his arms, and all of her hair promptly fell out, showering the first row in silvery strands that glinted in the spotlight. Some in the crowd shrieked, but Cody was oblivious. He pressed home with his kiss, even as her body writhed and twisted in his arms.

Cupidity's silky skin turned cracked and hairy, and bits of her perfect body crumbled off. Trying to kiss her, Cody looked as if he were wrestling an alligator, and the audience screamed in alarm. They shook one another in disbelief, and a boy near Mercury fainted and fell to the floor.

Finally Cody heard the screaming and realized something was wrong. When he drew back, he saw a shriveled, wizened cherub in a lumpy evening dress that was tight only across the belly. Cody screamed louder than any of the girls, and Mercury couldn't blame him. Grizzled, bald-headed Cupid looked like a lawn statue that had been left out in the rain too long.

"What's the matter?" asked Cupid in a gruff voice. "What's the matter, Codykins?"

The skater was clawing his way off the stage, as were most of his friends, when Mercury felt a tug on his sleeve. "Hi, Dad," said a familiar voice.

The god turned to see his oldest son. "Pan!" he exclaimed happily. "What are you doing here?"

"I had to drive the chariot," answered the satyr, "to get the ladies here. That mortal did it—she talked Venus into coming—but I guess we're too late."

"Where are they?" asked Mercury, peering over the heads of the panicked crowd.

"Near the stage!" The satyr pointed into the turmoil.

Laura froze on the steps leading up to the stage, and she didn't know whether to cry, laugh, or scream like everybody else was doing. They were going to be traumatized for years after seeing the hottest girl in the school morph into a gnarly little gnome. Laura had been expecting it, but even she could hardly stand to look at the creature that was left after Cupidity dissolved. This was like a Japanese horror movie, when the pretty moth turns into an ugly monster everyone wants to destroy.

When she tore her eyes away from the stage, Laura saw the horrified faces of Peter, Megan, Emma, and Jake. She wanted to run to Peter's side and comfort him, but they all probably figured they were losing their minds.

"Where's Cupidity?" wailed Cody, dropping to his knees and shaking his fists at the cherub. *"What have you done to her?"*

"Get a grip, dude!" ordered Cupid, scowling. "Everyone, settle down. I'm not done with my speech!"

"He still has no memory," said a voice behind Laura. She turned to look at the impossibly beautiful Venus, who now would have no problem being elected queen of this terrified mob. "Damn, I'm going to have to step in here, aren't I?"

Laura looked pleadingly at her. "If you do a good deed, I promise never to tell anyone."

Venus gave a hollow laugh. "You'd better not—that would ruin my reputation. First we have to break the love spells. Hand me an arrow."

"You have to be careful with them," warned Laura, feeling possessive about her magical weapon.

"Don't argue with me, mortal!" snapped Venus. "Who's the goddess here? I've done this before, okay? So hand me an arrow."

This time Laura quickly obeyed, fishing an arrow out of Cupid's quiver and handing it to the raven-haired goddess of love. With pandemonium, screaming, and shouting all around them, Venus held Cupid's arrow between her two clenched fists and chanted in an ancient tongue.

Maybe it was the fog machine or the strobe lights, but

the room began to spin. Strange flashes sparkled in the air, and Laura felt dizzy. She eased herself onto the steps as other students knelt in dazed confusion. Through blurry vision, she looked for Cupid and saw the grizzled cherub stagger and fall down. He was also under Venus's spell.

With a loud yelp, the goddess snapped the arrow in two, and the shaft disappeared in her hands. Laura still felt dazed, but the spinning went away. She staggered to her feet and looked at the goddess of love, who was breathing heavily.

"Mama!" yelled a raspy voice. "Mama!"

"Yes, my baby!" Venus leaped to her feet and ran up the stairs to embrace her frightened son, even though he was a shriveled cherub wearing a sparkly evening gown. "It's all right, baby, I'll take you home!"

The cherub pointed accusingly at Laura. "Mama, she's got my bow and arrows! She *took* them without asking!"

"No, you let Laura play with them," said Venus. "That's your friend, remember? But she will have to give them back now."

"Is that it?" asked Laura, taking the bow and quiver of arrows off her leather-clad shoulder. She felt oddly naked without them. "Everything is back to normal?"

Venus gave Cupid back his bow. "What's your definition of normal?" she asked. "I don't know how much they'll remember, but Cupid's spell is broken. Anyone in love now is honestly in love."

With those words ringing in her ears, Laura searched the area for Peter Yarmench. She spotted him backstage, arguing with Jake, and the two boys were almost back to blows as they had been on that afternoon so long ago.

"I caught you looking at her!" accused Jake. "You stay away from my girlfriend!"

Peter looked in confusion from Megan to Emma, and the girls gazed back at him. "Which one is your girl-friend?" asked Peter.

"Why, it's—" Jake paused, pointing first at the head cheerleader, then at the pale goth chick dressed in a spider-web black dress.

"It's me, dummy!" declared Megan, putting her hands on her hips. "I was only with Peter to . . . to make you jealous."

Emma just shook her head in confusion and looked as if she wanted to hide. "I don't know, Jake. I thought we had something . . . but it's up to you."

"Tell this ghoul to get lost!" insisted Megan, staring daggers at Emma.

Jake seemed to come to an epiphany, and he shook his head. "I don't think so. I need to look outside the box, like Cupidity told me. I'm with Emma." He rushed to the goth's side and put his arm around her waist. "See ya, Megan."

"Ack! Ack!" The queen bee could barely talk, and she started hyperventilating in shock.

Laura gazed in amazement at Jake and Emma as they hugged each other happily. Cupid's arrows made no difference to them—they were really in love. In fact, most of the mismatched romances at the Homecoming Dance seemed to be genuine.

Laura found herself gravitating to Peter's side. Did he really like her, or was he still lovesick and confused? He had just lost his date for the evening, and she knew how that felt.

"Peter, are you okay?" she asked with concern.

He looked appreciatively at her skintight leather ensemble. "Wow, that is some hot outfit! Do you always go to dances dressed like a biker babe?"

She smiled. "I didn't have a date, so I crashed this place with my motorcycle gang."

Peter looked around and whispered, "Would you hate me forever if I ditched my date and hung out with you?"

"No," she said with a grin, "but this is the last time you get to do that."

"Where's Cupidity?" yelled a forlorn voice. "Where did she go?" They all turned to see Cody Kenyon shuffling through the crowd of people, a dazed look on his face and a lopsided crown on his head.

"Dude," said Jake, "she bailed on you after you kissed some ugly little guy."

"Yeah," replied Emma. "I don't blame her."

In sympathy, Megan grabbed Cody's arm and escorted him away from the others. "Come on, Cody, let's ditch these losers. I'll take care of you."

"More music!" yelled the principal, trying to get the dance back on track. "Rockers, can't we have some more tunes?"

"Yes, Mrs. Waterbury," responded the lead singer, trying to gather up his band. "Come on, people, everyone off the stage but the musicians!"

Peter grabbed Laura's hand and led her down the stairs and across the dance floor, where they ran into Taryn and Chester. "Laura!" shouted Taryn with a delirious squeal. "I *knew* you'd make it to the dance, and you're here with Peter. See, I told you everything would work out!"

"Are you guys okay?" asked Laura with concern.

"Never better," answered Chester, gripping Taryn by the waist. "Laura, you have to wear kinky leather more often—you look hot." He gave Peter a playful thumbs-up sign.

Suddenly the band started playing again, and it was impossible to talk over the din. Hand in hand, Peter and Laura wound their way through the throng of people until they were outside, and the brisk night air felt like a welcome dash of cold water in Laura's face.

"Make a wish," said Peter, touching her arm. "There's a shooting star—a big one."

She looked up to see an impressive light flash across the night sky, although she knew it was too big and too bright to be a meteorite. "Apollo's chariot," she answered with a wave. "Good-bye, friends."

"I'm not going anywhere," said Peter, putting his arm around her. "I'm happy right here."

"Me too," agreed Laura, nuzzling his shoulder.

As Peter leaned down and gently brushed his lips against hers, Laura felt a shiver leap through her body. As they kissed for the first time under the glimmering sky, she realized that love didn't just come from a bow and arrow. Sometimes, it was written in the stars.

About the Authors

Deborah Reber is a writer, speaker, and recovering teen (not necessarily in that order). When she's not flipping through her tattered high school yearbooks and diaries for inspiration for her writing, she's running, gardening, hanging out with friends, or spending time with her family. She lives in Seattle with her husband, son, and big white dog. Visit her online at www.deborahreber.com.

Caroline Goode is a pseudonym.

Turn the page for a peek at
another sweet and sparkly romance:

Endless Summer
Jennifer Echols

Sean smiled down at me, his light brown hair glinting golden in the sunlight. He shouted over the noise of the boat motor and the wind, "Lori, when we're old enough, I want you to be my girlfriend." He didn't even care the other boys could hear him.

"I'm there!" I exclaimed, because I was nothing if not coy. All the boys ate out of my hand, I tell you. "When will we be old enough?"

His blue eyes, lighter than the bright blue sky behind him, seemed to glow in his tanned face. He answered me, smiling. At least, I *thought* he answered me. His lips moved.

"I didn't hear you. What'd you say?" I know how to draw out a romantic moment.

He spoke to me again. I still couldn't hear him, though the boat motor and the wind hadn't gotten any louder. Maybe he was just mouthing words, pretending to say something sweet I couldn't catch. Boys were like that. He'd just been teasing me all along—

"You ass!" I sat straight up in my sweat-soaked bed, wiping away the strands of my hair stuck to my wet face. Then I realized what I'd said out loud. "Sorry, Mom," I told her photo on my bedside table. But maybe she hadn't heard me over my alarm clock blaring Christina Aguilera, "Ain't No Other Man."

Or maybe she'd understand. I'd just had a closer encounter with Sean! Even if it *was* only in my dreams.

Usually I didn't remember my dreams. Whenever my brother, McGillicuddy, was home from college, he told Dad and me at breakfast what he'd dreamed about the night before. Lindsay Lohan kicking his butt on the sidewalk after he tried to take her picture (pure fantasy). Amanda Bynes dressed as the highway patrol, pulling him over to give him a traffic ticket. I was jealous. I didn't want to dream about Lindsay Lohan or getting my butt kicked. However, if I was spending the night with Patrick

Dempsey and didn't even *know* it, I was missing out on a very worthy third of my life. I had once Googled "dreaming" and found out some people don't remember their dreams if their bodies are used to getting up at the same hour every morning and have plenty of time to complete the dream cycle.

So why'd I remember my dream this morning? It was the first day of summer vacation, that's why. To start work at the marina, I'd set my clock thirty minutes earlier than during the school year. Lo and behold, here was my dream. About Sean: check. Blowing me off, as usual: noooooooo! That might happen in my dreams, but it wasn't going to happen in real life. Not again. Sean would be mine, starting today. I gave Mom on my bedside table an okay sign—the wakeboarding signal for *ready to go*—before rolling out of bed.

My dad and my brother suspected nothing, ho ho. They didn't even notice what I was wearing. Our conversation at breakfast was the same one we'd had every summer morning since my brother was eight years old and I was five.

Dad to brother: "You take care of your sister today."

Brother, between bites of egg: "Roger that."

Dad to me: "And you watch out around those boys next door."

Me: (Eye roll.)

Brother: "I had this rockin' dream about Anne Hathaway."

Post-oatmeal, my brother and I trotted across our yard and the Vaders' yard to the complex of showrooms, warehouses, and docks at Vader's Marina. The morning air was already thick with the heat and humidity and the smell of cut grass that would last the entire Alabama summer. I didn't mind. I liked the heat. And I quivered in my flip-flops at the prospect of another whole summer with Sean. I'd been going through withdrawal.

In past years, any one of the three Vader boys, including Sean, might have shown up at my house at any time to throw the football or play video games with my brother. They might let me play too if they felt sorry for me, or if their mom had guilted them into it. And my brother might go to their house at any time. But *I* couldn't go to their house. If I'd walked in, they would have stopped what they were doing, looked up, and wondered what I was doing there. They were my brother's friends, not mine.

Well, Adam was my friend. He was probably more my friend than my brother's. Even though we were the same age, I didn't have any classes with him at school, so you'd think he'd walk a hundred yards over to my house for a visit every once in a while. But he didn't. And if I'd gone to visit him, it would have been obvious I was looking for Sean out the corner of my eye the whole time.

For the past nine months, with my brother off at college, my last tie to Sean had been severed. He was two years older than me, so I didn't have any classes with *him*, either. I wasn't even in the same wing of the high school. I saw him once at a football game, and once in front of the movie theater when I'd ridden around with Tammy for a few minutes after a tennis match. But I never approached him. He was always flirting with Holly Chambliss or Beige Dupree or whatever glamorous girl he was with at the moment. I was too young for him, and he never even thought of hooking up with me. On the very rare occasion when he took the garbage to the road at the same time I walked to the mailbox, he gave me the usual beaming smile and a big hug and acted like I was his best friend ever . . . for thirty heavenly seconds.

It had been a long winter. *Finally* we were back to the summer. The Vaders always needed extra help at the marina during the busy season from Memorial Day to Labor Day. Just like last year, I had a job there—and an excuse to make Sean my captive audience. I sped up my trek across the pine needles between the trees and found myself in a footrace against my brother. It was totally unfair because I was carrying my backpack and he was wearing sneakers, but I beat him to the warehouse by half a length anyway.

The Vader boys had gotten there before us and claimed

the good jobs, so I wouldn't have a chance to work side by side with Sean. Cameron was helping the full-time workers take boats out of storage. He wanted my brother to work with him so they could catch up on their lives at two different colleges. Sean and Adam were already gone, delivering the boats to customers up and down the lake for Memorial Day weekend. Sean wasn't around to see my outfit. I was so desperate to get going on this "new me" thing, I would have settled for a double take from Adam or Cameron.

All I got was Mrs. Vader. Come to think of it, she was a good person to run the outfit by. She wore stylish clothes, as far as I could tell. Her blonde pinstriped hair was cut to flip up in the back. She looked exactly like you'd want your mom to look so as not to embarrass you in public. I found her in the office and hopped onto a stool behind her. Looking over her shoulder as she typed on the computer, I asked, "Notice anything different?"

She tucked her pinstriped hair behind her ear and squinted at the screen. "I'm using the wrong font?"

"Notice anything different about my boobs?"

That got her attention. She whirled around in her chair and peered at my chest. "You changed your boobs?"

"I'm *showing* my boobs," I said proudly, moving my palm in front of them like presenting them on a TV commercial. All this can be yours! Or, rather, your son's.

My usual summer uniform was the outgrown clothes Adam had given me over the years: jeans, which I cut off into shorts and wore with a wide belt to hold up the waist, and T-shirts from his football team. Under that, for wakeboarding in the afternoon, I used to wear a one-piece sports bathing suit with full coverage that reached all the way up to my neck. Early in the boob-emerging years, I had no boobs, and I was touchy about it. Remember in middle school algebra class, you'd type 55378008 on your calculator, turn it upside down, and hand it to the flat-chested girl across the aisle? I was that girl, you bi-yotch. I would have died twice if any of the boys had mentioned my booblets.

Last year, I thought my boobs had progressed quite nicely. And I progressed from the one-piece into a tankini. But I wasn't quite ready for any more exposure. I didn't want the boys to treat me like a girl.

Now I did. So today I'd worn a cute little bikini. Over that, I still wore Adam's cutoff jeans. Amazingly, they looked sexy, riding low on my hips, when I traded the football T-shirt for a pink tank that ended above my belly button and hugged my figure. I even had a little cleavage. I was so proud. Sean was going to love it.

Mrs. Vader stared at my chest, perplexed. Finally she said, "Oh, I get it. You're trying to look hot."

"*Thank* you!" Mission accomplished.

"Here's a hint. Close your legs."

I snapped my thighs together on the stool. People always scolded me for sitting like a boy. Then I slid off the stool and stomped to the door in a huff. "Where do you want me?"

She'd turned back to the computer. "You've got gas."

Oh, goody. I headed out the office door, toward the front dock to man the gas pumps. This meant at some point during the day, one of the boys would look around the marina office and ask, "Who has gas?" and another boy would answer, "Lori has gas." If I were really lucky, Sean would be in on the joke.

The office door squeaked open behind me. "Lori," Mrs. Vader called. "Did you want to talk?"

Noooooooo. Nothing like that. I'd only gone into her office and tried to start a conversation. Mrs. Vader had three sons. She didn't know how to talk to a girl. My mother had died in a boating accident alone on the lake when I was four. I didn't know how to talk to a woman. Any convo between Mrs. Vader and me was doomed from the start.

"No, why?" I asked without turning around. I'd been galloping down the wooden steps, but now I stepped very carefully, looking down, as if I needed to examine every footfall so I wouldn't trip.

"Watch out around the boys," she warned me.

I raised my hand and wiggled my fingers, toodle-dee-doo, dismissing her. Those boys were harmless. Those boys had better watch out for *me*.

Really, aside from the specter of the boys discussing my intestinal problems, I enjoyed having gas. I got to sit on the dock with my feet in the water and watch the kingfishers and the herons glide low over the surface. Later I'd swim on the side of the dock upriver from the gasoline. Not *now*, before Sean saw me for the first time that summer. I would be in and out of the lake and windy boats all day, and my hair would look like hell. That was understood. But I wanted to have clean, dry, styled hair at least the *first* time he saw me, and I would hope he kept the memory alive. I might go swimming *after* he saw me, while I waited around for people to drive up to the gas pumps in their boats.

The richer they were, the more seldom they made it down from Birmingham to their million-dollar vacation homes on the lake, and the more likely they were complete dumbasses when it came to docking their boats and finding their gas caps. If I covered for their dumbassedness in front of their families in the boats by giggling and saying things like, "Oh, sir, I'm so sorry, *I'm* supposed to be helping *you*!" while I helped them, they tipped me beyond belief.

I was just folding a twenty into my back pocket when Sean and Adam came zipping across the water in the boat emblazoned with VADER'S MARINA down the side, blasting Nickelback from the speakers. They turned hard at the edge of the idle zone. Three-foot swells shook the floating dock violently and would have shaken me off into the water if I hadn't held on to the rail. Then the bow of the boat eased against the padding on the dock. Adam must be the one driving. Sean would have driven all the way to the warehouse, closer to where they'd pick up the next boat for delivery.

In fact, as Sean threw me the rope to tie the stern and Adam cut the engine, I could hear them arguing about this. Sean and Adam argued pretty much 24/7. I was used to it. But I would rather not have heard Sean complaining that they were going to have to walk a whole extra fifty yards and up the stairs just so Adam could say hi to me.

Sean jumped off the boat. His weight rocked the floating dock again as he tied up the bow. He was big, maybe six feet tall, with a deep tan from working all spring at the marina, and a hard, muscled chest and arms from competing with Adam the last five years over who could lift more poundage on the dumbbell in their garage (Sean and Adam were like this). Then he straightened and smiled his beautiful smile at me, and I forgave him everything.

Feisty. Flirty. Fun. Fantastic.

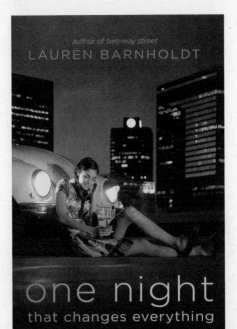

LAUREN BARNHOLDT

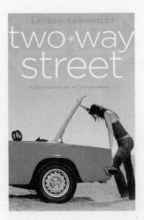

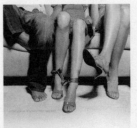

Girls you like.
Emotions you know.
Outcomes that make you think.

ALL BY

DEBCALETTI

When the pressures of prep school build up,
cracks can appear in the funniest places.

LEILA SALES

mostly good girls

From Simon Pulse
Published by Simon & Schuster

From **WILD** *to* **ROMANTIC,** *don't miss these* **PROM** *stories from Simon Pulse!*

A Really Nice Prom Mess

How I Created My
Perfect Prom Date

Prom Crashers

Prama

Love. Heartbreak.
Friendship. Trust.

after the kiss

Terra Elan McVoy

author of Pure

"I love this book. Like, love it love it.
My heart expanded when I
read it—yours will too."
—Lauren Myracle,
bestselling author of *ttyl* and *ttfn*

Pure

Terra Elan McVoy

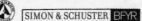

SimonTEEN

Simon & Schuster's **Simon Teen**
e-newsletter delivers current updates on
the hottest titles, exciting sweepstakes, and
exclusive content from your favorite authors.

Visit **TEEN.SimonandSchuster.com** to
sign up, post your thoughts, and find out what
every avid reader is talking about!